WEEPIN' TIME

WEEPIN' TIME

VOICES OF SLAVERY IN COASTAL GEORGIA

Historical Novel

Rand Wood Tuttle

iUniverse, Inc.
New York   Bloomington

Weepin' Time
Voices of Slavery in Coastal Georgia

iUniverse books may be ordered through booksellers or by contacting:

iUniverse
1663 Liberty Drive
Bloomington, IN 47403
www.iuniverse.com
1-800-Authors (1-800-288-4677)

Because of the dynamic nature of the Internet, any Web addresses or links contained in this book may have changed since publication and may no longer be valid. The views expressed in this work are solely those of the author and do not necessarily reflect the views of the publisher, and the publisher hereby disclaims any responsibility for them.

ISBN: 978-1-4502-0903-8 (sc)
ISBN: 978-1-4502-0905-2 (dj)
ISBN: 978-1-4502-0904-5 (ebk)

Printed in the United States of America

iUniverse rev. date: 2/10/2010

Slavery existed in Georgia for more than eighty years.
It created a complex social order for both black slaves
and their white owners – debasing for both races.
It was not a pleasant sight to witness—
truly a "weepin' time."

Contents

Preface

For the past twelve years, I have resided on property that was once part of Hampton Point, one of the plantations central to this story. Today, the landscape is covered largely by dense woodlands, with a canopy of magnificent live oak trees draped in Spanish moss. There are no signs of the highly productive cotton fields that occupied the land during the antebellum period. And with the exception of a few tabby ruins of former slave quarters and other buildings, there are no signs that a plantation ever existed here. If they listen carefully, observers can sometimes hear echoes of the statement made by Frances Butler Leigh at the end of this story: "It's almost as if Mother Nature has reclaimed the land and taken it back from the people she entrusted it to."

In their heyday, Hampton Point and its nearby sister plantation, Butler Island, were thriving enterprises. For nearly eighty years, upward of nine hundred black slaves toiled in the cotton and rice fields for the financial benefit of wealthy owners. Generations of both black and white people lived out their lives here—interacting closely with one another, while at the same time struggling to maintain their own values and identities. Slavery was the foundation on which these plantations were built—and the root cause of their demise.

Many times in the past, I have tried to visualize how things were here at Hampton Point during the plantation era. Certainly the existence of slavery was an evil that we today can condemn with utmost certainty. But what about the people, both black and white, who actually lived here during the period—how did they cope with the issue? And who were these people? … What were their thoughts and feelings? … How did they react to important events of their day? … As I thought about it, I had more questions than answers.

In search of answers, I read at least fifty books on the subject of slavery, visited historic sites, explored museums, and made innumerable queries using the Internet. I learned a great deal, but the materials I could access were mostly scholarly works of an historical nature, and they weren't sufficient to satisfy my curiosity about the lives of the people who had actually lived on the plantations. It seemed to me that recorded history contained a void in its handling of the personal aspects of the period. There were voices of both blacks and whites that were not heard. It was this void that led me to write this book.

The book is based on historical fact, but is nevertheless a fictional novel. The decision to make it such was due mainly to the scarcity of information pertaining to the lives of black slaves during the period—much more information exists for "white folk." To adequately tell the story of important black characters, therefore, required fictionalization. Some characters, such as the members of the Butler and King families, and certain slaves such as London, Frank and Betty are true real-life characters, while some characters, such as Aunt Mollie, Raylin, Christopher, and Martha, are not. In my view, the fictional and nonfictional elements of the story blend well and together portray what life on these plantations was really like. The reader will find that it was far different from the "moonlight and magnolia" atmosphere presented in many previous Southern novels.

In doing research for the book, I owe a great deal of gratitude to many authors whose publications I used to discern facts and develop an understanding of the antebellum period. Foremost is Malcolm Bell Jr., author of *Major Butler's Legacy, Five Generations of a Slaveholding Family*. His book contains a comprehensive history of the Butler family. It served as a principle source for many of the historical events discussed in this book, as well as a source for Butler family correspondence and other quoted materials. The contents of the chapter "Fanny Kemble" is based on her own publication, *Journal of a Residence on a Georgian Plantation in 1838—1839*, by Francis Anne Kemble. The introduction and footnotes, written by the editor, John A. Scott, provided valuable background information as well. Francis Butler Leigh's book, *Ten Years on a Georgia Plantation Since the War*, provided material for the chapters "Trying to Pick Up the Pieces" and "Come Hell or High Water," which cover the postbellum period. And the eyewitness account of the actual sale of Butler slaves, as documented in newspaper articles and the pamphlet, "Great Auction Sale of Slaves in Savannah, Georgia, March 2 and 3, 1859," by Mortimer Thomson, provided material for the chapter "Deeds of Cruelty and Wrong."

There are also many other publications that were used to gain valuable background information. The two most significant are *The Peculiar Institution, Slavery in the Ante-Bellum South*, by Kenneth M. Stampp; and *The Slave Community, Plantation Life in the Antebellum South*, by John W. Blassingame. Important others include: *Rice Gold*, by James E, Bagwell; *Them Dark Days*, by William Dusinberre; *Dwelling Place*, by Erskine Clarke; *Born in Bondage*, by Marie Jenkins Schwartz; *Reconstruction*, by Eric Foner; and *Slave Songs of the Georgia Sea Islands*, by Lydia Parrish.

I am aware that some readers may find the language used in the book offensive—especially the use of the term *nigger*. If so, I apologize, but my intent was to appropriately use the language that the characters speaking would have used at the specific time and place in the story. I have taken great pains to make the story as authentic as possible, keeping everything, including language, consistent with the period. If I had used language more acceptable in the twenty-first century, I feel the authenticity of the nineteenth century would have been compromised.

The antebellum slavery period, as well as the abortive Reconstruction period that followed, was a sad experience to witness. In writing this book, I immersed myself in this experience, and many of the beliefs I had held since childhood, about slavery and about the black race, were changed forever. Slaves called the experience a "weepin' time"—I now weep with them.

Rand Wood Tuttle
St. Simons Island, Georgia

CHAPTER 1—REIGN OF THE KINGS

"... fourteen ... fifteen ... sixteen..."

"Please, Massa, no mo'! No mo', please! I promise I'se do better—please ..."

"seventeen ... eighteen ... nineteen ... twenty!"

Rondo, a black male slave in his mid-twenties, was being whipped by a white overseer, Derek Thompson. Roswell King Sr. stood close by, watching.

Two months earlier, King had purchased Rondo at a slave auction in Savannah and had assigned him to work as a field hand in the rice fields. But, for some reason, he didn't adjust well to his new surroundings. His work ethic wasn't strong—he didn't complete his assigned tasks, complained about the quality of meals, and talked back to his driver. He showed signs of being a malcontent and a possible runaway. King had recognized these signs early on, and he knew Rondo needed breaking in.

During Rondo's first month on the plantation, the driver had given him ten lashes for insubordination. A second whipping had been administered just two weeks ago, in King's presence. At that time, King had strongly warned him that, if his attitude didn't improve immediately, the whippings would get worse. His attitude failed to improve, and on this occasion he'd received twenty lashes. The whipping didn't draw blood, but it raised large welts on his back, and he lay on the ground in a weakened condition. And his begging for leniency may have indicated he had experienced a change in attitude, which, in King's words, meant he'd been "conquered."

Looking at two male slaves who were standing nearby witnessing the event, King commanded, "Get him to his quarters." He then turned to face four other slaves who were sitting quietly on the ground, with wide-eyed, frightened expressions on their faces. They were new slaves who had been purchased that morning from an itinerant slave trader who had visited the plantation. They had been assembled so King could give them his traditional "plantation talk" on their first day in residence.

"I hope you learned something from what you just saw. That boy, Rondo, has been here two months, and he ain't learned nothing yet. That's the third whippin' he's got. And if he don't straighten himself out, he'll get more whippin's and they'll get even worse.

"You don't want the same punishment Rondo got, do you? Well, you don't have to get it, if you follow a few simple rules we got around here. First of all, you got to understand right here and now that I'm the boss—your master! And when I tell you to do something, you better do it fast, without questioning me—and do it with a smile on your face! The same goes when the overseer, Mr. Thompson, or a driver tells you to do something.

"Now, every day when the morning bell sounds, you gotta get up straight away and go directly to the place you've been assigned to work. You'll be given a task that you better finish before the end of the day, or you'll stay out in the fields all night till you do. Do you understand what I'm saying?

"And let me tell you one more thing. Don't ever try running away from this place. There ain't nothing but swamps all around here for miles and miles. They're full of snakes and 'gators, and no one can get through them alive. People that's tried have either died or come back here half-starved to death. And when they got back, there's been a big whippin' waiting for them. Do you understand?

"Okay, now get up and go with Driver Nero, here. He'll get you some tools and show you where your workplace is."

This incident took place at Butler Island, a rice plantation in the Altamaha River delta along the coast of Georgia. Butler Island and Hampton Point, a nearby cotton plantation on St. Simons Island, were managed by King for the benefit of an absentee owner, Major Pierce Butler. At the time, King had been manager of the plantations for a little more than one year.

King had given his "plantation talk" many times in the past. When he had first taken over as manager, he was struck by what he considered to be the lax manner in which the plantations were being run. He believed: "Niggers will try to get away with as much as they can, especially when rules aren't enforced." And being the new manager on the scene, he knew he'd be tested by the slaves. If things were to improve, he would have to act quickly to get the upper hand.

On the morning of his second day, he stood at the entrance to Settlement No.1 at Butler Island watching the slaves as they proceeded toward their places of work. When most had passed by, he made his way back through the settlement, cracking his whip at the laggards, to spur them on. Some slaves were struck by the whip, which quickly got their attention. At the end of the day, four field hands had failed to complete their tasks. They were each given ten lashes by a driver, in King's presence, and made to stay in the fields until dark to finish up. They missed their evening meals.

For the next three weeks, he made it a point to be "ever-present" in the fields, observing what was going on. Whenever he detected a slave causing a rule infraction, doing poor workmanship, or having a poor attitude, he ordered him whipped by the driver. King whipped a number of slaves as well, sometimes two or three in the same day. And on one occasion he went on a "whipping frenzy," whipping all the slaves in a field for working too slowly.

Observing his drivers over a period of time, he concluded that two of them lacked the ability to properly enforce discipline. He demoted them to being ordinary field hands, and replaced them with men of sterner character.

At the point where he felt he'd made progress in improving discipline, he turned his attention to enforcing other plantation rules that had previously been established by the owner, Major Butler, but which had long since been ignored. On a Saturday afternoon, after the week's work had been completed, the large plantation bell was rung as a signal for slaves to assemble in front of the overseer's house. King addressed the group:

"As you all know, we got rules around here that everyone has to follow in order to make this plantation work right. They've been in place ever since the plantation got started. The trouble is, most of you ain't been following them very well, and we're going to have to straighten things up a bit. So I'm giving you fair warning. From now on, all of you better pay attention and start following them, or you'll get severely punished.

"You know what the rules are: You cannot leave this plantation without a pass from the overseer. You understand that, don't you? You cannot visit any of the other plantations in the area—for any reason! And niggers from other plantations cannot set foot on this plantation either. You cannot sell any goods in the town of Darien, and you cannot purchase anything at the stores—especially liquor! … Now, listen up carefully. There's a new rule we're establishing, too. From now on, we're stopping all religious services held here on the plantation, and no one can attend church services over in Darien anymore." At that point, a loud murmur arose from the slaves. King continued, "Now, quiet down. I hope you all understand what I'm saying, 'cause if you don't, you'll be very sorry." King then walked back to the overseer's house and went inside.

Within only a short period of time, it had become apparent to everyone that Massa King, the new manager of the plantations, was the law of the land. To cross him in any way would result in severe punishment. This was exactly what King had set out to achieve.

*   *   *   *

King was thirty-nine years old when be became manager in 1802. He had previously lived in Georgia for thirteen years, but was originally from Connecticut. Prior to his new assignment, he'd been a merchant—marketing rice, cotton, and lumber—and a builder of commercial properties in the town of Darien.

He abandoned his existing business interests when he assumed the duties of manager, and he moved his wife and two sons into the newly constructed manager's house at Hampton Point. His initial salary was set at one thousand dollars per year, a sum more than twice the normal overseer's salary. And due to the self-sufficiency of the plantations—which provided food, shelter, and clothing—there was little need for him to incur additional living expenses. Most of his salary could be placed in savings.

This high income was an important consideration for him in accepting the position. But equally important was his admiration for the owner of the plantations, Major Pierce Butler. King was greatly impressed by the fact that the major had played important roles at the Constitutional Convention and in the U.S. Senate, was friends with such notables as George Washington and Thomas Jefferson, and was a person of great wealth. He basked in being associated with a man of such stature, always addressing him in correspondence as "Honored Sir."

*   *   *   *

During his first summer as manager, King elected not to evacuate Butler Island completely to escape the annual summer sickness. The sickness, called "miasmas," occurred in low-lying swamp areas along the coast where rice plantations were located. It was a highly infectious disease that most people felt was caused by atmospheric "miasmata" and night mists. Negroes were either partially or totally immune to the sickness and could work safely during the summer months. White people, on the other hand, were acutely susceptible. Once a white person contracted the sickness, he would experience a high fever, coupled with shaking chills and weakness. This condition would continue for up to two weeks, until he fell into a coma and died.

To avoid getting the sickness, white people evacuated the low-lying coastal region during the summer months and moved to locations at higher elevation where the sickness didn't occur. Typically, they'd be gone from late May to the first frost in late October.

Because he was right in the middle of making important operational changes, King felt his presence was needed at Butler Island. During the entire summer, therefore, he commuted daily to the plantation during daylight hours and then retreated to Hampton Point for the night. In doing this, he was away during the nighttime hours when people were more susceptible to the sickness, and he avoided getting it. But the experience of having to make the two-hour boat trip twice each day, drained him physically, and he didn't want to ever repeat it again.

While attending a livestock auction in Brunswick later that year, King had a chance meeting with the former manager of the Butler plantations, William Page. He explained his dilemma and asked Page how he had handled the situation when he was manager.

Page replied, "It certainly is a big problem, because it's very easy to catch the sickness if you're white. When I was manager, I resided at Hampton Point and went over to the rice plantation for only brief weekly visits—during the mid-part of the day when it was safe to be there. One day each week, Jack and I would meet and discuss what needed doing the following week, and, once that was agreed to, I just packed up and left the place. Jack took responsibility for carrying out the work plan."

"Who's Jack?"

"Driver Jack. He was the most experienced hand I had on the rice plantation. The major brought him down from Carolina when the plantation started up. Probably knew more about rice production then any white man."

"But he's a nigger! How could you trust a nigger to handle all that work when you weren't there?"

"Didn't think twice about it. He not only knew what he was doing, he was honest too—and liked having responsibility. I always used his advice whenever I made important decisions during the entire crop cycle."

King was taken aback by Page's comments. Having a nigger run the entire show was totally foreign to him. And, more surprisingly, he realized that Jack was one of the slave drivers he had demoted when he first took over as manager. He had felt Jack lacked the ability to properly enforce discipline. Nevertheless, he took Page's comments to heart. He knew if he were ever to get out of his dilemma, he needed to revisit the issue.

He did revisit the issue, and, after several conversations with Jack, he promoted him to "headman" for the entire plantation.

Jack's promotion placed him over the four other drivers on the plantation. In addition, he was given possession of a house outside the slave settlement, near the overseer's house. He proved to be trustworthy in King's eyes and remained headman for more than sixteen years.

$*$　　　$*$　　　$*$　　　$*$

Reflecting his management style, King established a rigorous system for controlling operations. At the end of each workday, drivers and other supervisors routinely reported to the overseer regarding what work had been accomplished.

This reporting session with Driver Sam was typical:

"Massa, forty-five of de forty-eight hands showed up today. De three missin' was Albert—he's sick in de infirmary, an' Alice an' Die—dey's lyin' -in. We got all de seedin' done in field eleven, an' we's hoein' grass after de sprout flow in fields thirteen an' seventeen—got 'bout half done in both fields. Only one hand, dat young boy, Chance, didn't finish his task—he still out in de fields, workin'."

This information was recorded in the plantation journal and checked for accuracy the following day by the overseer. Whenever he was present, King attended these sessions and periodically made his own assessment of the progress being made. Drivers rarely made false statements in their reporting, for fear of being punished themselves.

Of the four hundred-plus slaves resident at Butler Island, a little more than half were classified as field hands. This was a sufficient number to adequately handle rice cultivation during the crop cycle—with the exception of harvesting. The harvest was a labor-intensive activity that had to be completed within a narrow window of time each fall, in order to keep the rice from overripening. To supplement the field workforce during this critical period, King instituted a program whereby virtually every adult slave on the plantation was temporarily assigned to the harvest. This included guild shop workers, poultry minders, boatmen, and even house servants. The action caused consternation among the affected slaves—some feeling that fieldwork was below their dignity. Upon hearing grumbling from the slaves, King told them, "That's too damn bad. Harvesting's the most critical part of the plantation's operations, and we've all got to pitch in to get it done!"

He also found ways to make field hands more productive. Instead of having each family be responsible for preparing its own meals, he established centralized cookhouses at each settlement. Food was prepared twice daily for the entire slave community. The evening meal was eaten in the cookhouse, and the late-morning meal was transported to the fields in wagons. This greatly reduced the workload for women slaves, who previously had to get up early and stay up late after work to prepare meals for their families. It also ensured that everyone, especially children, received two meals a day.

In addition, King established a nursery for young children, which was run by an older female slave and several older children. This provided a place for parents to deposit their children during the day while they worked in the fields. It gave relief to the parents and eliminated distractions caused when small children were brought into the fields by their mothers.

Slave productivity was also enhanced, he felt, by either threatening to sell "problem slaves" to a slave trader or sentencing them to spend time at the plantation's penal colony at Five Pound.

Five Pound was a remote facility established by King on a small section of land on the western end of Little St. Simons Island, two miles west of Hampton Point. It had sheds for cattle, but no slave cabins, no cookhouse, and no amenities. A small crop of cotton was grown there under the direction of a driver who periodically came from Hampton Point. Slaves worked under prisonlike conditions and had to scratch out a meager existence by growing their own food or foraging in the woods. It was not a pleasant place to be, and slaves feared being sent there.

*   *   *   *

As part of his normal routine, King reported to the major on activities being carried out on the plantations, as well as on other issues he faced. He did this in the form of a weekly letter he wrote on Sundays. Each letter began with the salutation "Honored Sir," and ended with, "I am, Sir, your Faithful Servant," reflecting the esteem he had for the major. The letters focused primarily on work performed: "Completed rice harvest in Fields 18 and 19. With good weather, the remaining four fields will be completed within the next four weeks. Progress with threshing continues; 60 tierces pounded—will be shipped next week." Candid remarks about the treatment of slaves—especially runaways— were highlighted as well.

During his first six months as manager, there were eleven incidents of slaves running away—four more than during the entire previous year under the management of William Page. This situation didn't improve over the years and continued to be a significant problem for King, as reflected in these reports:

The gang of Negroes we got from Virginia has proven to be poor workers, and many have not responded to proper directions. One of them, named Albert, ran away and was captured in Savannah. I have retrieved him after having him punished at the jailhouse. He was made to walk the sixty-five miles back to Darien and arrived much swelled and none the smarter.

Jacob's boy, Sunday, broke into the barn and stole a half barrel of rice and ran off for two days. I gave him a severe whipping and let Jacob have him. As he is but a lad, I hope we can make him good.

Of the seven Negroes who attempted to leave since the beginning of the year, Nero was captured by Ben and Pompey and brought back within two days; Bacchus and Gay returned voluntarily after being in the swamps three days; Jeffery was picked up in Darien after six days; and the other three who attempted to get away in a log canoe were gathered in and returned the same day by the mail boat.

Giving you unfortunate news of four Negroes being drowned last Sunday. They were setting out unauthorized in the Eagle Boat, one of our dugout canoes: Jack Carter's Moses of about 18 yrs of age, Harry's boy Jacob about 16 yrs, Worster's boy Tipee of about 16 yrs, and Denna's Judy of about 14 yrs of age. They set out against an incoming tide in a strong northwest wind—a very dangerous condition in the broad reaches of the river. A vessel going by the cut saw a canoe in the river turned over with a Negro clinging to the top of it. But he drowned before they could git to speak. All the reply I made after hearing of this unfortunate accident was that their friends might find their bodies and bury them like dogs, for not one should have a coffin. I would sell the bodies to be *cut* to pieces by the doctors.

The Negroes are healthy and cheerful, except the fellow I mentioned to you some time past, named Chance, who doesn't seem to want to work. He worked a few weeks but has since sworn off again. I gave him a little whipping, but it had no effect. I shall take him home with me this evening (I think he is my match). He is a very likely lad of about 18 yrs of age, young enough to be conquered.

More often than not, the major responded to these reports in writing—usually giving criticism, directives, and advice to King. Being an absentee owner didn't prevent him from directing how the plantations were to be run. He wanted them run with military efficiency—slaves being kept under control at all times and subject to strict discipline. He tended to over-control operations, remotely, from his home in Philadelphia. King didn't like the major's intervention in day to-day management affairs, nor the criticism he received, but he proved adept at handling it. And, he made sure that every one of the many directives issued by the major was carried out to the letter.

*   *   *   *

On a warm December day in 1809, Roswell King Sr. and his son, Roswell King Jr., made the fourteen-mile boat trip from Hampton Point over to Butler Island in a dugout canoe manned by four oarsmen. It was the younger Roswell King's first visit to the island. They proceeded westward down the Hampton River until it intersected with Buttermilk Sound, and then turned northward. As they were about to enter the Altamaha River estuary, King Sr. turned to his son and said, "You'll see this place is quite a bit different from Hampton. We grow rice here, rather than the cotton you've been used to. The plantation's built on old marshlands and swamps that have been formed from all the black dirt that's been washed down the river. It makes good soil for growing rice. You can see now, we're starting to turn up the river here. It's the

Butler River, one of the four separate rivers the Altamaha splits up into here in the delta. Our old home in Darien's up north just apiece—'bout two or three miles."

As the boat came around a bend in the river, the plantation's landing came into view. Pulling alongside the wharf, King Sr. commanded, "Junior,"—referring to his son by his more common name that was used to differentiate between the two Roswell Kings—"take the rope, there, and jump out and wrap it around the pole, and pull the boat in close."

Junior did as he was told, and soon the two were standing together on the wharf, glancing around at all the activity that was taking place. "Come, let's take a stroll. I want to show you around a bit."

They walked up to a high point along the river dike and stopped to take a look at the scene. King told his son, "This whole plantation is below the river level at high tide. We're standing on what's called a "dike." It's a man-made wall that's been built all around the perimeter of the island to keep the river water out. It's anywhere from four to six feet higher than high-tide level, to protect against freshets coming down the river. See all those fields? They're dry now, 'cause we've just completed the harvest, but during most of the year they're flooded with water. Look up there along the dike—see that wooden structure? That's called a "trunk." It ain't nothing more than a big floodgate for letting river water into the fields and then letting it out again. When we want to flood a field, we open it up at high tide to let water in—it flows through all those ditches and canals you see there in the fields. When we want to drain the water out, we open it at low tide and the water flows back out into the river. Pretty simple, eh?"

"Why do you need to flood the fields?" asked Junior. "We don't flood cotton over at Hampton."

"Well, there's a couple reasons for doing it. First of all, rice's entirely different from cotton, and it needs a lot of moisture to grow properly— 'specially when the seeds are germinating. Second, the water protects the seeds, after they've been planted, from getting eaten by all the ricebirds we got around here—the birds don't like getting in the water. And, lastly, it keeps the grass from taking over the fields and reduces the amount of hoeing we have to do.

"We're right now doing repairs to the drainage ditches. In about a week or so, we'll burn off the stubble from this year's crop and start cross-hoeing the fields, getting 'em ready for next year's crop. In late March or early April, we'll start planting and do the first flow—that's what we call it when we flood a field. Soon as the crop gets about eight inches high, we'll drain the field and do some hoeing. Then we'll do another flow that'll last a month or so, drain it again, and do another hoeing. There are four flows in the whole process, up to the point of harvest in late September. Some planters around here do only three flows, but we find we get a better yield with four.

"When the rice is harvested, the plant stems are cut and get transported to the threshing area on canal boats. See—there's one over there. Threshing is when the rice gets shaken off the stems. It's all done by hand, and niggers don't like doing it. When that's done, it gets taken to the mill, where it's pounded to remove the husks from the kernels. We got two mills here, one driven by horses—that's it over there. The other's driven by tidal movements—it's up the river apiece.

"Hey, we better get going, we're supposed to have lunch with Mr. Thompson, up at his house. We can take a look at some of the guild shops on the way—they're not much different from what you've seen over at Hampton."

After lunch, King and Junior were standing in the open area in front of the overseer's house, when Junior asked, "Is this plantation as big as Hampton Point?"

"'Bout the same, I'd say. We got more acreage planted in cotton at Hampton than we got rice here. The number of niggers is 'bout the same though—a little over four hundred at each place. But this is where we make the most money. Rice growing's gotten more and more profitable over the years, and it's now doing better than the cotton.

"Rice growing's a bit more complicated than cotton, too, but once you get the hang of it, it's all about the same. It's how you manage niggers that's important. And believe me, that ain't easy sometimes. They're all a bunch of lazy, good-for-nothings that lie and steal from you every chance they get. You can get 'em to do work, but, as soon as your back is turned, they'll stop whatever they're doing. You've got to watch 'em all the time.

"There's all different kinds of niggers, too. There's those that fall all over themselves trying to be friendly and helpful; those that walk around with long faces and won't do any work unless you push 'em; and, worst of all, there are those that are mean and treacherous—won't do what they're told and are more likely to run away. You gotta handle them all differently, but in no instance can you ever trust any of them.

"We got plantation rules and work standards for niggers that have to be met in order to get all the work done around here. And you gotta be on your guard to keep 'em in line. That's where the whip comes in handy. I've tried using all kinds of incentives—like giving them better food and more time off, if they'd work harder—but everything I've tried ain't done any good. The only thing that seems to work is whippin' them, or threatening to whip them. It really gets their attention.

"Our rules permit a driver to whip a nigger as many as twelve times for any offense. The headman can do thirty-six and the overseer fifty. These rules are pretty much followed, but when an offense is really bad, I let 'em do more. Sometimes, when I'm present, I'll do the whippin' myself—but I prefer letting the drivers do it. Niggers know I stand behind whatever my drivers do, and being whipped by a driver is the same as being whipped by me.

"We use a cowhide whip. It makes a loud noise when you strike a nigger with it and scares all the others that's around. It can lacerate the skin pretty bad, though, so you got to be careful with it. You want it to hurt, but not do too much damage to the niggers, 'cause they're valuable property. And you really got to watch certain drivers to make sure they don't get carried away with using it, too. Seems like when you give one nigger some authority over another, he'll try beating him half to death."

"Sometimes when I see a nigger getting whipped, I think it's cruel," remarked Junior.

"Well, I can see why someone like you who ain't used to seeing it much, might think so, but it ain't cruel. You got to remember that niggers are an inferior race and they ain't too smart. They're not intended to be like you and me. They're not good for anything but being slaves, and the only way to get their attention is by whippin' them…. Just like your horse! Remember, when you were breaking him in, you used a whip. And even now, when you want him to run faster, you whip him. It's the same thing, niggers are dumb animals just like horses.

"There's only one exception to this rule on the entire plantation— Headman Jack. He's a pretty savvy fellow. Come on, let's see if we can find him, so's I can introduce you to him."

As the two walked down the main canal road toward the lower rice fields, King continued, "You're fourteen years old now, and I think it's time you started learning some about running a plantation like this. You know cotton operations pretty well, and it'd be good if you spent some time over here learning about rice, too. You've got the makings to be a first-class plantation manager if you want to be one. Someday you'll be able to take over from me."

✳   ✳   ✳   ✳

Early in his tenure as plantation manager, King had made the decision to halt all religious services for the slaves. It was one of the actions he took to initially establish control. Before taking it, though, he had sought Major Butler's approval:

> There is one plan I cannot forgo proposing (it is not much expense), which is to send me a full dozen fiddles, which will cost from one to two dollars each. I must try to break up so much preaching as there is on your estate. Some of your Negroes die for the Love of God and others through fear of him. Something must be done. I think dancing will give the Negroes a better appetite for sleep than preaching.

The major, whose opinion on religion for slaves coincided with King's, willingly provided the fiddles.

But despite the fiddles' popularity, King realized the slaves' religious fervor hadn't diminished over the ensuing years. Secret religious services and prayer meetings were held constantly in slave cabins throughout the plantation, and groups of slaves sneaked off on Sundays to attend services at "praise houses" set up for slaves on neighboring plantations. The religious movement was so pervasive that King finally decided to give in to it rather than continue to fight it.

At a gathering of all slaves, he announced, "As a reward for the good harvest we just brought in, you will be given the privilege of attending Sunday services over at the churches in Darien. Only those of you in good standing will be permitted to do this."

There was only subdued clapping and a few "thank you, Massas" heard in response to this announcement—everyone was in a state of shock.

Both churches in Darien permitted Negroes to attend services given for whites. They could sit in the upstairs rear balcony. These accommodations couldn't handle all the slaves who normally showed up on Sundays, so a special service was also held outside the churches following the white people's service.

Sermons for these services often centered on the role slaves played in society. Ministers made the point that slavery had been given divine sanction and that insolence was as much an offense against God as it was against their earthly masters. After all, the Bible stated, "He that knoweth his master's will and obeyeth it not, shall be beaten with many stripes." Sometimes two Negro preachers, the Reverend Sharper and the Reverend Jenkins, who were missionaries from up north, delivered the sermons.

The granting of this new previlege proved very popular with the Butler slaves, and many began attending services on a regular basis. After a while, though, King became uneasy over the large number of slaves leaving the plantations on Sundays. Most, he thought, had no religious intentions whatsoever and were merely using the occasions to socialize with slaves from other plantations—or to sell goods they'd stolen from his storehouses. He therefore changed the rule, limiting each slave's attendence at services to a maximum of one time per month; and as a substitute, he hired white ministers to come to Butler Island to hold services.

Due to the frequent unavailability of these ministers, however, services were held haphazardly, and he had to turn to using the two Negro missionaries. Their sermons had to be officially approved in advance by a white minister. Reverend Sharper became the more popular of the Negro ministers. He gave fiery sermons on occasion, and often his sermons deviated from the approved script and included double meanings. One meaning could be taken literally from the scriptures; the other, usually disguised, would relate the scriptures to the plight of the slaves' condition.

Services included the singing of spirituals with the whole congregation participating. Everyone clapped their hands and tossed their heads and bodies from side to side. The cookhouse, where the services were held, shook in all its joints.

King was comfortable with this arrangement—until, on one occasion, he heard slaves singing an old spiritual called "Better Days Are Coming":

> A few more beatings of de wind an' rain
> Ere de winters will be over
> Glory, Hallelujah!
> Some folk has gone 'fore me
> I must try to go an' meet dem
> Glory, Hallelujah!
> A few more risin's an' settin's de sun,
> Ere de winter will be over
> Glory, Hallelujah!
> Dar's a better day a-comin'
> Dar's a better day a-comin'
> Glory, Hallelujah!

King had heard this song before and had thought nothing of it. But all of a sudden, on this occasion, he felt the meaning was to signal a slave uprising. He forbade the slaves from singing it again, and, from that moment on, became suspicious of the religious teachings of Reverend Sharper. He felt the reverend might be preaching insurrection.

King's concerns deepened over the next several weeks, to the point where he terminated Sharper's services and had him escorted off the plantation. From that point on, religious services were limited to once-a-month trips to Darien and to whatever the slaves could do for themselves.

CHAPTER 2—THE EBO MAN

At the end of the workday, John and Mollie were relaxing on the log bench in front of their cabin, when Headman Jack and a young Negro man approached. "You two lookin' mighty fine this evenin'," said Jack.

"We is, an' what brings you to de settlement dis time of day?" replied Mollie.

"I'se come to git yo' help wid a small problem I'se got right here," said Jack, pointing to the young man. "Dis here is de Ebo Man Massa King bought over on St. Simons de other day, an' we's tryin' to figure out what to do wid him. I'se havin' a devil of a time doin' it."

"Why, dar somethin' de matter wid him?" asked Mollie.

"Yes, he cain't talk!"

"What you mean, ain't he got a tongue?"

"Well, he can talk all right, but what I means, he cain't talk our language. He's just come over from Africa and all's he can talk is some African language dat no one understands. He's been over at Hampton past three or four days, an' they couldn't understand nothin' he said, an' he couldn't understand nothin' dey said, neither. Everybody just done give up an' sent him over here. Dey ses he's better suited fo' rice work anyways, 'cause he's so strong. Massa King ses I gotta find a way to make a hand out of him, or he's gonna teach him to work usin' de whip. Dat's why I'se here."

"What you want us to do wid him?" asked Mollie.

"I wants John here to work wid him in de fields an' teach him a bit. Don't think he knows nothin' 'bout rice. An' I wants you to help him get settled in de quarters."

Mollie stood up, walked over to the young man, and looked him in the eyes. A smile beamed across her face, eliciting a slight, cracked smile from the young man. "What's his name?" she asked Jack.

"Don't know," replied Jack. "I'se told he come from some Ebo tribe in Africa, so's I'se been callin' him Ebo Man."

"What's yo' name?" Mollie asked the man, but got only a blank stare in return. "Well, he looks like a fine young man, but it'd be a heap of trouble tryin' to get him to understand things. I cain't 'member de last time we got someone direct from Africa here on dis plantation—maybe back in my Mammy's days. I'se sho' nobody 'round here speaks African. Most people don't even know how to speak Gullah no mo'—only de white folk's language. Don't matter none, we'll find a way to help him."

"Dat's mighty fine of you," replied Jack.

"Well, you gotta help too, Jack! You cain't just wash yo' hands of him and leave him here fo' us to deal wid."

"I knows. An' I'll do all I can. I'll tell Driver Nero not to assign him no task load till he gets de hang of de work, an' get him assigned to work 'longside John. I'll get him some new clothes an' some tools, too."

"Okay, he can stay here wid us in our cabin fo' a while—till he gets settled. After dat, we can move him in wid some other single men in de settlement," replied Mollie. Turning to the young man, she put her arm around his waist and motioned him to go into the cabin.

"Thank you," said Jack.

Mollie and John lived in Cabin #1 near the entrance to Settlement No.1 at Butler Island plantation. Mollie, a middle-aged woman of forty, was the head seamstress—a position in which she supervised four other women. She was notably the most respected female slave on the plantation—known for her frankness and honesty, and for her willingness to help others in the slave community. John, a field hand, was also well respected. He was a member of the Council of Elders, the formal, unsanctioned, governing body of the slave community. The fact that they resided in Cabin #1 was a sign of their standing in the community.

"What we gonna do wid him?" asked John, when they got inside.

"I don't knows," replied Mollie. "You needs to go see de head elder, Cassius, an' tell him what we got here. An' get him to pass de word to see if dar's somebody dat can speak de language of de Ebo tribe. I'll put de kettle on an' fix us all a cup of tea while you's doin' dat."

"I'se goin' right now," replied John.

John returned within twenty minutes and said, "Cassius is gonna send word out to all de settlements an' see if we got somebody who can talk to de Ebo Man. He ain't too hopeful 'bout findin' nobody, though. He gonna send word to de other plantations in de area, too."

"Dat's good," replied Mollie. "Pour yo'self a cup of tea. I been doin' some thinkin' while you's gone. What we ought to do is try an' talk Gullah to him. Dat's de closest language we got to African. Way back, it was used for talkin' between peoples from different African tribes dat was here on de plantation. Maybe it's close 'nough to de Ebo language dat he can understand it some."

"Dat might work," replied John.

"Well, I been waitin' fo' you to get back to try. It's been a long time since I spoke Gullah, an' you knows it a heap better den me," said Mollie.

"I'll give it a try."

Speaking to the Ebo Man, John pointed to himself and said, "Me John" and motioned him to respond. "Me John ... John."

"John," was the response.

"Good ... John," responded John, nodding his head. "Yes." He then repeated the process using "Mollie."

"Dat's good," said Mollie, "but dat ain't Gullah."

"I knows," replied John. "I'se only tryin' to git started."

He then picked up a small wooden chair and said "cheer." After waiting a few moments, with no response from the Ebo Man, he continued, "shut" as he pulled on his shirt—still no response. Going to the back door of the cabin, he opened it, shut it, and reopened it, saying "do'." He pointed to a rooster outside, "roostuh ... fedduh (feather) ... hass (horse) ... ribbuh (river) ... dut (dirt)—still no response. He then pointed to his teeth, "Teet ... dis is gonna be hard," he said in frustration. Pulling on Mollie's apron, he then said "Ap'un"—there was still no response.

"It don't seem like he knows no Gullah words," said Mollie. "Maybe we should just teach him English—least that way he can talk wid all de rest of de folk 'round here."

*   *   *   *

The plantation bell sounded the next morning a half hour before daybreak, signaling the start of the workday. "Wake up. We gotta get goin' fo' daylight," said John to the Ebo Man, shaking him gently. "You an' me is gonna be workin' out in Field #6 today."

After splashing cold water on their faces, the two men left the cabin and were immediately met by a group of other slaves walking slowly past on their way to the lower rice fields. John picked up his grubbin' hoe, which had been leaning against the cabin, and the two joined the parade out to the fields. "All des niggers is field hands," he said to the Ebo Man, not expecting him to respond. "We's ho'in grass fo' de stretch flow down in de lower rice fields." After they'd walked down the path along the main canal, past Fields No.1, No.2, and No.3, John spotted Driver Nero standing at the side of the path watching the procession of workers pass by. He said to him, "Driver Nero, dis here is de Ebo Man. Headman Jack's told me to teach him some about rice growin'."

"I knows 'bout him," responded Nero. "Understand he cain't speak nothin'—don't know how he's gonna work out here in de fields."

"Well, I think he's a pretty smart fella, so's maybe it won't take him long to learn," said John.

"I hope you's right. Don't want nobody out here who cain't understand orders. Here's de grubbin' ho' I got fo' him. See if you can get him to use it some. Headman Jack ses he ain't s'posed to get no set task—so he ain't gonna be doin' me no good out here. You can do all de teachin' you wants, just make sho' you finish all de work you's s'posed to do."

"I'll make sho' of dat," replied John.

There were eight other hands assigned to work in Field #6 that day. The field, some thirty acres in size, had been drained during the previous week, following the point flow. The rice plants were now nearly two feet tall, and approximately half the field had been previously cleared of grass.

When the two men entered the field, John greeted the other workers who were there and then marked off the rows he was responsible for hoeing. "Now, dat's a full day's job for an ol' man like me," he remarked.

Hitting the Ebo Man's arm gently with the back of his hand to get his attention, he began demonstrating the use of the grubbin' hoe. In an easy, controlled motion, he dug the blade into the ground directly behind the weeds—cutting the roots off just below the surface of the ground and then covering the weeds with the loosened dirt. He moved from side to side between two rows of rice, making sure he didn't disturb any of the new plants. He then proceeded to take a step forward up the row. When he finished going about six feet, he stopped and motioned to the Ebo Man to take over for him.

In a moment, though, he stopped him. "You's cutting too big a chunks! See," as he bent over and picked up a clump of dirt and broke it into smaller pieces with his hands, "dat's what you gotta do." A second attempt had better results, but more instruction on how to cut the main root was needed, and more instruction after that on how to work around the rice plants without damaging them.

The two men worked side by side the whole day, with John occasionally reworking portions of the Ebo Man's row. Overall, it was a satisfactory day. The second day was even better, and by the third, the Ebo Man had attained a degree of proficiency.

While Mollie and the Ebo Man were sitting by the fire on the evening of the third day, John burst into the cabin and said, "I'se got some good news! I was just wid Cassius, an' he told me dey couldn't find nobody on de whole plantation dat knows nothin' 'bout de Ebo tribe—dat's de bad news. De good news is he's found a woman over at Broughton plantation down de river apiece who might can help. De woman's mammy was from dat tribe a long time ago, an' she taught her some of de language when she was a youngun. She don't know if she can 'member much, but she gonna try."

"Well, mercy sakes," exclaimed Mollie. "Our prayers is answered. How we gonna get de Ebo Man to meet up wid her?"

"She's comin' here tomorrow night. Dey got someone to row her up from Broughton soon as it gets dark. Don't want nobody spottin' her leavin' dar or comin' here. De whole thing's bein' kept secret."

The next evening, a knock came at the cabin door. When John opened it, a strange man was standing there. "I'se Robert from Broughton; is everthin' okay?"

"Yes," replied John.

"Good, she's down at de boat. I'll git her."

A small woman in her mid-fifties appeared moments later. "I don't think I'se been spotted. My name is Athena. You must be John and you's Mollie ... an' dis here be our new young man all de way from Africa."

"*Aha m bu Athena*," she said to the Ebo Man.

When he heard these words, his face lit up, and he responded, "*Aha m bu Kunjar.*"

The two hugged each other and exchanged more words. Then Athena turned to Mollie and John and said, "He's from de Igbo tribe in Niger, de same as my mammy. Cain't make out all he's sayin', just some of it."

"Dat's plenty good," said Mollie. "I'se been dyin' to learn what his name is—ask him fo' me."

"It's Kunjar. He de son of Prince Kunfar of de Igbo tribe. I takes it he's a pretty important young man."

"Kunjar!" Mollie exclaimed. And seeing a broad smile come over the young man's face, she continued, "Dat's a good name. I won't have to be callin' him 'de Ebo Man' no mo'—dat's good. Ask him how he got here."

"He ses dat he and ten other men was taken prisoners when an enemy tribe raided dar village. He got sold to some white men and dey brought him here in a big ship. Dey landed on dat island off de coast here an' got took ashore in chains. His pappy, de Prince, was in one coffle, an' he was in 'nother. After dey been dar a while, his pappy stands up an' yells out dat Igbos never be slaves to white men. Den all de men in his coffle gots up an' walks into de water, yelling, 'Igbos free men!' He tried followin' him, but de others in his coffle wasn't

Igbos, and dey refused to go. He had to just sit dar an' watch his pappy drown.

"He ses he's lost here. Ain't got no family an' don't know where he's at."

"Well, you tell him he's at Butler Island plantation, in Georgia, in de United States of America. Massa Butler's his owner. Tell him who John an' me is, too, an' dat we's tryin' to help him get settled. An' tell him we's mighty sorry to hear 'bout his pappy," said Mollie.

"He knows you's his friends an' ses he likes you."

"Dat's nice," replied John. "Now, tell him who you is an' dat you don't live here—so's he don't s'pect you to be around much. An', while you's here, I'd like you to teach him some words dat he'll find useful— like rice, canal, water, trunk, barge, river ... full hand, half hand, an' quarter hand ... cookhouse, cabin, settlement ... driver, overseer, Massa King ... nigger ..."

The session continued well into the night—until Athena had to leave in order not to be detected on her way back to Broughton. Everyone was pleased with the results of her visit.

On their way to work the following morning, as they passed Field #6 where they'd been working previously, Kunjar exclaimed, "Dat?" as he went over to the dike that surrounded the field and scooped up water in his hands.

"Dat's water—dey let it in from de river to cover all de rice so's grass don't take over. It's de "stretch flow." It'll be drained off in 'bout a month's time," explained John, not knowing if anything he said was understood by Kunjar. "We's gonna start work in Field #7 dis mornin'."

Kunjar proved to be an intelligent individual, and within a month's time his command of the English language allowed him to carry on short conversations with other slaves in the community. His work ethic was strong, too, and he was made a full hand. John no longer had to give him instructions—that is, with one exception.

At the beginning of work one day, a field hand Jacob arrived in the fields a half hour late. He was given a whipping by Driver Nero for the infraction. When he saw what was happening to Jacob, Kunjar yelled "Stop!" and made a motion toward the driver. He was quickly restrained by John.

"Don't you do nothin'. It's none of yo' business. Jus' stay out of it!"

Later that day, Kunjar asked John why Jacob had been whipped and was told he had broken the rules. "Driver Nero mean man. He nigger too. No whip other niggers." This was the first time Kunjar had witnessed a whipping, but it wouldn't be the last.

*   *   *   *

At the end of the fifth month, Mollie said, "It's time now, Kunjar, fo' you to git off on yo' own. Dar's not much mo' John an' me can help you wid."

"What you mean?" responded Kunjar.

"I means it time fo' you to spread yo' wings a bit an' see what life's 'bout in dis settlement. I'se made arrangements fo' you to live wid some single men dat can show you 'round. Come, git yo' things, an' let's go up to dar place."

"Boys, dis here is Kunjar, yo' new cabin friend. Dis is London, an' Frank," said Mollie as an introduction.

"Welcome to our beautiful home," replied Frank. "Dar's room fo' two mo' here, so's you git yo' choice of de beds in dat closet."

"Good to meet you, Kunjar," said London.

"Me glad to be here. I'se seen you in de fields," said Kunjar, looking at Frank.

"Well, I'se out dar a lot tendin' trunks—could've seen me doin' dat," replied Frank.

"Yes, Frank's an important man 'round here. He's de head truck minder—de easiest job 'round. All he does is open and shuts trunks—don't do no work," interjected London, smiling.

"Lot more important den what you do—makin' tierces."

"Sit down, Kunjar. We'd like to talk wid you man to man an' find out mo' 'bout you—dat is, if Miss Mollie here will leave us alone," said London.

"I'se goin'! I'se goin'! Lawd help you, Kunjar, bein' wid des two."

That evening, a woman and two young men appeared at the cabin door looking for London. "Des folk is here fo' dar readin' lesson wid London," said Frank to Kunjar. "Why don't we just go out fo' a while? I think dar's somethin' goin' on down at the main campfire site dat we can go see."

When the two men were outside the cabin, Kunjar asked, "What's a readin' lesson?"

"Dat's when somebody learns to look at words dat's printed in a book an' makes sense out of it. You learn a lot of new things dat way—only, we don't talk 'bout it none. White folk don't like us niggers knowin' how to read, so we keep it a secret. Don't want you talkin' 'bout it neither. Now dar's a meetin' of de Council of Elders down at de campfire tonight. Don't know what dey'll be talkin' 'bout, but it should be interestin'. Let's go down an' see."

When they reached the campfire site, a group of about thirty slaves was standing in a large circle around the fire; seven men were seated on benches inside the circle talking among themselves. "De old man wid white hair sittin' in de middle dar is Cassius. He's de head of de Council—de others is members," said Frank.

"I sees John," said Kunjar.

"Yes, he's a member. De Council sets de rules for runnin' de settlements on dis plantation an' makes sho' dey is followed by everybody. Listen—Cassius' 'bout to say somethin'."

"Tonight we's here to see 'bout givin' a divorce to Helen here from her husband Joseph, who's over dar. Dis is de third, an' I hopes de last time, we gotta look at dis situation. It's caused a heap of trouble here in de settlement. Now, Helen you start by tellin' us why you wants a divorce," said Cassius.

Helen went into a long, emotional harangue about Joseph physically abusing her—to the point of hitting her on the arm, in the stomach, and on the face with his fists. This happened, she said, mainly when he got drunk. She still loved Joseph, but was afraid to live with him and wanted him out of her cabin. Two witnesses collaborated her story. And two more witnesses told of loud shouting coming from their cabin that disturbed the whole community.

Joseph, in his defense, said he was sorry for what he'd done—and that he loved Helen. He didn't want a divorce.

At the conclusion of the testimony, and after conferring with the other members of the Council, Cassius rose and addressed the gathering. "Gettin' a divorce is serious business an' shouldn't be taken lightly. De Lord joined des two peoples together in Holy wedlock, an' dat joinin' shouldn't be pulled apart by man—unless it's clear dat dey just cain't get along wid each other, or if one's hurtin' de other. And dat's de case in dis situation. It hurts de Council to grant a divorce, but we's gonna do it in dis case. Joseph, you gotta get out of yo' cabin an' find somewheres else to live, now! You both can consider yo'selves divorced on a trial basis fo' de next three months. At de end of three months, if either of you comes to me an' ses dey wants to remain divorced, it'll be final. Dat's our decision."

"Cassius is a smart man. I thought his decision was the right one," said Frank.

"Where I comes from, we don't have no divorces," replied Kunjar. "A man has many wives, an' if he don't get along wid one of dem, he jus' demotes her. She sleeps in a smaller hut after dat."

"I'se not sure I'd like dat. Findin' one good woman to live wid 'round here is hard 'nough fo' most men. Come on, let's go back to de cabin. London must be finished by now."

*   *   *   *

At dinner, two weeks later, Frank leaned across the table and said, "Listen to dis! My dear kind miss, has you any objection to me drawin' my chair to yo' side an' revolvin' de wheel of my conversation 'round de axle of yo' understandin'? What you think?"

"I don't understand what you's sayin'," replied Kunjar.

"Oh, don't pay no 'ttention to him. He's jus' practicin' what he's gonna say to a pretty gal he thinks he's in love wid. It don't sound very romantic to me," said London. "She's a high-class lady an' would probably get upset by such a crude remark."

"Well, how 'bout dis:

> If you was passin' an' saw me hangin' high
> Would you cut me down an' lie
> Or would you let me hang dar an' die?"

"I gotta admit I ain't got much experience wooing gals, but dat don't do much fo' me, neither," replied London.

"I still don't understand. What you doin'?" interjected Kunjar.

"Well, here in dis country, when you wants to get a girl's attention an' determine if dar's a chance of gettin' together wid her, you gotta start de conversation off wid a catchy remark. She'll probably play a little hard to get, even if she's interested—so's you gotta follow it up wid another remark to continue de conversation. All's I'se tryin' to do is practice some lines fo' when I sees her at de next shout. How's dis:

> Oh, when I first saw yo' lovely face,
> Laugh at me if you will,
> My heart jumped clean out of its place,
> I could not keep it still."

"Now dat's mo' like it," replied London. "I'll bet dat'll work jus' fine."

Then, turning to Kunjar, London continued, "Our friend Frank here saw dis young gal at the shout last month an' fell in love wid her. He ain't been de same since. All he can do is think of ways he can impress her when he makes his big move at de shout next Saturday. Her name is Betty, ain't it?" he asked Frank.

"Yes, Betty, a beautiful name—an' she's beautiful too," replied Frank.

"What's a shout?" asked Kunjar.

"It's a big party dat we has 'round here from time to time. Dar's lots of music an' everybody has a good time. Dar's dancin' too, but we don't call it no dancin' 'cause de white folk frown on us niggers dancin'. To make believe we ain't dancin', all's we gotta do is keep at least one heel on de ground at all times, an' shuffle our feet. Dat seems to satisfy de white folk. You gotta go to de one next Saturday. You'll like it," replied London.

✳   ✳   ✳   ✳

The shout was going strong when the three men arrived at the corn barn. The music was loud, and several couples were dancing in the middle of the floor, surrounded by others clapping and shouting to the music. Immediately, Frank spotted Betty and moved in her direction, separating himself from the other two.

Kunjar quickly got into the spirit of the event, standing in the circle watching the dancers and clapping to the music. He seemed to be right at home, although he didn't participate in the dancing itself. The dance steps and motions used in shuffling feet seemed complicated and foreign to him.

At a point when the musicians—two fiddle players, a banjo player, and a drummer—took a break, he went over to where the drum was standing idle. He began beating on it with his hands. The beat was similar to what the drummer had played during the previous dances, but with a short break and a more rapid burst inserted from time to time. It gave the music a wilder sound. As he played, people gathered around and started clapping; some danced.

When he saw their acceptance, he broke out singing an African song:

> Rochah mh moomba
> Cum bo-ba yonda
> Lil-aye tambe
> Rockah mh moomba
> Cum bo-ba yonda
> Lil-aye tambe
> Ashawilligo hamasha banga
> L'ashawilligo hamasha quank!

Most in the crowd had never heard a true African song before, but the tone, exclamation, and drum beat were much like what they were used to. Kunjar received a big ovation when he finished.

At the end of the evening, London and Kunjar walked home together. They couldn't find Frank anywhere and assumed he was busy escorting Miss Betty to her cabin. Whatever combination of sweet words he'd said to her must have worked.

*   *   *   *

The plantation bell rang at noon the following Saturday, signaling the end of the half-day work session. Kunjar stopped what he was doing and joined a group of field hands walking up along the main canal road to the settlement. He had worked hard during the week, and, feeling tired, was looking forward to having some time off.

Just as they were approaching the entrance, a commotion broke out inside the settlement. Some ten or so slaves were standing in a group, watching Massa Thompson, the white overseer, whip a female slave. As he got closer, Kunjar recognized the woman. It was Venus, a member of the overseer's housekeeping staff. Massa Thompson was yelling something about "stealing," and was beating her hard. Venus' husband was next to her, down on his knees, pleading with Thompson to stop. Tears were flowing down his face. Jonas, Venus' five-year-old son, ran around crying hysterically, "Stop! Stop! Dat's my mammy!" Instinctively, Jonas lunged at Thompson, trying to grab his whip.

"Get out of here boy, or I'll whip you an' yo' pappy too!" the overseer exclaimed, pushing the boy to the ground.

Jonas, half frightened to death, broke away and tried running from the scene. Kunjar bent down and caught him. He lifted him up and hugged him. The boy was hysterical and couldn't stop crying. "Now, now, everythin' gonna be all right. It's gonna be over soon. Yo' mammy's gonna be fine," said Kunjar.

The boy calmed down when the whipping stopped. And, after a moment, Kunjar let him to the ground, where he immediately ran to where his father was comforting his mother. Two women in the crowd assisted Venus as well, and they took the entire family into the nearest cabin.

That evening, Kunjar found himself walking aimlessly in the settlement. His mind was fixed on the whipping he'd witnessed earlier in the day. All at once, he spotted Cassius, the elder, sitting alone near a small campfire. He was staring into the flames, deep in thought.

As he approached him, Kunjar said, "Good evening, brother Cassius; mind if I sit down here next to you fo' a spell?"

Cassius, looking up at Kunjar, replied, "Don't mind at all."

Following a moment of silence, Kunjar remarked, "I'se at de Council meeting de other night. I thought yo' decision 'bout de divorce was wise." Then, after receiving a glance from Cassius, he said, "Where I comes from in Africa, our tribe has a council of elders, jus' like you does. Dey is de leaders an' makes decisions dat are best fo' de whole tribe—jus' like you does. Some pretty wise men sit on de council too." After another more prolonged moment of silence, he continued, "I s'pose you heard 'bout de whippin' dat took place in de settlement today.... It was de worst whippin' I'se seen in all de days I been here. Don't know what Venus done to deserve a whippin' like dat, but it must have been bad."

"She took a half cup of sugar from Massa's kitchen—dat's all!" was the response. "She got dat whippin' all for a measly amount of sugar— somethin' she deserved to have in de first place. Everybody's feelin' terrible 'bout what happened today—'specially since it took place here in de settlement."

Kunjar could tell that Cassius was in a tense mood and probably didn't want to discuss the matter. He nevertheless proceeded to ask the question that had been on his mind for weeks, "Cain't de Council do somethin' to stop all de whippin's dat goes on 'round here?"

"What you mean?"

"Well, der's a whole lot mo' of us niggers 'round here den dar is white folk. Why don't we all stand up to dem as a group an' git dem to stop?"

"You mean revolt against de white folk?"

"Yes, even if we gotta kill dem."

"Boy!" exclaimed Cassius. "I sho' can tell dat you is new 'round here! Sho' we could kill all de white folk on dis plantation—dar's only two or three of dem here. But dat ain't all dar is to it. Dar's thousands more white folk livin' in dis country dat would come in after us so fast yo' head would spin. Dey's got a big militia wid plenty of guns, an' canons, an' horses. Dey'd kill all of us, an' dat ain't no lie.

"De only reason we is slaves here is 'cause de white folk got de power to make us slaves. An' we ain't got 'nough power to change de situation."

"Dat mean we's gonna be slaves fo'ever?" asked Kunjar.

"I don't know. Everybody 'round here keeps talkin' 'bout gettin' dar freedom someday, but I ain't seen no signs of dat happenin'! Sho'ly, at my age, I'll never see it, but, someday, maybe. We just gotta be satisfied wid it happenin' when we's all in heaven. An' while we's still here on dis earth, we just gotta make de most of de situation," replied Cassius.

"If freedom ain't comin', why don't folk just run away an' get away from dis place?"

"Ain't no use in runnin' away, son. Fo' a nigger to get free, he's gotta get way up north—'bout a thousand mile. It ain't easy going all dat way through white folk territory. Dar's patrollers everywheres, an' if you ain't got no pass for bein' off de plantation, dey arrest you, an' even kill you fo' de bounty money. 'Sides, it almos' impossible to get through de swamps around dis place, wid all de 'gators and snakes dat's in 'em. Most peoples either dies tryin' or comes back in a few days starvin' to death and gets a big whippin'. I cain't 'member when de last nigger made it out safe.

"My advice to you, son, is not to be thinkin' 'bout runnin' away. Best to stay here an' make do wid what you got here in de settlement. Dis is yo' home—where yo' family is. I don't mean just yo' mammy an' pappy, but everybody else dat's here as well—we's all yo' family. We look out fo' each other. Sho' we got rules, but dar our rules, not de white folk's rules. De settlement is separate from de rest of de plantation, an' it belongs to us. What happens here ain't got nothin' to do wid de white folk.

"You been here 'bout a year now, ain't you? Well, you is just settlin' in, den. It won't be long 'fore you is a full member of de brotherhood. What you gotta do is learn our ways here in de settlement—an' on de outside, learn how to get 'long wid de white folk in dar world. It ain't easy doin' both, but when you learns how, yo' life sho' becomes a lot easier."

✳   ✳   ✳   ✳

"Whoooweee!" exclaimed Frank as he burst into the cabin. "Congradulate me, my fine friends. I'se gettin' married! Miss Betty's agreed to marry me, an' Headman Jack's given his approval."

"Dat's nice," replied London, still a bit groggy after being awakened from a sound sleep.

"It sho' is," added Kunjar.

"When's dis all gonna take place?" asked London.

"End of next month, right after de rice crop gets laid-by ... London, I wants you to be my best man, so's we gotta get us another preacher man to perform de ceremony. Hope we can get Reverend Sharper."

"I'se sho' we can," replied London.

The wedding was held over at Hampton Point, where Betty's family lived. Reverend Sharper did a marvelous job, declaring in a loud voice "I now pronounce you man an' wife"—to the clapping of all present. The dinner afterward featured roast chicken and ham, and both the bride and groom jumped over the broomstick safely.

It was the first time Kunjar had experienced a wedding in this country. The solemnity and formality were similar to what he'd experienced in Africa. But in Africa they made it more difficult for the bride and groom—they made them jump over the broomstick blindfolded.

"Who's dis God dey spoke 'bout in de weddin'?" asked Kunjar.

"He's de one who created de earth, de whole universe, all de people—you an' me," replied London."

"He's mighty powerful, den—same as Chukwu."

"Who's Chukwu?

"He's de mos' powerful Igbo god of all—above all de other gods—Anyamou, de god of sun; Ala, de goddess of earth; an' Igwkaala, de god of de sky. He's very kind, give everybody dar own *Chi*—his own spirit to guide them through life," replied Kunjar.

"Dat's 'bout de same. We call our god "God." But we think dar's only one god, an' he's responsible fo' de sun, de earth, and de sky as well. An' we call your *Chi*, de Holy Spirit."

"Igbos also believe dat when someone dies he enters Ndichie, an' he comes back in de spirit to help de people still on earth. Gives dem counsel," continued Kunjar.

"Dat's almos' de same as our heaven," replied London. "We believes when someone dies he goes to where God lives in heaven, an' is blessed wid a peaceful life fo'ever. Dar ain't no worries dar, an' dar ain't no slavery, neither—everyone's de same. Don't know if dar spirits ever comes back an' helps us here on earth, though, but sometimes I think dey do."

"I likes dis heaven of yours—sounds like a nice place."

"Well, you gotta start comin' to our church services on Sunday, den; you can learn mo' 'bout it. An' maybe come to de Bible lessons I holds on Wednesday evenin's, too."

"I think I'll do dat," replied Kunjar.

✶   ✶   ✶   ✶

One morning, while John and Kunjar were walking to the fields together, John remarked, "Kunjar, you's a great blessin' to us older field hands. We really appreciates you helpin' us wid our tasks. You is now de best worker in de fields—mighty strong, an' on some days when we ain't quite up to doin' our work, you's always dar helpin' us out. Dat's mighty nice of you."

"I'se happy to do what I can."

"We's 'bout done hoein' followin' de stretch flow—'bout ready fo' de harvest flow now. Won't be havin' much to do in de fields fo' a while. But don't worry; dar'll be plenty for us to do. Just 'cause all de white folk is gone, it don't mean Headman Jack won't find a heap load of things to keep us busy," said John.

"What you mean, all de white folk is gone?"

"Ain't you noticed? Dar ain't a white man to be found nowheres on dis plantation. Dey's all gone to 'scape de summer sickness. It's called "miasmas," an' it makes white folk mighty sick—most die from it. Nobody knows what causes it—only dat it comes every summer to de low area along de coast here. Niggers don't get de sickness; only white folk do."

"You mean de white folk go away an' leaves dis whole place just to de niggers? How long dey gone fo'?" asked Kunjar.

"Better part of five months, from late May till de first frost in October."

"Dat's durin' de start of harvest season. Who's running de place when dey's gone?"

"Headman Jack is. He's a good man an' knows what he's doin'. Best rice grower in de whole area," replied John.

"But he's a nigger."

"Don't matter none. De white folk trust him, an' he does a good job fo' dem. Us niggers get treated better when he's in charge, too. But don't get me wrong; he makes us work just as hard as de white folk do."

"I knows Headman Jack is fair in his dealin's. But ain't it strange dat de white folk trusts a nigger to run de whole place. Dey don't trust niggers to do nothin' else," said Kunjar.

"It's strange, ain't it? S'pose dey don't have no other choice 'cause of de sickness. Come on, we better get to workin' now."

That afternoon, Driver Nero yelled at one of the field hands, "What's wrong wid you, nigger? Why don't you do what I tells you?" He started whipping the man. The action occurred no more than thirty yards from where Kunjar was working, and it immediately caught his attention.

After witnessing the whipping for a while, Kunjar yelled out, "All right, Driver Nero, dat's 'nough!"

Stopping and turning toward Kunjar, Nero responded, "What you mean, nigger? Dis ain't none of yo' business. Stay out of it. I'se in charge here, an' I can do anythin' I wants."

"No, you cain't!" replied Kunjar as he started moving in Nero's direction. "De rules on dis plantation ses a driver can give a nigger only twelve stripes wid de whip. You just finished givin' dis man thirteen. I counted dem. Dat's too many already. Now, stop!"

Nero was taken aback by the boldness of the man coming toward him—and the man's size and apparent strength didn't escape his notice, either. In a half-apologetic manner, he said, "Oh, you is right. S'pose I lost count."

The incident was over. Within minutes, Nero left the field and didn't return again that day.

That evening, Mollie sat patiently on the bench in front of her cabin. She was waiting for Kunjar to finish his meal in the cookhouse and pass by her place on the way to his cabin. When he appeared, she called to him, "Kunjar, you got a minute? Come over here and sit wid me a spell."

"Evenin', Miss Mollie, you's lookin' mighty fine."

"Well, I ain't feelin' so good—mighty sorry 'bout what I been hearin'. Heard you had a run-in wid Driver Nero today. Dat right?"

"No, it was jus' a small thin'. Nothin' come of it."

"Well, you's lucky. If Massa King was 'round, he'd have you whipped fo' what you done. He don't cotton to no nigger challengin' de authority of his drivers—you understand dat?"

"Yes, but de driver was wrong, an' I needed to set him straight," replied Kunjar.

"It don't matter if he's right or wrong. You ain't got no business interfering wid what no driver's doin'. I don't care if you is de son of a prince, or de King of Africa, fo' dat matter. When you is outside dis settlement, you's nothin' but a nigger, an' you better act like one, too. Otherwise somethin' bad's goin' to happen to you. You understand what I'm' sayin'?

"Yes, ma'am."

"Good, now go on home an' think 'bout it some mo'."

As she watched Kunjar walk slowly up the road toward his cabin, Mollie couldn't help thinking how much she cared for the young man. He was a good person, a little headstrong, and not quite adjusted yet to living under slavery. She hoped she'd taught him a lesson and hadn't been too hard on him in doing it. He still needed some settling down … maybe finding him a good wife would help.

*   *   *   *

For over a week, Mollie sat in the cookhouse observing all the young women who came in for meals. She knew the one who'd be right for Kunjar would have to be smart, in order to gain his respect; be strong so she could stand up to him; and be cute, too. After observing several from a distance, she picked three who she thought might do. She then made a point of sitting at the same table with each of them during meals to get to know them better. Through this process, she eliminated one of the three, thinking she wouldn't be able to manage

Kunjar very well. Her first choice was Betsy, a sixteen-year-old with good looks and a sharp wit. Patience, a seventeen year-old, was her second choice. She decided to concentrate fully on Betsy and hold Patience in reserve.

The next day she made it a point to walk past Betsy's cabin, and, seeing Gloria, Betsy's mother, sitting outside on the doorstep, said, "Why, hello Gloria. I ain't seen you fo' quite a spell. How you been?"

"Been a little sickly, but I'se feelin' better now," was the reply.

"Sho' missed you an' yo' younguns at Sunday church. Been prayin' fo' you."

"Thank you kindly. 'Less somethin' unexpected comes up, I'se plannin' on being dar dis comin' Sunday."

"Dat's good … an' make sho' you brings Betsy an' Gilbert 'long, too."

"I'll do dat."

"Good seeing you," said Mollie as she waved good-bye.

At church the following Sunday, Mollie sat near the cookhouse doorway, so she could exit quickly after the service. She wanted to commandeer a position just outside, where she could intercept people as they came out. When she saw Gloria, she exclaimed, "Well, sho' is good to see you again. An' Betsy here, you sho' is lookin' mighty pretty. Gilbert, you's growin' up a lot, too. Sho' is a nice day, ain't it?"

Before Gloria could respond, Mollie spotted Kunjar and said, "Hello dar, Kunjar—come over here, dar's some folk I wants you to meet. Dis here is Betsy, an' her mammy, Gloria, an' her brother, Gilbert."

"It's nice to meet you all, "said Kunjar.

By the smile on Kunjar's face, she could tell he was somewhat attracted to Betsy. "It's such a nice day," she said. "John and me is plannin' to have some watermelon after church up at our cabin. We'd sho' be pleased to have you and yo' family join us, Gloria."

"I think we'd like dat."

"Good." And, turning to Kunjar in an apparent afterthought, she said, "An' you can come too, if you'd like."

"I'd be mighty pleased," was his reply.

As they walked toward the cabin, Mollie placed her arm on the back of Gilbert's shoulders and directed her attention to Gloria, inquiring about her recent illness. This forced Kunjar and Betsy to walk together. They seemed to get along well, and there was laughter intermixed in their conversation. Mollie inwardly smiled as she watched them.

Betsy and Kunjar were married exactly four months after the day they met. And a son, John, was born to the couple a year later.

A week after John's birth, Kunjar wrapped him in a small blanket and took him outside for the first time. He showed him off to everyone he could find in the street. "Dis is my son! Dis is my son, John! He's a beautiful child. He grow up big and strong." He was still excited when he reached John and Mollie's cabin at the end of the row.

"He sho' is a handsome child—look just like his pappy," exclaimed Mollie.

"Bet he'll be strong like his pappy, too," said John.

"We's named him John after you, 'cause you's my good friend," said Kunjar. An' when we gits a girl, we's gonna name her Mollie, too."

"Dat's awfully nice," replied Mollie. "But dis youngun don't need to be out here in de hot sun much longer. You'd better take him back to yo' cabin."

As they watched Kunjar walk up the settlement road with baby John, Mollie turned to John and said, "We sho' done a good job wid our Ebo Man, didn't we?"

Chapter 3—The Major's Coming

In early September of 1810, Quash, the mail delivery boy, returned from his regular Friday trip to the Darien Post Office. When he entered the plantation office, he handed the packet of mail to Roswell King, who was sitting at his desk. Glancing through the letters, King noticed that one of them was from Major Butler. He'd been expecting it. Almost without fail, the major had responded in writing to the weekly reports King submitted. And, more often than not, these responses contained criticisms of how operations were being carried out. King didn't like receiving the letters, and he mentally braced himself as he opened this one.

The contents surprised him. Instead of one of his usual responses, the major announced that he and members of his family were planning a visit to the plantations in November, and they would be holding a gala event with seventy invited guests in early December. Their stay would be short, however, lasting only until the end of January. The letter included detailed instructions for actions King was to carry out prior to their arrival, including making arrangements for the plantation's schooner, the *Roswell King*, to meet their party in Charleston on November 3.

"Oh my God," thought King. "He hasn't been here in over four years. Why does he have to pick the busiest time of year to come? It's right in the middle of harvest season! This is really going to muddle things up."

In a flurry of activity, King began reassigning hands to prepare for the major's arrival. Lawns and shrubbery around the Big House would need to manicured; the house and guest cottages had to be spotlessly cleaned; linens, dishes, and silverware would have to be brought out of storage; repairs would have to be made to the house; draperies and rugs in the main drawing room would have to be replaced; stables would have to be cleaned and painted; hogs would have to be butchered and smoked; and the live fish holding tanks would have to be filled. And—most importantly, according to the major's instructions—work on the new racing boat had to be completed on time.

The work proceeded on schedule, although at the expense of planned progress on the rice harvest at Butler Island. Some thirty Butler Island slaves were temporarily assigned to the preparation activities at Hampton Point. King didn't want the cotton harvest at Hampton to be delayed, since the major would be spending the bulk of his time there—he wanted things to appear as normal as possible.

Exactly at three o'clock in the afternoon on November 5, the *Roswell King* pulled alongside the landing at Hampton Point. The passengers—the major, his daughter Frances, and two Negro servants, Gina and Mary—were greeted by King, his wife and sons, and an assembly of fifty or so slaves, who were all clapping and cheering.

As they began walking toward the Big House, the crowding of slaves all around them impeded their progress, and they could hardly take a step. Edging his way through the crowd, the major greeted various slaves individually, some of whom he'd known for years. Men took off their hats and bowed to him, women curtseyed. Everyone was smiling, and the noise was deafening. The procession up to the Big House rivaled the return of a conquering emperor in Roman days. The major was delighted.

When they finally reached the house, the party ascended one of the two broad curving staircases that lead up to the main entrance on the second level. Upon reaching the landing, the major turned to the gathering and raised both his arms high in the air to acknowledge the cheering. He then turned and entered the house.

The off-loading of the ship's cargo took more than three hours. In addition to the passengers' personal luggage, there were over fifty cases of wine, twenty cases of brandy, twenty cases of rum, four barrels of sugar, one hundred and fifty boxes of candles, four crates of dishes, and a myriad of miscellaneous items, including boxes of cigars, hunting rifles, spices, two carriages, and Gallant Fox, the major's prize stallion. All were needed for the upcoming gala.

When the party entered the Big House, Frances exclaimed, "It's beautiful! It's been a long time since I've been here, and it's even better than I remembered it. I love the high ceilings, the tall windows, the piazza, the fireplace—all of it!"

"I'm glad you like it," said the major. "Perhaps, Mrs. King, you'd be good enough to show Frances around the place, so she can gain a perspective of it all."

"Yes, I'll be happy to. Come with me—we can start here in the main drawing room."

The major then turned to King and said, "I've got to see the boat. Where is it?"

"It's at the boathouse near the landing. It's all ready," replied King.

"Good, let's go take a look at it."

When he saw it, the major gasped, "My word, it's beautiful!" The forty-foot-long dugout canoe was resting on carpenter's workhorses inside the boathouse. Its shellacked emerald green finish glistened brightly, and the wording *Shamrock II* painted in yellow stood out prominently on its bow. The sides were as smooth as wet ice.

"This here is Marcus and Jupiter, the two carpenters who've done most of the work on the boat, Major," said King.

Shaking the two men's hands, the major replied. "You've done a fine job. I hope it's as fast as it looks. The last time I won a regatta was with a boat named *Shamrock*, which is a good luck symbol for Irishmen like me. I'm hoping *Shamrock II* brings me equally good luck in the upcoming race."

"Well, she's a mighty fast boat, Massa. I think she'll do you proud," said Marcus.

"She's a lot bigger than the last one—eight oars instead of six. It must have taken a pretty good-sized cypress to make it."

"Yes, Massa, de best tree we could find over on de mainland. Took us nearly four months to carve it all out, 'nother two to smooth it down. Look here, you can see de bottom's a little flatter den usual, and dis runner dat goes from midship to de stern will make it plane better. It's built jus' like de plans in de newspaper you sent us," replied Marcus.

"Well, Mr. King, let's get it ready. I want to give it a try first thing in the morning. The crew's ready isn't it?"

"Oh yes, they've been training for some time."

The major appeared at the landing immediately following breakfast the next morning, dressed in dark blue trousers, white shirt, and yachting cap.

"Good morning, Major," said King. "Let me introduce you to Pompey. He's our most experienced boatman and head crew member. The other crew members are over by the boat. The course we've laid out for the regatta is exactly one mile long, ending right in front of the Big House. We've had to put the starting line downriver apiece, around the bend there. The starter will fire a pistol at the beginning of each race. We can hear it from the Big House, so we can time it."

"Good, let's get started. I'll take the helm and head for the starting line."

A couple of minutes after the boat had disappeared around the bend, a shot was heard. Moments later, the boat reappeared, being powered by the eight crewmen rowing in unison as fast as they could. Crossing the finish line, the major raised his arms high in the air, and yelled, "Boy, that was fast!" After maneuvering the boat over to where King and Marcus were standing at the finish, he asked, "Well, how'd we do?"

"Six minutes and four seconds," replied King.

"That's almost the exact same time du Bignon had when he won in the last regatta, isn't it? I was hoping to do better than that. Come, let's try it again."

The result of the second try was six minutes, five seconds. The major was disappointed when he disembarked at the landing.

"I'se don't know what de problem is, Massa; maybe de tide is a little stronger den usual today. When we's been practicin' we's been makin' better time den dis—usually 'round five minutes an' fifty seconds," remarked Pompey.

"Well, that would be more like it. We'd win if we could be that fast," exclaimed the major.

"You've been getting that time using Pinder at the helm," interjected King. "He's a small boy, who don't weigh much. That might have something to do with it."

"It might," replied the major. "But wouldn't it be cheating to use someone like him in the race? The owner of the boat is supposed to be at the helm, isn't he?"

"Not necessarily, Massa," replied Pompey, "Things has changed some since you was here last. Some do and some don't."

"Then why don't we give it a try using this boy Pinder?' said the major.

The result with Pinder at the helm was five minutes and forty-eight seconds, despite the crew being tired from all the previous rowing. "That does it," said the major. "Pinder is our man. We will not settle for anything less than first prize in the regatta!"

*　　*　　*　　*

While making his way back from the landing to the Big House, the major noticed a small chaise, drawn by two fine black horses, coming down the oak-covered drive that led to the house. He stood at the end of the drive and waited for the visitor.

As the chaise drew near, he recognized the driver, John Couper, an old friend and owner of the neighboring plantation, Cannon's Point.

"Good Morning, Major. I'm glad I found you at home."

"Good morning, Mr. Couper. It's a pleasure to see you again. How have you been?"

Couper, dismounting from the chaise and signaling his lackey, who was trailing on horseback, to take charge of the horses, replied, "Well, for the most part, I've been in excellent health. But two weeks ago I was foolishly standing on a cotton wagon and got knocked off accidentally when they were loading a bale. Darned if I didn't hurt my leg. It's not all that bad, but the doctor refuses to let me ride a horse until it's completely healed. That's why I'm in this darn contraption. Makes me look like an old man."

"Well, come in the house; I'll give you something to drink that'll make you feel as young as you please."

"Oh, no—thank you very much. I don't have time for that. I've just come over for a quick visit to extend an invitation to you. You being one of the original planters on this island, I'm sure you remember all the camaraderie we had back in the early days at those special dinner meetings we organized. Well, we've formalized these meetings a bit, and we now call ourselves a club—the St. Clair Club, to be exact. It's a name that was chosen to reflect the place where we meet. Our next meeting's a week from this Thursday, and we'd be delighted if you'd join us."

"That's very nice of you, Mr. Couper. I remember those dinner meetings vividly and enjoyed every one of them. I'd be delighted to join you."

"Good. It's settled then. And how are you finding things on our beautiful island?"

"Very well, thank you, but we've just arrived, and I haven't seen much yet."

"We certainly have nice weather for you, and there's lots of new things to see, too. And that reminds me. It was your friend, Thomas Jefferson, who got me interested in planting olive trees here on the island. I took his suggestion and imported two hundred trees directly from France, and they're all doing quite nicely. It looks like I'll have a whole new crop to manage. You ought to come over and take a look at them."

"Well, I'd like to see what you've done. I would never have thought one could make a profitable crop out of olive trees on this island, though."

"Then you must come over and see for yourself. How about lunch the day after tomorrow?"

"I'll be there."

$$\ast \qquad \ast \qquad \ast \qquad \ast$$

The loud tolling of the plantation bell woke the major at five thirty on the morning of his luncheon with Couper. It was the signal for slaves in the nearby settlement to begin their workday. All able-bodied hands were to be at their workplaces by daybreak. The major arose quickly and went outside onto the piazza, making his way around to the side of the house. From that vantage point, he could view a portion of the slave settlement on the far side of the overseer's house. He heard muffled voices and could dimly see movement occurring in the settlement. Then, as the six o'clock hour approached, there appeared to be a lot of scurrying around, and he heard a driver's voice shouting commands to laggards. It seemed the workday would begin on time without incident.

After breakfast, he walked down to the boathouse and took another look at *Shamrock II*. It still looked good to him. And seeing the crew assembled near the landing, he told them to keep training hard. "It would be good to knock a few seconds off your record time," he told them.

"Oh yes, Massa," replied Pompey. "We's just waitin' fo' the tide to get right 'fore we continue wid our trainin'. Pinder, here, is gettin' real good at de helm, an' he's workin' us hard. He gonna make you a good driver someday."

The major walked up the stone path along the river, past the Big House, to the equestrian complex.

The complex covered a six-acre area. It included two stables large enough to accommodate twenty horses, a carriage house, a paddock, an exercise ring, and two fenced pastures. The buildings' architecture matched that of the Big House. They were painted white, as was the fencing. It was an impressive sight.

A bustle of activity greeted the major as he arrived. Horses had just finished their morning feeding and were being let out into the pastures by stable hands. Seeing Ishmael, the head stable master, the major said, "Good morning."

"Good morning, Massa. You sho' picked a fine day fo' takin' a ride."

"I did indeed. The horses seem to be in good condition."

"Oh yes, Massa. Includin' Gallant Fox, dar's ten horses, an' dey's all ready fo' when de company comes."

"Good, and we've got room to stable maybe ten more for the guests who bring their own horses, right?"

"Yes, Massa, we got twenty stalls, an' by doin' a bit of squeezing, we can handle 'bout twenty-five horses."

"Well, I'm just going to take a look around. Saddle up Gallant Fox for me, so we can get started. I want to give him some exercise after that long trip he had from Philadelphia."

The major and Ishmael rode their horses down the clamshell road that led south through the plantation, passing cotton fields that had been stripped bare during harvest. At a point three miles down the road, they reached the main entrance to the plantation. It had a large black iron gate set off by two ten-foot-high tabby columns. Low tabby walls extended in a semicircle forty feet to either side. Continuing a half mile down the road, they came to an intersection, and, taking a sharp left-hand turn, they proceeded in a northeasterly direction up the Cannon's Point Road. The plantation house was a mile away.

As he rode, the major's thoughts turned to his luncheon host, John Couper. He and Couper had been among the first to establish plantations on St. Simons Island nearly fifteen years earlier, and they'd been friends ever since they'd met.

Couper, he was thinking, was friendly with everyone. He was an affable old Scotsman who had come to this country as a young boy and made good as a businessman and planter. Tall as a tree, he was probably six foot three or four. With his red hair, he looked more Irish than Scottish. His good humor and charm made him more Irish, too. He would probably fit right in as an Irish lord --- may be the reason they got along so well. He's a renowned horticulturist too. It was no wonder Jefferson had picked him to experiment with olive trees—he'd imported more plant varieties into this country than perhaps anyone else. With good results, too. The major certainly liked him as a friend and enjoyed being in his company.

As they proceeded up Cannon's Point Road, the riders passed large cotton fields that had been completely harvested. About a quarter of a mile from the house, however, the scene changed abruptly. At that point, the surface of the road turned from clamshells to small white pebbles. Palm trees of various kinds appeared along the roadside, and the grass on both sides of the road was well manicured. Large orchards of lemon, lime, orange, and pomegranate trees stretched as far as they could see to the east. Down by the river were groves of olive trees. The lemon trees were in fall fruit, and there was a lemon scent in the air. It was as if the two riders had entered a totally different world.

The plantation house was large, standing three and one-half stories tall. Its first level, an English kitchen, was made of tabby. The levels above were of wood, painted white, with dark green shutters. A broad flight of stairs led from the stone drive up to the main level at the river entrance, where a wide piazza wrapped around to the sides of the house.

A young livery boy, dressed in uniform, was waiting for them at the base of the stairs. "Good morning, Massa," he said. "Massa's 'spectin' you. You's to go right up."

Just as the boy finished saying these words, Couper appeared on the piazza and called down to them. "Good morning, Major. Please forgive my not greeting you down there in person, but my bum leg makes it difficult for me to manage these stairs. Please come up."

As they entered the house, they were met by Couper's wife, Rebecca, and his sixteen year-old son, James Hamilton Couper. "I'm sure you remember my wife and son," said Couper.

"Indeed I do—it's a pleasure to see you again, Mrs. Couper. But I'd be hard pressed to recognize this young man. He's grown so much since I last saw him."

"That he has," replied Couper. "And gotten a bit smarter, too. He's been up north to college this past year, and he's home now for a short break before he heads back."

"Major, won't you please come into the drawing room and sit down a spell? Lunch will be ready shortly," said Mrs. Couper. "Here, have some of my homemade orange punch. It'll help relax you after your ride in the warm sun."

"Thank you." After taking a sip of the punch, the major remarked, "This is delicious. I remember it from years past."

"Thank you, Major. Mr. Couper may be famous all over the South for his horticultural work, but I'm equally famous for my orange punch."

"I can understand why," said the major.

After lunch, the major and Couper went outside and began walking along the river. "I'm sorry to be going so slowly, but my leg is acting up again," said Couper. Then he abruptly stopped and added, "Have I ever shown you this?"

"No. What is it?" replied the major.

"It's what I call our Constitution tree stump. Back a number of years ago, a young man was going around the island searching for oak trees to make lumber to build war ships for the country's newly organized navy. When he came here, he saw a large, beautiful live oak growing right here and said that it was just the shape he needed for the sternpost for the new *U.S. Constitution*. He said it was the most important part of the ship, and he was having difficulty finding just the right piece of wood for it. He was very persuasive, and I let him cut it down. It got shipped up to Boston, where the ship was built.

"And you know why the *U.S. Constitution* is called 'Old Ironsides,' don't you? Here, feel the wood. The live oak is made of the heaviest, most dense wood of any tree alive. When the British fired cannon balls at it, they just bounced right off.

"The amazing thing was that right after the *Constitution* captured the British frigate *Guerruere*, this bay tree started growing out of the old stump. It's grown pretty big, now. I thought this was so unusual I wrote a piece about it in one of those agricultural journals, and I got hundreds of letters back from readers. Many wanted a piece of the old stump, so I sent them some small items like paperweights and inkwells I made from the wood."

"Well, that's very interesting, Mr. Couper. And, as a matter of point, I was a member of the U.S. Senate when the act to establish the navy was passed, and I voted in favor of building the *U.S. Constitution*, as well as other ships for the navy. But I had no idea the wood came from here," replied the major.

As the men continued their walk, Couper remarked, "The olives trees start about here and cover more than six acres along the river. The soil has a great deal of calcium from all the clamshells that's buried in it. It matches the soil in their native region in France. They seem to thrive being near the water.

"It's been six years since we planted them. The first year we didn't get any fruit, but the yield has been improving ever since. We've done a bit of grafting and planting of seedlings too—increased the number of trees to nearly six hundred now. This year we'll get more than 150 gallons of olive oil, and, with no domestic competition in this country, we'll get a good price for it."

"It's amazing that you could do all this. There certainly is a big demand for olive oil in this country, and I thought we could only get it from Europe," said the major.

"I've been trying to get other planters along the Georgia coast here interested in growing the crop, and I've had some success. If you'd be interested, I'd be happy to supply you with sufficient seedlings to get you started."

"Well, that's very kind of you. I'll have my manager, Mr. King, take a look at it for me."

As the major was preparing to leave, Couper said, "There's a great deal of interest being shown around here over your coming to our meeting next week at the St. Clair Club. Everyone's anxious to see you again.

"That's very nice; I am anxious to see them as well. I'm looking forward to the event," replied the major.

"I think it will be a splendid evening. If you wouldn't be too embarrassed by riding in my chaise, I could pick you up on the way, and we could both go together."

"It would take more than that to embarrass me, Mr. Couper. I'd be delighted."

"Good. We'll have to leave a bit early, me being the designated host and all. Need to make sure that all the preparations are made correctly. I'll be at your place around eleven o'clock."

✳   ✳   ✳   ✳

Coupr picked the major up on time, and the two men headed down the clamshell road toward the St. Clair Club, which was located midway down the island. They were accompanied by two of Couper's lackeys and one of the major's, who followed on horseback.

When they had proceeded a short distance past the Hampton Point entrance, the major, while looking at all the surrounding cotton fields, remarked, "It amazes me to see all this cotton growing on such a small island. It's been a good year for all the planters, I'm sure."

"Yes, it has." replied Couper. "Everyone's planted as much as they possibly could. This island is fourteen miles long and anywhere between two and three miles wide, and there's hardly a square foot of it that doesn't have cotton growing on it. Wasn't long ago that a great deal of the island was still covered by woods—mainly live oaks and myrtles. There was some good hunting then, but not anymore.

"There are fourteen plantations in all. This makes us a good bit different from all the other barrier islands along the coast—like Cumberland, Jekyll, and Tybee. All the others are owned by just a single family, with only one plantation on them. We're more of a community here, which adds a lot more spice to the social life.

"For being such a little place in a remote part of the world, we've got quite a diverse, and, shall I say, sophisticated population. We've got Englishmen, Scotsmen, and Frenchmen living here—all college-educated professional men. They include former statesmen, military professionals, college professors, and businessmen—with varied interests in fields like philosophy, religion, arts, and science. It all adds up to a very stimulating group. It's never difficult to find someone willing to intelligently discuss just about any subject you choose.

"Most of the planters are members of our club, and you'll see them today. I believe you'll recognize most of them, possibly with the exception of the two Wyllys, who are new. There'll also be two other guests besides yourself—Thomas Spaulding of Sapelo Island and Monsieur Christopher Paulan du Bignon of Jekyll."

"I know them both well," said the major.

"Good," replied Couper. "It's Thomas Spaulding who should get the credit for the growth of the Sea Island cotton industry in Georgia and Carolina. His father, James, was actually the first person to plant the cotton from seeds he got from a friend in the Bahamas. But it was Thomas who turned it into a profitable crop and promoted growing it in the region. We all owe a debt of gratitude to him for doing it.

"Look there! See that old wagon trail going through the field? That leads over to the old town of Frederica. Dates back more than seventy years to General Oglethorpe's days. Hard to visualize that a thriving community was there once with more than a thousand residents. Nothing there now … I suppose it's a sign of how things change in this world. By the way, speaking of change, I'll bet you haven't seen our new lighthouse at the south end of the island, have you? You'll have to go and see it. It's magnificent—more than seventy feet tall now. It's almost finished—be commissioned next March."

Couper steered the chaise into a drive leading to a large old house a hundred yards off the main road.

"Here we are, the world-famous St. Clair Club. Well, maybe not 'world-famous,' but certainly one of the most delightful meeting establishments in the South. It's the old Sinclair Plantation home; been kept up quite nicely over the years. It's owned by some distant member of the Wylly family, and, for the past two years or so, it's been our meeting place. As you'll see, it is a most welcoming meeting place indeed.

"The main entrance is around front, but we need to go in at the lower level here in the back. I've got to check on how things are going in the kitchen."

The two men were met by a flurry of activity as they entered through the basement door. Waiters and kitchen staff were busy preparing food, removing dishes from pantries, and polishing silverware. "This is Johnny, Sandy, and Ol' Dick. They're waiters from Cannon's Point. And Lydia over there is mine, too. The other two are on loan from Major Page and are here to help out," said Couper. "Where is Sans Foix?"

"Here I is, behind dis curtain," called out a voice.

"Oh, I see now," said Couper. "Sans Foix! Stick your head out and say hello to Major Butler."

"I'll surely do dat." And, in a few seconds, a black face appeared around the side of the curtain, sporting a broad smile. "It surely is a great pleasure to see you again, Massa. I hope you's been well."

"I have, and it's good to see you again," replied the major.

"Sans Foix is preparing his famous boneless turkey dish for our dinner this evening," interjected Couper. "It's a big secret how he's able to remove all the bones from the bird and get it back into its original state, looking new again. That's the reason for the curtain. He doesn't want anyone to see how he does it."

"A secret, indeed," replied the major. "I remember it well. It's one of the best meals I've ever eaten. Your reputation as the best chef in all of the South is well deserved."

"Thank you, Massa. I hopes you likes tonight's meal just de same."

"I'm looking forward to it."

Couper and the major proceeded up to the main level of the house. "This is our dining room; the table seats fourteen ... the next room over here is our library. It has a cozy sitting area near the fireplace, and, as you can see, we have quite an extensive collection of books. They cover a great many subjects—from history, to geography, to agriculture, and philosophy. It would be hard to find its equal anywhere in the South," said Couper.

"It certainly is an impressive collection."

"The other main room on this floor is the game room. We've got two billiard tables, a snooker table, card tables, dart boards—and whatever else one needs for entertainment. Listen, I hear horses outside. Some members must be arriving."

In a few moments, the front door burst open, and in walked Alexander Wylly and his son, William. Still brushing some of the road dust from his clothes, the elder Wylly remarked, "What's that old lady's chaise doing out there alongside the house? I thought we only let men attend these meetings."

"Oh, I'll admit it's mine. I've gone and hurt my leg, and the doctor won't let me ride a horse for a while," replied Couper.

"I know—I was only teasing. Word around these parts is you got hurt picking up a three-hundred-pound cotton bale all by yourself."

"Not quite, but that story will suffice. I'd like you to meet Major Butler."

"Oh, yes. I'm pleased to meet you, Major. I've heard a great deal about you. This is my son, William."

"It's a pleasure to meet you both," replied the major.

Within minutes, the rest of the members arrived: Major William Page of Retreat plantation, the former manager of Hampton Point; Dr. William Fraser of Lawrence plantation and his son John; George Braille of Village plantation; Raymond Demere of Black Banks plantation; Benjamin Cates of Kelvin Grove plantation; William Armstrong of Pikes Bluff plantation; and Daniel Heysward Brailsford of Broadfield plantation. Two guests were also among the arrivals: Christopher Paulan du Bignon, owner of Jekyll Island, and Thomas Spaulding, owner of Sapelo Island.

There was a great deal of comradeship shown among the men, and all were delighted to renew their acquaintance with the major.

Everyone was still crowding together in the entrance hall when the loud voice of John Couper rang out, "Gentlemen, I'm sure we'd all do better if we moved into the game room."

"Yes, the Wyllys are here to challenge the Frasers in a game of snooker. We want to reclaim some of the money we lost last time," said Alexander Wylly.

"I'm looking forward to a good game of billiards." remarked another. "And I some smart cards," remarked still another.

As the group began moving into the game room, Couper turned to the major and said, "Well, do you fancy a game of billiards, Major?"

"I don't play the game very smartly, but I'll be a good spectator."

"Perhaps you'd rather adjourn to the library. We could get ourselves a cup of Mrs. Couper's orange rum punch and try to solve some of the world's problems around the fireplace. I have some fine cigars that would put us in the right mood for a good discussion."

"I'd like that very much," replied the major.

"And, if the two of you don't mind, I'd like to join you," interjected George Braille.

"As would I," added Benjamin Cater.

After lighting their cigars and receiving a cup of orange rum punch, the four gentlemen settled into deep, comfortable chairs surrounding the fireplace. Braille, exhaling a big puff of cigar smoke, began the conversation.

"I must say, I've had a very perplexing morning. This past week we've had three Negro children born on our place, and I'm having a dickens of a time finding a sensible name for any of them. With 140 Negros, all the good names seem to have been taken. For the likes of me, I can't think of any new ones."

A general chuckling erupted among the group, with Couper responding, "I know exactly how you feel. I've long since used up all the common names like Joe, Sam, and Sue, as well as classical names like Caesar, Nero, and Pompey. I'm now onto Biblical names—Abraham and Moses. Where I'll go next I haven't the slightest clue."

Braille interjected, "I've heard of one plantation owner in Mississippi who asked his sister to do the naming for their Negroes and she came up with Alexander de Great, General Jackson, Walter Scott, Napoleon

Bonaparte, and Queen Victoria. Now that's carrying it a bit far, don't you think?"

"I must say," said the major, "your problems pale in comparison to mine. I've got nine hundred Negroes, and it's an impossible task to assign them all names. I've given up long ago and let the Negroes choose for themselves. In recent years I've found that names like Betty and Mollie have become popular. I think we have at least eleven Mollies on the place. We've had to call them Mollie One, Mollie Two, Mollie Three, and so on; even a Jack's Mollie. And there's at least one named for each day of the week, and each month as well."

"I let my people choose their own names, too," said Cater, "and I've noticed a bit of a trend lately, as well. There are fewer and fewer Negroes choosing African names for their children. There aren't very many Quashes, Quaninas, or Jubas anymore. English names are more popular."

"That's right. It's probably because each new generation is becoming more and more Americanized, don't you think?" said Couper.

"Yes," replied Cater. "We've been banned by the federal government from importing Negroes into this country for over three years now, and Georgia hasn't allowed imports for more than ten. It's forced us into relying on a high birth rate to home-grow our labor force. Although I suppose we still get some from Virginia, where there's a lot of Negro breeding going on."

"The tobacco planters in Virginia and Maryland have worn out their land, and it's not very productive anymore. They are either selling off their Negroes or moving them to new plantations in Kentucky and Tennessee, and some even to Alabama," said Couper. "It may be a source of new hands in the short term, but, in the long term, we'll have to rely totally on growing our own."

"In the main, I think we're doing a good job of that here on the island," said Cater "Our Negro population seems to be increasing nicely. But I'm not certain that's the case on plantations in other parts of the state. What's been the experience on your rice plantation, Major?"

"Well, our operations are still expanding, so we've been continually bringing in new people. But our Negro birth rate has improved some, and we're now operating nearly at a break-even. There's no question that the work is far more demanding on our rice plantation than it is on our cotton plantation, though, and life expectancy is considerably shorter, too. The damp working conditions don't help any, and I'm no longer as convinced as I used to be that Negroes are totally immune from the 'summer sickness.' More and more of them seem to be affected by it."

"That's why I prefer being a cotton farmer instead of a rice farmer. It's much less risky," said Cater.

"Yes, it is," replied the major. "But much less profitable as well."

"You know, there's something about the practice of Virginia planters that disturbs me a great deal, especially those who operate breeding stations where they sell off young Negroes," said Couper. "I feel it's an inhumane practice. I don't think there's a single planter in Georgia who would sell any of his Negroes if he didn't have to. Oh, yes, if there's a need to settle an estate, Negroes may have to be sold, and maybe an occasional recalcitrant hand or habitual runway, too. But Negroes here are nearly always sold as part of a family unit, not as individuals."

"You're right," replied Cater. "Georgia planters are more humane."

"I agree wholeheartedly," interjected the major. "And I would add one more thing on the federal government's ban on importing slaves. The U.S. Constitution permitted importing for a period of not less than twenty years, which, at the time, seemed like an eternity. I was a member of the Constitutional Convention when the provision was voted on and a member of the U.S. Senate four years later, when Congress made the twenty-year period the absolute limit. In both instances, the instigation for the time limit came from northern abolitionists. These provisions passed easily, and I'm not sure if we Southerners realized the impact they would have in the long term. It's my opinion, they were the first steps taken in a far-reaching plan abolitionists have for completely eliminating slavery in this country. Since their passage, we've had additional legislation that's banned importing slaves into the District of Columbia, which wiped out one of the country's largest slave-trading markets. And the ban on importing slaves countrywide is being enforced more rigorously now. I feel we will need to brace ourselves against an onslaught from the abolitionists in the future, and I'm afraid their movement is growing in strength."

"I couldn't agree with you more, Major," said Braille. "It may require us taking matters into our own hands and breaking the blockade against slave imports."

"Now, don't let us forget what happened the last time we tried something like that," interjected Couper. "That illegal slave runner who came to this island a few years ago tried hiding his ship in Dunbar Creek. And when he off-loaded a bunch of Igbo slaves, a number of them drowned themselves in the creek in protest. It was a total disaster. Word spread all over the island and spooked every Negro here. They even call the place where it happened 'Ebo's Landing' and claim it's haunted. There's not a single one of them who'll go anywhere near there."

"That's because Negroes are all very superstitious," replied Braille.

"I'd call them plain ignorant," interjected Cater. "It goes far beyond being superstitious. I can't tell you how infuriating it is to have to explain how to carry out every task you want them to do in minute detail—and then, in the end, have them just stand there and stare at you as if you hadn't said a word. It's sometimes easier just to do the job yourself."

"I've found them to be a bit of a paradox," Couper broke in. They often appear ignorant when you're trying to explain something to them—but very crafty and intelligent in the way they try to get out of work or steal your property."

"You're right," replied Cater. "It's almost as if they have two different personalities. One that shows allegiance, and another that constantly tries to sabotage your operation by stealing from you or running away. You'd think because of all the good things we do for them, they would show greater appreciation and loyalty. We give them all the necessities of life—food, clothing, shelter, and medicine. How can they not understand this?"

"In the main, I believe it's their inherent ignorance that keeps them from doing so," replied the major. "Most of them fail to comprehend conceptual ideas and have no inclination to better themselves in the world. In reality, they are an inferior race that has become totally dependant on white society for their existence and well-being. White society has assumed the role of protector and benefactor for these people and now must accept the burdens that go with that role."

"I think we'd all agree with you, Major," said Braille. "And, based on the present condition of the Negro race, it's a role we'll have to keep playing for some time to come. The true realities of the situation make a mockery of all the talk we hear from northern abolitionists about the need to emancipate them."

"Amen, Mr. Braille." said Cater. "Can you imagine what would happen if we Southerners turned all our slaves loose—all one million of them? My God! It would turn the entire South into a gigantic African country. These people are devoid of moral rectitude and haven't a clue how to govern themselves. It would be a disaster. White people would either voluntarily leave or be driven out of their homeland. All the hardships whites have endured to develop this land and wrest it from British tyranny would have been endured in vain."

"I agree, gentlemen," replied Couper. "Moving too quickly to emancipation would be wrong. I oppose the position of northern abolitionists and disagree with their contention that slavery, per se, is immoral. Slavery has been present since the beginning of mankind. It's existed by the will of providence—and justified in the Bible by patriarchs and prophets from the day of Abraham to the period of St. John's Revelation. It should not bother any man's conscience that he owns slaves, especially under the benevolent conditions that exist here on this island.

"But that doesn't mean that we can't move toward eventual emancipation for Negroes. It's just that we must proceed carefully in preparing for such an occurrence. And this, in my opinion, can only be done through enhancing their religious understanding and sensibilities."

"And just how would you propose to do that?" asked Carter. "We've all at one time or another tried bringing preachers—white and black— onto our plantations. It hasn't worked. Negroes tend to mix their African superstitions with the Gospel and get confused about religious principles. And the ministers incite insurrection. I don't know of any planter who lets them give sermons to their people anymore."

"I, for one, won't let those so-called ministers set foot on my property," remarked the major.

"Well, we might start taking a closer look at what the Reverend Charles Colcock Jones has been doing up in Liberty County," replied Couper. "He's devoted his life to ministering to the Negro community, and I believe he's made good progress. He's developed what he calls a 'catechism' that uses a series of verbal questions and answers to teach biblical concepts and to explain the role slaves have played throughout history. According to some of my friends who live up there, he's had a calming affect on the Negro population, and they are very pleased with his work. I'm hoping he'll publish his methodology so that it can be spread more widely in the South. I think it would be applicable here."

"With all due respect, Mr. Couper, teaching religion to Negroes may indeed help them become more enlightened individuals, but, in my view, there is no better way to advance their character development than through the enforcement of proper discipline. Rules of behavior are necessary for running a plantation, and they should be established and followed to the letter," said the major.

"And when Negroes don't follow rules to the letter?" asked Couper.

"Then there must be some form of punishment handed down. I don't mean this has to be in the form of a whipping necessarily, but whipping is the most effective type of punishment. It certainly gets the message across to them," replied the major.

"I concur that discipline is necessary, but whipping as punishment should be used sparingly," said Couper.

"Yes. I agree," interjected Braille. "Plantation rules should not only set the standards of behavior but should be used for instructing Negroes as well. In some cases, infractions can be overlooked or handled with only minor penalties. I prefer, in most cases, to merely withhold privileges rather than whip a Negro—whipping should be the punishment of last resort. Most Negroes seem to understand kindness, and, if you treat them well, they'll treat you well."

"I wish I could believe that, Mr. Braille," replied the major. "But my experience tells me otherwise. It's my opinion that most Negroes respond only to either the fear of being punished or to the punishment itself. And that punishment is the lash. My plantations are run very much like a military operation—strictly by the book. The intent is not to overlook any infraction. If one Negro gets away with something he shouldn't, others will try to do the same, which places the entire system in jeopardy.

"I would agree, however, that whipping can be counterproductive if it's carried to extreme. A Negro is valuable property, and excessive whipping can damage that property. And to prevent this from happening, I've placed strict limits on how many stripes a driver or overseer can give a Negro."

"I suppose we all walk a fine line between dealing out too much or too little punishment for infractions," replied Couper. "But I would say, Major, your approach to maintaining discipline seems a bit more severe than what's used by others on the island. In your case, though, it's probably warranted. All the rest of us live on our plantations year-round. This gives us ample opportunity to observe the actions of our Negroes and establish a more personal relationship with them. You, on the other hand, are an absentee owner who can't maintain the same degree of personal interaction. The only way you can be assured that discipline is maintained is to set rules and charge your overseer with enforcing them."

Ting! Ting! Ting! Couper's waiter, Johnny, moved through the house ringing a small silver dinner bell.

"Oh, that means our meal is ready. Come, let's join the others, before they eat everything in the place," said Couper. "We can continue our discussion over dinner, or switch to a more pleasant one such as the high prices we're getting for this year's cotton crop."

When everyone had gathered in the dining room, the designated host, John Couper, made the seating assignments around the large table in a manner that would "ensure good conversation and comradeship." The room had a cheerful atmosphere. A great wood fire burned in the fireplace, and scores of candles, placed in bright brass candlesticks on the table, lit the room. The dishes were of blue East India china.

Couper sat at one end of the table, with the major on his left and Thomas Spaulding on his right. A round of white wine was served, and Couper stood to propose a toast. "It is with great pleasure that we welcome three distinguished gentlemen here with us tonight: our old friends, Major Pierce Butler, Mr. Thomas Spaulding, and Monsieur Christopher Poulan du Bignon. To your good health, gentlemen."

Amid cheers of "Hear, hear," all the members stood and joined in the toast.

"And I would also like to present another toast: to President James Madison. May he have the wisdom and courage to guide our young country to the position of prominence it deserves! Now, let's begin."

The first course consisted of two soups, a crab and corn chowder, and a chicken mulligatawny. Red wine followed, along with the main course. Large covered silver plates were positioned around the table; they contained fish, shrimp pies, crab in the shell, pork roast, mutton, and boneless roast turkey. Everyone helped himself to whatever he wished.

The conversation around the table was lively. At the far end, it centered on the virtues of Moliere. In the middle, Alexander Wylly recounted his recent travels to the Creek Indian territory. And, at the head of the table, the major, John Couper, and Thomas Spaulding engaged in a discussion about crop rotation, a new concept that was being tried to revitalize agricultural land.

Following the main course and dessert, the chef, Sans Foix, was brought out and given a standing ovation for what everyone considered to be an excellent meal. It was then time for brandy and cigars.

Couper again rose to speak. "As you all know, as acting host on this august occasion, I am privileged to have the honor of selecting the main after-dinner topic for discussion. I have been thinking long and hard about this for weeks now and planned a presentation on the 'care, feeding, and propagation of the palmetto palm.' I'm sure this would be of great interest to all of you, since the palm grows like a weed all over this island. But rather than put everyone to sleep within a matter of minutes, I decided to do something different. Our good friend, Major Butler, as you all know, played a key role during the early history of our federal government and is very knowledgeable about what's happening at that level. I didn't want the occasion of his being here to pass without gaining some of his insights. So I've asked him to give us his views. Major Butler ..."

"Thank you, Mr. Couper. As many of you know, I'm no longer an active member of the U.S. Senate, so I'm not directly involved with events that are currently taking place in Washington. But you can be assured I keep my finger on the pulse of what's happening.

At the beginning of our dinner this evening, we drank a toast to President Madison. I think I will begin my remarks by addressing some of the more significant problems he is now facing in the middle of his first term in office.

As a result of all the warmongering that's been going on between Britain and France over the past three years, Britain has recently taken steps to block shipping from neutral nations to the continent of Europe. They have intercepted our vessels and confiscated our cargos and seamen almost at will, and, despite our warnings, they continue to do so. The situation has become serious and could result in our breaking relations with Britain. If that were to occur, it would have a devastating affect on our cotton trade.

"There's been some talk of our establishing an embargo that would prevent shipments of American goods being made to England, despite the failure of a similar action taken some years ago by President Jefferson. This talk is getting serious, but, right now, it's a game of wait and see. I don't think there are sufficient votes in the Congress for Madison to declare war against Britain, but that's a possibility, too. We in Georgia need to rally our congressmen to vote against any such action if it were ever proposed. Our cotton would sit and rot on the docks of Savannah if either an embargo or war took place.

"Now, looking at some of the domestic issues Madison is facing, it's my opinion …"

*   *   *   *

At ten o'clock a bell rang, alerting members that the meeting was at an end. Reluctantly, some of them rose from the table and began preparing to leave. A few remained, crowding around the major—still wanting to ask questions. Finally, Couper prodded all of them to leave. The meeting was over.

The last to leave were, of course, Couper and the major. Two lackeys, holding pine-knot torches, preceded them on horseback as they rode home in the chaise. Another lackey brought up the rear with another torch.

"A delightful evening," said the major.

"I'm glad you enjoyed it," was the reply.

*   *   *   *

After breakfast the next morning, the major took a stroll outside, down the path that led from the front entrance of the Big House to the river. The sun had come up over Little St. Simons Island, and the smell of orange blossoms from the nearby fruit orchard permeated the air. It was a beautiful day. When he reached the embankment, he paused and gazed out at the scenery. Miles and miles of marsh grasses, light green in color, lay before him. It was one of the most beautiful sights he'd ever seen. On the far western horizon, he could dimly make out the masts of several ships docked in the port of Darien, some five miles away. He marveled at how far a person could see in the low delta country.

His eyes then focused on a point of land just south of where the ships were docked. This, he imagined, was where his rice plantation was located. He felt a rush go through his body and thought how fortunate he was to own such magnificent property. It, along with Hampton Point, had made make him a very wealthy individual— arguably the wealthiest man in America. He inwardly smiled when the name Butler Island crossed his mind. He thought it reflected the island's proper status—as did the name Butler River, which he had registered for the channel of the Altamaha River that passed by the north side of the island.

Turning around, he paused momentarily when he caught sight of the Big House at the far end of the garden path; he marveled at how grand it was. His thoughts then turned to his former wife, who had died thirteen years earlier just prior to the completion of the house, "What a shame Mary isn't here to enjoy this. It's exactly what she wanted." He then began walking in that direction.

"You all look very nice in your uniforms. Each of you has two uniforms and you must wear a clean one every day. That means you've got to have one of your uniforms washed and ironed every night. Take them to Glandy at the laundry building; she'll handle this for you. Do you understand? You must also take a bath every day and wash your hands several times during the day as well. You'll be wearing white gloves, but you must always have clean hands. You must also remember to wear your shoes at all times."

Frances was addressing the group of waitresses, maids, and waiters who had been selected to serve guests at the upcoming gala. She had just finished inspecting them individually and was admonishing them with last-minute instructions. The servers were all lined up against the dining room wall while she spoke. The women were wearing neat black dresses that reached to their ankles, with white cuffs and collars, small black bonnets with white ruffles, and white aprons. The men wore black trousers and jackets, white shirts, and red bow ties. And each server wore black leather shoes.

Frances continued, "We have only three days left before the guests arrive, and we still have a lot to do to get ready. You should all know what your jobs are by now, but does anyone have any questions? Okay, then, remember that all the guests who are coming are very important people. Be courteous to them and always smile. If they ask you to do something—no matter how trivial—always say 'Yes, Missis,' or 'Yes, Massa,' and go do it as quickly as you can. If you don't understand exactly what they're asking for, go see House Mary—she'll know.

"Okay, you can take your uniforms off now, and get on with your work."

Frances left the dining room and walked out into the main hall, just as the major was coming in through the front entrance. "What is all this?" he asked.

"It's our new dining table, or, rather, five dining tables we've strung together to make into one. We can't feed all our guests at one time in our normal dining room—it's too small—so we're moving it all out here in the hall. Even so, it'll still be a bit crowded," replied Frances.

"My goodness, have we invited that many people?"

"Yes, we have, and I'm glad you're here. I want to go over some of the planning with you. Let's go into the drawing room."

Once the two were seated near the fireplace, Frances, looking over a sheath of papers she was holding, said," We have received acceptances from fifty-seven adults. We can expect possibly seventeen children and at least thirty-five servants to be accompanying them. That means we have to be prepared to handle more than one hundred people during the ten-day period."

"My Lord! How are we going to accommodate all those people?" asked the major.

"I'll get to that, but first I want to cover how we're going to get them all here. Elizabeth will accompany Dr. and Mrs. Rush from Philadelphia to Charleston, arriving in late November—probably by the twenty-sixth. We are to have the plantation schooner there to pick them up on December first. At the same time we'll pick up the Middletons, Pinckneys, and Brailsfords. The members of the Shakespearean cast and orchestra we've hired will board the schooner then, too. The ship will make a stop at Savannah and pick up the Berriens—arriving here on December third. The rest of the guests are all local, and they will come either by their own boat or carriage.

"Now, how we accommodate them all is a complex issue. Although there are twenty-six rooms in this house, there are only seven that are suitable for use as guest bedrooms. Elizabeth and I will double up and share one of them. And I've assigned the others to the Rushes, Middletons, Pinckneys, Pages, Spauldings, and du Bignons—our most honored guests. We'll stick six other families—particularly those with children, in the three guest cottages out back. We can fit one family upstairs and another downstairs in each cottage. I've also made arrangements with the Coupers to take in four families at Cannon's Point. A boat will be stationed at their place to provide transportation for the guests across Jones Creek, so they won't have to go the long way around. After that, we're depending on the rest of them to go back to their own homes on the island after each day's activities—although the Frasers have agreed to accommodate some of them if necessary. I think that should do it."

"I'm certainly glad you're handling all this! It looks fine to me."

"Now, let's talk about the overall schedule of events," said Frances. "Of course, the whole ten days is really focused on the regatta that's to take place on Sunday. It's the main event of the gala. But we've got a lot more events planned as well.

"On the first day, which is a Sunday, too, people will be arriving at all hours of the day, so we'll keep things informal. We'll serve a buffet dinner on the piazza, and the Shakespearean cast from Charleston will perform *MacBeth* in the drawing room for our evening's entertainment.

"Overall, there'll be five formal sit-down dinners in our newly enlarged dining room during the gala. These will be followed by dancing in our old dining room, which is now mainly vacant. We have a five-piece orchestra.

"Early on Tuesday morning, there will be a hunting expedition for men, over on Little St. Simons Island. I understand that deer and boar are plentiful this time of year. The ladies will go by carriage down to Retreat Plantation at the far end of the island and be the guests of Mrs. Page for lunch. We'll get to see the new lighthouse while we're there.

"Wednesday night, there'll be Negro boxing at the stables for the men. We'll have drinks and cigars there to enhance the event. Negro wrestling will be on Friday night. A buffet dinner will be served on the piazza on both of these evenings.

"On Saturday evening, we'll put on our own performance of *Midsummer Night's Dream* with authentic costumes. Our Shakespearean cast will coach us in this, and we'll have tryouts for various parts earlier in the week. There are quite a few parts in the production, and almost everyone can get involved. It should be a lot of fun."

"I already know what part I would like to play," remarked the major.

"That's fine, but you'll have to earn it. I think the competition will be fierce! Now, for the children, we'll have organized games every day and a clown and mime for entertainment. There will also be a special event for them on Wednesday, when they'll take a cruise completely around the island in the schooner, stopping in Darien and Brunswick.

"There will also be a variety of activities scheduled on an informal basis each day. Tea will be served both on the piazza and in the sunken garden at eleven o'clock and at two o'clock. A string quartet will play music on the piazza during tea, as well as during the hour before dinner. And we'll have horseback riding, fishing, boating, and croquet available all day at the beck and call of guests. On a couple of occasions, I'm sure I'll be able to talk Mr. Couper and Mr. Fraser into reading poetry to the ladies out under the live oak trees as well.

"And, finally, the regatta, which I know holds your greatest interest. It will be held on Sunday between noon and two o'clock. This is the time, I'm told, when there will be a high tide but little movement of the water one way or the other—perfect for the race. We'll have a festive luncheon down at the river's edge, near the finish line, so everyone can watch the races. In the evening, we'll have an outdoor pig roast by the river, as well. This will be followed by a choral performance by our Negro singers. The actual presentation of the regatta trophy to the winner will be held over to the following evening's dinner—as a grand finale. And that's it!"

"I'm really astonished by what all you've done! I think this will be the grandest event this little island has ever witnessed."

"You bet it will," replied Frances.

*   *   *   *

The gala went off almost without a hitch. Everyone had a good time. Some highlights included:

The men's hunting expedition on Little St. Simons Island proved successful. Raymond Demere shot a two-hundred-pound boar and William Fraser an eight-point buck. Three days later, Benjamin Cates shot a sixteen-point buck.

Daniel Brailsford's Negro, Maxi, easily beat all comers in the boxing event. He was crowned champion and awarded one hundred dollars in prize money.

The performance of *Midsummer Night's Dream* was a huge success. Dr. Rush played the part of Demetrius, the jilted lover. Oberton, the King of fairies, was played by Major Page, and Puck, the mischievous elf, was played by William Fraser. The major played the part of Nick Bottom, a stage-struck weaver who gets his head turned into that of a donkey but gets his girl in the end.

There were eleven entries in the regatta, two by Monsieur du Bignon. They were all colorfully decorated boats, with crews dressed in bright uniforms. As each entered the water, they rowed up past the finish line to be formally announced and viewed by the excited onlookers. Loud cheers were given for each. *Shamrock II*, of course, with its crew dressed in white uniforms and green sculling caps, drew the most applause and was the sentimental favorite. The eleven boats were divided into three preliminary heats of four, four, and three boats. The winners of the three heats then had a runoff to determine the champion. *Shamrock II* easily won its heat, beating the next-fastest boat by a full length. And, surprisingly, both of du Bignon's boats won their heats, but by lesser margins. The times for all three heats, though, were nearly the same. The major was pleased with his win, but it was obvious that du Bignon had made improvements to his boats as well, and he was a bit worried.

The championship race came down to a duel between *Shamrock II* and du Bignon's *Liberty*. It was a neck-and-neck finish, which had the three judges huddled for over ten minutes trying to determine the winner. After an emergency supply of brandy was delivered to sharpen the judges' eyesight, the winner was finally announced—*Liberty*. Although disappointed, the major took the loss magnanimously, announcing to all present, "Monsieur du Bignon, the best boat has won. Congratulations on a magnificent victory!"

This was the first time in a very long time that one of the major's boats had been this competitive in a regatta. And as a reward for their gallant effort, he gave his eight crew members and coxswain, Pinder, ten dollars each.

✴   ✴   ✴   ✴

It had been an exhausting ten days for everyone involved with the gala. Afterward, both Frances and the major looked forward to a more relaxing time during the remainder of their stay.

Despite their desires to the contrary, this would be the last time either of them would ever set foot on the Georgia plantations.

CHAPTER 4—WAR OF 1812

In support of its ongoing war with France, Britain began intercepting American vessels on the high seas to prevent shipments from reaching France. She impounded cargoes on captured ships and impressed American sailors into the British navy. Although in a weak financial and military position, the United States responded to these "outrages" by declaring war against Britain. With little breathing room following the Revolutionary War, therefore, the country again found itself in a military conflict with Britain, in the War of 1812.

During the first two years of the war, fighting was concentrated in upper New York State and in the Chesapeake Bay region—including Washington DC. There was little impact on the State of Georgia.

This changed abruptly in early 1815. Britain's war with France ended, and thousands of British troops were redeployed from European operations to the American war effort. Britain's immediate new objective was to capture the city of New Orleans in order to gain control of the Mississippi River. In support of this operation, Admiral Sir George Cochran was ordered to vacate his position in the Chesapeake Bay and move southward to the coast of Georgia. This movement was intended to draw American forces stationed in the south away from the military assault that was about to take place at New Orleans. The admiral was to create havoc along the coast—capturing as much territory as possible, liberating slaves, and fomenting internal rebellion.

On January 10, 1815, British forces invaded Cumberland Island, the southernmost barrier island along the Georgia coast, some twenty-five miles south of St. Simons Island. They met no resistance. The following day, they captured the city of St. Mary's on the mainland and then began moving northward along the coast. On January 13, three

British frigates sailed north up the inland waterway to the old town of Frederica on St. Simons Island. They fired two warning shots to alert people in the area and then landed a battalion of Royal Marines. Again, there was no resistance. British troops moved freely about the island.

Roswell King was greatly disturbed by the invasion and wrote Major Butler on January 20, advising him of the situation:

> I fear that this is the last letter I shall write to you for a time, and I write this day for fear the Enemy will be here before my usual day of writing. With all my exertions I have only got to Market 216 Tierces rice, and all the old crops of cotton. The first 30 bales of new cotton I put on board Mr. Couper's sloop under deck, and by stupid management it never started, and is now on board up the river as high as it can go, and I have 57 bales more in boats as high as I think will be safe and I must build a house to keep it out of the weather. I expect the Enemy will take all the rice we have pounded out, which is about 300 tierces. I have stopped pounding rice and ginning cotton and drove the oxen back. By what I learn from Cumberland and St. Mary's, we shall not have any kind of stock left that they can catch or Negro that they can persuade away.
>
> The British have landed 2,500 troops near St. Mary's—1,600 are black. Deserters from the neighboring plantations are swelling their ranks. Your Negroes, however, truly behave well.

The very next day, thirty-six Royal Marines, led by naval officer Lieutenant Alexander Horton, reached the southern boundary of Hampton Point plantation. They proceeded up the road toward the Big House, passing the slave settlements at Busson Hill and Jones Creek. These settlements were deserted. Slaves had become frightened by the invasion and hidden in the nearby woods.

When the marines reached the grounds of the Big House, they were met by King standing erect in the middle of the road. Crowded around behind him were fifty or sixty slaves, all with frightened expressions on their faces.

"My name is King. I'm the manager of this plantation. What can I do for you?"

"Good afternoon, Mr. King. I'm Lieutenant Horton of His Majesty's Royal Navy. Under terms of war, we have captured this island and are now in the process of securing the land area. We are here to scout the contents of your plantation and to give a message to your Negroes. We hope there'll be no resistance to our doing this, but if there is, we are prepared to deal with it."

"Be assured sir, there'll be no resistance, and you are free to look around."

On a signal from Lieutenant Horton, the marines began moving about the premises, examining facilities and taking notes on the contents they found. In less than an hour, they reported back.

"Well, you seem to have quite an operation here," said Horton.

"Yes, we're a self-contained plantation."

"Tell me, why haven't my men been able to find any horses or oxen here, like we have at other plantations?"

"That's because we don't use them here," replied King. "The last ones died about six months ago, and we now do everything by hand."

"That's very interesting. Would you please gather all your Negroes together in a group? I'd like to address them."

When the slaves had assembled, Horton began to speak, "I'm Lieutenant Horton of the British Navy. I am your friend, and I've come to bring you some good news. If you would like, you can become free persons—no longer be slaves. Yes, that's right, we are offering you freedom. You will be able to do anything you like and not be under the control of your master any longer.

"We are offering freedom to all of you who want it. We will not force you to take it. If you want to be free, all you have to do is go down to the Frederica wharf and board one of our ships. We will first take you to our camp on Cumberland Island, and, within four weeks after that, you will be in Canada, where you can live as free people."

A great murmur erupted among the slaves, with many showing excitement.

"Now, remember, we will take only those of you who go willingly. Each of you must decide for yourself if you want to be free. For those who do, it will be the best day of your lives. If you don't choose to go, you will never get another chance. You'll remain here being a slave until the day you die.

"We want you to think about this. We'll be back here tomorrow morning to answer any questions and begin taking you to our ships. This is a glorious day God has made for you. God bless you all."

At that point, Horton led the marines back down the plantation road in the direction of Frederica.

King had stood dumbfounded all during Horton's speech. When the British left, he gathered his wits and addressed the slaves, "That's the biggest bunch of hogwash I've ever heard. They're nothing but a bunch of liars. You know how badly they treated your parents on those godforsaken slave ships that brought them over here from Africa, don't you? If you get on one of their ships, you'll probably die from starvation or some disease. And they won't be taking you to Canada, either. They've got in mind selling you as slaves in the West Indies."

Word of what had happened spread quickly, and there was a great deal of excitement throughout the plantation. The whole slave community congregated around campfires, talking among themselves—no one bothered to sleep that night.

The next morning, only a few slaves reported to work at the usual time. And when Lieutenant Horton and his marines returned midmorning, there were more than two hundred gathered on the Big House grounds.

Again King stood in the middle of the road as the marines approached, blocking the way. "You cannot proceed any farther," he said in a loud, commanding voice. "This is private property. We are all civilians here and are not part of the war effort. By the law of nations, you cannot attack or destroy civilian property. And the Negroes here, sir, are personal property of the owner. You are therefore not allowed to confiscate them in any manner."

"I am not aware, Mr. King, of the 'law of nations' you refer to. I am merely following orders. And, as a matter of fact, we are not confiscating your Negroes. We are offering them a proposition, which they can freely choose to take or not take."

"No matter what, you can proceed no farther. You must go back to where you came from."

"No, Mr. King, we are here to carryout our mission. You can either get out of our way and let us proceed, or I will have you arrested."

When King refused to move, two marines arrested him and placed him in hand irons. As he was being led away, he turned and yelled to Horton, "Do what you please. These Negroes will never leave this plantation."

Lieutenant Horton then began meetings with small groups of slaves, explaining in more detail what the British plans were and answering questions. Midafternoon, when he felt there was a lull in the activity, he stood and addressed the entire gathering. "We are taking all the materials and supplies that we've collected here back to our ships now. If any of you would like to come with us at this time, you are free to do so. The rest of you still have time to think about it some more. But remember, you have only two more days to do so. Our ships will leave on the evening tide the day after tomorrow."

Without saying a word, two slave families picked up their belongings, which they'd gathered in blankets, and followed the troops down the plantation road.

*　　*　　*　　*

After the troops had left, the slave community was abuzz. Everyone was talking about "freedom" and about the shortness of time they had in which to decide. Word went out that there would to be a meeting of the Council of Elders that evening at Busson settlement to discuss the matter—"everyone be there!"

That evening, the Council members sat on benches near a large campfire. Hundreds of slaves gathered around in a big circle. There was a great deal of murmuring among the group, until Harold, the head elder, rose to speak. Then all became quiet.

"We's all here to talk 'bout de freedom offer de navy man told us 'bout. I knows dar's lots of interest in de matter, an' peoples got different opinions 'bout it. We's here to hear both sides. So's, we'll let one person talk at a time, an' everyone listen to what he ses. Do you understand? Okay, who wants to talk first?"

Jupiter, a young man in his twenties, was recognized. "Dat navy man dat come here is just like Moses. He done come to lead us to de promised land!"

Jake, a tanner, piped up, "I been livin' on dis plantation ever since it got started. I cain't tell you how many niggers I'se seen tryin' to 'scape an' git to Canada. Dar plenty more dat tried over on Butler Island, too. None of dem has ever made it. Dar's just no way out of here. Georgia's a long ways from Canada—an' dose dat tries gets caught, and brought back, an' whipped half to death. One time I wanted to 'scape, myself, after my wife Helen got whipped by Massa King. All's I could do was just stand dar an' watch. I couldn't do nothin'. I was nothin' but a slave, not a true man. It would have been different if I'se free. Now dis navy man is gonna make it easy fo' us to git to Canada an' be free—widout havin' to take de chance of gettin' caught an' bein' brought back here. I ses dis is de opportunity we's all been waitin' fo', an' we better take it while we can. Won't be no other chance in our lifetime."

Rascal, an older slave, put in, "I'se mighty old now—been livin' a long time. Ain't got much to do, 'cept clean out de cabin an' mind a few chickens. Ain't got much longer to live, neither. But I'se tellin' you one thing. All my life I'se wanted to be free—almost couldn't think of nothin' else. Never got de chance, though. Now, what dis navy man is offerin' is de answer to my prayers. De Lawd has finally heard me an' is showin' me de way. I'se surely goin' to take it—even if I dies on dat ship."

Others rose to express their views, both pro and con ... "Thar's goin' to be a lot of dying on dat ship." ... "We ain't gonna get 'nother chance." ... "It's too cold up in Canada fo' niggers; we'll all die up dar." Slaves clapped when each speaker finished, and "amens" were heard.

At one point, though, a hush came over the crowd. A visitor had come among them, and a pathway was cleared for him to approach the Council. It was old Tom, the head driver from the neighboring plantation at Cannon's Point, who was well known and respected by most of the slaves at Hampton.

"Good evening, brother Tom; what brings you over here tonight?" asked Harold. Tom was a devout Mohammedan who had been a slave on a British plantation in the West Indies. "I'se come here to give you some advice dat's based on my own experience. It's de same dat I'se given to my own people 'cross de way." He then described the inhumane treatment slaves had suffered under British owners in the West Indies. He compared his treatment under the British to what he'd experienced here on St. Simons Island—the treatment here had been far better. He told them not to trust the British, and strongly urged them not to accept the offer. When he finished speaking, he left and went back to Cannon's Point.

Old Tom's speech threw a damper on the enthusiasm that had built up during the meeting. Shouts still reverberated for freedom, but now there were expressions of doubt and indecision as well.

Harold stood up and addressed the crowd. "De Council has made de decision not to take a stand one way or de other 'bout acceptin' de navy man's offer. We's goin' to leave it up to each of you to make de decision fo' yo'self."

A sense of relief came over the crowd, and the slaves began making their way back to their cabins. It was a decision favored by all, but most welcomed by those who were leaning toward accepting the navy man's offer. Even if the Council had decided to reject the offer, many slaves would have left anyway. Now, however, their decision would be much easier. Since there was not a consensus for everyone to stay, they wouldn't have to feel they were deserting those who would be left behind—breaking the unity of the slave community.

Knowing they had only two days in which to accept the offer, the slaves devoted the whole next day to discussions among friends and family members. Within the community, slaves were polarized. They felt very strongly about either going or not going. In some cases, a wife or husband was adamant about leaving, which forced the other partner into a decision to leave as well.

Sometimes, families split. A case in point was the family of House Mary. Mary, together with her two sons, Silas and John, her daughter Raylin, and John's wife and two sons, had gathered in her cabin throughout the morning. Silas and John were excited over the prospect of gaining freedom and were eager to accept the offer. They tried hard to convince everyone else in the family to do the same.

All of a sudden, Mary, who'd been listening for some time, had heard enough. She said, "Dat's 'nough talk. I'se made up my mind. I ain't goin' nowheres. I'se too old to be goin' on no ship way up north, where dar ain't nothin' but snow an' ice. Lawd knows, I'd die. 'Sides, when de major comes back here, who's gonna look after him? I'se the only one 'round here dat knows how to run de Big House. He'd be lost widout me."

"Oh, Mammy, you must change yo' mind an' go wid us, so's de whole family can stay together," said John.

And Silas interjected, "'Sides, it's been five years since de major's set foot on dis island. He's gettin' old too, an' he may never come back."

"I don't care!" snapped Mary, as she stood up and left the cabin.

"Oh no no!" moaned Silas, "Dis is gonna break up de family." Then, looking at fifteen year-old Raylin sitting quietly in the corner, he asked, "An' what 'bout you, Raylin?"

"I ain't goin' neither!"

"Why? Why?" asked Silas.

"'Cause I ain't gonna leave Mammy here alone. She gettin' on in age now, an' who gonna take care of her when she's down if I ain't here? 'Sides, I ain't got no complaint 'bout de way things is. I'se got a good job an' I likes what I'se doin'."

The members of Mary's family went their separate ways.

In another family, a recalcitrant bricklayer, Sancho, refused to leave. As a result, he was stripped of all his clothing and blankets and left naked by his mother, while the rest of the family went off to join the British.

The overwhelming choice was to accept the navy man's offer. The word "freedom" was on everyone's lips. By late afternoon, groups of ten or more were leaving the plantation on their way to the British ships at Frederica. Some sang an old spiritual as they went:

> Oh Canaan, sweet Canaan
> I'se bound fo' de land of Canaan
> I thought I heard dem say,
> Dar was lions in de way
> I don't 'spect to stay
> Much longer here.

Run to Jesus—shun the dangers
I don't 'spect to stay
Much longer here.

By the next morning, the plantation appeared deserted.

*   *   *   *

Meanwhile, on Butler Island, the slaves were all in a stir. They were aware of what was happening at Hampton Point and kept wondering what was taking the British so long to get to them. All work had stopped, and many slaves wanted to commandeer the plantation's boats and join the Hampton slaves. Few boats were available, however, and the prevailing opinion was to be patient and just wait for the British to show up. The British never did.

*   *   *   *

Roswell King returned to Hampton Point on February 4, following his release from confinement. He found the place stripped to its bare bones. Virtually all tools used by guild workers, household goods, wine and rum, farm animals, cotton, and silverware were missing. And, more importantly, so were most of the slaves.

There were only eight field hands left on the entire plantation—not a single shoemaker or tanner, only three blacksmiths and two bricklayers. In all, 138 slaves were missing—two-thirds of the entire slave population.

King was livid! "What kind of gratitude is this? You treat niggers humanely, give 'em food and shelter, medicine, and this is what you get in return? When I get 'em back, they'll be ruled with a rod of iron to make 'em more responsible human beings. I'll teach 'em good behavior before the year's out."

Later, King learned that Hampton Point wasn't the only plantation on the island to be hit hard by the British. Neighboring Cannon's Point lost sixty slaves and Hamilton plantation 238. In total, the British had nearly two thousand slaves in custody.

King went to British headquarters on Cumberland Island and requested to speak with the Hampton slaves who'd been taken there. This request was granted by the commanding officer, although most of the slaves had already been transported to Bermuda on their way to Nova Scotia. The results of his efforts were reported to Major Butler:

> I tried to reason with some of the most sensible of the Negroes not to be so foolish and deluded as to leave their comfortable homes and go into a strange country where they would be separated and probably not live half the year out. I found none of the Negroes insolent to me; they appeared sorry, solemn, and often crying. They, however, appeared to be infatuated with their newfound freedom, to a degree of madness. When I endeavored to reason them out of their folly, some said they must follow their daughters, others their wives. I found my reasoning had no effect on the set of stupid Negroes, half intoxicated with liquor and with nothing to do but think their happy days had come.

King, along with his nineteen-year-old son, Junior, began the long struggle to reestablish the plantation's routine, with only one-third of their slave workforce intact.

*   *   *   *

All the war activity along the Georgia coast—beginning with the British invasion of Cumberland Island through to the removal of slaves from St. Simons Island—occurred during the months of January and February 1815. Unknown to all participants, this activity had taken place after the War of 1812 had been formally concluded. A peace treaty had been signed in Ghent, Belgium, on December 24, 1814. This was followed by formal ratification on February 17. Communications regarding the treaty hadn't reached Georgia in time to stop the process. Word didn't come until early March—one day before the British had planned to sail up the Altamaha River and take over Butler Island.

The fact that all the slaves had been taken from St. Simons Island at a point in time after the war had officially ended lent credence to demands made by the island's plantation owners for the British to return the slaves forthwith. However, these demands fell on deaf ears. Admiral Cockburn, the British commanding officer, agreed only to return those who "had sought protection under the flag of England" following the formal treaty ratification on February 17. This had no effect on any of the Hampton slaves—all had left prior to this date.

*   *   *   *

The value placed on Hampton slaves taken by the British was sixty-one thousand dollars. The major was livid! And his anger was directed at both the British and at Roswell King. King, he thought, had used poor judgment in not relocating the slaves to the mainland, where the British wouldn't have found them. After all, he had done this with boatloads of cotton and rice and oxen. Why hadn't he done it with the most valuable property of all? He considered it a case of total mismanagement on King's part.

Following the incident, the major appeared to lose confidence in King's ability to manage the plantations. He became overly critical of everything King did, and, at that point, he seriously considered finding a replacement for King. But in correspondence with William Page, his former manager at Hampton, he was told that it would be difficult to find an adequate replacement, and he was advised to move slowly in this regard. The link between King and the major, therefore, proceeded on a tenuous basis.

King, however, was not stupid, and he could see his tenure as plantation manager would come to an end at some point in the foreseeable future. He began setting the stage to make the separation palatable. Over the next three years, he directed more and more of his attention to his own personal business interests in and around the town of Darien. With a gang of twenty-six of his own slaves, he built and then operated a small rice plantation, located upriver from Butler Island; he bought and operated a sawmill in Darien; he acquired rental properties within the town limits; and he became a director of the newly chartered Bank of Darien. More importantly, he methodically transferred more and more of the responsibility for managing the Butler plantations to his son, Junior.

The major became annoyed with King's outside interests, and, at one point, queried him about the amount of his rental property income—stating that he thought it was about $4,000 per year. The response King gave was, "No, the rents are $2,025—the same as I make as manager of the plantations."

Since the major hadn't specifically asked about his other interests, King didn't tell him how much he made from either his rice plantation or sawmill operation; nor did he explain how he came up with the thirty thousand dollars he'd needed for these investments. What the major didn't know wouldn't hurt him.

In the same response, however, King informed the major, "I have given up the management of your estate to my son, but my mind and advice is as much devoted to it as ever." This was a roundabout way of saying, "I quit!" And, in no uncertain terms, the tie between the two men was severed.

After receiving "lukewarm," but not negative references from John Couper and William Page regarding Junior's ability to take over as manager, the major decided to give him the job. The major's health was beginning to fail, and he felt he had no other choice in making this decision.

Chapter 5—Raylin

"No, Raylin! That's not how the dessert spoon and fork should go! How many times do I have to tell you this? Here, this is the way—on either side of the dinner plate."

"But, Miss Frances ses dey should go up top de plate like I got 'em. Dat's how she taught me," replied Raylin.

"I don't care how Miss Frances taught you. She doesn't live here, and I do. And, besides, I'm the mistress of this house, and you must do things the way I tell you to do them. Do you understand?"

"Yes, Missis—but it de wrong way."

"Why, you insolent nigger! Take this!" she exclaimed, slapping Raylin across the back of her head.

Raylin, attempting to duck out of the way, bumped into the side of the dining table, knocking off two water glasses, which broke on the floor.

"Now, see what you've done! Get out of here—out of my sight. I never want to see you again!"

Raylin stooped down to pick up the broken glass.

"No no. Out! Out! Get out of here."

*   *   *   *

Raylin, fifteen years old, had been on the housekeeping staff for nearly five years. At the time of Major Butler's last visit to Hampton Point in 1810, her mother, Mary, had enlisted her to help out in preparing for the festivities that had taken place at the gala. And the major's daughter, Frances, who had served as hostess for the event, had taken a liking to Raylin. She had dressed her up in a pretty white and black maid's uniform and instructed her on how to greet people and perform various service functions. Frances had been impressed with the brightness of her personality and her willingness to learn—so much so that when she was leaving to return home to Philadelphia, she had instructed that Raylin be permanently added to the housekeeping staff. This had been a big break for Raylin, and she made the most of it—she learned to clean, do laundry, sew, and serve guests.

The confrontation over the placement of the dessert fork and spoon wasn't the first time she had had a run-in with the plantation's mistress, Mrs. Roswell King Jr. During the past several months, there had been growing tension between the two, the cause of which puzzled Raylin.

One evening, while Raylin was lighting Junior's cigar for him in his study, Mrs. King had come in and, seeing her standing there, had abruptly ordered her out of the room. And there had been several incidents where Mrs. King had complained about her appearance and ordered her to keep the front of her dress buttoned up to the neckline. Another time she told her, "Don't swish your bottom all around the place while menfolk are in the house." It seemed to Raylin that she couldn't do anything to please her mistress.

That evening, a knock came at their cabin door, and Mary got up from her chair near the fireplace and answered it. Standing in the doorway was Driver Morris, who asked, "Raylin here?"

"Why, yes," said Mary. "She's right here, come in."

"Good, I'se glad I caught you. De missis has told me she don't want you workin' up at de house no mo', and she wants me to put you to work out in de fields. So, tomorrow morning I wants you to report to Field #4 down at Busson, to help with de plantin'."

"Oh no!" exclaimed Raylin "I ain't no field hand!"

"What you mean, she ain't workin' at de house no more? I'se de head housekeeper, an' I ses she is! De missis never told me nothin' 'bout dis," exclaimed Mary.

"All I knows is what she told me," replied Morris. "An' we can sho' use some help wid de plantin'."

"Well, Morris, you listen to me. She ain't goin' to no field tomorrow. I'se gonna get to the bottom of dis, an' if necessary find her 'nother job.

An' fo' sho' it ain't goin' to be as no field hand. You can count on dat! Now go on, an' mind yo' own business."

"Okay, but you'd better git dis settled soon. I'll be back tomorrow evenin'," replied Morris as he left the cabin.

"My gracious, what's happened between you an' de missis, child?" asked Mary.

"I just broke two glasses," said Raylin, crying. She then went on to tell about some of the other incidents that had occurred recently.

"Well, child, I wish you'd told me 'bout des things sooner; I could have warned you. You know, you is fifteen years old now an' just comin' into womanhood. Lookin' mighty nice, I might add. An' menfolk is gonna start lookin' at you in a different way. Dat includes white menfolk, too. I think maybe de missis thinks Massa King's got his eye on you, an' she's jealous 'bout it. Breakin' a few glasses don't mean much to her, but havin' a pretty young gal 'round her man makes her mighty leery. It's happened in de past. She had April whipped real bad when Massa took a shine to her. Believe me, doin' field work is a lot better den gettin' whipped.

"Now, Massa King presents a real problem, an' maybe it's best you don't work at de house no mo'. What to do, though, is de next question, an' I ain't got no answer right yet. I'se gotta sleep on it. We'll talk 'bout it in de mornin'."

*   *   *   *

"Now, get up, Raylin. We's gotta get movin'. It'll be daylight soon. I wants you to get all yo' things packed up in a blanket. We's gonna catch de first boat over to Butler Island soon as de tide's right. We's gonna pay us a visit to yo' Aunt Mollie. Now, get goin'!" barked Mary.

"Why's we doin' dat?'" asked Raylin, half-asleep.

"Don't mind 'bout dat now; we gotta catch de boat."

As their boat reached the mouth of the Hampton River and turned northward into Buttermilk Sound, Mary turned to Raylin and, in a low voice, said, "Mollie and me was close as sisters when we's growin' up. We still is, even though we been livin' apart for almos' twenty years— her at Butler Island and me at Hampton. She's a mighty fine woman an' got a lotta influence over things dat goes on at Butler Island—bein' de head seamstress an' all. I'se sho' she can help us find you a good job over dar dat'll keep you out of de fields."

"But, Mammy, Butler Island's a dirty ol' place. I cain't live dar. 'Sides, I don't want to leave Hampton."

"If you wants to stay out of de fields, honey, you ain't got no other choice. Butler Island ain't all dat bad. De folks dar is all nice—dey'll make you feel right at home. Probably a lot more eligible men dar, too—if you's ever of de mind to get married. Since all de folk left wid de British navy man last year, dar ain't hardly none left at Hampton no mo'. If you stay, you'll probably end up bein' an ol' maid," replied Mary.

"Well, you's sho' right 'bout dat. Ain't seen a single man worth a second look."

After disembarking at Butler Island, the two women walked down past the long row of guild shops that were brimming with activity. "Dar's de storehouse. Dat's where Mollie does all her sewin'. We'll probably find her dar," said Mary.

Opening the storehouse door, they entered a large room with clothing piled high along the walls—men's trousers in different sizes, shirts, dresses, blouses, and shoes. In the back of the room, two women were seated at sewing machines; two others were turning large wheels on the end of each machine to provide power, and another was off to one side cutting material. "Mollie," yelled Mary over the loud noise.

"What?" answered a large woman, stopping her machine. Upon recognizing who had come into the room, she said, "My goodness, is dat you Mary? An' Raylin too? What brings you over here to Butler Island? Ain't church day is it?"

Hugging Mollie, Mary said, "No, it ain't church day. We's here on important business, an' we gotta talk wid you."

"Okay, sho'. I can stop what I'se doin'." Turning to a women in her work group, she said, "Hilda, you take up the sewin' where I left off, an' Joanna, you stop doin' de cuttin' and turn de wheel fo' her. I'll be back in a bit."

As they walked toward the door, she remarked, "We's nearin' de end of de "spring allotment"—makin' clothes fo' all de hands. Gotta finish by de end of next month, or dar'll be a lot of unhappy folk 'round here. Ain't got much time left, so's we's all workin' hard."

Once outside, Mollie asked, "Now, what can I do fo' you fine ladies?"

"Well, we got a heap of troubles," replied Mary. "You know Raylin here's been workin' in housekeepin' over at Hampton, just like me, fo' 'bout five year now." After receiving an affirmative nod from Mollie, she continued, "Well, she done reached de age where Massa King's been givin' her de eye. Ain't nothin' happened yet, but Mrs. King's got jealous an' thrown her out of de house. Wants her to work in de fields."

"Massa King up to his ol' tricks, is he?" asked Mollie.

"Yes, an' I don't want nothin' to happen to her. That's why I'se comin' to you fo' help. If Raylin can get a job over here, she'd be as far away from him as she could get—an' be outta trouble."

"I agrees. What kinda job does she want? We ain't got no "big house" over here, an' dar ain't much need fo' housekeepers."

"I knows, but there's got to be somethin' 'sides bein' a field hand," said Mary.

"Come to think of it, I could use some help wid all the sewin' I'm doin'. One of my gals is in a 'lusty' condition too—won't be workin' much longer. You ever done sewin', child?'

"Some," responded Raylin. "Done stitching, but I ain't never used a sewin' machine."

"Dat's all right; you'll do," said Mollie. "I'll need to get permission from Headman Jack. Don't think dat'll be no problem, though; he owes me a heap of favors."

"Oh, dat's truly great, Aunt Mollie—thank you kindly," exclaimed Raylin.

"Dat's okay. Now, you go take yo' belongings up to my cabin—it's de first on de right. Since yo' Uncle John died last year, I been livin' dar by myself—'cept when I takes in some women who's havin' family problems. Dar's plenty of room, so's you can stay wid me."

"Thank you again, Aunt Mollie," replied Raylin.

"Yes, thank you. I really appreciates what you's doin'," said Mary.

"Now I'se gotta get back to work, so's I gotta say good-bye. Raylin, I'll see you when I'se done, an' we can talk den," said Mollie as she turned and headed back into the storehouse.

"Well, darlin', I'se sure gonna miss you, but I'll keep in touch. I knows you'll be all right here, an' Mollie'll take good care of you."

"Good-bye Mammy," replied Raylin, with tears in her eyes. "Thank you."

Mary watched Raylin walk up through the entrance to the settlement until she disappeared from sight. "Thank you, Lawd," she said quietly. "She's a mighty fine gal; help her all you can." She then walked back to the landing to wait for the next boat heading to Hampton.

✳   ✳   ✳   ✳

Raylin's training as a seamstress began at a very rudimentary level. Her first job was to turn the large wheel on the end of a sewing machine, which gave it power. The wheel moved easily, especially at high speeds, but less so when there was need to constantly stop and start during intricate sewing maneuvers. When her arms grew weary, she'd trade off with another worker—usually sewing buttons on shirts or cutting clothes from patterns. The whole group was under a strict deadline to complete the spring clothing allotment, one of two such allotments given to all hands during the year. Aunt Mollie had little time to give her instructions on how to operate a sewing machine but promised to do so once the allotment was finished. Raylin liked being in the environment and learned a great deal on her own by observing the others.

The clothing distribution took place on a Saturday afternoon. Slaves from all four settlements—men, women, and children—formed in long lines, starting in front of the storehouse and stretching back as far as the clearing in front of the cookhouse. Clothing was piled high on makeshift benches, and, as the slaves passed by, they received one item of clothing after another, depending on their gender, size, and occupation. By the time a slave made it completely through the line, his or her arms were piled high.

As part of the process, Raylin handed out trousers to male slaves. She performed this task enthusiastically, always with a smile on her face.

Several men struck up conversations with her as they passed by, asking her name and where she was from. She enjoyed the experience and, more importantly, got to see firsthand what the young male population looked like. Of course, it was sometimes difficult to distinguish between good-looking young men who were single and those who were married, but, overall, she was encouraged by what she saw.

Later that evening, while Raylin and Mollie were sitting in their cabin, a loud knock came at the door. It was Driver Nero, saying that the couple in cabin #14 was fighting again and the neighbors were complaining. Without saying a word, Mollie left the cabin to go to the scene. In less than thirty minutes, she returned with a young mother, Gabriella, and her two small children. Gabriella looked like she'd been beaten—the side of her face was swollen, and she was crying.

Mollie washed her face with soap and water, and, after she had calmed down, told her she could stay with her that night. She would deal with Ham, Gabriella's husband, in the morning. She then put her and the two children down to sleep in Raylin's bed.

"I'se sorry to put you out so," Mollie said to Raylin. "I'll get some extra blankets an' make a bed fo' you next to the fire. You'll be cozy there."

"Dat's fine," replied Raylin. "I sho' feels sorry for Gabriella; she must have a mean husband."

"Dat's a fact. Dis ain't the first time dis has happened, neither, an' tomorrow I'se gonna give him a piece of my mind. An' if he don't improve, I'se gonna bring him up 'fore the Council for punishment he won't ever fo'get."

"You know, Aunt Mollie, I'se been here six weeks now, an' dis is de third time I'se seen you get right in de middle of some problem here in de settlement. I can't even count how many womenfolk has asked you for advice, too. Peoples sho' do depend on you to keep things goin' right 'round here."

"Well, honey, someone's gotta do it. An' being as old as I am, I s'pose people thinks I'se had 'bout every kind of problem dar is an' knows how to deal wid them. I like helpin' folk an' feel pretty good when things turn out right."

"You're a real good woman, Aunt Mollie. I sho' hopes I turns out half as good as you."

"Now, now, child, dat sho' wouldn't be hard to do. An', by de way, speakin' 'bout you, didn't I see you playin' up to all dem good-lookin' young men dat come through de clothin' line today?"

"Well, I wouldn't 'xactly call it playin' up," responded Raylin, blushing. "I was just tryin' to be friendly—'sides, dey was playin' up to me more dan I was playin' up to dem."

"Oh, yes! I noticed dat, too. Dar's quite a few eligible young men on dis plantation. Some would make a good catch fo' a pretty gal like you—an' some wouldn't. Maybe tomorrow at dinner I can point out some of de good ones to you an' see what you think."

"I'd be much obliged, Aunt Mollie."

A light rain shower came up the following evening, and the slaves in Settlement No.1 crowded into the cookhouse to eat their supper. Mollie and Raylin had gotten there early and taken seats at a corner table, where they could see everyone as they came in through the door. "Dat's Jacob" said Mollie as a man in his early thirties entered. "He's maybe too old fo' you, too set in his ways. Alex, de man next to him is over thirty, too ... Oh! Dar's Justice. He might be one worth lookin' at—he's a field hand an' mighty han'some ... Dat's London; he's an apprentice cooper—a little older den you, but good-lookin' ... Oh my goodness, dar's Tony; he's a real ladies' man an' mighty good-lookin', don't you think?"

Raylin held her opinions about the men Mollie identified, until they'd left the cookhouse and were walking back to their cabin. "Dar's a good many attractive men 'round here. It might be hard decidin' which is de right one," said Raylin. "But, at first sight, dar's four dat appeals to me—Justice, Tony, London, an' Michael."

"Dey appeals to me too. You gotta good eye fo' men. Dey's all good-lookin'."

"Bein' good-lookin' helps, but de man I wants gotta be smart, too. He's gotta want to make somethin' of hisself, not jus' be a good-for-nothin' wid no ambition."

"I cain't agree mo' wid you, child. It looks like you gotta good head on yo' shoulders, too. What we gotta do, honey, is find out a little more about des men—you know, what makes dem tick inside. An' maybe we can begin doin' dat at de shout comin' up a week from Saturday. I'se sho' dey's all be dar."

"Okay! I didn't know dar's a shout comin' up. Dat's excitin'. I sho' likes to dance," exclaimed Raylin.

*　　*　　*　　*

"Raylin, you sho' is lookin' mighty pretty," said Mollie as they were getting ready for the shout.

"Well, thank you, Aunt Mollie. I'se sho' excited—been practicin' all my dancin' moves. I'se plannin' to knock de eyeballs outta all de men."

"I'se sho' you will, honey, but let me help you a bit. I wants you to wear dis headband dat I got when yo' Uncle John was alive. It's de brightest dar is on dis plantation, an' it'll make you stand out 'bove all de rest. Des beads'll help too."

"But what will you wear?"

"Don't you worry none 'bout me. I'se only goin' to watch a bit. You's gonna be de big attraction."

"Thank you—I cain't wait fo' it to start."

By ten o'clock, people began gathering in and around the hay barn, waiting for the festivities to begin. Then, the slow beat of a drum sounded, followed by the strumming of a banjo. Two fiddles cut in, and the music began getting faster and faster. People started whooping and hollering and whistling. All at once, a couple burst out from the crowd into the middle of the barn and started waving their arms and gyrating their bodies, moving slowly around the room, shuffling their feet. The crowd encircled the couple and began clapping to the beat of the music. The shout had begun!

One dance followed another—sometimes with everyone dancing, sometimes small groups, and sometimes a few couples only. Raylin was very conspicuous and caught everyone's eye.

At midnight, the dance she'd been looking forward to took place. It was a "ring shout"—for single men and women only. Men formed in an outer ring and women on the inside. At specific intervals, each woman would move from one man to the next, dancing with each one, until she had moved completely around the ring. It was Raylin's opportunity to get better acquainted with each of the men she was interested in.

By chance, she was paired with London for the first dance. "Good evenin', Mr. London," she said. London may have mumbled some response, but the music started, and it was unintelligible. Raylin's dance moves were animated and sexy—London's were stiff and unimaginative. She felt no magic or connection while they danced and was disappointed by what seemed a lack of interest on his part. When the music stopped, she looked him straight in the eyes and gave him a smile that would have melted any man's heart—and, without saying a word, moved on to the next man in the ring.

She had fun as she made her way around, especially when she got to Justice, who told her she was a "beautiful dancer."

At the end of the ring shout, London was despondent. He had been attracted to Raylin the whole evening but was too shy to show it. He knew he hadn't made a good impression.

Seeing their forlorn friend, Frank and Betty urged London to forget what had happened and get his courage up and begin a conversation with Raylin. He became determined to do so. But just as he was about to approach her, he was stunned to hear Justice, who had reached her moments before he did, saying, "Miss Raylin, it is dark outside, and, wid no moon, dar's a distinct possibility dat evil demons is roamin' 'round out dar. A pretty gal like you will need protectin' goin' home."

"Well, Mr. Justice, where is I goin' to find any protectin' like dat?"

"Miss Raylin, I was born to be a protector of pretty women. I'll gladly offer you my services."

"Well den, Mr. Justice, I'll gladly accept yo' kind offer."

*　　*　　*　　*

A month following the shout, word was passed through the community that a meeting of the Council of Elders would be held at the main campfire site in Settlement No.1. It would be on Thursday at nightfall. There had been a great deal of discussion among the slaves over several community problems of late, but there was no indication of what topics would be addressed at the meeting. Raylin went as an observer.

The first issue was a trial for a man accused of stealing another man's chicken. After several witnesses testified against him, he was found guilty and ordered to pay the owner two dollars and perform four hours of work on the weekend, cleaning drainage ditches in the settlement. A second man accused of a theft was found innocent. The head elder then gave a lecture on why slaves shouldn't steal from one another, and warned of severe punishment for those who were caught doing it. "We's all brothers, an' we gotta stick together, if we's gonna survive under de white folk's rule."

It looked to Raylin that the Council was addressing only minor issues—not what she had expected. And when the head elder asked if there was any further business to come before the Council, she abruptly stepped out from the crowd and raised her hand.

"Oh, Miss Raylin is dat you? You's new in dis community, ain't you? You probably don't know dat women don't usually speak at des meetin's—only de men."

"Yes, I'se new here, an' I'se sorry to cause any irregularities fo' yo' meetin', but I'se s'prised you ain't addressin' one of de mos' urgent problems facin' dis community, an' I'd like to raise it as an issue."

After conferring with the other Council members, the head elder said, "Well, Miss Raylin, you seem mighty determined, so's we's willin' to make an exception in dis case. What is it you want to say?"

"I want to speak fo' all de women in de community. I'se sure everybody here knows de change in de work rules dat's been made by Massa King in givin' new mothers only three weeks off from workin' followin' de birth of dar chillun—instead of four weeks." At that point there was total silence. Continuing, she said, "Dat ain't right. Three weeks ain't 'nough fo' a woman to get back her strength, an' makin' her go back to work so soon is only goin' to do her harm—de child too. Dis past week Angela, here in dis settlement, collapsed after jus' two days in de fields. She's back in de infirmary an' no tellin' how long it'll take her to recover. De week 'fore dat, two women from de other settlements collapsed too. If de women on dis plantation is gonna keep havin' babies, we gotta do somethin' to protect dar health, or dey gonna die."

A murmur and some muted clapping came from women in the crowd. "I'se recommendin' dat we does somethin' to get Massa King to change his mind an' put back de four-week period. Maybe a work slowdown or somethin' like dat."

Raylin then moved back into the crowd and waited for a response. After some discussion among the Council members, the head elder spoke, "De situation dat you describes is of great concern to us. De kind of action you purpose, though, is mighty risky and would cause many of de brothers an' sisters here to get whipped. We needs to proceed carefully, so's the Council will take de matter under advisement. De meeting is now over. Thanks fo' comin'."

A loud murmur broke out from the crowd, and the women all gathered around Raylin and thanked her for speaking out.

As the crowd started to disperse, she began making her way back to her cabin. When she heard a voice call out from behind her, "Oh, Miss Raylin," she stopped and turned around. It was London.

"I wants to tell you dat what you done tonight was very courageous. Not many men would have been brave 'nough to do what you done, an' I'se sure no other woman would, neither."

"Thank you, but it was only a small thing."

"Oh no, Miss Raylin. It ain't small at all. There ain't much thought given 'round here about de concerns of women, an' you made everyone stand up an' take notice. I think it's a big thing."

"Why? You concerned 'bout women, Mr. London?"

"Certainly; de Bible ses we's all created equal—men and women. Dat means women should be treated same as men."

"Really? Tell me mo'."

"I'll be happy to. May I walk wid you to yo' cabin?"

*   *   *   *

"Aunt Mollie, I done completely changed my mind 'bout Cooper London. At de shout, I thought he was a dull person—not very smart. But he ain't like dat at all. Last night he walked home wid me, an' we sat outside talkin' fo' 'bout an hour. He's a smart man an' very kind too. Make a good catch. Trouble is, he's either shy, or he don't have no interest in me."

"Well, honey, I'se glad to hear you say dis. He's always been at de top of my list, an' I was awful disappointed wid yo' reaction to him at de shout. He'd be a fool not to take a shine to you, honey—de only problem is, he don't know it yet. I think we gotta help him a bit."

"What you mean?'

"Well, if he's as smart as we think he is, we gotta approach him on an intellectual level. You need to start goin' to church on Sundays and readin' de Bible."

"I don't understand."

"Well, Cooper London, he's workin' toward becomin' a preacher. He helps wid the Sunday services when de minister comes over from Darien, an' he teaches de Bible on Wednesday evenin's. You is goin' to show some interest in what he's doin'."

"I don't know much 'bout the Bible, Aunt Mollie. We never had church services over at Hampton, an I'se only been to church in Darien a couple times. Ain't never read de Bible, neither. I cain't read."

"Really? Well, I'll just have to read it to you. An' you and me is goin' to church next Sunday."

The Sunday service was held, as usual, in the cookhouse. Mollie and Raylin, dressed in their finest, found seats in the middle of the congregation. By prior arrangement, Reverend Sharper, the minister who performed the service, had his star pupil Cooper London deliver the sermon. It was a tolerably good sermon on Daniel's experience in the lion's den. London stressed the point that the Lord puts all people, including those at Butler Island, in difficult situations to test their faith.

Following the service, members of the congregation filed out past Reverend Sharper and London, making small talk and shaking hands. When Mollie came up to London, she said, "Brother London, dat was a mighty fine sermon you gave."

"Well, thank you, Miss Mollie," replied London. And, turning to Raylin, he asked, "Did you like it, too?"

"Best sermon I ever heard on de subject," she replied.

"I'se happy to hear you say dat. It sho' is a pleasure havin' you at our service dis mornin'."

"It's a beautiful day out today," interjected Mollie. "It'd be a shame to waste it. Would you like to join me an' Raylin fo' a little walk down along de canal?"

"I'd be delighted. I'se been meanin' to talk to Miss Raylin 'bout comin' to our Bible lessons on Wednesday evenin' anyway."

*   *   *   *

Raylin and London's courtship lasted six months, and the two were married on the January 15, a Sunday. Reverend Sharper performed the ceremony.

They would have liked to marry sooner, but Massa King's approval of the union was contingent upon London completing a sufficient number of tierces to accommodate the year's rice crop. This took until the end of December. All the additional approvals required for the marriage—from Headsman Jack and, most importantly, Raylin's mother, Mary—had been obtained early on.

Raylin was a beautiful bride, dressed in white. Betty, her bridesmaid, wore a large, beautiful peach colored dress she had borrowed from Aunt Mollie, to partially disguise her pregnancy. London and his best man, Frank, wore black suits and top hats. It was a fun-filled occasion, capped off with a dinner of barbequed goat provided by Headman Jack, and, of course, the traditional jumping of the broomstick. At Frank's insistence, the broomstick was held at an elevated position twelve inches above the ground, and the couple was made to jump over it backward. Raylin cleared it, but London's left foot struck the broomstick on the way down. Immediately, everyone knew which of the two would "rule" the family home.

The couple resided with Aunt Mollie during the first year of their marriage. London, with the assistance of several carpenter friends, worked during slack periods to construct a cabin for him and Raylin. It was located on the newly developed third row of the settlement. He also built a table, a number of chairs, and a bed to provide basic furnishings for the cabin. Move-in day coincided with their first-year anniversary.

If London thought that once he'd completed his cabin his life would become easier, he was greatly mistaken. Massa King promoted him to full cooper, and he was given responsibility for overseeing the work of the other coopers in the shop. Over and above this, Reverend Sharper, who preached at Butler Island, came into conflict with Massa King, who thought he was preaching insurrection to the slaves. He was run off the plantation and never came back, which made London the sole minister for Butler Island.

To help London with his new responsibilities, Raylin began acting as his assistant—arranging weddings and funerals, setting up for Sunday services, and, most importantly, helping the needy in the community. She would make sure that confined and elderly persons had sufficient firewood during cold days and nights and that the sick received care and medicine.

After a year of working in the sewing group, she was promoted to seamstress—as a full hand. She had become one of the most accomplished seamstresses in the group and was often assigned the more difficult tasks—such as sewing buttonholes in men's shirts. Once when Junior came into the sewing area to inspect the goods, he remarked how well the buttonholes had been made. He was impressed when Mollie told him Raylin had done them.

*   *   *   *

"Look right here at my 'notchin' stick',—'bout time for somethin' to happen," exclaimed London. "Dis is de thirty-ninth week."

"You don't have to tell me 'bout dat. Look how big I is," replied Raylin. "I'se got a feelin' it's gonna be a big child—been movin' 'round a lot."

Raylin and London were about to have their first child, and the expectant father was a nervous wreck. He knew too well the dangers of childbirth for both the mother and infant, and he had taken all the precautions he could think of to ensure that everything would go smoothly. He had recorded each important event during Raylin's pregnancy on his "notchin' stick": the date of conception, date of quickening (when she first felt movement), first outward signs, first pains—and he was about to record the occurrence of labor itself.

Raylin's pregnancy had gone smoothly. She was fortunate in being a seamstress, where the stress from physical exertion was far less than for the women field hands. Aunt Mollie and her co-workers had seen to it that she did only light sewing tasks, and they covered for her when her condition didn't permit her to complete her work. Mollie also sewed clothing and blankets for the new infant. London made a cradle.

"Now you make sho' an' tell me when you gets de first pains. I'll get you real quick over to de infirmary," said London.

"Oh no, you won't!" replied Raylin. "I'se havin' dis child right here in our cabin. I ain't goin' to dat dirty infirmary wid all de sick people 'round dar. 'Sides, de nurse dar is so busy takin' care of all de other folk, she'd forget I'se havin' de baby. You better get dat idea out of yo' head, 'cause I'se stayin' right here."

"How's you gonna do dat? I cain't do no birthin'."

"Don't worry, I'se already taken care of dat. Elvira, de midwife from over in Settlement No.2 has agreed to help wid de birthin'. All you gotta do is let her know when it's happenin'," replied Raylin.

"I sure hope she knows what's she's doin'."

"She does. She's done it a hundred times—even helped Betty wid her child. So don't worry."

In the middle of the night during the following week, Raylin began experiencing labor pains. At dawn the next morning, she told London he'd better get Elvira quickly. And, after stopping to alert Mollie about what was happening, he ran the half mile to Settlement No. 2.

Elvira, after calming London down, told him to go back home; she'd be there as soon as she got all her things together. She appeared at the cabin, with her seventeen-year-old daughter, Elsey, about an hour after London had returned. "What's taken you so long? She's really hurtin'," he exclaimed.

"Calm down now, everythin's gonna be all right," she said. After taking a brief look at Raylin, she ordered London to help Elsey bring in the blankets, bowls, and sheets that were in the back of her mule wagon. "An' get de ax, too," she added.

"What you gonna do wid dis ax?" inquired London.

"I'se gonna put it under de bed—it'll cut de pain. Now, put some more wood on de fire and warm dis place up a bit. An' you get out of de way while Elsey an' me straightens thin's up some and gets everythin' ready. Go outside and do somethin' useful. Raylin wants her mammy, so get somebody to go fetch her. An' you can tell Mollie she can come in whenever she wants."

The baby, a healthy boy, was born at four o'clock in the afternoon. Raylin's labor went smoothly, and it seemed the infant knew he had to wait until his grandmother arrived before he made his appearance. It was merely five minutes after Mary got there that the moment occurred. At the time, the cabin was crowded with interested observers: Mary, Mollie, two seamstresses, Julie and Cassie, Betty, and the two midwives, Elvira and Elsey.

Immediately after the birth, Elsey began cleaning up the cabin, burning the afterbirth in the fireplace and sweeping the floor. She did this carefully, so as not to disturb the ashes in the fireplace or sweep under the bed—to prevent bad luck from occurring. Elvira cut and tied the infant's navel cord. She then placed a piece of linen she'd browned in a skillet of grease directly on the navel, and wrapped a piece of flannel around the baby's middle as a "belly band" to prevent infection.

London, who had been nervously waiting outside the cabin with Frank during all this activity, was then let in. "My, what a beautiful baby—a son! I'se truly de happiest man alive!" he exclaimed.

"His name is Christopher," replied Raylin.

*   *   *   *

Raylin stayed in her cabin during the three-week confinement period she was granted. And fortunately, being a seamstress, when she began work again, she could take the infant with her and place him in the cradle London had built. In this way, she was immediately available when it came time for breast-feeding.

A few weeks later, Junior came into the storehouse on the occasion of one of his inspection visits. After seeing Raylin breast-feed the infant, he remarked that he hoped too much time wasn't being lost from her sewing work. And, if there was, he'd have the baby moved into the nursery. Immediately, Mollie rose from her sewing machine and exclaimed, "Now, you ain't got no call to say nothin' like dat! She's doin' a fine job—an' ever since I'se been head seamstress 'round here, we ain't never missed doin' our work on time. An' you knows dat!"

Sheepishly, Junior backed off, saying, "I know, I know—I was just thinking out loud." Minutes later he exited the storehouse without saying another word.

Raylin and London had three additional children. Mary, born a year after Christopher, lived only a year and a half—she died from cholera. Bran, a second son, was born a year after Mary and, like Christopher, would live to maturity. A second daughter, Betty, died within a week of her birth.

✶   ✶   ✶   ✶

"Thank you, Hannah," said London. He was picking up seven-year-old Christopher and five-year-old Bran from the slave nursery. "Hope dey behaved demselves today."

"Dey did. Dey is pretty good playin' wid de other chillun," replied Hannah.

"Don't know how you manage wid all de chillun you got here—must be thirty or forty."

"Dey sho' is a pretty crop of little pickaninnies, ain't dey? Wouldn't be able to handle dem all if I didn't have Patience and Cloe as my helpers. Dey's both twelve years old now and mighty good wid de younguns. When chillun get to be the age of yo' two, dey ain't much bother. Dey play games a lot, an' all I gots to do is to keep dem from gettin' into trouble."

"Well, if dey ever gets in trouble, you jus' let me know, an' I'll take care of it."

"Oh, I will; don't worry 'bout dat."

"Good, an' thanks again."

When they reached their cabin, London instructed his two sons, "Its time now you did yo' chores. Christopher, you got a load of sweepin' to do. When you gets done wid doin' de insides, sweep around out here in front of de cabin, too. Bran, me an' you is gonna clean out de fireplace. When we's all done an' yo' mammy gets home, we'll go to de cookhouse an' get us somethin' to eat. Okay?"

"Yes, Pappy," they both replied.

The meal that evening was sparse—a serving of cooked rice and collard greens. London's portion was supplemented with a small piece of pork, and the two boys were given as much milk as they wanted. The cook, Helen, promised that the next night's meal would be better. It would be either fish or oysters.

Aunt Mollie sat with them during the meal and afterward went back to their cabin for an evening visit. While Christopher and Bran were off playing, the three adults sat on a bench in front of the cabin, watching. Mollie finally said, "You sho' got two fine boys dar. Dey seems to get along real good wid each other—an' wid de other chillun, too."

"Thank you." replied London.

"We's very proud parents," interjected Raylin. "Dey don't seem to give us much trouble, an dey's always helpin' each other when dey needs it."

"I knows it's mighty early to tell, but from what I sees, I thinks Christopher's gonna be de smart one," remarked Mollie. "Oh, I don't mean dat Bran is dumb, by no means. But Christopher, he's somethin' special. He's got a good brain in his head. Bran'll be de stronger of de two. You can tell dat by his size. He's two years younger den Christopher an' almost as big."

"I think you's right," said London. "Dey is both good boys, but dey sho' is different."

"Lookin' at dem playin' like dat, you can tell dey's enjoyin' demselves," said Mollie. "Dey's feelin' comfortable bein' here in de settlement. Don't get to see many white folk back here, do dey?"

"No, dey don't," replied Raylin. We ain't got many white folk on de plantation. Most of de time, dar's only Massa Thompson an' his wife; Massa King, when he's 'round; and a few workers from the mainland from time to time. Dey almost never comes back here in de settlement."

"Dey is still innocent den," said Mollie. "Dey probably think dat de whole world is made out of niggers. Don't got no idea dat dis is a white man's world, and dey is white man's slaves."

"You's right, Aunt Mollie. London an' me ain't told dem much 'bout slavery. We thinks dey's too young to be concerned 'bout dat now."

"Well, child, what you been doin' is right, but dey's gettin' to the age now when dey is gonna find out fo' demselves. An' dey is gonna be in fo' a rude awakenin'. You and London gotta be prepared fo' dat, 'cause it's gonna change dar lives real good, an yo's too."

"I know you's right Aunt Mollie."

✳   ✳   ✳   ✳

One evening a few weeks later, when Raylin was putting the boys to bed, the three of them kneeled at the side of the bed and recited their usual nighttime prayer:

Now I lay me down to sleep,
I pray de Lawd my soul to keep
If I should die befo' I wake,
I pray de Lawd my soul to take
Bless Pappy, bless Mammy,
Bless Massa King, an' bless me.
Amen.

"Now, into bed you go," said Raylin. You need to rise an' shine early tomorrow. By de way, Christopher, I could use some help at de sewin' shop tomorrow, an' I was wonderin' if you'd like to go to work wid me an' help some."

"Yeah!" I sho' do! I'se always wanted to go to work!"

"Me too, Mammy, me too!" exclaimed Bran.

"No, not you, Bran; you's a little too young yet, but yo' turn will come soon. Christopher will come wid me in de mornin' and you'll go wid Pappy to de nursery as usual. Now, good night, you two."

"Good night, Mammy," they replied.

At midday the following day, Raylin had to leave the sewing shop to take some newly finished linens to the overseer's house, and she took Christopher with her. On the way, she was surprised to see Junior coming in the opposite direction. She knew they'd have to pass him. As he approached, she stopped, pulled Christopher off to the side of the path, and dropped the package of linens she was carrying. "Get dat hat off yo' head an' smile when he gits here," she ordered Christopher.

She then curtsied as Junior passed and said, "Good day, Massa." Junior merely nodded his head and kept walking.

Raylin picked up the linens and resumed walking toward the overseer's house.

"Who dat man, Mammy?" asked Christopher.

"Dat's Massa King. He run de whole plantation here," she answered.

"He de same Massa King I say in my prayers at night?

"Yes, he is."

"He seem like a nice man. Is he Mammy?"

"No!—I means … sometimes he is, an' sometimes he ain't …. Let's go in de house now."

When they were leaving work later that same day, Raylin and Christopher heard a disturbance near the entrance to the Settlement, where a small crowd of spectators had gathered. In a loud voice, a man was yelling, "You dumb nigger, dis is what you get fo' breakin' tools."

As they came up to the gathering, they could see Junior standing in the middle of the crowd watching Driver Nero administer a whipping to a middle-aged woman. The woman's back was bare. The crack of the whip startled Christopher, and he could hear moans come from the woman each time the whip struck her. He couldn't control himself, and in an excited voice exclaimed, "Mammy, why is he hitting her like dat?"

"I don't know, son."

"He hurting her. Make him stop! Look, dar's blood on her back!"

"I cain't—just be still!"

Christopher began crying and became hysterical—to the point where Raylin had to grab him and lead him away. He cried all the way to the cabin and went immediately to bed.

Later that evening, London and Raylin gathered the boys, and all four of them sat around the table in their cabin. London began, "I knows what you seen today wasn't a pretty sight—"

"Why did de man beat her like dat, Pappy?" cried Christopher. "He was real mean—he hurt her bad."

"Can't say fo' sho' why he did it, son. I s'pose she broke a plantation rule an' was being punished fo' it—just like you gets punished when you break a rule in dis cabin."

"I knows it hurts when I get punished, but you ain't mean about it. Why didn't someone stop dat man? Massa King was standin' dar— why didn't he stop him?"

"Truth is, son, it was Massa King who told de man to whip her in de first place. He don't like it when any of us niggers breaks a plantation rule. You see, he owns us, an' he can do just 'bout anythin' he wants to us. We's his property—his slaves. Dat's why we always gotta follow his rules an' do what he tells us to do."

"I don't understand. Why's we his slaves?"

"Well, to answer dat question, you gotta go a long way back in time—all de way back to yo' great-gran'pappy. When he was a young man, he used to live in a faraway place called Africa. He lived free an' did whatever he wanted. Den, one day, some white folk come and captured all de black folk in his village an' brought dem over to dis country an' sold dem to de plantation owners in Carolina. Yo' great-gran'pappy became de property of ol' Massa Bull, who made him a slave 'cause he had de power to do it. Otherwise, Massa Bull would have killed him.

"Ever since den, all de family down de line to you an' me has been slaves too—'cause we belongs to a white man, an' he's got de power to kill us, too. Now, it ain't easy being a slave, 'cause we ain't got de freedom to do what we wants. We always gotta do what de white folk tells us to do."

"White folk is better den us niggers, ain't dey?"

"Oh no, dey ain't! We's jus' as good as dem—even smarter, maybe. De only reason dey can make us slaves is 'cause dey is more powerful den we is. Dar's a whole lot more of dem in dis country den dar is of us, an' dey got all de guns an' horses. We ain't got nothin' to fight 'em wid. 'Sides, dey is all organized into militias dat are trained to fight. We ain't trained at all, an' wouldn't be no match fo' dem, even if we had guns.

"If us niggers had our freedom we'd be jus' de same as white folk. We'd all be equal."

"When will we get our freedom?"

"Well, dat's a hard question to answer. It ain't gonna be easy. You 'member from yo' Bible lessons dat de Israelites was all slaves when dey was livin' in Egypt, don't you? Dey was slaves for a long time before Moses lead dem out of Egypt to de promised land. In de end, de Lawd looked after dem an' preformed miracles to allow dem to 'scape.

"I believes de Lawd is lookin' out for us niggers too, an' someday we'll be set free. It may not be today, or even tomorrow, but someday it'll come. Maybe, fo' some of us, it won't be in our lifetime, but fo' sho' it'll be in heaven. In de meantime, we just gotta make do de best we can."

✶   ✶   ✶   ✶

As Raylin, London, and the two boys were walking home after church one Sunday, Raylin said, "Now, don't you boys forget dars a chillun's campfire meetin' dis afternoon. You don't want to miss it. Uncle Abraham's gonna tell some good stories."

"We ain't forgot, Mammy—wouldn't miss it fo' nothin'," replied Bran. "His stories is really funny."

Bran and Christopher arrived at the campfire just as Abraham was tuning his banjo. They joined about ten other children around the same age, who were sitting on the ground waiting for their favorite "uncle" to begin.

Abraham began playing a soft, slow tune on his banjo, and, in a soft voice, overlaid the music: "You knows what happens when de preacher man comes to pay a visit, don't you? Yes, we do a lot of prayin' and singin', but what else? Dat's right, we has a big supper prepared fo' him.

"Well, whenever de preacher man comes here, you ever notice how all de poultry birds 'round 'bout gets real excited—'specially de rooster?

"De rooster say: Preacher comin'! Preacher comin'!

"De guinea hen say: I knowed it; I knowed it!

"De goose say: Tell it; tell it!

"De duck say: Hah, hah, hah!

"But de turkey gobbler is a wise ol' bird. He git fussed at all de noise, an' when de rooster kept sayin': 'Preacher comin', preacher comin',' he sputtered, schu-u-un! An' say: 'What de heck do I care? You better watch out fo' yo' neck!'"

Finishing with a loud strum of the banjo, Abraham exclaimed, "Whew-eehh! Dat turkey gobbler sho' is a smart bird, ain't he? Bet he went an' hid out in de piney woods when de preacher man come, don't you? If someone's gonna git cooked fo' supper, it sho' ain't gonna be him. Dem other birds ain't so smart, is dey?

"You know somethin'? I'll bet every one of you is pretty smart too—even smarter den dat ol' turkey gobbler. You know why? Cause you gotta brain. An' if you use it, you can outsmart anyone you wants, even de white folk. But if you don't use it, you'll end up just like dem other birds—a cooked goose!

"Now, anybody 'member what story we told last time? Dat's right—Brer Rabbit an' de tar baby. Dat's a good 'xample 'bout someone usin' dar brain when dey's in trouble, ain't it? 'Member, ol' Brer Fox, he tricked Brer Rabbit into gettin' his hands an' feet all stuck up wid de tar baby. Now, dat wasn't smart on Brer Rabbit's part, was it? But he got tricked into it.

"Ol' Brer Fox had him trapped, didn't he? He couldn't decide what to do wid him—cook him for supper, hang him, or drown him. Brer Rabbit was sho' in a pickle, but he had his wits 'bout him. He kept beggin' Brer Fox to either cook him, hang him, or drown him, but, 'Please, please—don't throw me in de briar patch.' He made it sound like being thrown in de brier patch was de worst thing dat could ever happen to him. An' Brer Fox wanted to do de meanest thing he could, so he threw him in dar! Den what happened? Sho' 'nuff! Dat's exactly what Brer Rabbit wanted—'cause dat's where his home was. He liked being in de briar patch best of all, an' he thanked Brer Fox fo' throwin' him in dar. He done used his brain to outsmart Brer Fox, didn't he? An' he got outta trouble 'cause he did."

Strumming his banjo, Abraham continued, "Now, I'se gonna tell you 'nother story 'bout Brer Rabbit. Dis time 'bout his meetin' up wid Brer Bear. It all happened some time ago, on a hot summer's day.

"Brer Rabbit was walkin' 'long a dirt road near de piney woods when he spotted a well. He was thirsty, an' when he got to de well, he found dar was two buckets in it—one went up when de other went down. Brer Rabbit says to hisself, 'Dar's some nice cool water down at de bottom of dis well. Think I'll jus' get in one of des buckets and lower myself down an' get some.' He did just dat, an', after he got his fill of water, he tried pullin' hisself up by the rope—but he wasn't strong 'nough to do it. He was stuck down dar at de bottom. 'Maybe if I make some noise,' he thought, 'somebody dat's comin' by will hear me an' pull me out.' So he started singing and splashing de water 'bout.

"It wasn't long 'fore ol' Brer Bear come along an' heard him singin'. He stuck his head down de well an' saw Brer Rabbit. "What you doin' down in dis well?" he asked.

"I'se down here drinkin' some of dis cool water," replied Brer Rabbit, "Does you want some?"

"Well, dat'd be real nice; how do I get it?" asked Brer Bear.

"All you gotta do is get in de bucket and come down here where I is."

"Now, you know dat Brer Bear is a lot bigger an' heavier den Brer Rabbit is, and when he gets in de bucket he goes down. An' halfway down, he meets Brer Rabbit comin' up in de other bucket. When Brer Rabbit reaches de top, he gits out of de bucket, looks down at Brer Bear, an' says, "Dat's de way things go in dis world. Some of us is goin' up, and some is goin' down. Thanks fo' de lift; I'll be seein' you later.

"Now, tell me, what happened in dis story?" asked Abraham. "Dat's right—he used his brain to get out of trouble. Ol' Brer Bear, he was much bigger an' stronger, but Brer Rabbit was smarter den him, wasn't he?

"You gotta 'member dis. Dar's gonna be times in yo' life when you'll meet up wid someone bigger and stronger den you. An' when you does, you gotta use yo' brain. You understand?

"Tell me, when you's been around white folk, have you ever listened to dem widout ears, or looked at dem widout eyes? No, I s'pose you ain't never done dat. Well, when you's around white folk when dey is talking between demselves, dey don't want you listening in on what dey is sayin, do dey? Now, if you is gonna act like dis ..." Abraham stood up and bent over, glaring at the children, with his face turned toward them, his eyes opened wide, and his hands cupped behind his ears—"You is gonna get into trouble."

The children erupted in laughter.

"You'll sho' hear what dey is sayin', won't you? But you'll get in a heap of trouble for it. Now, dar's 'nother way of doin' it, where you can hear just as good, an' keep outta trouble at de same time. It's called listenin' widout ears and seein' widout eyes. Look, watch me now. I'll pretend I'se doin' some hoein' while de white folk is talkin'." He turned sideways to the children and, without saying a word, moved his arms as if he had a hoe in his hands. His head and eyes were fixed on where the head of the hoe was hitting the ground. Shortly, he moved to a position where his back was turned to the children. "See dat?" he continued. "Now, I was de same distance from de white folk as b'fore, an' I could hear dem talkin' just de same. I just pretended I wasn't listenin' an' dey didn't even notice I was dar. Now, when I did dis, was I usin' my brain? Dat's right!

"Well, we got just 'bout 'nough time left to sing us a song. It's one of my favorites, "My Old Missis Promised Me." It goes along wid de subject of freedom we been talkin' 'bout from time to time. You know it, so join in de chorus:

> My old missis promised me,
> Shoo a la a day,

"Now stop! Wait a minute. Come on now—you can do better dan dat. Let's start again, now.

> My old missis promised me,
> Shoo a la a day,
> When she die, she set me free.
> Shoo a la a day,
> She lived so long her head got bald
> Shoo a la a day,
> She give up de idea of dyin' a-tall.
> Shoo a la a day,

Good! Dat's all dar is. Everybody enjoy de day."

✱   ✱   ✱   ✱

"I had a talk dis mornin' wid Headman Jack," remarked Raylin. "He says you boys is gettin' to de age now where you can be useful 'round de plantation. I told him dat you ain't quite twelve years old yet, Christopher, an' you, Bran, ain't ten, but he says dat's old 'nough.

"Christopher, he wants you to be a water boy fo' de field hands down in de lower rice fields. You gotta fetch fresh water in a bucket from de river an' take it to dem when dey needs a drink. Wid de hot days we been havin' 'round here, dis is an important job."

"Oh boy, I'se gonna be a full hand, like all de other men 'round here," replied Christopher.

"Now, slow down. You's still mighty young to be a full hand. 'Sides, dis job is just to get you started. It'll be in de fields, an' it ain't the best job, 'cause it don't take much thinkin'. Wid yo' brains, we gotta find a better job fo' you in de guild shops 'fore long, so's you can put dem brains of yo's to good use—like yo' pappy does."

"When do I start, Mammy?"

"Tomorrow morning at sunup. I'll take you wid me an' introduce you to Driver Nero. He'll show you what to do.

"Now, Bran, in another week we's gonna complete de firs' sprout flow on some of de fields. An' dat's when we 'spects rice birds to start flockin' in here an' eat up all de new rice plants. Headman Jack wants you to be part of de scarecrow crew. You an' some other chillun will run an' chase de birds away 'fore dey eat everythin'. It'll be like playing a game."

"Good, I'll be a full hand too," replied Bran.

One evening, a week later, London asked Christopher, "How's it goin' out dar in de fields?"

"All right," replied Christopher, "I know how to do it all now, an' most of de field hands has stopped complainin' 'bout not gettin' 'nough water. Driver Nero's stopped yellin' at me, too."

"Driver Nero?"

"Yes, in de beginnin' he was always yellin' at me to move faster in givin' out de water. He really scared me once when he cracked his whip at me, but he never struck me wid it. Cain't say de same for some of de other field hands. Seems he's always whippin' somebody for doin' somethin' wrong. De white overseer, Massa Thompson, he do de same thing."

"Field hands seem to get into trouble a lot. Dey is always breakin' plantation rules," said London.

"Yes, mainly fo' workin' too slow an' talkin' back to de driver. De whippin's sometimes is bad, but it don't do no good. De hands speed up when he's yellin at dem, but, as soon as he goes away, dey slow down again an go on sayin' bad things 'bout him."

"Dat's usually de way things is 'round here," replied London. "When de drivers an' white folk is around, we act de way dey wants us to act. When we's alone, 'specially here in de settlement, we acts de way we wants to act.

"As you get older, you'll learn how to deal wid de white folk. Dey is different from us. An' dey got dis peculiar notion dat us niggers should be happy bein' dar slaves. Dey wants us to go 'round smilin' all de time, an', mo' important, pay dem de proper respect dey feel dey deserve. It seems dey is happy when dey thinks we is happy. An' when dey ain't happy, dat's when all de trouble starts.

"So, what us niggers gotta do, including me and you, is always make dem think we is happy. When we see dem, we gotta smile, tip our hats, say good mornin' or good afternoon, an' step out of dar way as dey's goin' by. Now, dat don't mean we is happy, but we can't let dem know it.

"Doin' what white folk tell you to do is another thing dat'll keep dem happy, too. If you get asked to do somethin', always do it de best you can wid a smile on yo' face, even if you ain't happy doin' it.

"You always got to keep in mind dat de white folk got all de power, an' dey can punish you wid de whip for anythin' dat crosses dar mind. So when you deal wid dem, try not to do nothin' dat'll make dem cross wid you—you understand?

"Now, it ain't de same when white folk ain't around. You can say or do most anythin' you want den. Dat's 'specially true when you's back here in de settlement. Dis is our home, our own property—white folk don't come back here much. We's free to do whatever we wants. Dis is 'cause no word ever gets out to de white folk 'bout what happens here. Nobody, includin' me an' you, ever tells dem what goes on. It's strictly our business.

"All de niggers dat live here are our uncles and aunts, our brothers and sisters. We's one big family, an' we all stick together. Help and protect each other, too. Even if one of de family does somethin' wrong dat upsets de white folk, we never tells on him. An' if de white folk ever asks us 'bout it, we tells dem we don't know nothin'.

"An' dar's another thin' dat comes to mind. Most white folk thinks dat niggers is dumb—which you an' me knows ain't true. So, if we's ever in trouble 'bout somethin', it sometimes pays to act like you is dumb an' don't know what de white folk is talkin' 'bout. Dis gets dem all befuddled, an dey goes off an' leaves you alone. It's a good trick to remember—works most times.

"Now, you got any questions 'bout what I been telling you?"

"How do I learn all des things, Pappy?"

"Best way is to jus' keep yo' eyes an' ears open to what's goin' on 'round you. Notice how de older folk act here in de settlement, an' how dey act when dey is talkin' to de white folk. You can learn a lot from dem. You'll learn a lot from yo' own mistakes too, 'cause it ain't all dat easy dealin' wid white folk. Dar moods change a lot, sometimes from one day to de next."

"I knows I gotta git a lot smarter den I is, Pappy. I wants to be as smart as you. Want to learn to read, too."

"Well it's a little too early to start learnin' to read. Maybe when you's thirteen or so, we'll start teachin' you."

*   *   *   *

London had for nearly twenty years been the primary reading instructor for the slaves on Butler Island. Under Georgia state law, it was illegal for him to conduct reading classes for Negroes, and it was a practice frowned upon by Massa King. The classes were therefore conducted in secret. Each year, beginning in January, London would select three slaves who had expressed interest in learning, and he would take them through a year-long program that in the end enabled them to read simple sentences and passages from the Bible. Classes met for two hours every Monday night—usually at the cabin of one of the students. The course of study was rigorous and, provided a student kept up the pace, he was allowed to continue in the program. If he failed to do so, he was dropped from the class. In some years, all three of the students "graduated," but in other years, no one did.

When Christopher was thirteen, he was admitted as one of the three students. At the first class session, he and the other students were given a copy of *Webster's Blue Back Speller* as their primary resource material during the course. The course began by having the students memorize the alphabet, and moved on to syllables and consonant combinations, whole words, and, finally, phrases and sentences.

Christopher did well—even to the point where he helped one of his fellow students "graduate." However, two years later, his brother Bran failed to complete the course. Bran didn't adjust well to formalized learning. None of his friends knew how to read either, and he didn't see the need for it in his life on the plantation.

At age fourteen, Christopher became an apprentice to Engineer Ned, who operated the plantation's rice mill. Ned was reaching an advanced age, and, when he retired, Christopher would be in a position to take over from him. It was one of the most prestigious jobs on the plantation, and both Raylin and London lobbied hard with Headman Jack in order for him to get it.

Bran, who had initially wanted to be a field hand, became an apprentice carpenter, upon the insistence of his mother. His heart wasn't in the job, and it lasted only two years. He was made a field hand.

Both brothers remained close friends as they grew up, and their ties to their family were strong. London and Raylin provided much of the "glue" that held the slave community together, and the family was held in high esteem.

Raylin continued serving as adjunct nurse for the sick, sitting up nights with some. She helped many recover from serious illnesses—but when her good friend and mentor, Aunt Mollie, become ill, she was unable to help her. Mollie failed to respond to treatment and died following a two-week illness. Raylin was heartbroken.

"I'se sorry to hear 'bout Mollie," remarked Headman Jack. "I knows how close you two was."

"She was one of de most beautiful people I'se ever known in dis world. I don't know what I'se goin' to do widout her," replied Raylin.

"I knows what you mean." After fidgeting around a bit, Jack continued, "De reason I come by is because I'se tryin' to decide what to do wid her cabin. It's de number-one cabin in de row. An' I was wonderin' if you'd be interested in havin' it."

"Why, Jack, dat's de best cabin in de whole settlement! Why you wantin' to give it to me?"

"Well, I s'pose it's 'cause yo' husband is de preacher 'round here, an' it'd be a good place fo' him to keep his finger on what's goin' on in de settlement. But, mo' important, it's a place dat's befittin' de new head seamstress on de plantation."

"What you mean? You makin' me de head seamstress?"

"I s'pose dat's 'xactly what I means."

"My gracious, dat sho' is good news! Jack, you sho' knows how to make an ol' gal like me happy. An' if dat's de case, I'd be honored to live in Mollie's cabin."

"Good. Here's de keys to de storehouse—guard 'em wid yo' life. I'll be dar early in de mornin' to tell all de others 'bout yo' new promotion."

"Thank you, Jack," exclaimed Raylin; she gave him a big hug and kissed him on his cheek.

CHAPTER 6—PASSING THE TORCH

On a cold evening in early February 1822, the major was helped to his bedroom on the third floor of his Philadelphia mansion by his daughter Frances and a servant. He never left the bedroom again, dying on the fifteenth of the month. He was seventy-seven years of age.

The Philadelphia press took little notice of the event, with only a one-line obituary appearing in the *Daily Advertiser*: "Died on Friday morning last, in the seventy-seventh year of his age, Major Pierce Butler."

Although somewhat lacking in accuracy, a "more befitting" obituary—one that would have pleased the major more—appeared in the *South Carolina Gazette* on March 2.

> Died at Philadelphia on the 15th of this month. Major Pierce Butler in the 77th year of his age. Major Butler was one of the four delegates from South Carolina who were sent to Philadelphia on the adoption of our present glorious Constitution. This honor was conferred upon him, as a feeble testimony of the greatness and high opinion of his countrymen for his Revolutionary services. He was several years a member of Congress, and his mind and influences were always devoted to his country's good. The wealth which fortune had bestowed upon him was used for purposes of beneficence, and his talents and generosity were universally acknowledged.

A month later, Frances wrote Roswell King Jr., informing him of the major's death and requesting that all future correspondence regarding the plantations be directed to her. "For the present, there will be no changes made in how the plantations are being managed."

Junior, of course, informed the slaves at Butler Island and Hampton Point. The news created quite a stir, and there was a genuine outpouring of affection. For many, the major had been the only master they'd ever known—the cornerstone on which the plantations were built. They felt they had lost the person on whom they anchored their very existence. Prayers were offered on his behalf, and many cried.

But then the questions began: "Who gonna take his place?" … "What gonna happen to dis plantation? Will it be sold?" … "Dey gonna sell us niggers? Will dey split us all up?" … "Massa got chillun, ain't he?" All of a sudden, the slaves' sympathy for their former master abruptly shifted to anxiety over what would happen to them. They knew that when masters at other plantations had passed away, their plantations had often been split up or sold to pay debts or because there was no heir. For over a week, Junior was bombarded with questions and false rumors. He constantly had to reassure the slaves that everything would be all right. "The major's got children who will inherit the property," he told them. "One of them is a son, and he'll be running it in the future—don't worry! There ain't going to be any changes."

The situation quieted down, but lingering questions remained, such as: "What dis son of his like?" … "He got somethin' to do wid de government, too?" … "How come he never been to Georgia?" … "When we gonna see him?"

*   *   *   *

The major was buried in the Butler family tomb at Christ Church in Philadelphia, in a private ceremony. Many Philadelphians found it amusing that his corpse was secretly transported to the graveside under cover of darkness in predawn hours. But this amusement paled in comparison to the shock they experienced when the contents of his last will and testament were made public. On the day before he died, the major had signed one of the most bizarre wills that had ever been executed in America.

At the time of his death, he had four adult children—a son, Thomas, and three daughters: Sarah, Elizabeth, and Frances. Both

Thomas and Sarah were married and had children. Elizabeth and Frances were spinsters.

His relationship with Thomas had been strained for a number of years prior to his death, and the two had not been on speaking terms.

Hoping to have his son develop into a man of high standing, like himself, he had enrolled him, as a small child, in an exclusive boarding school in England and kept a firm hand in directing his educational program. Thomas had remained in England for a period of eleven years, never seeing either his mother or father during the entire time. His boyhood totally lacked any warm parental affection. In addition, he hadn't met his father's expectations academically, and he had been constantly bombarded with criticism for his lack of achievement. It had caused him to resent his father.

The situation didn't improve once he returned to America. Within months, friction developed between the two—to the point where he left the Butler homestead to escape the domineering influence of his father. He later married the daughter of a wealthy plantation owner from the French West Indies—over the major's vehement objections.

The major's relations with his oldest daughter, Sarah, weren't any better. They, too, were not on speaking terms. Sarah was a highly intellectual woman, strongly independent, and almost as stubborn as her father. She never could, or would, yield to the tight parental control he tried placing on her. Against his strong objections, she had married James Mease, a Philadelphia doctor and son of the local tax collector. The couple had six children, five living to adulthood.

Fortunately for the major, he was able to maintain cordial relations with his other two daughters, Elizabeth and Frances. As adults, they both continued to live with him in Philadelphia and cared for him in his old age.

As would be expected, the major's relationship with each of his four children greatly influenced the inheritance he passed down through his will:

Frances and Elizabeth were given a lifetime interest in the two main Philadelphia residences, the in-town mansion and the country estate. And the crown jewel of all was a lifetime interest in up to 75 percent of the profits derived from the Georgia plantations. A provision was also made that if the income from these plantations should be diminished through either revolution or insurrection, or other similar calamity, other assets in his estate could be sold to meet their financial needs.

Sarah was given the sum of $67,667 to be held in trust—"free from the control and influence of her husband." There were stipulations attached to this grant that prevented her from making any further claim against the estate.

Thomas was given the sum of $20,000 and several miscellaneous land parcels in Pennsylvania and Tennessee.

The fact that the major's sole male heir, Thomas, was given so little came as a surprise to many. Under normal circumstances, it would have been expected that he'd be the natural heir to the bulk of the estate. His being ignored was a slap in the face from his father. But this wasn't the biggest surprise. The will contained two other surprises of even greater significance.

The first was the fact that none of his children were to inherit the main assets of his estate—the two Georgia plantations. Elizabeth and Frances were granted a lifetime interest in the properties, but that was all!

The second, and more intriguing, was the manner in which the plantations were to be inherited, and by whom. The major gave them to three of his grandsons: Thomas Mease, John Mease, and Butler Mease—the children of his daughter Sarah. Their inheritance of the properties, however, was made contingent on each of them dropping the surname Mease and adopting the name Butler—"They shall, as they respectively arrive at the age of sixteen years, or within twelve months after my demise, cease to use the name Mease and respectively take, assume, and use the surname Butler." If any one of the three grandsons refused to meet this condition, his share would be given to the others. And if all three refused, the bequest would pass to his other grandson, the son of Thomas Butler.

The will itself was complex and tightly written, indicating it had been drawn up well in advance of the major's death. The fact that he hadn't signed it until the day before he died reflected his desire for a last-minute reconciliation with Thomas. He had sent word to Thomas of his failing health and his desire for such reconciliation, but this never came about. Instead, because he did not respond to his father's wishes,

Thomas lost the inheritance he would have otherwise received under the terms of a prior will.

It didn't take Thomas long to arrive in Philadelphia following his father's death. When the terms of the will were made known, he was distraught. He had been denied the inheritance he felt was rightly his, and he sought to contest the will.

He proposed an alternative method for distributing the estate assets, whereby each of the four children—himself, Sarah, Elizabeth, and Frances, would share equally in the income, and ownership would be distributed in four equal parts. Elizabeth and Frances were willing to go along with this plan—the stumbling block was Sarah.

Thomas told Sarah, "I received a letter from Frances advising me of Father's illness and that he had requested I return home with my family. It was my intention to comply with this request, but due to the illness of my daughter Anne, I couldn't do so immediately. I wrote to Frances telling her of the situation, but, before my letter reached Philadelphia, Father had expired. If the timing had been better, I would have stood to inherit a substantial portion of the estate. It would be unfair now if I were left out of the inheritance."

To substantiate his position, he referred to correspondence the major had sent to each of the siblings some years prior to his death:

If you should love me, unite closely together. Allow not for a moment one thought, one impression, derogatory, from the most unreasoned friendship and affection to gain admittance among you. It is a last request of a fond father that you live in union. Let no earthly consideration induce a separation while you remain single. In every sense, in every light in which I can be viewed, it is in your interests to live together, and closely united by ties of friendship and affection.

This letter contained a compelling argument in support of Thomas's proposed plan. How could Sarah, or anyone else for that matter, fail to see that it expressed the true wishes of their father?

No one could, but Sarah rejected the proposal anyway! There were no warm feelings between her and Thomas. They had never gotten along and hadn't spoken to each other in years. And, besides, it was her sons who stood to inherit the plantations—her legacy.

After obtaining outside legal advice regarding the futility of proceeding without Sarah's support, Thomas reluctantly gave up pursuing the matter.

*   *   *   *

In the year of the major's death, 1822, his oldest grandson, Thomas Mease, was eighteen years old. He therefore had twelve months in which to decide whether or not to change his name to Butler to qualify for the inheritance. He did not wait that long—he immediately declared his unwillingness to do so. He felt it would be an affront to his father, and he urged his younger brothers to follow in his footsteps. John Mease, the second oldest, was sixteen, and, following his brother's lead, he refused to change his name, as well.

The third grandson, Butler Mease, was twelve years old and had four years in which to make his decision. And when it came time, he became a Butler! For him, the aura of so much wealth was too alluring to pass up. And, in an act that would have made his grandfather proud, he took the name of Pierce Butler.

Being the only one of the three grandsons to qualify for the inheritance, Pierce Butler, at age sixteen, began receiving income in the range of fourteen thousand dollars per year. This was three times the income earned by the most successful lawyers in the city of Philadelphia. And what's more, he didn't have to lift a finger to earn any of it.

Six years later, being envious of Pierce's wealth and lifestyle, John Mease—the second oldest of the Mease boys—recanted and changed his name to Butler as well. Pierce welcomed the move, and, in an act of extreme generosity, agreed to share the inheritance with him on an equal basis. The two brothers, thenceforth, became partners in the plantation business.

*   *   *   *

Neither Elizabeth nor Frances knew anything about the operations of the Georgia plantations. It had been over twelve years since either of them had set foot on the properties. The newly christened Pierce and John Butler were even less knowledgeable, having never been to Georgia. Collectively they knew that the current manager, Roswell King Jr., had held the position for four years prior to the major's death, and they therefore assumed his performance in the job was satisfactory. They also knew he conscientiously submitted regular reports on the plantation's operations and forwarded payments reflecting the income earned.

As long as the payments they received from Junior remained at an acceptable level, they were satisfied that the operations were being carried out adequately and were disinclined to get more deeply involved. All control over how the plantations were run, including the treatment of slaves, was left in the hands of Roswell King Jr. The Butler family, in effect, surrendered all responsibility for running the plantations and became totally dependent upon him.

Chapter 7—Junior

The sixteen-year relationship between Major Butler and Roswell King Sr. ended abruptly and acrimoniously in1818. The major, in deteriorating health, couldn't leave his residence in Philadelphia and was forced to select a replacement for King without any face-to-face encounters with prospective candidates.

During the previous three years, King had promoted his son "Junior" as his eventual successor, and had slowly allowed Junior to take over management of the operation. At the time of King's resignation, Junior appeared to be the only available candidate. Still, the major had reservations. He wrote to John Couper,

> Mr. King has notified me of his intention to do for himself—not knowing how to do better, I think of trying his son, but, before I do, I wish much of your opinion as the advisability of such a measure. He is young, and the trust is considerable to be placed in so young a man. I am truly at a loss; and I wish to have your unreserved opinion.

Couper's response was ambivalent and didn't help the major's decision process much: "He stands high in my opinion, as a correct youth, full of activity and ambition to be a planter to please you. His last two crops, though, have been badly managed—due, I believe, to poor supervision on the part of the drivers." Nonetheless, Junior, at age twenty-two, was hired.

The transition from father to son didn't go as smoothly as the major would have liked. Hearing of problems early in Junior's tenure, he wrote,

It is requisite and essentially necessary that I should be minutely informed on what is doing—what has been done—and what you propose to succeed the work doing. It is all important to myself and children who may come after me that the estate be directed in the most correct and perfect manner—that activity, without severity, should prevail in every part of it—that every individual discharge a reasonable duty. I fully rely on you being before time (not behind it) in your own work. I depend on you selling 200 tierces of rice before Christmas.

Junior failed to meet the major's demand to sell two hundred tierces before Christmas, prompting another letter,

I found no difficulty in managing the estate when I was there last. And, if I were to reside constantly on the estate, I would have everything go on with the regularity of clockwork. With very little trouble, I would keep always before time; activity without pressure should always prevail everywhere. I would, I know, make good crops when not disturbed by hurricanes and still have many leisure hours. You are a young man. You have not yet established a character in the society around you. Believe me, as you manage the trust committed to you, so you will be thought of by your neighbors. If all things go on with order and increasing industry, you will be esteemed and respected by your neighbors and will acquire my future friendship. If any of your neighbors make better crops, or if they evidence more system, you will be thought lightly of, though it may not be expressed.

In further correspondence, referring to reports of the success John Couper's son was having in the use of "systematic management techniques," he warned Junior, "If you allow young Mr. Couper to overtake you, I shall be very much mortified."

Junior's management style mirrored that of his father. Plantation rules were strictly enforced, with violators being punished. From the standpoint of the slave community, there was little or no difference between father and son.

Junior continued his father's practice of reporting to the major on a weekly basis. His "Dear Honored Sir" letters, however, were not as comprehensive as his father's, often with important events minimized or ignored completely. After the major died, he directed his letters to the major's daughter, Frances, who assumed responsibility for the estate. The letters were addressed, "Dear Miss Butler, Madam."

*   *   *   *

Within a few years, Junior fully mastered the job of plantation manager. His crops, in terms of quantity and quality, had no equal in the coastal region. He proved to be both a stickler for detail as well as an innovator in adopting new methods to improve the production process.

One of his most significant innovations was the installation of a steam-driven rice mill at Butler Island. Since the early days of the plantation, there had been two rice mills—one powered by horses, the other by tidal movements. These were primitive facilities. The rice harvest was usually completed in late fall, but due to the limited capacities of these mills, was not fully processed until June the following year. Often, large quantities of rice were shipped as "rough rice," with the husks still on, instead of as the more profitable "clean rice."

The new steam-driven rice mill was built on soft marshy soil adjacent to the main boat landing. Workmen needed to drive hundreds of pilings below the surface to stabilize the ground, and construction took more than a year to complete.

From the beginning, though, the mill was a huge success. Junior reported:

> We get steam at about 7 am and glow off at 7 or 8 pm without any interruption, unless throwing in or out of gear the millstone, which takes about three minutes. Have never gone over 12 or 13 hours daily. By pushing I can get 150 tierces weekly.

The mill produced more than three times the output of the two older mills combined—yet the slave operators were less fatigued. And to cap off this success, Junior contracted with other planters in the area to do their milling as well, resulting in a significant profit for the Butlers.

The hand-threshing operation, performed immediately prior to the milling process, couldn't keep pace with the new mill, so Junior installed steam-driven threshing devices as well—all to the delight of the slaves, who had hated doing the threshing by hand.

✳   ✳   ✳   ✳

One day, in making a periodic inspection of fieldwork activity, Junior was walking along the dirt road that bordered the southernmost cotton fields at Hampton Point. When he stopped to observe a group of slaves thinning plants near the edge of the road, his eyes focused on a female slave in her late twenties. He began walking toward her.

"Aletha," he said as he reached her, "you've been rated a half hand for some time now, haven't you?"

"Yes, Massa, 'cause I'se 'spectin.'"

"You don't look it; how long you been a half hand?"

"Oh, I don't know, Massa … not long. I'se due to be showin' anytime now."

Junior, although feeling something was odd, didn't press the issue and left the field. That evening he had the overseer check the plantation journal. He was astonished to learn that Aletha had been classified as an expecting mother for a period of eight months. And still she wasn't showing any sign of pregnancy. "That damn nigger!" he exclaimed. "She's been pulling the wool over our eyes, so's she can get out of work!" A further review identified three other women at Hampton who had been given lighter tasks over five months ago and still weren't showing any outward signs of their condition—and three women at Butler Island as well.

Junior was furious! He didn't like being taken advantage of by anyone—especially niggers. He ordered all the "pregnant" women back to work as full hands, and each of them was given extra weekend duties as punishment.

He then went to the infirmary where the "lying-in" women were being cared for. Seeing two women sitting up with their backs against the wall, holding newborn infants, he ordered them to stand up. One of the women, who had given birth just two days earlier, couldn't move, but the other stood up as directed. "You look strong enough to be working," he said. "Why are you still in here sitting around doing nothing?"

"Massa, my baby's born just three weeks ago. I ain't completed my four-week confinement yet."

"Well, you're looking strong enough to me. You don't need four weeks."

Turning to the head nurse, he said, "Sackey, from now on I want all the women out of this place within three weeks' time after they deliver. You understand? We'll try getting 'em light duties somewhere near the nursery, so they can nurse, but that's all."

"Yes, Massa ... But, Massa, some of des women is mighty weak after just three weeks. Some's got women's problem, and dey bleed a lot. Stickin' 'em back in de fields too soon only make things worse."

"I don't care, Sackey. I'm sick and tired of these niggers using their pregnancies as an excuse to get time off from work. They think up all kinds of reasons why they can't work. I won't take any more of it, and that's it. From now on, the pregnancy leave is limited to three weeks. And, furthermore, pregnant women won't have their task reduced till they start showing signs—not before."

Junior walked out of the infirmary, unaware of the added misery his actions would cause women slaves on the plantation.

*   *   *   *

On a particularly warm spring day, a gang of slaves was working in Field #6 in the lower section of Butler Island. The hands were tiring under the heat of the sun. Raylin's son, Bran, was working close by Kunjar, and, stopping to wipe his brow, said, "It sho' will be nice when dis day is over. I likes bein' out in de sun, but days like dis is just too much."

"You sho' got dat right. I'se lookin' forward to a cool drink of water—wonder where dat water boy is at?" replied Kunjar.

All at once, a loud voice rang out, "What you doin' down on de ground nigger? Git up!"

It came from Romulo, a young, overachieving driver who had recently been assigned to the gang. He was standing over a young woman who had succumbed to the heat and fallen to the ground. "Git up, I said!" continued Romulo, as he cracked his whip. "I been watchin' you, an' you ain't done hardly nothin' all day. Look, you ain't done half what you's s'posed to." At that point, Romulo raised his hand as if he were about to strike the woman with his whip.

"Stop!" yelled Kunjar from a distance as he began running toward the driver. "Don't whip her! Cain't you see she's wid child an' 'bout ready to give birth anytime now?" Pointing at Kunjar with his whip hand, Romulo replied, "Nigger, you stay out of dis an' git back to work. It ain't none of yo' business." He then struck the woman with the whip.

Kunjar grabbed the end of the whip and said in a strong voice, "You ain't gonna whip dis woman no mo'. She needs to be taken to de infirmary where she can have her child. You better understand dat right here and now. I'll finish all de work she cain't do."

Junior had witnessed the last part of this incident from the embankment at the end of the field, which was some two hundred feet away. He came riding up on his horse and dismounted, whip in hand. "What's going on here?" he demanded.

Pointing to Kunjar, Romulo said, "Dis nigger's tryin' to stop me from whippin' her. She ain't done her job. Look here, he got hold of my whip."

"Let go that whip, boy! What's the matter with you? You know you can't interfere with my drivers."

"I'se jus' tryin' to point out to Driver Romulo here dat dis woman is wid child an' 'bout ready to deliver. It'd be wrong to whip her in dis condition. Don't mean to interfere. I told him I'd finish her work, so's everythin' would be all right."

"Boy, that ain't no excuse. You deserve a good whippin' yourself," replied Junior, as he let the end of his whip uncoil to the ground.

Seeing the whip uncoil, Kunjar's entire body suddenly became tense. With his fists clenched, he took a step toward Junior—bringing the two within three feet of each other. Looking him directly in the eyes, he said in a firm voice, "Dar ain't no man alive dat's gonna whip me. I'll fight him to de death first, wid my bare hands."

Junior froze. Kunjar was at least six or seven inches taller than he was and muscular, with broad shoulders—capable of killing any man he fought. Following a lapse of several seconds, while still looking Kunjar in the eyes, Junior called out to Driver Romulo, "Let this event pass. It ain't much, anyway. This boy says he'll do her work after he finishes his. Make sure he stays here till it's all done—understand? And get this nigger woman to the infirmary." He then turned, walked back to his horse, and remounted. Pausing for a moment, he looked out over the rice field and saw the other slaves in the gang standing motionless, gawking at the scene. "What are you looking at?" he yelled. "Get back to work!" Immediately everyone got busy.

Junior knew he had lost a confrontation with a slave—a crack in his armor of superiority. To make matters worse, it had been witnessed by other slaves. Riding out of the field, he vowed to himself never to let it happen again.

All the field hands chipped in to help finish the pregnant woman's task, and in the late afternoon they walked back to the settlement as a group. As they entered, they began singing,

Hate dat sin dat made me moan
Eli, I cain't stand!
John's on de isle of Pat-te-nos
Eli, I cain't stand!
Take one brick out of Satan's wall
Eli, I cain't stand!
One of des days I'se goin' away
Eli, I cain't stand!
Won't be back till judgment day
Eli, I cain't stand!

Hearing the singing, Raylin came out of her cabin to find out what was going on. Seeing Bran in the group of field hands, she asked in a loud voice, "What's happenin'? Why's everybody so happy?"

Bran pulled away from the group and told her, "We's celebrating a miracle. Brother Kunjar saved a pregnant woman from gettin' whipped. He's a hero!"

"What you mean? How'd he do dat?"

"He stopped Driver Romulo from whippin' her after she fell. When Massa King come along to find out what was goin' on, he told him he would fight him to de death 'fore he'd let him whip him. An' ol' Massa King, he backed down. Nobody's ever seen him do dat b'fore."

"I'se afraid somethin' like dis might happen someday. Massa King's not de type dat'll let dis pass," replied Raylin.

Within hours, everyone on the plantation had heard a detailed account of what had taken place. Kunjar became an instant hero, and a celebration was held in his honor the following Saturday night. Raylin, although concerned over what Junior might do in retaliation, joined the festivities. It seemed as though the entire slave community had gained a higher level of self-esteem.

★   ★   ★   ★

One day during the early afternoon, Junior walked up behind a female slave who was hoeing in the plantation vegetable garden and said in a low voice, "Minda."

"Oh!" replied the startled woman. "Dat you, Massa? I didn't know you's there. You frightened me."

"It's time, Minda. You know what I want."

Dropping to the ground, Minda exclaimed, "Oh no, Massa, not today. I'se not feelin' well—got female problems, hurtin' real bad. Please, not today."

"Nonsense! Get up!"

"No, no Massa, please!"

Junior grabbed her by the arm and pulled her to her feet. "You ungrateful nigger. You know I treat you well—you've got the easiest job on the plantation. Now let's go!"

He pulled her by the arm over to the hay barn at the edge of the garden and flung her against the door. Minda was crying, but she reluctantly opened the door. Once inside, Junior tore off her clothes and raped her.

This was the third time he'd done this to Minda, and it wouldn't be the last. She had become his latest "fancy" and, before he would get tired of her, she would bear two children by him. Several other slave women bore his children as well—Judy, Scylla, Martha, and Betty.

Having sexual intercourse with female slaves was one of his favorite pastimes—just as it had been his father's before him. The women he favored received "benefits," such as being assigned light tasks or given trinkets. None of them, though, entered into the relationship willingly. They became submissive only through fear of being whipped.

Seeing a large number of mulatto children on the plantation, Pierce Butler once wrote to Junior asking for an explanation. Junior's response was most interesting:

> Today I received yours of the 19th inst. The information you desire regarding Judy and her mulatto son, Jim Valient, etc., I will give as well as I can from recollection. Some time about August 1814—see Births & Deaths Book—three women had mulatto children: Viz Sophy, Judy, and Scylla. As that was contraband trade, they were sent to Five Pound and remained there until 1819, when your grandfather visited the estate and moved Judy and Scylla, who had husbands, elsewhere. I think this punishment was at the express desire of your grandfather. I was absent at the time the groundwork was laid; therefore cannot say anything further on the subject, only that it was a subject of surprise that one so young and small should have a child. Why does Judy complain of her banishment to Five Pound? A thing that cannot be undone. Also Cassie, when I was at Butler Island, she complained that I whipped her when she was pregnant and when the child was born it had whip marks on it. Negroes invariably give their own version to their subjects; only give ear and you will have ripped up complaints of 30 years standing, even punishments that their grandfathers sustained; they impose a heavy task on you if they think you might right wrongs that they have had inflicted.

Intentionally or unintentionally, Junior misstated the year in which the mulattos were born as 1814. This placed the events at a time during his father's tenure as manager, not his own. And by stating that he "was absent at the time the groundwork was laid," he denied any responsibility whatsoever. He then deftly changed the emphasis of the discussion to that of not paying attention to the complaints of slaves.

Pierce Butler must have been satisfied with this response, since he made no further inquires. However, this wasn't true with Junior's wife, Julia. She was jealous of the slave women her husband became involved with. And on the occasion of both Judy's and Scylla's confinements, she entered the infirmary with the overseer and supervised the whipping of the two women. She was irate!

Junior, of course, felt no paternal connection with the mulatto children he fathered. Throughout the south, mulatto children were considered a normal part of slave society—not associated with the purity of the white race. Most plantation mistresses in the South, though, seemed to know who the father was of each of the mulatto children on every plantation in their immediate vicinity—that is, except their own. The ones on their plantations must have "dropped out of the sky."

✳   ✳   ✳   ✳

Raylin was sitting on the bench outside the storehouse eating her morning meal when Junior approached. She instinctively rose and politely said, "Good morning, Massa."

"No no, don't get up. I want to sit down a spell," said Junior.

After a moment or two of silence, Raylin said, "You's lookin' mighty troubled Massa—somethin' matter?"

"Well, nothing more than usual, I reckon. But it's sure hard to take one step forward when you're always taking two steps back."

"What you mean?"

"The dang child mortality we got here on this plantation is what I mean—it's twice what we got over at Hampton. We had two die last week, and when I was at the infirmary just now, I found another dead. If it ain't the measles, it's the cholera—but the disorder they get in the summertime's the worst. I think there's something in the drinking water around here that does it," replied Junior.

"Summertime's when de miasmas hits around here, too," said Raylin. "Peoples say us niggers don't git it—only white folk, but I'se seen a lot of niggers get it too—some died. Maybe younguns get it too—maybe even more den older folk."

"The miasmas certainly affects white people. That's why we all leave the rice plantations along the coast here during the summer," replied Junior. "But all the medical evidence we got says niggers are immune. It goes to show that nigger children are immune, too."

"Well dey sho is gettin' somethin'. I grew up over at Hampton, an' I ain't never seen no child gettin' sick durin' de summertime over dar. Why's dat?"

"I don't know. But Hampton's on high ground, ain't built on swampland like this place, and white people don't get sick over there, either. There's·something about the miasmas, that it only affects people in the low swamp areas, not on high ground."

"Well, maybe we needs to find us some high ground 'round here too, den."

"There ain't none. This island's all swamp, most of it below river level at high tide."

"Dat place up de river a piece in de piney woods where de overseer goes in de summertime—it's on high ground ain't it?"

"Yes. That's Woodville, but so what?"

"Well, what if we moved all de chillun up dar durin' de summertime? Wouldn't dat git dem out of de swamps—an' be better fo' dem?"

"Yes, it would. We'd need to build a new nursery and cookhouse for them, though. It might work. But wait a minute, wouldn't all the mothers get real upset about having their children taken away from them during the summer?"

"Probably dey would. But if dey realized it'd protect dar children from de summer sickness, they'd be okay wid it. Maybe dey could visit dem on de weekends, too."

"You know, Raylin, sometimes I think you're a genius. You've hit on something that's worth trying."

Well, I ain't no genius, but it might work."

Seeing that Junior was in a receptive mood, Raylin reopened an old topic of discussion, "Maybe if we did somethin' 'bout changing de confinement time for new mothers back to four weeks, dat'll help some too."

When he heard this, Junior's face became flushed, and he stood up abruptly. "Now, damn it, Raylin, we've gone over this time and time again, and I told you never to bring it up again. Nothing's going to change—get that straight right now. Next time you mention it, you'll get a good whipping!"

Junior's whole demeanor had changed dramatically, and Raylin realized she'd made a mistake. Standing up quickly and pointing to her lips, she said, "I knows. I knows, Massa. My lips is sealed. Dey won't speak 'bout it never again."

Picking up her lunch piggin, she backed away toward the storehouse door. "I'se truly sorry, Massa." She opened the door and quickly went inside, getting out of Junior's sight. "Wheew!"

Once she settled down, she realized she'd gotten carried away by her success in helping the children. She'd forgotten there was a line that existed between a slave and his master that should never be crossed—no matter how strong the relationship is between them. On this occasion, she knew she had crossed it.

*   *   *   *

On a bright fall day, a small boat arrived at the Butler Island landing. One of the three passengers was a short, stocky white man of about fifty years of age. He wore an old, wrinkled plaid shirt and vest, a broad-brimmed hat, and brown shoes with soiled white spats. He appeared coarse and ill bred, and had a whiskey-tinted nose and tobacco-stained mouth and fingers. His name was Amos Hinckley; he was a well-known itinerant slave trader who operated along the Southeastern coast. Accompanying Hinckley were two muscular Negro men dressed in dark blue trousers and jackets.

"Where's Mister King?" he asked as he disembarked. After being told he was at the rice mill, he headed in that direction.

Junior had been expecting him. The two huddled together in conversation for a half hour before shaking hands on a deal.

This meeting occurred during the rice harvest season, and most hands were engaged in fieldwork. Kunjar was working in an upper section, cutting rice stalks with a hand sickle. When he got word that Headman Jack wanted to see him right away down at the rice mill, he stopped what he was doing and hurried in that direction.

As he approached, he noticed Jack standing in the yard in front of the mill with two Negro men dressed in blue. Taking off his hat as he spoke, he said, "You wanted to see me, Headman Jack?"

"Kunjar, I'se sorry—" But before Jack could finish his sentence, the two Negro men grabbed Kunjar, pulling his arms behind his back and clamping iron cuffs on his wrists. One of the men then restrained his arms, while the other strapped on leg irons. Kunjar was taken totally by surprise and found himself in a position where he couldn't move.

"Kunjar," Jack repeated, "I'se sorry, but you's been sold to a slave trader who's gonna take you far away from dis place."

"Why?" demanded Kunjar. "What has I done to deserve dis? I got a family—wife an' two chillun dat I'se responsible fo'. I cain't leave dem."

"I know, I know," replied Jack. "Ain't nothin' you done. Just that Massa King has made up his mind dat it's de best thing fo' him to do. I tried talkin' him out of it, but no use."

Just then, the door to the mill opened and out walked Hinckley. "Well, well. It looks like we got us a good-looking nigger." After feeling Kunjar's biceps and pinching his cheek, he said, "Bring a good price in New Orleans, too."

Turning to look back at Junior, who had remained standing in the doorway of the mill, he said, "It's a fair deal for both of us." He then motioned to his men to begin walking toward the boat.

Kunjar stood motionless, glaring at Junior. He knew exactly what had caused the situation—the incident with Driver Romulo four months earlier. In his eyes, Junior was the lowest form of human being to walk the earth. If the two were ever to meet again, he vowed he would kill him without any hesitation. Junior, seeing the look in Kunjar's eyes, turned away and went back into the mill.

As the boat carrying the party pushed off from the landing, Kunjar heard children playing in the slave nursery near the river. He yelled out to his two sons, "John, I loves you! London, I loves you!" There was no response; they hadn't heard him. His thoughts then turned to his wife, Betsy. "I loves you too, Betsy," he said in a low voice, knowing she was far away in a rice field and wouldn't hear him even if he yelled.

That evening, Jack, along with Raylin and London, informed Betsy of what had happened. She was distraught, and so were her two sons. The whole slave community mourned for months.

✳   ✳   ✳   ✳

On August 21, 1831, an event took place far away in Southampton County, Virginia, that sent shockwaves throughout the South—the Nat Turner Rebellion. Nat Turner, known as "the Prophet" among his slave brethren, had been a docile, highly religious individual all his life; he had never given his master any trouble. But through a series of "spiritual signs," he believed he'd been given divine direction from God to free his people from bondage.

Starting with a handful of trusted friends, he killed all the members of the white family living on his plantation. He and his followers then moved from one plantation to the next, freeing slaves and picking up new recruits—and killing every white man, woman, and child they came across. The white militia in the area mobilized quickly, and the rebellion was put down in a matter of forty-eight hours. But, by that time, fifty-seven whites had been killed.

In retaliation, fifty-five slaves suspected of having been involved in the uprising were executed by white officials, following a perfunctory trial. And nearly two hundred other slaves, who had nothing to do with the uprising, were beaten and murdered by angry white mobs, with no interference from the white officials.

Nat Turner himself eluded capture for more than two months, but was finally caught hiding in a cave. He was tried for murder on November 5, 1831, was convicted, and was hung on November 11. His body was beaten, beheaded, and quartered.

Within a matter of weeks, news of the event reached the slave community at Butler Island. Alice, a young slave woman, was secretly passed a small envelope containing clippings from Richmond and Savannah newspapers during a church service in Darien. She was told to have the clippings passed on to Hopeton, Champney, Broadfield, and Hampton plantations as soon as possible.

That night, a meeting of the Council of Elders was held at the main campfire site in the settlement. More than two hundred slaves attended. The head elder, Cassius, read aloud each of the newspaper articles, giving vivid details of the events.

The news created a huge commotion among the slaves. Many wanted to take up arms and follow the lead of Nat Turner. But cooler heads prevailed. "De white folk is just too powerful fo' us to beat in a fight. Dey'd kill us all." The decision of the Council was to follow a wait-and-see policy. What had happened in the Nat Turner affair had occurred in Virginia, a long way from where they were in Georgia. If more activity occurred closer to home, they'd revisit the issue.

Nevertheless, the event created a feeling of jubilation among the slaves. For the first time ever, some of their kind had actually tried to fight back against the white folks' supremacy. Maybe others would, too. Singing lasted into the wee hours of the morning.

The rebellion caused white people all over the South to become anxious, and many questioned whether this was the first sign of a general slave uprising. Had the dam that had heretofore held slavery firmly in check been cracked open? Planters on St. Simons Island held a meeting at the St. Clair Club to discuss collective measures that could be taken to guard against a local occurrence. Out of this meeting came a new method of communicating between plantations in cases of emergency.

Despite being manager of the largest plantation on the island, Junior was not among those invited to the planters' meeting. He was not a member of "the Club." Although always treated cordially by members, he was looked down upon as an uneducated hired hand— not part of the island's aristocratic society. This attitude on the part of the planters had always been taken by Junior as a personal affront. He felt he had plantation management skills superior to any other planter on the island and should be recognized and accepted as an equal. He harbored jealousy and resentment over the issue.

On the other hand, he was invited to attend a meeting of plantation owners on the mainland, which was held at Midway, in Liberty County. Thirty-five planters attended. So did Colonel John Marshall of the state militia and Roger Griswold, assistant to the governor. Both of these men came from the state capitol in Milledgeville to lend support for any pending crisis.

The consensus at the meeting was that no immediate danger of a slave uprising existed in the area. There were, however, signs of agitation among the slaves, and feelings were strong that something needed to be done to put them to rest. A show of military force in the area was deemed appropriate. Colonel Marshall agreed to send in a fifty-man cavalry unit for a limited time. Twenty-five men would be stationed at Midway and twenty-five at Darien.

Within days, troops were bivouacked in the main city park in Darien. Daily, they rode around the area in a large group, sometimes galloping in mock pursuit of an enemy. On Sundays, they were positioned near the two churches in town, where they were highly visible to slaves attending services from the outlying plantations— including Butler slaves.

Reports of these activities were brought back to Butler Island— dampening any thoughts the slaves might have had about starting a local rebellion. But the coup de grace came the day a boatload of soldiers, dressed in dark blue uniforms, arrived at the plantation. Responding to commands from their leader, they fell into formation on the landing and marched in full view of the slaves to the overseer's house. The overseer guided them on a tour of the rice mill, guild shops, and nearby rice fields—pointing out various features of the plantation. When this was completed, the soldiers fell back into formation, marched to their boat, and departed.

It was an impressive show of force that made it clear to everyone that white folk were powerful. No further discussions about starting a rebellion took place after that. Nevertheless, Nat Turner's rebellion was remembered and discussed for a long time afterward by the slaves— they cast him as a hero.

Nat Turner also left a lasting impression on white planters in the area. They would never again feel completely at ease over their ability to control large numbers of slaves. The possibility of a slave rebellion caused many of them, including Junior, to keep loaded pistols at their bedsides at night.

✳   ✳   ✳   ✳

In terms of size, number of slaves, and crop production, the two Butler plantations were among the largest in the South. And, they had a reputation for being well managed. In recognition of these facts, the editor of the *Southern Agriculturist* asked Junior to submit an article for the journal's December 1828 edition, entitled "On the Management of the Butler Estate." Junior responded enthusiastically to the request.

His article covered various aspects of plantation management, with heavy emphasis given to the handling of the slave labor force. Some of his statements were true, but many were not. He seemed to be telling his readers that the plantations' efficiency was due primarily to the use of "paternalistic" management techniques. This couldn't have been further from the truth.

The article was written in the form of a letter.

Dear Sir—Your letter of the 29th August came to hand on the 8th inst. Nothing would afford me more satisfaction than to impart the little knowledge I possess of Southern Agriculture and plantation economy, if such would benefit others. We are all dependent on each other, and each should contribute his mite.

Disregarding deplorable living conditions, hospital care, and treatment of slaves on the plantations, he devoted a large portion of the article to what he described as "the welfare of the Negroes:"

The reputed good condition of the Butler Estate has been the work of time, the diligent attention to the interest of said estate, and to the comfort and happiness of the slaves on it.

No person of any age knows more the nature of these persons than myself; since childhood I have been on this place, and from the age of eighteen to this time have had the active management; therefore I speak with confidence. Negroes have a perfect knowledge of right and wrong. When an equitable distribution of rewards and punishments is observed, in a short time they will conform to almost every rule that is laid down.

A master does not discharge his duty to himself unless he will adopt every means to promote his interest and their welfare.

I find at Butler's Island, where there are about one hundred and fourteen little Negroes, that it costs less than two cents per week in giving them a feed of okra, soup with pork, or a little molasses or hominy, a small pie. The great advantage is that there is not a dirt-eater among them.

Young Negroes are put to work early, twelve to fourteen years old; four, five or six in a group rated a hand. It keeps them out of mischief, and by giving light tasks, thirty to forty rows, they acquire habits of perseverance and industry.

I have no before-day work, only as punishments; every hand must be at work by daylight.

A hospital should be on each plantation, with proper nurses and apartments for lying-in women, for the men, and for a nursery; when any enter, not to leave the house until discharged.

The labor of pregnant women is reduced one-half, and they are put to work in dry situations.

Elaborating falsely on the "trials" and punishment given slaves, and on the use of slave drivers, he wrote:

More punishment is inflicted on every plantation by the men in power from private pique than from a neglect of duty. This I assert as a fact; I have detected it often. To prevent abuse, no driver in the field is allowed to inflict punishment until after a regular trial. When I pass sentence myself, various modes of punishment are adopted; the lash, least of all—digging stumps, or clearing away trash about the settlements, in their own time; but the most severe is confinement at home six months to twelve months or longer.

An order from a driver is to be as implicitly obeyed as if it came from myself, nor do I counteract the execution, (unless directly injurious) but direct his immediate attention to it.

The lash is, unfortunately, too much used; every mode of punishment should be derived in preference to that, and when used, never to lacerate.

It is a great point in having, as principle drivers, men that can support their dignity; condescension to familiarity with general slaves should be prohibited.

Despite his dismal record of runaways, sometimes several at a time, he boasted:

In ten years I have lost, by absconding, forty-seven days, but of nearly six hundred Negroes.

And, finally, he gave credit to his father:

To Mr. R. King, sen'r, more is due than to myself. In 1802 he assumed the management. The gang was a fine one, but was very disorderly, which invariably is the case when there is a frequent change of manager. Rules and regulations were established (I may say laws), a few forcible examples made after a trial in which every degree of justice was exhibited. These first steps established the foundation for good discipline and orderly operations.

Junior took a great deal of pride in his published article. It was his first attempt at building his own reputation among a wide spectrum of his peers. It placed him, he felt, on a more equal footing with his aristocratic neighbors on St. Simons Island.

CHAPTER 8—HEADMAN FRANK

It was late afternoon when field hands finally completed seeding Field #16 at Butler Island. On a signal from Driver Nero, Frank partially opened the inlet trunk leading from the main canal, and water slowly poured onto the field. Using wooden boards, the hands diverted the water so that it flowed mainly down a small ditch at the edge of the field before entering between the rows of newly planted rice. Once the water was smoothly flowing down the rows, the trunk was opened wider—making the flow faster, but not fast enough to disturb the planted seeds. At the point when the entire field had a shallow covering of water, the trunk was opened fully, and the water poured in rapidly. Then, as the water reached a depth of eight inches, the trunk was closed and the water shut off.

This process took a little more than four hours and was done while the Altamaha River was at high tide. It was the sprout flow for Field #16. This flow would remain on the field for about ten days, giving the newly planted seeds time to germinate and sprout to a height of six to eight inches. The sprout flow was the first of four separate floodings during the rice cultivation cycle, and it was the most difficult to administer, since great care had to be taken not to disturb the newly planted seeds. On this occasion, the flow had gone well, and Frank was pleased.

On his way home, he stopped by the cookhouse to pick up his evening meal, which the cook had saved for him in a wooden piggin. He then proceeded up the row of cabins to #9, on the right-hand side of the settlement road.

When he entered, he was greeted by his wife, Betty, and their two children: Ishmael, age three, and Phoebe, age one.

"Pappy, Pappy, you's home," exclaimed Ishmael as he ran and grabbed Frank by the legs.

"I sho' is," said Frank as he lifted Ishmael with one arm, while carefully balancing his meal in his other. "Sho' good to see you!" He handed Betty his piggin and gave her a kiss. "Sho' good to see you, too," he said.

"Come and set down and eat yo' dinner and tell us how yo' day went," said Betty.

"Well, it went real good. De flow on #16 went widout a hitch—best I've done! You know yo' ol' man is gettin' pretty good at bein' a trunk minder, don't you? Heck, when I first started doing it, Headman Jack used to always be dar looking over my shoulder. Now he don't even show up no mo'."

"I know it. I'se awful proud of you. We's all proud of you," said Betty.

As a young boy, Frank had been trained as a carpenter, specializing in the construction of trunks. Four years ago, though, he had been made a trunk minder. It was a role he had adapted well to, and within just two years he had been promoted to head trunk minder, responsible for operating trunks on the entire plantation. He had an innate ability for determining the appropriate timing for flooding and draining operations. And Headman Jack relied heavily on his judgment in making those decisions.

$$\ast \qquad \ast \qquad \ast \qquad \ast$$

A week later Frank came home late again. When he opened the cabin door, he was shocked to find Betty wrapped in a blanket, cowering in the corner of the room, crying. Raylin and London were there trying to comfort her.

"My goodness, what's wrong?" he asked as he rushed to her side, taking her in his arms.

Betty was hysterical and couldn't speak. Raylin quickly interjected, "Somethin' terrible's happened; she's been raped."

"Raped! How? Who?" demanded Frank.

"By Massa King," replied Raylin.

"Oh no! My dear, dear wife, I'se so sorry," said Frank, as he hugged her even harder. "Don't you worry, everythin's gonna be all right."

It took several minutes before Betty calmed down enough to speak. "I don't know how it happened. I'se busy doin' my work hoein' in de tomato garden, when Massa King come up and ses he wants me to go wid him into de hay barn. I thought it was mighty strange, but I followed him in. Once we's inside, he started grabbin' at me and tearin' my clothes. He said he'd been eyin' me fo' some time and he wanted to have me. I tried fightin' him off, tellin' him I was a married woman and couldn't do what he wanted. It didn't matter none to him. He said if I didn't submit he'd beat me, and take my chillun' away from me, too. I just didn't have no choice."

"Dear, it ain't yo' fault," said Raylin. "Massa King's an evil man. He don't have no regard fo' no human bein'."

"It ain't right fo' him to do something like dis," said Frank in a strong voice. "He cain't just take 'nother man's wife and do anythin' he wants wid her. He's gotta be punished!" Standing upright, with his fists clenched, he added "I'se gonna kill him! I'll do it wid my bare hands if I have to."

Seeing rage in Frank's eyes, London rose quickly, put his arm over his shoulder, and said, "Calm down now, Frank. You gotta keep yo' senses 'bout you. It ain't gonna do no good to go off yo' rocker."

"Go off my rocker? What would you do if de same thing happened to Raylin, here?"

"I'd do nothin'. I couldn't do nothin'. An' neither can you. De white man's power is too great. You must never fo'get dat he owns you. He owns all of us, an' we gotta do what he tells us, or he'll hurt us all. We is niggers, an' that's all dar is to it."

"But he deserves to die fo' what he done!"

"I know, I know. An' if you killed him, what do you think would happen den? You'd be hung up at de nearest tree 'fore you could blink an eye. Den what would happen to Betty an' yo' chillun? Who'd look after dem?"

"I knows you's right, London, but it pains me not to get even wid dat evil man."

"I knows, but it best you let things lie."

＊　　＊　　＊　　＊

Frank succeeded in not having any contact with Junior for several days following the incident. He didn't know what he'd do if they met.

A week later, he didn't find Betty at home when he again arrived late from work—no children either. He began searching the settlement, asking everyone he met if they knew her whereabouts. Eventually, he found the children at the cabin of the head nursery keeper. She had taken them home with her when Betty hadn't shown up to get them at the end of the day. Betty couldn't be found anywhere.

Finally, through a contact Raylin had with a member of the housekeeping staff, word came that Betty was with Massa King at the overseer's house. Frank was livid, and fearful for her well-being, but he managed to control himself. All he could do was hope that she'd be all right ... and wait up for her. It was near midnight when she came in through their cabin door, crying. She had been raped again.

This time he knew he couldn't remain passive. Something had to be done to punish this man and stop him from ever doing it again.

Four days later, Frank arose from his bed shortly before midnight and went outside. It had rained earlier that evening, and heavy clouds were still in the sky, all but covering the full moon. He thought, "Dis is perfect—jus' 'nough light to see by and dark 'nough not to be seen." He knew the river would be at high tide in about an hour and he would have to hurry.

He quickly made his way up the river dike, heading to the western rice fields. He passed the first main canal and continued up along the river for about a mile. When he came to the second main canal, he began following it in a southerly direction. At Field #21, he opened wide the trunk used for draining the field. He then proceeded down the canal, opening the drainage trunks for the next four fields as well. When this was done, he walked up through the last field to the far end and opened the inlet trunk to the field. He did the same for the other four fields.

At that point, he was standing directly in front of the main river trunk, which was used to let in water from the river to the entire plantation. The river level, now at high tide, was some five feet above the level of the rice fields, and when he opened the river trunk to its maximum extent, water poured through the opening with tremendous force—it was as if a dam had burst. It immediately flooded the perimeter canal and rushed through the inlet trunks Frank had opened in the five fields—causing severe damage to the crops.

Frank stood there for a moment admiring the results of his efforts. Then, concern for his own safety jolted him into action. He began running down along the river dike, so no one would spot him near the scene. When he reached the settlement, he stole his way along the backs of the cabins until he reached # 9. He entered quietly, so as not to awaken any of his family.

He lay in his bed the rest of the night, eyes wide open, imagining the destruction the heavy flow was doing to the rice fields. His feelings were mixed, however. He knew the damage would greatly trouble Massa King and felt satisfied that he would have his revenge. On the other hand, he also felt a degree of remorse. It was the very first time in his life he had deliberately acted to harm anyone or anything on the plantation.

Just before dawn, the plantation bell rang. It wasn't the slow tolling normally used to awaken the slaves. It was a rapid clanging reserved to signal an emergency. It caused all the slaves in the settlement to rise quickly and go out into the streets to investigate. Everyone was excited, and people were scurrying around everywhere, trying to find out what was going on.

When Frank got out into the street, he saw Headman Jack hurrying toward him.

"We's got flooding in de western fields. De river dike must have broke somewheres upstream. I wants you to take some men and go down and open de exit trunk at de main drainage canal and try an' get some of dis water out of here. Me an' Driver Nero will go up along de river dike and see where de problem is. Hurry! We's still at low tide, but it won't last long."

Frank quickly commandeered an empty rice barge, and, with two other slaves, began poling rapidly down the main canal toward the exit trunk at the far end of the plantation.

There were two main canals that traversed the western fields in a north-south direction, paralleling each other. These were connected to each other at the far end of the plantation by the perimeter canal. After the river water had flooded the five rice fields, it had poured out into the more westerly of the main canals and then into the other canal, as well. And when the whole system had become saturated, it had overflowed the banks into No. 3, and No. 4 slave settlements. As Frank poled past these settlements, he could see women and children standing in the doorways of their marooned cabins with forlorn looks on their faces. It was an outcome he hadn't anticipated when he had devised his plan for revenge.

Shortly after they opened the exit trunk, most of the water had drained from the canals. At that point, Frank made his way up along the western canal to survey the scene. All five of the rice fields had been severely damaged. In the two that had been recently planted, the seedlings were completely washed out, and in the others, there were deep gullies, with no signs of the neat rows of rice plants that had existed the day before. The drainage trunks along the main canal were inundated with mud, and the canal itself was filled with dirt. A hurricane couldn't have caused more damage. When he sighted Headman Jack at the far end of one of the fields, he went in his direction.

"Dar ain't no break in the river dike," remarked Jack, when he saw Frank. "Someone's done deliberately opened all des trunks to cause de floodin'. We closed de main river inlet, so no more water can get in, but de damage has all been done."

"Dis sho' is a disaster," replied Frank.

"It sho' is, an' Massa King's gonna be mad as fire when he learns 'bout it."

Along with Driver Nero, the two men began surveying the damage in more detail. In all, 170 acres of crops had been completely destroyed. Two inlet trunks were partially damaged. All five of the drainage trunks were completely covered with mud and would have to be dug out before any damage could be assessed. Over one-half of the main canal would have to be reditched and the five rice fields reterraced. It would be a massive undertaking, requiring more than four months to complete. About one-fifth of the plantation's total rice crop was lost.

Junior was livid when he heard the news. With most of the damage being near Settlements No. 2 and No. 3, he suspected someone living there was responsible, and he ordered his drivers to interrogate every resident in an attempt to find the culprits. The interrogations were met only with silence from the slaves. The slave community either didn't know anything or wouldn't talk about it. In retaliation, Junior ordered the food rations for both settlements cut in half for an entire week. And to satisfy his need to punish someone, he personally whipped the two drivers in these settlements, giving them fifteen lashes each.

Frank felt sorry for the punishment given the innocent residents of the two settlements. But, on the other hand, he had little respect for either of the two drivers who had been whipped. They were mean-spirited in their dealings with slaves, and they deserved what had been handed them. For his part, no one seemed to even suspect him of any wrongdoing. And he made it a point to make himself useful, and visible, in helping bring order back to the operations of the plantation.

Overall, he was pleased with the outcome of his little escapade. Although severe destruction had been done to the plantation he loved, it was made right again over a period of four months. And, more importantly, he had extracted revenge on Massa King—just where it hurt the most. Rice production fell drastically that year, and Junior was placed in the embarrassing position of having to explain the incident to the Butler family. All during the rebuilding process, he was preoccupied with matters other than having sexual contact with Betty. No further advances were made.

*   *   *   *

In the late fall of that year, Frank was busy making rounds of the lower rice fields, inspecting the condition of the crops. All the fields had been under flood conditions for more than two months, and he was attempting to establish the best time to drain each field prior to the harvest. Looking up, he was surprised to see Headman Jack approaching. "Good mornin'," he said.

"It is a good mornin'," Jack replied. "Dis crop is lookin' mighty good. Gettin' near harvest time, ain't it?"

"Yes sir, dis here field oughta be drained by de end of dis week. An' we got two more down de way dat's ready, too."

"Dat's good … An' how you been?"

Frank's instincts perked up at this question. Rarely was Jack ever concerned much about his well-being. Why was he asking? "I'se okay, I s'pose," he replied.

"Dat's good, 'cause dar's somethin' I wants to talk over wid you. Massa King's wantin' to replace Driver Benton. He thinks he's gotten too headstrong in de job and gives out too much punishment fo' de good of de hands. He's nearly killed two field hands lately, whippin' 'em half to death. Massa an' me has talked a lot 'bout who should be de new driver, an' we feels you'd be de best man. An' I'se come to offer you de job, if you wants it."

Frank was dumbfounded, but he immediately responded, "Jack, dar ain't no way I'd be no driver! I'se grown up wid all de people in de settlement. Dey is my family—I loves 'em. No way could I use a whip on any of dem! 'Sides, I got a good job, an' I likes what I'se doin'."

"I know it's a good job—important, too," replied Jack. "But a driver's job is even mo' important. De whole plantation is run by drivers. An' when you consider de well-being of yo' family, it'll be mo' important to dem, too. Dey'll live in better quarters an' get better food. An' yo' wife Betty, she'd like it better too. She'd be made a half hand on a permanent basis. Dat'll make her job easier and give her mo' time to take care of yo' chillun."

"All dat sounds good," replied Frank, "but drivers gotta use whips, an' I ain't gonna do dat to nobody I knows and loves."

"You'd be surprised to learn how little a driver needs de whip. Dar are other ways to get people to work widout hurtin' dem. You're intelligent, an' you'd find hundreds of ways to do it. 'Sides, we wouldn't make you de driver where you lives, in Settlement No. 1. It'd be out in Settlement No. 4, where you don't know de people as well. De work force is smaller out dar, but dar's some good workers. They'd get de job done fo' you.

"Right now, we're building a new cabin out dar where you an' yo' family can live. It's a lot bigger den de one you got now, an' you won't have to share it wid nobody, neither.

An' one mo' thing … Massa King don't go out in dat section much. He knows if he's got a good driver, he don't have to. An' if dat's de case, it's likely he won't be messin' no mo' wid yo' wife, neither."

Frank was stunned by Jack's comment. Did he know of Betty's problem with Massa King? How could he? Was he trying to solve two problems all at once by offering him the job? Or worse yet, did he suspect him of doing all the damage to the rice fields, and trying to solve three problems?

"You think 'bout it, an' talk it over wid Betty some. I'll see you tomorrow."

Frank and Betty talked that night, and they decided he would take the job. Betty's main concern was the possibility that they would be outcast from the rest of the slave community. But this concern was overshadowed by Frank's desire to protect her from the advances of Massa King, especially now that she was expecting their third child.

Jack was pleased with Frank's decision.

As driver, Frank would be responsible for the 152-acre section at the far western end of the plantation. Settlement No. 4, located adjacent to the section, had sixty-one resident slaves, of which twenty-six were either field hands or ditchers. It would be his job to produce the rice crop in this section and make sure that trunks and drainage ditches were maintained in working condition. He would operate under general directions given by Headman Jack and each day report back to him on the progress made. He would ride a mule the one and a half miles back and forth to the overseer's house, where the daily progress meetings were held.

On the day before it was to be announced that Frank was the new driver, he and Jack met and drank tea together.

"Beginnin' tomorrow," said Jack, "you's gonna be de boss man of yo' settlement. De peoples needs a leader, an' you's gonna be it. It's a badge of honor, so carry de responsibility best you can. Now, I'se gonna give you a bit of advice dat I hopes you follows.

"First of all, always 'member dat de amount of work to be accomplished fo' each task by a full hand, half hand, or quarter hand is written in stone. Don't ever try changin' it, neither. Everybody knows what de work rules is—dey's been set ever since dis plantation got started. It'd cause all kinds of trouble if dey got changed.

"Second, you gotta 'member dat you is de boss, an' you gotta act de part. You gotta dress better den dey do, talk better dan dey do, an' issue orders in a strong voice. 'Spect yo' orders to be carried out to de letter, an' follow up to make sho' dey is. An' you must never show no familiarity wid yo' hands, neither. You is a step above dem—not dar equal. Also, never do any of de work yo'self, unless it's an emergency—always get de other hands to do it fo' you. An', by de way, always carry yo' whip wid you, as a sign of yo' authority.

"We got lots of rules on dis plantation—from gettin' to work on time in de mornin' all de way to behavin' right in de settlement. Dey gotta be followed by everybody. It takes discipline to make sho' dey is. An' maintainin' de right amount of discipline will be yo' biggest job. Niggers always try an' get away wid somethin' dey shouldn't be doin'. I'd say don't be too hard on dem fo' breakin' de small rules, but enforce de important ones. Yo' life will be a lot easier if you do dis.

"Now, when you gotta discipline somebody—an' make no mistake 'bout it; you'll have to do dis—try usin' some method other den whippin' dem. Sometimes de loss of privileges, reduced meal rations, or de loss of new clothing does wonders in correctin' bad behavior. Whippin' should be done as de last resort and never to de extent dat it damages a hand where he cain't work no mo'. Plantation rules ses you can whip a nigger wid up to twelve lashes. But if de offense is really bad, I'll turn my head in de other direction an' let you give him up to twenty.

"Every day after work, you gotta come over to de overseer's house and report on what's been done. An', for yo' own good, I'll warn you—never give no false information 'bout it. De overseer keeps records on what you report, and, from time to time, he goes out in de fields and checks on you. If you've lied about it, he'll order me to give you a whippin' you won't ever forget. Understand?

"One other bit of advice—you gotta keep yo' eyes and ears open to what's going on 'round you. You'll find if dar's any trouble brewin' it's better to put a stop to it early on. Don't wait till later.

"Oh, one mo' thing. You gotta get up early in de mornin' an' ring de bell to wake up all de hands. It's one of those added tasks dat goes wid de job. Most hands'll get up quickly and head fo' the fields. But some won't. You'll get to know who de laggards is pretty quick, and you'll have to chase dem out of dar cabins to get 'em going.

"Now I'se done a lot of talkin', and I hope you understand it all. You got any questions?"

"No, I don't think so, but it sounds complicated," replied Frank.

"Well, I'll be checkin' on you from time to time to see how you's doing. If any questions come up, just ask 'em. I'll be glad to help as much as I can."

"Thanks; I'se sure I'll be needin' a lotta help."

Frank's first day as driver went smoothly. Jack was with him during the morning and then left him on his own. Field hands worked steadily, but, as often as they could without being detected, they snatched glimpses of their new driver as he moved among them. Most recognized Frank from seeing him function as the head trunk minder, and they knew he was skilled in that job. But they wondered: What kind of driver would he be? How much did he know about working a crop? Would he work them harder than the last driver? Would he be quick to use the whip? On his part, Frank intently watched each hand work. How steady was he? Did he do a good job? Was he a potential troublemaker? Each side, management and labor, sought to size the other up.

Hands performed their work well on the first day, and all tasks were completed by four o'clock in the afternoon. The same was true on the second, third, and fourth days. But on the fifth day, a Monday following the Sunday break, problems began to appear. Isaac, a man in his mid-thirties, didn't complete his task; he complained of a severe stomachache. The next day, two others did the same thing. And two days after that, the whole gang broke out into a song with a slow rhythm:

> Breddren, don' get weary, breddren don' get weary,
> Breddren don' get weary, Fo' de work in mos' done.
>> Keep yo' lamp trim an' a'burnin',
>> Keep yo' lamp trim an' a'burnin',
>> Keep yo' lamp trim an' a'burnin',
>>> Fo' de work is mos' done.

Frank cracked his whip as loud as he could to get their attention. "Stop dat singin' right now," he said in a loud voice, "an' speed up what you's doin'. Dat song's too slow for workin', an', at de rate you's goin', we ain't gonna finish till midnight. Now, get on wid it." His face was flushed as he spoke, and everyone knew he was angry.

That evening, Frank described the happenings over the past few days to Headman Jack.

"Dey is testin' you, boy!" exclaimed Jack. Dey wants to know what kind a man you is, an' how much dey can get away wid. Make no mistake; niggers will try an' get away wid as much as dey can. It's best you stand up to them right away and show 'em who de boss is. If you don't, they'll run all over you."

Deep down, Frank knew Jack was right. He'd hoped fair treatment and logic would suffice. However, it looked like he'd been wrong and he'd have to change his methods.

The next time a slowdown occurred, and it became evident that several hands wouldn't complete their work by the usual quitting time, Frank just bided his time. Jacob and Quimby, two of the more reliable hands, completed their tasks around three-thirty in the afternoon and were preparing to leave the field.

"Where you goin'?" asked Frank in a loud voice.

"We's done our work, and we's goin' back to our quarters," replied Jacob.

"Oh no, you ain't," said Frank, "Cain't you see dat everyone out here ain't finished what dar s'posed to be doin'? No one's gonna leave dis field till all de work's done. You understand?"

"But, Driver Frank, we's done our tasks—we can go now," said Jacob.

"You's right, you's done yo' tasks, an' you don't have to do no mo', but you ain't leavin' dis field no way." Cracking his whip, he commanded, "Go down to the end of the row an' sit an' wait till the rest of de hands is finished."

Reluctantly, the two proceeded to the end of the row and sat down. A murmur came over the rest of the hands as they overheard the conversation. As each hand finished his task, he went and sat down at the end of the row and waited.

It was nearly six o'clock when the last task was completed. Frank followed the gang back to the settlement, noting that there was a great deal of agitation among the hands who had completed their work early. A sly, satisfied grin came over his face. He thought it would be some time before anyone tested him again.

Frank whipped a slave for reporting to work an hour late one morning. Lateness was a serious breach of rules and highly visible to all hands. It was the first time he'd ever struck another man with a whip. He had resisted doing it, but, under the circumstances, he knew he had to. It was a lesson for the man and reenforcement for the others who'd witnessed the event.

That evening, when he told Betty of the incident, tears came to his eyes. "It ain't right fo' no man to strike 'nother wid a whip. I'se ashamed of what I done."

Betty replied, "I know it's hard fo' you to believe, but you done de right thing today. Dis plantation's got rules that we all must follow to make it work right. When one person don't follow the rules, it hurts us all."

"I understand dat. But what I don't understand is why some niggers is always tryin' to break de rules. You'd think dey'd know it'd be easier on dem if dey just followed de rules. Dar lives would be better, too, if dey took a little pride in what dey did. Some does, but mos' don't."

"I agrees, but let's don't worry no mo' 'bout it tonight. Come, let's have our supper."

Unlike the rest of the slaves in Settlement No. 4, Frank and Betty ate their meals in their cabin, not at the cookhouse. This was a decision they made after the first night they lived in the settlement. Innocently, on that night they had gone to the cookhouse for supper, and, after getting their meals, they had sat down at an empty table near the center of the room. As more and more slaves came in, all the tables in the room filled up, except theirs. Eating alone brought home vividly the isolation they would feel living in the settlement. Having familiarity with a driver was against one of the unspoken rules of the settlement. A driver gave his allegiance to the owner, not to the slave community. He was not to be trusted.

Betty, whose job was to run the children's nursery, interacted frequently with other mothers in the settlement and formed friendships. The women would even, on occasion, pass word to her of things going on in the settlement that Frank should be made aware of. And Frank's children, Ishmael and Phoebe, played freely with the other children and were accepted by them. It was Frank himself who was isolated from the community.

He had known from the beginning that being a driver would impose new difficulties in his life, and he was prepared to face them. But on a completely different front, he found himself totally unprepared ....

Betty was with child and went into labor. With the assistance of a midwife, Frank helped bring the child into the world. Everything with the birthing went well. The only problem was, the child was not black—only half black. A mulatto! When she saw the infant, Betty went into hysterics. It was clear that Frank wasn't the father. The true father was Massa King, who had raped her.

"Dis is awful. It cain't be true!" exclaimed Betty, sobbing. "It ain't our child. It belongs to dat evil man, Massa King! Give it to him—I don't want it!"

Frank was stunned. He handed the infant to the midwife and hugged Betty, trying to comfort her. "Now, now, honey, settle down. Everythin's all right." He held her tightly, lying beside her for nearly an hour without saying a word. Then, sitting up at the side of the bed, he said, "Dis child is yo' child, an' because I'se yo' husband, he's my child, too. What happened wid Massa King is in de past, an' what's important now is de well-being of dis small boy. De Lawd has given him to us an' 'spects us to rear him up to be a good man. We cain't let de Lawd down. I loves dis little critter as much as I does our other chillun, and I aims to be a good father to him."

"Oh, Frank, I'se so ashamed. I don't know how I'se gonna face de world wid a half-white child."

"You mustn't worry, honey; dars lots more chillun just like him on dis plantation, an' a heap mo' all over Georgia. Dey's fine human bein's—nothin' to be 'shamed 'bout."

Betty calmed down. And, after some thought, she said she would name the boy Renty. Throughout the rest of her life, she would never acknowledge to anyone in the slave community who the true father was, although it was obvious to everyone.

Over time, whipping errant slaves became a normal part of the discipline Frank handed down. At home, he practiced whipping a post in a manner that made the whip crack before landing. It was a technique he used on slaves who committed minor infractions or who were normally well behaved. It had a lesser impact on the slave's body and didn't result in lacerations. However, on some occasions, for infractions of a serious nature, he used the whip with the intent of inflicting pain. On those occasions, he no longer felt any remorse afterward.

Above all, he tried to be fair in his dealings and treat everyone equally. He became a keen observer of slave behavior and of life in the settlement. And, from experience, he learned which infractions should be overlooked and which should not.

As part of his duties in the settlement, he handled a variety of problems. Once he broke up an argument between a married couple who had been creating a disturbance for several nights, and assigned them to separate cabins—to the delight of the couple's neighbors. He was able to gain approval from Massa King for a young man in his settlement to marry a girl from Settlement No. 2, and he attended the couple's wedding ceremony. And based on his observations of the physical capability of each slave, he made selective changes in their task assignments to distribute the workload more equitably.

On Sundays, he and Betty routinely attended religious services conducted by Cooper London. They would hitch their mule to a flatbed wagon and ride the one and a half miles to the cookhouse at Settlement No. 1, where the services were held. Occasionally, others from the settlement rode with them.

In time, Frank became respected by the slaves in his settlement— to the point where they would frequently refer to themselves as "Driver Frank's people."

It had been at the beginning of the harvest period when Frank first became the driver at Settlement No. 4. The job started out in a hectic manner, and it was all he could do to get the harvest completed on time.

During the following year, though, he was responsible for the full crop cycle—from preparing the ground through to harvesting. During this process, he observed the operations more carefully, and, in so doing, identified two areas where significant improvements could be made. Firstly, the section he was responsible for consisted of fields that varied in size from ten to fifty acres. He felt that if the fields were divided uniformly at twenty acres apiece, it would provide for more efficient operations. All hands could be used to quickly prepare or weed grass in a single field, with the next flow being done immediately afterward. This would reduce the amount of time rice birds would have to attack the seedlings, and the harvest could be scheduled more optimally. He was able to convince Headman Jack and Massa King that this idea had merit, and they gave him additional hands that winter to reconfigure the rice fields.

The second area involved the preparation of fields during the winter months for seeding. The process required field hands, using grubbing hoes, to dig up the soil by hand. Three separate passes were required. Frank proposed acquiring an old plow from Hampton Point and using his mule to do the plowing. Headman Jack was skeptical about the idea, because he thought the plow would run into too many cypress roots buried underneath the surface. He didn't think it would work, but he agreed to try it.

In plowing with the mule, cypress roots weren't much of a problem. The real problem arose when the crusted surface layer of the ground was broken by the plow. It uncovered a layer of damp soil that became soggy under the feet of the mule. The animal got bogged down in muck. As a result, the experiment was abandoned.

Undismayed, Frank begged Headman Jack for an ox the following year, arguing that it was better suited for the conditions. Jack reluctantly conceded. The ox had little trouble handling the soggy ground, and the new experiment proved a huge success. Previously, it had taken eighteen hands a total of five days to prepare a single twenty-acre rice field. Using the ox and plow, it took one hand only six days.

The crops in Frank's third full year as driver were laid-by three weeks earlier than in any other section. It was becoming evident that he was the best driver on the plantation.

*   *   *   *

Headman Jack stood at the bottom of a gangplank at the boat landing. He was barking orders to hands loading three hundred-pound tierces of rice onto a schooner. The hands had rolled a tierce up to the top of the gangplank and were attempting to tilt it up on its end for positioning on deck. The weight proved too much for the men to handle, and they lost control. The tierce suddenly rolled back down the gangplank, and before Jack could get out of the way, it struck his side and rolled over the lower part of his left leg. The blow badly crushed his ankle and foot. The injury was so severe that the lower part of his leg had to be amputated.

A few days later Frank visited Jack in the infirmary.

"How you doin'?" asked Frank.

"Not bad fo' an old man wid only one leg," was the reply. "How you?"

"Oh, okay. De plantin's goin' good. We started seedin' in two fields yesterday an' will do de flow tomorrow, when de tide's right."

"Dat sounds good … Seems dat you enjoys being a driver. Dat right?"

"Yes, I s'pose so. Got its good points an' bad."

"I knows what you mean…. You knows dis injury of mine is gonna cause me to retire from being headman, don't you?"

"No, I don't."

"Well, it is. I won't be able to get around much no mo'. 'Sides, I'se sixty years old and not as spry as I used to be. It just seems to be de right time fo' me an' de missis to become poultry minders or some such thing."

"I'se sorry."

"You don't need to feel sorry fo' me. I'se had a good run. 'Sides, it'll open up an opportunity fo' you to take my place as headman, if you wants to. I'se talked wid Massa King, and he agrees wid me; you's de best man fo' de job. I think he'll be talkin' wid you 'bout it real soon."

Junior met with Frank the next day and offered him the job. Along with it came better housing—he'd live in the headman's house next door to the overseer—better food and clothing, a house servant, and a cash bonus if there was a good crop. Frank readily accepted.

✻   ✻   ✻   ✻

It was late spring when Frank was made headman. All the rice fields were under water awaiting termination of the stretch flow. And mosquitoes were beginning to show up in the low-lying fields. This was the sign for all white persons on the plantation to vacate the premises and head to higher ground. The summer months were the "sickly season" for white folk, and they feared the miasmas.

In mid-May, Frank was left in charge of the entire plantation. He was responsible for the final stages of growing the crop and beginning harvest—a big responsibility. This had to be done largely without any supervision. The white overseer would visit only three times during the summer, arriving in the late morning and departing before dusk on the same day. Massa King wouldn't show up at all. This was the first time Frank, as headman, had been given this responsibility. It presented new challenges, which he was prepared to face.

One evening, a week after the white folk had left, Frank entered Settlement No. 1 and walked down the street to the main campfire site. There were a large number of slaves standing in a ring around a bonfire. In the center of the ring sat the Council of Elders. When the crowd realized Frank was in their midst, they made way for him, and he walked to where the Council members were sitting. The appearance of a headman at such a meeting had never occurred before, and there was a great murmur among the crowd. Everyone became silent, though, when Frank spoke,

"Good evenin', gentlemen."

There was no reply, only a nod of the head by the white-bearded Cassius, who was the head of the Council.

"Is it all right if I takes a seat here on dis bench? Dar's somethin' I'se come to discuss wid you." He sat down after receiving another nod from Cassius.

Frank had known each member of the Council all his life and had been good friends with some before he became a driver. The Council members included his best friend, Cooper London; engineer Ned;

Cassius; Noah, a boat builder; and field hands representing each of the four settlements, including Jacob from Settlement No.4.

"I'se come to reestablish some old friendships an' try an' start our new relationship on firm ground," he said. "It don't make no sense for neither me or you to get off on de wrong foot. You knows Massa's gone fo' de season an' left me in charge. His leavin' don't change nothin', though. Dar's a heap load of work to be done 'round here. An' me an' you is gonna have to work hard to git it all done. I'se gonna do my part an' I'se askin' you to cooperate wid me an' do yo' part. I don't want to have to do nothin' harsh to persuade you."

Frank stopped talking and waited. There were stunned looks on the faces of the Council members, and they began looking at each other and whispering. Finally the whispering stopped, and Cassius looked up at Frank and said "If we cooperate wid you, what's in it fo' us?"

"What do you want?" replied Frank.

"We wants better food—mo' meat in our diet, an' better clothes, an' mo' time off from workin'."

Frank sat there for what seemed an eternity contemplating the request—with all the Council members staring at him intently. Finally, he said, "You's asking a lot for doin' somethin' you ought to be doin' in de first place. But dar might be somethin' I can do to meet yo' demands. I'll make sho' you gets better clothin' at de next distribution at Christmas time—clothin' dat's made out of better material and stitched stronger. An' somethin' nice fo' de ladies, too. I'll guarantee it'll be good quality, an' last longer.... I don't know fo' sho' what I can do in the way of gettin' you mo' meat, but I'll give you my word dat I'll do de best I can to see dat you gets it. Now, as far as gettin' mo' time off from workin', dar ain't no way I can do dat. De amount of work to be done fo' each task's been set in stone since dis plantation got started. No way it's gonna change now. We is tryin' to improve de way we does things, though. Next winter we'll start plowin' with de ox in de lower section—same as we do now in the western sections. An' Massa King's been talkin' 'bout buyin' a threshin' machine. If he does dat, there'll be no need to do all de threshin' by hand. Dat'll make yo' work a lot easier den it is now."

Again, Frank abruptly stopped talking and waited. And, again, there was whispering among the Council members. Cassius finally said, "It seems you got a deal. We'll make sho' we holds up our end of de bargain."

"Good," replied Frank as he rose and shook the hand of each member. When he finished, he left the gathering, and a great murmur erupted among the crowd.

As he walked in the darkness back toward the entrance to the settlement, a wide, tight-lipped smile stretched across his face. In the days just prior to this encounter, he had made the decision to improve the clothing and meat rations for the slaves. But instead of merely announcing his decision, he thought it would be better to have the slaves earn the new privileges through bargaining—a favorite custom of theirs. In this way, the community as a whole would hold up their end of the bargain, and ensure that individual members were kept in line. He planned to go to Darien with Raylin in a few days to pick out samples of new material for clothing and have her make new suits for a few field hands as a sign of his good intentions. And, at the next livestock auction, he would purchase a number of new breeding sows and a large number of extra piglets for fattening.

Over the years, rice production on the plantation increased steadily. And Frank became an indispensable cog in the operations. He was trusted fully by Junior and respected by the slave community. He and his family seemed happy and enjoyed a good life. But things weren't all roses.

On the occasion of his taking a boat trip to Savannah, with Junior, to purchase slaves, Frank was looking forward to a period of relaxation during the voyage. While Junior was lounging in the upper-deck parlor, he found a comfortable place to lie down on the lower deck among cotton bales.

From this vantage point, as the ship pulled out of Darien harbor, he could see steam rising from the Butler Island rice mill in the distance. "Good to see dat smoke rising," he thought. "We got de rice poundin' started early dis year an' it looks like we's gonna have a good crop. Last year we produced over a million pounds of clean rice, an' we's gonna do even better dis year. Massa King's always braggin' dat we produce de best rice quality of all de plantations in Georgia, an' we's always gettin' folk comin' here to see how we does it. Massa takes a lot of pride in what we do ... I takes a lot of pride, too, 'cause I think we does a good job.

"Butler Island's a beautiful place. It's been my home all my life. I loves de different seasons an' seein' all de crops spring up and come alive. De Lawd knew he should make me into a farmer, an' I sho' enjoys bein' one.

"I'se sure de owners is happy, too. Dey must be makin' lots of money on all de rice dat's grown here. But I cain't say fo' sho', though, what de owners is really thinkin'—I's never met any of dem. "S'pose I treats Massa King as de owner. He de only one 'round here dat ever talks to de real owners, an' he gives out all de orders. Ain't no question he de most knowledgeable plantation manager 'round des parts. He knows everythin' dar is 'bout growing rice and cotton. I'se sho'ly learned a lot from him. An', over de years, I think we had a good relationship. I knows he depends on me to do things right, and I tries hard never to let him down.

"Down deep though, Massa King's truly an evil man. I cain't never forgive him for rapin' Betty—an' a lot of other women on de plantation, too. He got no respect fo' niggers. Seems he enjoys whippin' 'em, an' he don't care if he hurts 'em bad. Whippin ain't right! No man's got de right to punish 'nother man wid a whip. On de other hand, though, some niggers do dumb things, even mean things, dat deserve some kind of punishment. I don't know if it's 'cause dey is stupid or dey is just fightin' de system.

"De system, slavery—it ain't right, neither. Dar ain't nothin' more valuable to a man den havin' his freedom. He wants to make choices fo' hisself—not have dem made by other folk. Conditions ain't good neither—bad clothing, food, an' medicine. It's unhealthy stompin' 'round in de cold, damp swamp soil dat rice plantation's made out of—powerful lot of folk die.

"In my way of thinkin', it'd be a whole lot better if de land belonged to de folk dat works it, not just to de rich white folk livin' up in Philadelphia. But, how you go 'bout makin' a change like dat ain't easy. Wid so many niggers an' only a few white folk livin' on de plantation, I s'pose it'd be easy 'nough to stage a rebellion an' kill all de white folk. But dat won't work. All de white folk would do is send in de state militia wid a lot of guns and cannons an' kill all us niggers. It'd be de same as dey done wid Nat Turner up in Virginia.

"I s'pose it's all in the Lawd's good hands, an' everythin' will come right at de time he chooses. Don't look like nothin's goin' to happen in my lifetime, though.

"Here I is de headman fo' de whole plantation, an' I ain't no better off den a common field hand. I'se still a slave. I could be whipped or sold tomorrow if Massa King decided to do it. Worse yet, it could happen to my wife an' chillun. Dar's no one on de whole plantation dat wants his freedom more den me. But I ain't gonna get it, an' no one else is gonna get it, neither. We just gotta do de best we can under de conditions.

"Just like he done wid de Israelites in Egypt, de Lawd's put us here fo' a reason, an' we just gotta make de most of it. An', just like he done wid Moses, he's given me de most difficult job of all. I'se right in de middle of everythin'. I'se got to make de white folk happy by workin' all de niggers hard. An', on de other hand, I'se got to protect all de niggers from the evil doin's of de white folk an' try to make things better fo' dem at de same time—even when dey don't 'preciate what I does fo' dem. It ain't easy keepin' a balance between de two. I gotta pray hard fo' de Lawd to give me de guidance an' strength to handle de load."

At that point, Frank turned over on his side and began gazing aimlessly out at the water passing by.

Chapter 9—Runaway Slave

When Raylin completed her work for the day, she locked the door to the storehouse where she did her sewing. Putting the key in her apron pocket, she turned and walked toward the slave settlement. Her mind wasn't focused on anything in particular, so she hardly noticed the field hands coming in from the lower rice fields walking alongside her. She was about to go into her cabin at the end of the first row, when she heard a plaintive voice call out from behind her, "Oh, Raylin!"

Turning around, she saw a young, slender female walking twenty feet or so behind her, holding a grubbin' hoe over her shoulder. She had an anguished look on her face. Raylin recognized her immediately and said, "Martha, child, what you cryin' fo'?"

"I feels miserable Raylin. I'se got a terrible hurt right here," putting her clenched fist over her heart, "an' I knows I'se gotta do somethin' 'bout it 'fore it drives me crazy."

"Well, child, just come on in here an' sit down a spell an' tell me what's ailin' you." Wrapping her arms around Martha, Raylin guided her through the door of her cabin and sat her down on a wooden chair, pulling another chair close by.

"Raylin, I ain't got no other family livin' on dis plantation, an' you's the only one I can talk to. I'se fed up to my neck wid livin' here. Massa King's de meanest man dat ever drew a breath. I hope he dies soon, so's he can go an' live wid his brother, de devil."

"Now, now, child, it cain't be all dat bad. What's he gone and done to you?"

"He's killed my child, and now he's tryin' to kill me!"

"How's dat?"

"When I'se pregnant dis past springtime, he made me work a full task, not half task, like most women like me. It was too much fo' me to handle, an' de days I didn't finish, he'd whip me bad. I didn't go to de hospital till de bleeding come. De baby was born dead. An' just three weeks after dat, he puts me back in de fields as a full hand. Whippin's ain't stopped, neither."

"I'se really sorry, child. Tell me, who's de father? Is he as heartbroken as you is?"

"De baby ain't got no father."

"What you mean, he ain't got no father? Oh! You means Massa King's de father?"

"Yes, ma'am."

"Den Massa King killed his own child."

"Yes, ma'am. Two years ago, when I'se barely fifteen years of age, my ol' master sold me to a trader who auctioned me off on the blocks in Savannah. He told everybody I'd make a good 'fancy,' so's he'd get a better price. Massa King bought me for six hundred dollar and brung me here. I didn't want to submit to him, but he made me. He got awful mad when I come down wid child, and dat's when all de trouble started."

"Child, you've been through some hard times."

"Too hard! Nobody deserves to live like I do. It ain't what de Lawd intended for no human bein'. An' I ain't gonna take it no mo'. I'se gonna run away from dis place. Massa King's gonna start de rice plantin' next week, an' I ain't gonna be 'round to help."

"Now, slow down, child, dar ain't no use runnin' away. Where you gonna go? De only place is de swamps, an' dat ain't no good. Peoples dat go in dar either dies or comes back here an' gets whipped half to death. It ain't no place fo' a young child like you, an' it ain't gonna do you no good no how."

Martha rose with a jolt, and, looking down at Raylin, responded in a strong voice, "I don't care. I cain't keep livin' in dis place—anythin's better den dis."

Raylin, seeing the flushed look on her face, stood up and gave her a hug. "I sho'ly don't blame you fo' wanting to leave dis place, but shouldn't you think on it a bit mo'? It's a mighty big decision."

"No! I'se made up my mind fo' good. I'se leavin' tonight!"

"Child, you sho' seems determined, an' if you's set on goin', I'll help you best I can. But dar ain't no way you can leave here tonight. De driver will see you is gone first thing in de mornin' an' be on yo' trail like a bolt of lightnin'. He'll catch you an' have you back 'fore dark.

"It's a whole lot better if you wait till Saturday night. Dar ain't no work on Sunday and you won't be missed all de way till Monday mornin'. An' wid all de confusion dat'll be goin' on 'round here with startin' rice plantin', you probably won't be missed till late on Monday. Dat'll give you plenty of time to get a long ways from here 'fore dey can do nothin' 'bout it.

"We's got some gettin' ready to do 'fore you go, too. You'll need a heap of things to take wid you, if you is goin' to survive out dar all by yo'self. Make sho' you takes a blanket; you'll need it to keep warm at night. I'll get you some good clothes out of de storehouse, an' some food from de cookhouse—maybe a knife, too. London can get a boat. Now, let's see, today is Wednesday, so's we got three days to get ready.

"Now, you go on home, an' be back here right after supper on Saturday. We'll get you started soon as it gets dark. An' make sho' you don't tell nobody else 'bout dis. You knows how word gets 'round. Now git, an' put dat pretty smile back on yo' face."

It rained during the day on Saturday, and the sky was still overcast when supper ended. There was a coolness in the air that caused most of the slaves to retreat to their cabins when they finished eating. Only a few lingered in the streets, engaging in small conversations. No one in the settlement noticed a slightly built woman come out of her cabin midway up the row carrying a blanket wrapped up in a bundle. She walked down past the row of cabins, heading toward the entrance to the settlement in a slow, but deliberate, manner, not acknowledging any of the people she passed.

Christopher, Raylin's oldest son, sat waiting in the shadows between the last two cabins in the row. He watched Martha walk through the settlement, concentrating on seeing if her movement caused any concern among the other slaves. When she got near, he spoke to her in a low voice, "Martha, dis is Christopher; come over an' sit down on dis log a minute." She did as she was told. Christopher continued, "Be still, now; I want to make sho' no one is followin' you."

In a short while he seemed satisfied, and he said." We can go in now." They stood up and entered the cabin.

Inside, two candles were burning on a table in the main room. Raylin and London were sitting there waiting. When they saw Martha, they stood up and hugged her, admonishing her to speak only in a low voice.

"How is yo', child?" asked Raylin.

"I'se fine."

All four sat down at the table. Looking her in the eyes, London asked Martha, "Are you really sho' you wants to go through wid this?"

"I'se sho' as de Lawd made me. I wants to get as far away from dis place as I can possibly get—all de way to Canada."

"Now, child, dat might be askin' a little too much. You know how far Canada is from Georgia? It's a mighty long ways, an' you cain't get dar from here no how. Years ago, runaways used to hide on board de ships docked at Darien, and dey made it out of here goin' north. Dey got at least as far as Savannah, an' maybe some got all de way to Canada. But, nowadays, de patrollers knows dat dis is de best way out, an' when a runaway is loose, de first thing dey do is search all de ships an' catch 'em. Dat means de way out of here goin' north is closed fo' good. De only way you can get out nowadays is by headin' west through de swamps."

Seeing Martha grimace, London was quick to add, "Dat ain't all dat bad, now. Dar's two maroon camps down in the Okefenokee near the Florida border, where dar's niggers like us livin' free. If you gets to one of des camps, Massa King will never find you.

"Of course, child, de biggest problem you got in gettin' dar is makin' it through de swamps dat's just upriver from here. Dey is mighty dangerous, an' de goin' ain't easy."

"I knows I can make it," replied Martha, "I just gotta."

"Well, den, we found a small bateau fo' you to use. It's de best kinda boat fo' gettin' 'round in de swamps. Dar's no moon out tonight, neither. It'll be dark 'nough so's no one will see you leave—cain't ask fo' a better situation. Now, de most important thing fo' you to remember is dat you gotta get as far away from dis place as you can 'fore dey find out you is missin'—so dey won't be able to catch up wid you. By Monday mornin' you gotta be a long ways from here. You understan' dat, child?"

"Yes."

"Good. I'se gonna give you a bit of advice I wants you to follow. First, all de travellin' you does has gotta be done at night, never in de daylight. Travellin' in daylight is too risky; you might get spotted. An' dar's 'nother thing fo' you to remember. When you's goin' upriver, you gotta stick to de north side, 'cause dat's de side where de river's not so deep an' it's easier polin'. I'se gonna repeat dat, 'cause it's important: stay on de north side of de river. You'll be able to duck into the swamps quick if someone's comin'. In some places de swamps go back miles from de river, other places not far at all.

"Now, just as you starts out from here, de river splits into two branches at the west end of Butler Island. Take de north branch. De south branch goes close by Hopeton plantation, and somebody's likely to spot you goin' by dar. De two branches comes back together 'bout two mile upriver. After dat, dar ain't no mo' plantations for miles and miles—only swamps.

"Dis time of year, dar's Oconee boxes floatin' downriver to Darien. Dey's carryin' big loads of cotton to de docks. You gotta get out of dar way when dey go's by and hide in de swamps. Dar's at least one white man onboard, an' it won't do no good to have him spot you. An', let me add somethin' else. Don't ever trust no white man you comes across, no matter how much he says he'll help you. Dey is nothin' but white trash, de lowest form of humans alive. Dey'll lie to you, an', first thing, dey'll turn you in.

"Now, gettin' to de Okefenokee, you gotta leave de river and go south through de piney woods—'bout forty mile. De place you leaves de river is 'bout twenty mile upstream from here, where de first big creek comes in from de south. You'll recognize it, 'cause it looks like a big fork in de river. You can take de bateau up de creek 'bout a mile till it nearly runs out. At dat point, dar's a trail dat leads south past some cotton farms, but mostly through piney woods. You can sneak into de quarters at any of de farms, and de niggers dar will help you an' give you food. Just tell dem you is lookin' fo' 'Uncle John.' Sooner or later, maybe in two of three days' time, Uncle John will find you and take you to one of the maroon camps in de Okefenokee. Yo' journey will be over."

Martha listened intently, trying hard to remember everything London was telling her. She realized there was a great deal more to being a runaway than she had thought. If she were going to make it, she'd better follow London's advice to the letter.

London added, "I s'pose I don't got to tell you de swamps is full of snakes and gators. Dey's dangerous, an' you gotta keep a close eye out fo' dem."

She wondered how London knew all this, and she was tempted to ask how he'd learned it. But she knew it was better not to, and she merely accepted his advice.

Raylin interjected at this point, "I'se got some food fo' you to take. Dar's eight ears of corn, some cornbread, cooked hog rind, and peas. It'll be 'nough to get you started. Got you a new slip an' scarf, too. An' here's a big kitchen knife. You gotta be careful wid dis now, it's mighty sharp. It'll come in handy."

"You got any questions?" asked London.

"No, I'se set to go."

"Good," said Raylin. "Christopher, here, will help you wid all dis stuff, an' show you where de bateau is. It ain't far—up just passed de horse rice mill."

"I think it's safe to go now; it's plenty dark out," said London. "De tide's comin' in, an' it'll make it easier goin' upriver, least fo' a while. You gotta be careful goin' through de settlement—don't want nobody to see you. But don't worry much 'bout goin' by driver Romulo's cabin. It's Saturday night, an' he's down at de overseer's house drinkin' rum." He gave her a hug and told her, "God will look after you—be brave."

Raylin then gave her a hug and said, "I'll be prayin' fo' you, child."

Martha put her arms around the necks of both London and Raylin and said, "Thank you; thank you both. I'se do greatly appreciates all you's done fo' me."

The candles were blown out, and Christopher opened the cabin door. After looking up and down the street, he said, "Come on, de coast is clear." And the two figures slipped out into the darkness.

They passed through the settlement and then made their way along the river dike to the horse rice mill, without passing anyone on the way. Christopher pulled the ten-foot bateau out of the tall cordgrass, where it had been hidden, and pushed it into the river. After he had placed the food and Martha's belongings in the front of the bateau, he said, in a low voice, "I'se slippin' de knife in along de side here underneath de back rib of de boat. Dat way it won't get lost, an' it won't cut you." He then helped her get in and handed her the pole.

Martha tried to raise herself up to stand in the rear of the boat, but her legs wobbled so badly the bateau almost capsized, and she lost the pole. She had often seen rice barges being poled in the plantation's canals, but she herself had never poled a boat before. Standing up on a small floating object for the first time, without any firm support, unnerved her, and she fell to her knees—grabbing onto the sides of the bateau for dear life.

Christopher saw the frightened look on her face and said to her, "Standin' up ain't difficult once you get used to it, but you'd better pole sittin' down to start wid. It'll be easier." He grabbed the blanket, folded it into a seat cushion and placed it in the rear, and helped Martha get settled. As he handed the pole to her for the second time, he said, "Remember, you gotta cross over an' stick close to de north side. It'll be easier polin'. Is you ready?"

"Yes."

"Good luck," he said, and he gave the bateau a push out into the middle of the river. The incoming tide seemed to catch the bateau, and it started to move slowly upriver. It wasn't long before Martha was out of sight, and Christopher could no longer hear any movement in the water.

On the next day, which was Sunday, the usual hustle and bustle of slaves getting ready to go to church on the mainland took place in the morning. Plantation rules permitted slaves to attend church once a month at either of the two white churches in Darien. Each of the slaves who wished to attend was assigned a particular Sunday of the month, and approximately thirty slaves were making the trip this Sunday. Half came from Butler Island and half from Hampton. Hampton slaves had been transported to Butler Island enroute to Darien, and when they met up with the Butler Island slaves, the whole scene looked more like a raucous social event than a religious one. The noise and confusion didn't subside till the last boat to Darien cast off.

For those slaves living on Butler Island who weren't scheduled to go to Darien, a local religious service was held in the cookhouse, with Cooper London serving as minister. Forty slaves were in attendance on this Sunday, including Headman Frank and his wife, Betty. Frank and Betty weren't regular attendees, but they attended often enough so that little notice was given them when they did. On such occasions, though, Cooper London always made it a point to more closely follow the guidelines of the white minister's catechism in preaching the Gospel message.

Following the service, the attendees gathered outside the cookhouse in small groups, as was their custom, greeting one another and exchanging gossip. After a while, they slowly began breaking up and meandering toward their cabins in the settlement. Raylin and Betty, along with three other women, were in the last group to begin moving. They were followed by Frank and London, walking abreast of each other, at the end of the procession.

After they'd gone along the path a little way, not saying a word to one another, Frank, without turning to look at London, asked in a subdued voice, "Is everythin' okay?"

London, without looking at Frank, replied, "Yes, she done got away clean."

"Good, may de Lawd protect her."

When they reached the fork leading up to the headman's house, they met Betty, who had broken off from the group of women up ahead and was standing there waiting. Frank turned to London and said, "Good sermon—thank you." He and Betty then walked up toward their house, and London continued on to the settlement.

It appeared to everyone as just another typical Sunday at Butler Island.

*   *   *   *

No one could have been more frightened than Martha when she, in a tiny bateau, was pushed abruptly out into the river in pitch-black darkness. Her whole body tensed, and her mind froze; it was as if her heart had stopped beating. It was the push of the tide that finally signaled to her that she needed to do something. In a jerky motion, she grabbed the pole and shoved one end deep into the water, expecting to be propelled forward by the motion. But the water was too deep for the pole to reach bottom, and her momentum almost caused her to lose the pole. She nearly panicked, but she was able to gather herself. Her only thought was to reach the other side of the river—the north side. Laying the pole down inside the bateau, she began paddling frantically with both hands. She succeeded. And, after having gotten to the north side, found she could reach bottom with the pole as long as she stayed within ten to fifteen feet of the shoreline. A sense of urgency then set in, and she began poling as rapidly as she could.

It wasn't long before she reached the west end of Butler Island and could see the fork in the river London had told her about. She took the north fork as he had directed. Proceeding on, she fell into a comfortable rhythm, raising the pole into a near-vertical position, then lowering it to the river bottom and pulling with overlapping hand motions until her hands reached the end of the pole. Later, she tried kneeling in the bateau instead of sitting. This worked better. She got more leverage with each stroke, and it was less taxing on her back muscles. Taking short breaks periodically to recharge her energy level, she kept up a steady pace throughout the night. London's admonition, "Get as far away as possible," constantly rang in her ears and pushed her onward.

Daylight the next morning was a mixed blessing. She was afraid to stop, but she was exhausted and needed rest. Spotting an opening in the swamp, she turned and followed a small stream inland. Within a short distance, it opened into a large pond encircled by mature cypress trees growing out of the water. Multiple side streams led in from various directions. She took one of these streams up far enough to be out of sight of the river and tied the bateau to a tree.

The sun was now starting to come up over the horizon, giving a pleasant aura to the scene. She was feeling good about her accomplishment during the night, "I'se come at least five mile," she thought, "maybe mo'." Without any hesitation, she lay down in the bateau, pulled the blanket completely over her body, and fell asleep.

When she awoke, the sky was overcast, although a faint outline of the sun could be seen directly overhead. She knew it was about midday. The first thing she noticed when she sat up was the pain in her shoulders and lower back. She had used muscles in poling that she hadn't used as a field hand at Butler Island. A little rubbing helped, but it didn't make the pain go away.

Reaching over the side of the bateau, with cupped hands she splashed water on her face to clear her mind. And, feeling hungry, she pulled an ear of corn and a piece of cornbread out of her food stash and devoured it. The corn was uncooked and tasted stale, but it didn't bother her. She was still hungry when she finished and thought about getting more, but she decided against it. "I'd better save what food I got, best I can. I don't want to run out 'fore I find some mo'."

She then looked around to take in her surroundings. The gray sky made the water in the swamp look gray, too, and she thought the area was a bit uninviting. Nonetheless, knowing she had several hours to wait before it would be dark enough to continue her trek upriver, she decided to do a bit of exploring to see what a swamp really looked like. Seeing the large pond not far away, she began maneuvering the bateau in that direction.

Just as she was approaching the last cypress tree before entering the pond, she heard a big splash that startled her. It seemed to come from out near the middle of the pond. Her eyes quickly focused on a large dark object. It was the spinelike back of an alligator—maybe ten feet long—floating on top of the water. Its large beady eyes were staring directly at her. "Oh my Lawd!" she said to herself. Then she noticed the head of another alligator not far from the first one, with eyes fixed on her as well—and two more just beyond that one! She knew instantly that she'd entered a gator pool, where a bunch of alligators were living. They seemed to be very protective of their home.

Instinctively, she backed the bateau up to a point where she could maneuver it through the thicket of cypress trees without going out into the pond. Zigzagging around trees, she went parallel to the edge of the pond, down to a point close to the river. She then made a quick dash out into the pond and down the little stream to safety in the river.

She had escaped danger, and, feeling a sense of relief, sat there resting in her bateau. Then, all of a sudden, she realized she was out in the middle of the river in broad daylight—where she shouldn't be! She began poling furiously, until she came to an area with low-lying bushes, about a hundred yards upstream, and darted in for cover. She remained there, and vowed to herself never to go exploring in the swamps again.

The rest of the day passed without incident. The bateau's hard wooden bottom wasn't ideal for sleeping, and occasionally she got out and stood in the shallow water to stretch and regenerate her circulation. Her thoughts often focused on whether Driver Romulo had discovered she was missing. Each time, she had to remind herself that today was Sunday, and he wouldn't even be looking for her yet. Everything was all right.

By dusk, she was eager to get started. In the process of maneuvering the bateau toward the river, she stood up in the rear to pole. Wobbly at first, she slowly gained confidence and felt sure she had mastered the technique. But, when she reached the river, her courage waned, and she once again knelt down to pole.

After she had gone only a short distance, she reached the point where the two branches of the river came back together after splitting off just west of Butler Island. Her heart sank when she realized where she was. London had said this would occur two miles upstream from Butler Island. "I thought I made at least five mile polin' las' night—I'se made less den half dat!" A sense of panic set in, and she began poling more vigorously.

As daybreak came, she knew she had made better progress than the night before, and she felt good about it. At a small opening in the swamp, she pulled in. She found a bushy area not far from the river and tied up the bateau. The water there was shallow, and she thought the low-lying, tangled bushes would make it uninviting for alligators. It wasn't long before she was asleep.

But sleep didn't last. Hardly two hours later, she was awakened abruptly by the whopping and hollering of men's voices. It startled her, and her first thoughts were of seeing Driver Romulo and Massa King coming after her. Keeping low in the bateau, she raised her head to see what was going on. She was relieved when she discovered the voices were coming from upriver, which wasn't the direction from which Romulo and King would be coming. But she knew there was still danger.

In a few moments, a boat came into view, followed closely by two others. They were Oconee boxes, flat-bottomed raft-like structures piled high with cotton bales. Each had two or three men on board, who were manning poles and the rudder. The men were shouting back and forth to each other, giving instructions and exchanging insults. In comparison to the quiet solitude she'd experienced thus far on her journey, the noise reverberated over the entire area and was deafening. She could hear every word that was spoken.

Although she was hidden behind low-lying bushes, she realized the place she had tied up to was no more than fifty feet from the river. The boats were so close to her as they passed she felt she could reach out and touch them. If any of the boatmen looked in her direction, they would certainly spot her. But they passed by without suspecting anything. An hour later, a second group passed by, followed by another and another—six groups in all. It was a harrowing experience for Martha, hunkered down in her bateau all day—not daring to change her position for fear of being seen. Even that night, while she was poling upriver, she listened intently for the sound of boats coming down the river; and she was more cognizant of places along the swamp's edge that could be used for a fast entry in case of an emergency.

Despite her anxiety, she managed to make good progress. The next morning, she was more deliberate in choosing a place to tie up. From now on she would tie up only in areas having thick, low-lying bushes, where the bateau could be slipped underneath and be out of sight. And, furthermore, it would be at least fifty yards from the river. That way she wouldn't have to worry about alligators or boatmen.

The plantation rain gauge had shown rainfall of one-half inch on Saturday. This hadn't deterred Junior from his plan to start rice planting on Monday. Six lower rice fields and four western ones had been previously prepared, and they'd be dry enough to work in. Everything seemed ready to go, when on Sunday night three more inches of rain fell. It inundated the rice fields, making it impossible to send field hands in to work. They'd be wallowing around in mud up to their calves and not getting anything accomplished. On top of this, more rain was expected. It didn't look as if the planting could begin until the following Saturday at the earliest. A whole week would be lost.

The delay angered Junior. He spent the entire morning on Monday reassigning field hands to tasks that didn't require them going into the fields. It had been hectic, and he wasn't happy with his drivers, who didn't seem to appreciate the urgency of the matter.

It was late morning, just as the slaves were beginning to enter the cookhouse for their first meal of the day, when Driver Romulo approached Junior, who was standing at the entrance to the rice mill. "Massa, Massa—she's done gone! I cain't find her nowheres."

"What do you mean? Who's gone?"

"Martha, dat no 'count field hand. Cain't find nobody dat's seen her. She done run away fo' sho'."

"You certain? Did you look through all the quarters?"

"Yes, Massa."

"The infirmary?"

"Yes, Massa."

"How about the guild shops? The storehouse? The fields? The overseer's house?"

"Yes, Massa. I done looked everywheres. So has de other drivers. We cain't find her nowheres."

Just then, Boatman Quarterman came up to where the two were standing and said, "Good day, Massa. I done checked all de boats, like Driver Romulo told me, an' I done found one missing—a small bateau. I truly don't know where it's gone off to; hardly nobody ever uses it no mo'."

"Damn! That ungrateful nigger," exclaimed Junior. "She's run off into the swamps. After all I've done for her, this is the gratitude she shows?" Looking at Romulo, he commanded, "Take a couple of boats and search up the river and see if you can find her. If you don't find her soon, come on back before dark. There ain't no use wasting much time looking. She don't know these swamps. Either the snakes'll scare her half to death, or she'll starve and come crawling back here. Mark my words—she'll be back here soon, begging me to forgive her. I give her three days, no more than four."

Even the thought of having a slave run away made Junior livid. It was a sign that discipline on the plantation was faulty. And, heaven forbid, if one slave ever got away with it, others might try as well. Glancing down the road toward the entrance to the slave settlement, his eyes caught sight of the last of the slaves going into the cookhouse, and he started off in a huff in that direction.

Throwing open the cookhouse door, he stood there in plain sight of all the slaves. Immediately, everyone stopped talking, and a deadly silence came over the group. "I understand the field hand Martha has run away and gone into the swamps," he said in a loud voice. "Let me tell you, if I ever find out that any of you here helped her get away, I'll give you a whipping you'll never forget. There ain't no way she's going to make it through those swamps alive. And when she comes back, there ain't going to be no skin left on her back from all the whipping she'll get!" He then turned abruptly and stalked out of the cookhouse.

The news of Martha's running away came as a big surprise to all but a few of the slaves present in the cookhouse. As soon as Junior left, a great murmur erupted, with everyone trying to talk at the same time. "What she go an' do dat fo'?" "How'd she get away?" "Bet she's gone to Canada." "She can't make it—only die out there in de swamps." "Least she's free from dis place." "She's got her freedom." "Dey gonna send de dawgs after her?" Only after Driver Romulo ordered them to get back to work did the murmur subside.

The news spread like wildfire throughout the other settlements on the plantation, to Hampton Point, and to neighboring plantations along the Altamaha River as well. That night, despite the cool dampness, large groups of slaves gathered around campfires, talking till the wee hours of the morning. Many expressed concern for Martha's well-being, fearing something bad might happen to her. And a great many prayers were said. But the overall feeling, expressed by almost all the slaves, was one of subdued joy. One of their own had broken her bondage. Martha was free, just like every one of them wanted to be. She had shown courage in reaching out for freedom, and she was a hero.

The next day, a special lift appeared in the step of every slave, and work seemed to get done with more enthusiasm than usual. All over the plantation, whenever slaves were out of earshot of drivers, you'd hear them singing one of their favorite songs:

> Run, nigger, run, de patroller ketch you,
> Run, nigger, run, it's almos' day.
> Dat nigger run, dat nigger flew,
> Dat nigger tore his shirt in two.
> Dat nigger he sed, 'Don't catch me,'
> But git dat nigger behind de tree.
> Dat nigger cried, dat nigger lied,
> Dat nigger shook his old fat side.
> Run, nigger, run, it's almos' day.

*　　*　　*　　*

It was afternoon when Martha awoke. A group of Oconee boxes was going by, but she hardly noticed them. She knew she was far enough away from the river to be out of danger. More came by that day, and she didn't give them a second thought.

Today she decided to do a bit of housekeeping. She removed her slip and washed it the best she could by rubbing it together in the water, and she hung it on a bush to dry. Next came a bath for herself. The water was clear and cool—and felt good.

Thinking about Butler Island, she knew they must have discovered her missing by now. "It don't matter none," she thought. "I'se way too far away fo' dem to catch me now." At that moment, a blank look came over her face. "I'se been gone a long time, but I cain't recall exactly how long it's been. It all seems blurry." It took her a minute or so, before she realized she'd been gone three nights. Since she had left on a Saturday night, today must be Tuesday. "My Lawd, I'se all turned 'round. My nights, when I does all my work, is like days, an' days, when I does my sleepin', is like nights. I sho' better do a better job of rememberin' what day it is, or I'se gonna lose all track of time." She grabbed her knife and cut three notches in her pole. "Dar—I'll do dis every day from now on."

During the night, she stood up to pole for long stretches at a time. This helped considerably, since she was now far enough upriver that the incoming tide gave no assistance. Again she made good progress. In the morning, she chose to stop in an area that was covered with old cypress trees, their grotesque roots growing out of the water like big balls of twine. Large vines hung down between the trees, nearly touching the water in places and giving the area an eerie feel. Nevertheless, she spotted a place about seventy yards inland that looked hospitable, and she proceeded in that direction.

The low vines made it impossible for her to remain standing, so she knelt down in the bateau to pole. As she was approaching the place where she had planned to tie up and not concentrating much on what she was doing, the top end of her pole hit an overhanging vine. The force of the collision knocked a dark object off the vine into the middle of the bateau. It made a dull-sounding *thud* as it landed, causing Martha's body to jolt upright.

It was a black snake, about three feet long, so thick in the middle that a hand the size of Martha's couldn't reach around it. Its dark skin had distinctive bands wrapped around and across its yellowish stomach, and it had a triangular-shaped head, signifying it was poisonous.

The snake was stunned by the fall and by the shock of being abruptly awakened from its sleep. Almost immediately, though, it sensed danger and recoiled, sliding forward in the bateau up against the forward rib. Its fangs were exposed to attack whatever danger it encountered. By the white lining of its mouth, Martha knew it was a cottonmouth, and she thought it was about ready to bite her. She was frightened, and her heart beat rapidly.

Reaching down at her knees, she grabbed her blanket, and, by slowly shifting her weight back onto her toes, she was able to pull it out from underneath her. Her heart was still pounding, as she slowly unfolded the blanket and brought one end of it up to the height of her shoulders to form a shield between her and the snake. Then, instinctively, she threw the blanket over the snake, completely covering it. Miraculously, the snake didn't move.

"Lawd, how is I gonna git dis snake outta here?" she asked herself. "If I'se not careful it'll bite me right through dis blanket." She reached back and pulled the knife out from the side of the bateau. Then, holding it in her right hand, she pressed the blade down on the blanket at a point between her and the snake—to act as a barrier in case the snake crawled under the blanket toward her. Only a third of the blanket actually covered the snake, so, with her free left hand, she folded the remainder as best she could into layers. And then, taking a deep breath, she flipped the bundle over on top of the snake and pressed down at the place where she thought its head was—still the snake did not move.

She then pulled the knife out from the blanket, and, using the point, reached over and lifted the blanket from the back part of the snake. She could see a portion of its body coiled up. Again she took a deep breath and started cutting at the snake. Although the knife was sharp, she had positioned it where it came into contact with two or three parts of the snake's body at the same time, and it didn't cut all the way through. Blood splattered everywhere. The snake began whipping around wildly, its body slamming against Martha's arm and the sides of the bateau. She nearly lost control and had to use both hands to hold its head down. She finally took the knife and again attacked the snake's exposed body—this time with success; she cut off a large portion. While it was still wriggling, she grabbed it and threw it overboard.

The rest of the snake, including its head, was still under the blanket, actively jumping around. She let up on her grip and slowly lifted the blanket to take a look. The knife cut had been made about ten inches below the head. The snake was still full of life and wriggling like a cut earthworm—its mouth open and fangs exposed. She then bulked the blanket up as a shield and started stabbing at the snake with the point of the knife. After several attempts, she pierced the snake with the knife, and she flipped it overboard. She watched it sink slowly down in the water, still with its fangs exposed. At that moment, a great sense of relief came over her.

The encounter left blood splattered everywhere—on the bateau, blanket, knife, and on Martha. She didn't care. She was just grateful it was over. Retrieving her pole that had fallen overboard during the encounter, she left the area and went back downriver to a more hospitable location.

*　　*　　*　　*

Midmorning on Thursday, a boat manned by two Negro oarsmen pulled up to the main landing at the plantation. A tall, burly white man climbed out onto the dock. He was wearing high riding boots, loose-fitting riding pants, and a large brown floppy-brimmed hat. When he asked the whereabouts of "Mister King," he was told he could find him in the area over by the storehouse, "just down a piece."

As soon as Junior saw the man coming toward him, he knew exactly who he was, or at least the type of man he was.

"Mister King?" enquired the stranger.

"Yes."

"I'm Bill Mortimer, from up in Liberty County. I'm down here chasing two runaway niggers who burned down a rice mill in our area. Been chasing them for four days now, havin' a devil of a time catching 'em. They've been spotted down in this neck of the woods, possibly trying to get to Florida. You ain't seen anything of them, have you?"

"Nope. They'd know better than to come anywhere near here. I've seen the notice posted at the Darien post office, though. They're wanted dead or alive, ain't they?"

"Yep. The owner's damn mad about what they done. It's going to cost him a pretty penny to rebuild the rice mill they burned down. He's offered a five-hundred-dollar reward to anyone who catches them.

"The last time anyone's seen 'em was up about four miles west of Darien. They was headed into these swamps you got around here. That's why I'm here. I hear you know these swamps 'bout as well as any in these parts, and I've come to ask you to join our patrol. We got three men from Liberty County, and we picked up one more from Darien who's got some good-looking nigger dogs. You'd make five. What do you say?"

"Well, ain't been on a good nigger hunt with dogs for some time—think I might enjoy it. Been on lots of patrols, though—it's the only way to keep niggers from wandering all over the place. Burning a man's property ain't nice, and these niggers deserve to be caught and punished. It'll keep others from doing the same thing. Besides, with all the rain we've been having, can't get in the fields to start planting, anyway. When you want to get started?"

"First thing in the morning. We'll meet up on Ol' Musgrove Road, 'bout three miles out of Darien—where it meets up with the river. The dogs'll be waiting there."

"That's good. I'll be there. I'll bring one of my men who knows the swamps real good, too. If they're in there, we'll find them. I got me a nigger runaway somewhere up there, as well; maybe we'll find her, too."

"Thanks; see you in the morning," replied Mortimer. He shook Junior's hand and walked off in the direction of the landing. Junior took a glance around and then headed toward the blacksmith shop.

The next morning, Junior and Amos rode up the Ol' Musgrove Road on horses they'd gotten at the Darien stables. Amos was a former slave driver who had been demoted to field hand for his overzealous whipping of a slave. He had accompanied Junior on a number of patrols in the past, and was adept at figuring out how runaways reacted when they got into unfamiliar swamps.

The two were the last to arrive at the meeting place and were greeted by the barking of a large yellow dog that wasn't sure they belonged there. Looking at Junior, Mortimer said, "Good, we're all here. We can get going." He didn't introduce Junior to any of the others, as if it didn't matter. One man in the group, though, seeing that Amos was a Negro, said, "I didn't know we was going to have no sixth person to share the reward with. And I ain't going to share nothin' with no nigger."

Junior quickly jumped in, "He's with me. He knows these swamps better than any man alive, and he'll be useful in tracking through some of the remote places we'll be going into. Any sharing of the reward he gets will come out of my share." This seemed to settle things down, and all the men in the group became more relaxed.

Junior recognized the owner of the dogs. He was Samuel Quicker, a craggy-toothed man of about fifty, who was known for his hard living and whiskey drinking in Darien. His dogs had the reputation of being the best nigger dogs in the county, and Quicker claimed they'd never failed to get a runaway they were after. He had four dogs in all, each a powerful animal weighting ninety pounds or more. They were mixed breed, possibly bloodhound and sleuthhound, with dirty yellow coats—the meanest looking dogs Junior had ever seen.

Sensing the chase was about to begin, the dogs were becoming excited. Quicker said, "They sure is spillin' for some nigger meat." He unleashed them and gave the command, "Ketch!"

The dogs made rapid circles around the horsemen, sniffing the ground, and then they started spreading out, as the horsemen headed west along the river. They were soon far ahead of the horsemen, but their loud yelping and sometimes baying permitted the men to track where each dog was. At times, the distance between dogs seemed as much as a quarter of a mile, but they knew the terrain well and would periodically cross each other's paths in a manner that completely covered the area being searched. The horsemen stuck mainly to the riverbank and sandy trails through the swamp, where their horses could maintain their footing.

By noon, the party had searched the entire lower swamp area where Mortimer said the fugitives had been spotted—some five or six square miles. They'd found nothing.

While the group was resting by the river, Amos mentioned to Junior that there was an adjacent section of swamp a little farther north of where they were, and that he knew a shortcut for getting there. Junior then announced to the group, "It don't look like they stopped to hide in these here swamps; they must have kept going upriver. The river takes a big bend up a piece and doubles back on itself. We can take a trail that cuts off the bend and meet up with it 'bout four miles upstream. We might catch up with them if we take it."

"Call in your dogs, Quicker," said Mortimer, "and let's get going."

*   *   *   *

Earlier that same day, Martha had spotted a pleasant-looking opening in the swamp just as she was planning to stop for the day. After poling the bateau in, she noticed that the swamp didn't go back very far inland, maybe a hundred yards at most. A sand ridge, two or three feet above the level of the water, ran parallel to the river and then abruptly turned and ran down to the river's edge about sixty yards upstream from where she was. A thicket of palmettos grew on the landward portion of the ridge, with only sand on the portion stretching to the river. It was a protected lagoon with plenty of brush for hiding the bateau. She tied up for the day, and it wasn't long before she was asleep.

She was awakened around noon by the baying of dogs far off in the distance. It sounded as if they were chasing something, and her heart started racing when she thought they might be after her. But the more she thought, the more she realized that it wasn't possible. She had come much too far from Butler Island for them to be chasing her way out here in the swamps. The dogs must be chasing deer for some hunter who lived in the area. Nevertheless, she kept her ears attuned to the activity, hoping the dogs would turn and go off in a different direction. "Dey mus' know dar's no deer in dis here swamp," she thought.

Then, all of a sudden, she was startled by what sounded like a large animal charging through the palmetto thicket up on the ridge. Two men, apparently runaway slaves, came into view, running along the sand ridge. They had terrified looks on their faces and were running as fast as they could. They passed within a hundred feet of Martha—so close she could see the sweat on their faces. If they'd stopped at the top of the ridge, they would have surely seen her, she thought.

The two men kept running until they reached the river. She could barely see them through the bushes at that point, but she sensed they stopped for a split second to look up and down the river, and then they waded in and began swimming across. The sound of the dogs now seemed a lot closer, and their baying indicated they were on the trail of some prey.

Martha was terrified. She didn't know what was going on around her, but she felt her life was in danger. All of a sudden, she realized her bateau could be seen from the sand ridge, and she decided she'd better do something about it. She quickly got into the waist-deep water, pushed her blanket down into the bottom of the bateau where it couldn't be seen, and then shoved the bateau as far into the bushes as she could. Only a small portion of the end stuck out. She then laid down on her back in the water, up close to the bateau, and submerged herself so that only half her head remained above water, enough to breathe and to see what was going on.

She barely had time to do this before a large dog came crashing through the palmettos along the same path the two men had taken. When it reached the river, it plunged in without hesitation and began swimming after the men, who by this time were about three-quarters of the way across. Two more dogs came crashing through the palmettos, and then another, on the trail of the first dog.

When one of the men reached the other side, he scampered up the six-foot embankment on his hands and feet. He stopped for a spilt second at the crest, looked back at the dogs, and then started running again—disappearing from sight. The second man had made it to the other side, and was trying to get up the embankment, when the first dog caught him from behind just as he was reaching the crest. The dog knocked him down and began attacking him furiously, tearing his clothes and skin. The man fought back but was no match for the big dog. When the other dogs reached the scene, they joined in the attack. It seemed they were trying to kill the man by ripping him apart.

At that moment, a group of horsemen galloped up to where the dogs had crossed the river, passing directly by Martha. "Dey's patrollers!" she thought. She could hear them yelling and whopping it up, "They got 'em; they got 'em good." "Kill them damn niggers!" It was like a raucous party for the men, more exciting than a cockfight.

Martha was terrified, but she remained still in the water. Her eyes focused on the men. And then, all of a sudden, she recognized one of them, and her heart stopped! "Oh no, it cain't be—but it is—it's Massa King! He's come to get me," she thought. "What am I goin' do?"

She then heard King yell out to the other riders, "We can't cross here; we gotta go upriver a quarter mile. There's a place up there where we can ford across and then double back." The celebration abated, and the riders turned their horses up along the river. In a minute, Martha could no longer hear or see any of them.

A half hour later, she heard horses and men's voices coming from the other side of the river. A horseman appeared near the top of the far bank, and, looking down at something on the ground, he called out in a loud voice, "We got one run up a tree and the other's over here. He looks half dead."

"Hold the dogs back, and get him out of the tree; I've got some irons that'll hold him real good," said another man.

It seemed to Martha that it didn't take long to quiet the dogs and get the man out of the tree. Most of the conversation she could hear between the men was about what to do with the man who was "half dead." He wasn't in any condition to be easily moved out of the swamps. Then a loud gunshot rang out—the matter was resolved. The horsemen, four dogs, and a man walking in chains then began moving upriver in the direction of the fording place. All but one were in a happy mood.

Martha didn't move a muscle during all this activity. And she remained lying in the water for over an hour after the men had left, for fear they'd come back along the ridge that passed near her. She was thankful they didn't.

It was dusk when she finally pulled herself out of the water. She was shivering violently and wrapped herself in the blanket and laid down in the bateau. She got no sleep that night, and no thought was given to continuing her trip upriver.

The next day, she lay on her back in the bateau, looking up at the sky. Turkey buzzards were circling overhead. They had discovered the dead man's body across the river and were flying lower and lower in anticipation of a rare feast. At daybreak, she had thought about crossing over and trying to give the man a decent burial, but she had decided against it—it was just too dangerous. Now it was too late. The turkey buzzards were having their way.

All day she could hear the buzzards squabbling among themselves, but it didn't faze her. The awful sight of the dogs nearly killing a human being kept repeating itself over and over again in her mind. It still terrified her. She thought it was the cruelest thing she'd ever seen, and she vowed she'd kill herself before letting dogs like that be unleashed on her.

She also kept wondering why Massa King was with the patrollers. It just had to be because they were looking for her—why else would he be with them? They had probably gotten distracted when they found the other two runaways. "If he uses dogs to git me, dar's nowheres in dis swamp I can hide," she thought. "He's bound to find me." The thought of the patrollers coming back haunted her, and she remained nervous the whole day— frequently stopping to hold her breath so she could listen for distant sounds more intently.

That night, while poling upriver, she felt weak, and she stopped to eat the last piece of cornbread in her food stash. She realized then that she was out of food. Her progress wasn't good, despite her intentions to make up for the day she had lost because of the dogs. The place where she stopped the next morning was quite different from the places she'd stopped before. It was more open, the water seemed clearer, and, for the first time, she noticed blossoms on some of the bushes. More sunshine came through the trees, too. Her spirits brightened a bit, and she wandered aimlessly through the waterways, enjoying the pleasant scene.

After tying up, she found herself looking down in the water at numerous fish passing under and around the bateau. "What a good meal you'd make," she thought. Taking her knife, she stabbed down at the fish, attempting to spear one. She couldn't—the fish were too quick. After several attempts, she gave up. "Don't know what I'd do even if I caught you. I ain't got no way to start a fire fo' cooking. An' you wouldn't taste good raw." Then, after cutting the seventh notch in her pole, she lay down and went to sleep.

It was midafternoon when she awoke. The sky was heavily overcast, and it looked as if it would rain. She had a few hours before she would start out again, so she used the time in trying to wash the snake's blood off the bateau and off her clothing—to no avail. Giving up, she lay back and enjoyed the scenery until it was time to go.

About an hour before dusk, she poled the bateau out into what looked like the main waterway through the swamp. Turning left, she followed it for about fifty yards and then came to an abrupt stop. From where she was, she couldn't see or hear the river, and, more worrisome, she didn't recognize any of her surroundings. She turned around and headed back in the opposite direction. After a while, she began to panic. She didn't recognize anything in that direction either, not even the place where she had tied up during the day. The heavy overcast made it impossible to locate the sun to get her bearings, and she was left to her own reckoning to find the way back to the river. She tried going down a different waterway that led to the left, then one to the right—to no avail. "Glory be, I'se plumb lost. I'll never find my way outta here. Lawd, please help me," she said. With pitch-black darkness coming on quickly, she began shivering with fear. The only thing she could do at that point was tie up and wait for morning.

Morning didn't come any too soon. She was ready to go at the first light of dawn. She knew it was critical for her to find the river—her life depended on it. But, to her dismay, the sky was still heavily overcast, and there was no sign of the sun at all. She tried retracing in her mind the route she'd taken coming into the swamp, but it was all a blur. She looked intently at the water to detect any sign of a current that might point in the direction of the river—the fish in the water and the birds in the sky—nothing helped.

In desperation, she randomly chose a waterway and began following it in whatever direction it was heading. She had been on this course for almost an hour, when, all of a sudden, a small beam of sunlight broke through the clouds and lit up the whole area. It startled Martha, but she knew instantly that the light was coming from the east, since it was still morning. "My Lawd, I'se been going in de wrong direction," she said out loud. She immediately turned around and started back toward the south. The beam of sunshine began to fade, so she concentrated hard on maintaining a perspective of where south was on the horizon. As she poled through the swamp, she kept her head constantly facing in that direction, regardless of which way the bateau was pointing at the time. It worked, and in time she came to the river. As soon as she saw it, she sat down in the bateau and smiled. "I ain't never seen nothin' more beautiful den you, Mister River. Thank you, Jesus."

*   *   *   *

The notch Martha carved on her pole that day was the eighth. That meant it was Sunday. Back at Butler Island, there was the usual Sunday service conducted by Cooper London. With no person of authority in attendance, he felt free to express himself more openly in his sermon. He spoke on the book of Exodus and Moses leading the Israelites to freedom by parting the waters of the Red Sea. He emphasized the bondage the Israelites had lived under for many years, and how, with God's help, their path to freedom had led them through dangerous waters. He pointed out that the Israelites had been brave to place their trust in God, and, in the end, they had been rewarded by gaining freedom.

"Glory to God," extolled London. "May all our brothers and sisters who place dar trust in Him be rewarded." When they heard this, nobody had any doubt that London's remarks referred to their sister, Martha. The whole gathering immediately responded, "Amen. Hallelujah, brother. Hallelujah, sister. Hallelujah!"

Following the service, everyone seemed to linger outside the cookhouse a bit longer than usual. All wanted to be brought up to date on Martha's situation. "It's a week since she's been gone—she mus' have made it through de swamps by now." "I heared dey sent de dogs in after her, an' dey couldn't catch her." "De Lawd is sho' lookin' after her." "I bet she makes it." "Wouldn't it be nice to be free like her?"

The atmosphere was electric—everyone felt good about Martha's chances of making it to freedom. As the first people showed signs of moving on to the settlement, a man in the crowd started singing a familiar spiritual. Everyone joined in as they proceeded:

> No more rainfall for wet you, hallelujah!
> No more sunshine for burn you.
> Dar's no hard trials;
> Dar's no whips a-crackin'.
> No evildoers in de kingdom;
> All is gladness in de kingdom

As soon as the procession entered the settlement, they broke into:

> Oh, gracious Lawd! When shall it be
> Dat we poor souls shall all be free?
> Lawd, break them slavery powers;
> Will you go along wid me?
> Dear Lawd, dear Lawd, when'll slavery cease;
> When we poor souls'll have our peace?
> Dar's a better day a coming,
> Will you go along wid me?
> Dar's a better day a coming,
> Go sound de jubilee!

*   *   *   *

That night Martha felt weak, and she poled only a half mile before stopping. She was exhausted and was experiencing a sharp pain in her stomach. She hadn't eaten in two days. A short way up a small creek, she found a pine tree growing on a sandy ridge and tied up. It was pitch-dark out.

In the morning, she looked around and found that the tree she'd tied up to was on a hammock, a small island in the middle of the swamp. The hammock was no more than a hundred feet long and twenty wide, but it had pine and oak trees growing on it, some of which were twenty feet tall.

She walked up a slight rise to a small clearing to have a look around. It was the first dry land she had set foot on in over a week. There were signs of a campfire having been set in the clearing sometime in the past, but she paid no attention to it. She was intent on finding out if there was something around to eat, and she was delighted when she discovered a clump of bushes with small red berries on them. Without any hesitation, she began stuffing them in her mouth and chewing them. The berries had a harsh taste, and when they reached her stomach they gave her a dull pain. But she kept stuffing them in her mouth anyway, until the pain became unbearable.

Thinking there must be something better, she began exploring the rest of the hammock. It didn't take her long to reach the other end, and when she got there she turned around and headed back. Midway, she spotted a few pine nuts scattered on the ground and bent over to pick them up. As she reached down, she heard a loud, shrill rattling sound that caused her to stop dead in her tracks. Without moving any other part of her body, she lifted her head—and found herself staring into the face of a ferocious-looking rattlesnake just six feet away from her. It was four feet long, coiled, and ready to strike. She had never seen a rattlesnake before, but she had heard about them from slaves she'd met from Hampton Point. He was the ugliest thing she'd ever seen.

Slowly—very slowly—she straightened her body up and took a step backward. She then remained motionless. And, in a few minutes, the snake's tail stopped rattling, and its body became less tense. Then, without even looking at Martha again, it slithered off into the bushes. Martha relaxed and sighed, "Thank you, Jesus." She then picked up a handful of pine nuts and slowly tiptoed her way back to the clearing, keeping a watchful eye out for other snakes.

When she got to the clearing, she sat down on a log, near the remains of the old campfire, and devoured the pine nuts. "Dar don't seem to be much food 'round here, an' dis place ain't as safe as I thought," she said to herself. Glancing at her bateau, she said out loud, "You's the only safe place I got. You sho' has been good to me."

Looking down at where the old campfire had been, she dragged her foot through the ashes. "Wonder if some runaway nigger like me set dis fire?" she thought. "Did he make it to freedom, or did he bog down in des swamps, like me? Bet he starved to death, maybe right here on dis hammock." Then her thoughts turned to her own situation. "It don't look like I'se going to make it out of des swamps, neither. It's just too hard goin'. I been at it nine days, an' alls I got to show for it is de pain in my stomach an' a lotta heartache."

When she had made her escape from Butler Island, she had known it was the biggest undertaking of her life and there'd be hardships along the way. Her trials, though, had been much more difficult than she'd anticipated. She was now on the brink of starvation, with her very life in danger. Yes, she wanted her freedom, but at what cost?

"Lawd, it ain't been too many years ago dat I didn't know being black or white made no difference. I thought we's all de same. From de very first day I learned I was owned by a white man, an' I'd be his slave fo' de rest of my life, I hated slavery. An' I fought against it every chance I got. It ain't right fo' a person to own 'nother. An' de whippin's! Lawd, why should anyone have to put up wid such cruelty? If you'd give me de answer to dis, least I'd understand.

"I always wanted to be free, an' now I is. But it ain't what I 'spected, Lawd. I cain't stay here on dis hammock wid no rattlesnakes. I cain't keep goin' upriver; no tellin' how far de Okefenokee is from here, an' dars more of what I been runnin' from up dar, anyways. 'Sides, I ain't got de strength fo' it. An' if I stay in des here swamps, I'll get hunted down by dogs or starve to death. I s'pose I ain't got no choices dat are any good, an' I'se comin' to believe I'd be better off bein' where I come from than dyin' out here in de swamps.

"I can still remember what my mammy tol' me when I'se a small child, "Freedom won't come to people like us in our lifetime, only when we gets to Heaven." I got de feeling she was right. Please Lawd, give me de courage I needs to go back to Butler Island and take my punishment. I ain't got no other choice."

*   *   *   *

It was on the eleventh day following her escape when she poled her bateau up to the riverbank behind the slave settlement at Butler Island in broad daylight. She knew the settlement would be deserted, with all hands working in the fields, and she made her way to her cabin unnoticed. After depositing her belongings and burying her knife outside, near the back corner of the cabin, she made her way to the cookhouse in search of food.

When April, the cook, saw her, she exclaimed in a loud voice, "My Lawd, you is back! An' lookin' 'bout as sickly as a ghost. When's de last time you had somethin' to eat, girl?"

"Dunno, maybe four days."

"Well, you set yo'self down here in the back of de kitchen where nobody'll see you, an' I'll fix you somethin' to eat. How does cornbread, black-eyed peas, and ham sound?"

Martha gobbled down everything that was put in front of her, and, afterward, a broad smile appeared across her face.

It was now late afternoon, and field hands who had finished their tasks were beginning to straggle past the cookhouse on their way to the settlement. Martha watched them from inside without letting them see her. At a little before five o'clock, Driver Romulo had finished pushing the last of the field hands to complete their work and was walking toward the settlement. With whip in hand, he walked in the same arrogant manner he always did. Martha watched him make the long trek up from the fields, and, as he was about to pass the cookhouse, she stepped outside and shouted, "Driver Romulo, I'se come back!"

When he saw her, a shocked look came over his face. "Well, I'll be! Massa King was sho' right. De little nigger woman has come crawling back home." He grabbed her by the arm and marched her up to the overseer's house, where Junior was staying. "Massa, Massa, I'se got a surprise fo' you. Please come out," he called out in a loud voice.

In a minute, a man's face could be seen peering through the window in the door. The door slowly opened, and Junior stepped out, pulling his suspenders up over his shoulders. "Well, well, the ungrateful nigger bitch is back, is she?" he said. "Did all those snakes chase you out of the swamps, or are you starving to death?" When he got to where he was standing face to face with Martha, without warning, he gave her a hard blow to the side of her head, knocking her to the ground. "You've always been a complainer 'round here, no good for nothing. Get up! If you think that's all the punishment you're getting, you're sadly mistaken." Looking at Romulo, he commanded, "Tie her up to the whipping post and assemble the niggers. She's going to get a whipping she'll never forget."

When all the slaves had been rounded up, Junior came out of the overseer's house dressed in a black suit, a wide-brimmed black hat, and high black leather boots. As he approached the gathering, the slaves made a large opening for him to pass through. Martha, stripped to the waist, was tied to the whipping post, her hands held high above her head by a rope that passed through a ring near the top of the post. Her toes barely touched the ground. Junior turned and faced the gathering, and, in a loud voice, said, "As you all know, this here nigger has been a runaway for eleven days. Running away from your master is the worst sin a nigger can commit. If a white man did it, he'd be shot dead. Martha here has got to be punished for her sin, and we're here to do it." He then turned to Driver Romulo and said, "Give her sixty lashes!"

Romulo administered the whipping, making sure the last lash was just as hard as the first. Martha never cried out or asked for mercy. Blood started running down her back after the thirtieth lash, and her body fell into unconsciousness just before the sixtieth. Many of the onlooking slaves couldn't bear the sight, and either turned their heads or closed their eyes and prayed.

Junior stood watching intently, his feet set wide apart, body erect, with his clenched fists resting on his hips. He did not flinch. When it was over, he told Driver Romulo to send her to Five Pounds in the morning. Then, turning to the slaves, he said, "You see what happens to a nigger when she tries to run away? Learn from this, and don't ever try it yourself. You'll get the same punishment if you do." He then walked directly back to the overseer's house.

A grave silence fell over the slave community. No one wanted to talk about what had just happened, and most went directly back to their cabins. Raylin cried bitterly the whole night.

Chapter 10—Changing of the Guard

In early January 1837, Junior received a letter from his father, postmarked from Macon, a small town in the interior of Georgia. He wrote that he would be returning from his sixth trip to the interior, and he wanted to review his findings with him and his brother, Barrington. There were some "exciting prospects" that could be taken advantage of, if they were interested. He'd be stopping by Barrington's plantation, South Hampton, on his way home, and he suggested the three of them meet there on January 15.

Junior was aware of his father's interest in properties up in the northwestern part of the state. He knew he'd made several trips there as an agent for the Bank of Darien and had identified several valuable tracts he was personally interested in acquiring. But there'd been problems in gaining access to the land from the Cherokee Indians who occupied the territory, and he'd been unable to close on a deal. Maybe, he thought, the situation had changed and "Daddy" had made some progress.

South Hampton was located in Liberty County, fifty miles north of Darien. Junior, on horseback, left for the meeting at dawn on January 15. As he rode, his thoughts weren't on his father's deal, but rather on his younger brother, Barrington, and the relationship they shared.

He and Barrington had both married well to women from Liberty County. Junior's wife, Julia, was the daughter of Colonel Audley Maxwell, a respected planter in Liberty County, who was still living. Julia would eventually inherit a number of slaves—maybe twenty or so—when her father died, but the family plantation itself would be passed down to the colonel's eldest son. Junior and Julia's fortunes wouldn't be improved significantly. Barrington, on the other hand, had married the daughter of James Nephew, who some ten years ago had decided to retire from being a planter. And, at that point, he had sold his 1,950-acre plantation to his daughter and son-in-law for a nominal sum. Instantly, Barrington had become a respected planter. This was the status that had eluded Junior all his life—despite his superior knowledge and plantation management experience. He harbored resentment and jealousy over this fact.

When Junior arrived at South Hampton, he was warmly greeted by his father and brother. It had been several years since the three of them had all been together, and there was a great deal of camaraderie between them.

After dinner, the three got down to serious discussions. King told his sons that he had found several large tracts of land lying between the Chattahoochee River and a rapidly flowing creek called Vickery Creek. It was a hilly area covered by virgin pine and oak forests. The Cherokees had recently moved west out of the area under an agreement with the State of Georgia, and the land, currently owned by Mr. Fannin Brown, could be purchased cheaply.

"The area is so beautiful, I'm positive people will be attracted to it, and there's potential for constructing several towns," said King. "And if we were to become the developers of these towns, we'd make a lot of money. But, even so, the real money's to be made in the construction of mills alongside the creek. The water force is sufficient to generate power for a cotton mill or flour mill. There aren't any other mills in the entire northern region of the state—we'd have a monopoly. No telling how rich we'd be! And the creek can support more than one mill."

"That sounds great, Daddy," exclaimed Barrington, with Junior nodding his head in agreement.

"I've negotiated an option to buy the property from Mr. Brown, and I'm planning to close the deal in the next couple of months. The problem is, I think the total project is a little too big for me to handle alone. So, I'm offering you boys a chance to join in with me. I'd be proud to have you as my partners."

"Count me in, Daddy," exclaimed Barrington. "I've been itching to get into something new for years now."

King, getting no response from Junior, asked, "What about you, son?"

"I don't know Daddy. I've been a rice and cotton planter all my life. It's all I know. I'm damn good at it, and I like what I'm doing. I'm just not sure I want to give it all up for something I don't know anything about."

"I can understand your feelings, son," replied King. "Remember, before I became a plantation manager, I did a lot of construction work in Darien, so it's not something that's totally new to me. You, and me, and Barrington, here, would be a team. We'd learn from each other and help each other out. We got brains, and we work hard. There's really nothing we can't do together."

"I know, Daddy. I guess I just gotta think about it a bit before I decide."

"That's all right; you do that," replied King, in a voice showing his disappointment. "It'll take us about six months to marshal all the equipment and materials we'll need to start construction. You've got till then to make up your mind if you want in on the deal."

The next morning, Barrington walked out to the stables with Junior to assist him in saddling his horse for the journey back to Butler Island. "I'm committed to Daddy's plan," he remarked. "I think it will make us all rich, so I'm hoping you decide to get on board, too."

"I know. I just don't think it's the right thing for me. I don't want to hurt Daddy's feelings, so I'm going to give it a lot of thought. Got Momma to consider, too. I talked to her last week, and she said she ain't going up north with Daddy on this adventure. She's staying right here on the coast. Someone's got to look after her, if she does."

"Well, look, I hope you join us—but, if you don't, I'd be willing to make you a deal on South Hampton here. I'd sell it to you at a fair price."

Junior's interest perked up at this comment. "That's mighty nice of you. I'll take that into consideration as well."

Junior's mind was reeling on the ride home. He was almost certain he wouldn't join the new venture, if there were some way he could get out of it without hurting his father's feelings. But what to do otherwise was the big question—stay in his current position as manager of the Butler plantations, or strike out on his own and buy South Hampton? Did he have enough money? He had to do some serious thinking about these possibilities.

✶   ✶   ✶   ✶

Junior did purchase South Hampton from his brother instead of joining his father's venture. The price was $17,600. And, as it had done for his brother, ownership instantly conveyed to him the status of a respected planter. He made friends easily among Liberty County's elite. His efficient management of the property also enabled him to stand out among his peers, and he became wealthy in the process. Finally, he had the status he so desperately wanted.

The new wealth didn't stop with Junior. Roswell King Sr. and Barrington successfully established a thriving township, Roswell, in northwest Georgia, along Vickery Creek, and this attracted several wealthy families to the area. The Roswell Manufacturing Company, a cotton mill founded by the Kings, became a thriving enterprise as well. It eventually reached a two hundred-loom capacity and made them both rich. The mill also helped draw workers to the region, swelling the town's population.

Junior, of course, resigned from his position as manager of the Butler plantations. This caused a great deal of anxiety for the owners, Pierce and John Butler. They had never before taken any interest in the operation of the plantations, nor even set foot on the properties. With Junior's departure, it now appeared they would have to get more deeply involved.

Chapter 11—Fanny Kemble

After viewing a performance of Romeo and Juliet starring Frances Anne Kemble, a New York City theater critic wrote, "I am quite satisfied that we have never seen her equal on the American stage." And on September 23, 1832, Henry Berkeley, a bon vivant chum of Pierce Butler's, wrote to him from New York,

> Why don't you come here and see the Kembles? Charles is the best and most finished actor you have ever seen, and Fanny is superior to anything that can be imagined. The working of her fine face and the subdued and smothered voice of intense passion which she brings forth with the eye of fire is only met with once in a man's life. In person, she is pretty, rather tall, large legs and feet, large arms—never mind, you will fall in love with her, for she is right lovely to look upon.

It didn't take Pierce long to make the trip to New York from his home in Philadelphia. Upon seeing a performance of the father-daughter Kembles, he was spellbound. He was infatuated with Fanny and became a regular "stage door Johnny," attending every performance. He courted Fanny relentlessly for nearly two years, even accompanying her on the Kembles' American tour of Boston, Philadelphia, Baltimore, and Washington DC. In June 1834, he proposed marriage.

Fanny and her father, Charles, had not come to America with the intent of finding an appropriate marriage partner. Their reason was more basic—they needed money. Money would help restore the operations of the family-owned theatre, Covent Gardens, in London. The theatre had been Charles' mainstay for over thirty years, but it had recently fallen on hard times. Low attendance, brought on by a financial crisis in England and an outbreak of cholera, had forced the theatre to suspend operations.

The Kembles came from a long line of actors who had graced the London stage since the days of Queen Elizabeth. They were widely recognized as being the class of their profession. An Aunt of Fanny's, Sarah Siddon, was the queen of the English stage for decades, unequaled in her performances in Shakespearian roles. Fanny had ascended to her aunt's place of prominence and had become the idol of the theater-going public. The whole world seemed to be at her feet.

Her fame preceded her to America, and she became an overnight sensation. Within two years of touring, the Kembles amassed sufficient funds to place their theatre back on firm footing. But, at this point, when they were about to return to England, Fanny decided to forgo her acting career in favor of marrying Pierce Butler. Her father, Charles, returned to England alone.

Her marriage to Pierce promised financial security, something she had lacked most of her life, as well as a place in society where she could meet and interact with individuals at the same intellectual level as herself. But despite her being twenty-five years of age and highly intelligent, her decision to marry Pierce proved naive.

Prior to their marriage, they had never discussed the source of Pierce's wealth. And when it became evident to Fanny that it was based on slavery, her abolitionist views sharpened and clashed strongly with those of her husband. One year after their marriage, she wrote to a friend:

> The family into which I have married are large slaveholders; our present and future fortune depends greatly upon extensive plantations in Georgia. But the experience of every day, besides our faith in the great justice of God, forbids dependence on the duration of the mighty abuse by which one race of men is held in object physical and mental slavery by another. As for me, though the toilsome earning of my bread were to me my lot again tomorrow, I should rejoice with unspeakable thankfulness that we had not to answer for what I consider so grievous a sin against humanity.

The subject of slavery was a constant irritant during the early years of their marriage, which was a stormy affair. Fanny, through reasoning based on moral conviction, hoped to change her husband's views—to the point where he would emancipate his slaves. Pierce staunchly defended slavery and thought Fanny's views were based on ignorance of the facts.

Pierce's last living aunt, Elizabeth, died in 1836. Under the terms of his grandfather's will, full ownership and control of the Georgia plantations passed to him and his brother, John. This new responsibility, as well as Roswell King Jr.'s resignation as manager of the plantations, caused the two brothers to make their first-ever visit to Georgia, to inspect operations. Fanny wanted to accompany them, but they denied her the privilege. However, the following year, when Pierce planned to make the trip alone, she was granted permission. Pierce relented on this occasion, in part because he felt that first-hand experience with slavery would moderate her views.

On December 21, 1838, Fanny; Pierce Butler; their three-year-old daughter, Sarah; their new baby, Frances; and their Irish nurse, Margery O'Brien, left Philadelphia enroute to Georgia. They traveled by train to Wilmington, North Carolina, and from there they took a steamship to Savannah, with a brief stopover in Charleston. Their final leg down along the coast of Georgia to the small port of Darien was in a steam packet, the *Ocmulgee*, which arrived on December 30.

Fanny was sitting in her cabin, gazing out a porthole, as the *Ocmulgee* pulled alongside the town dock. From her position, she could see a line of small, irregularly shaped buildings that comprised the town of Darien and, beyond that, low, reedy swamps stretching far into the distance. "We have now certainly reached the outermost limits of civilization," she thought. "Mr. Butler's plantation must be somewhere out there in the swamps. I am looking forward to seeing it and have come with no prejudices against what I may find there. On the other hand, I know I have prejudice against slavery itself, for I am an Englishwoman, in which the absence of such a prejudice would be disgraceful. I want to observe carefully and objectively the situation as it truly exists, and I am prepared to find conditions that mitigate the general injustice of the system. I will keep a journal of my findings."

As the party went out on deck in preparation for disembarking, they were greeted by shouts from Negro men in two brightly painted boats that had pulled alongside. They stood yelling, whistling, and jumping about in an excited manner.

"Oh, Massa! How you do, Massa?" shouted one man.

"Oh, Missis! Oh, Lily Missis! We too glad to see you," shouted another. The affectionate shouts of welcome enlivened Fanny. They were being greeted like royalty.

In what turned out to be a mass of confusion, Fanny and the others were seated in one of the boats and their luggage in the other. The party then set out for Butler Island, two miles away. They crossed over the Darien River and entered a canal, or "cut," that transversed one of the delta islands. Man-made dikes with unkempt grass growing in spots bordered the canal. At the far end, they intersected with the Butler River, and the scene changed. Thick groves of cypress trees with limbs draped with gray moss lined the riverbanks.

At the intersection, the boat took a westerly turn, passing a large brick chimney structure and several wooden buildings belonging to the plantation. All were closed, since it was Sunday. As they came around a small bend in the river, the plantation's main landing came into view, and they saw a schooner docked alongside the wharf. An oarsman took up a large conch shell and signaled their arrival.

By the time they reached the landing, a large crowd of Negroes— more than one hundred— had gathered to greet them. They were jumping all around, dancing, shouting, laughing, and clapping in ecstasy. They crowded around the group like a swarm of bees, pulling and tugging at their clothing, kissing their hands, pushing and shoving them. If it hadn't been for the efforts of Mr. Oden, the overseer, who cleared a path for them, they wouldn't have been able to take a single step.

"My goodness!" said Fanny, after they had reached the overseer's house and gotten safely inside. "That was a sight to behold!"

"Well, I thought it was a bit frightening," remarked Margaret O'Brien. "They nearly smothered the children."

"You shouldn't be worried; they're just happy to see you and want to make you feel welcome," said Oden. "They certainly wouldn't do anything to harm you. But now, let me officially welcome you to Butler Island plantation. It's a pleasure to have you here."

"Well, thank you, Mr. Oden. If what we've seen so far is any indication, I'm sure our stay here will be a very interesting experience," replied Fanny.

*   *   *   *

The Butler party shared living quarters in the overseer's house with Mr. Oden. The house was a small wooden structure consisting of three apartments and three closets. The main apartment, measuring fifteen by sixteen feet, served as a sitting and dining area combination. Its walls were plastered, but not painted. Another room of similar size served as the Butler's bedroom. It was separated from the main apartment by a dingy wooden partition covered with hooks, pegs, and nails, to which an assortment of hats, caps, and keys was suspended in irregular fashion. The doors had wooden latches, which were raised by means of small pieces of string. The third apartment was a chamber with a sloping ceiling situated above the sitting room. The nurse and children used this as a bedroom. Of the three closets, one was used by Mr. Oden as his bedroom, another for his office. The third adjoined the Butler's bedroom and was used as Pierce's dressing room, as well as an office where he gave audiences to Negroes. All of the interior walls were thin, and a sound made in any part of the house reverberated throughout the whole structure. Fanny was a bit dismayed by the accommodations, but she was determined to make do.

Just before dawn the following morning, Fanny was awakened by the clanging of a large bell. Immediately afterward, she heard noises in the house, as Mr. Oden moved around getting ready for the day's activities. And a short while later, she heard groups of people passing by the house on their way to work in the darkness.

When daylight came, she arose, got dressed quickly, and went outside to observe what was going on. She met Mr. Oden standing in the middle of a large open area in front of the house.

"Good morning," he said.

"Good morning to you, too," she replied. "You certainly start work early around here, don't you?"

"Oh yes, ma'am. Our hands need to be at their assigned places before daylight. That way we can get as much done as possible before the heat of the day is upon us."

"Everyone seems to be working now, even at this tall brick structure near the house here. What is it, anyway?"

"Well, ma'am, that's our steam rice mill, the best of its kind in these parts. It's used to do pounding during the final stages of rice production. Would you like to see how it operates?"

"Yes I would."

"If you'd like, I could take you on a short tour of the plantation as well."

"That would be grand; let's do it."

Oden showed Fanny the rice mill, the nearby blacksmith and cooperage operations, and the cookhouse. He then explained the general structure of the plantation—its system of dikes, trunks, and ditches, and the number and location of slave settlements, barns, and agricultural operations. They then took a tour of the nearby rice fields.

Upon seeing the mosaic of rice fields, divided by small dikes and canals, Fanny exclaimed in a despondent voice, "I don't suppose I'll be able to do much horseback riding here."

"No, ma'am," was the reply. "These dikes aren't good for much other than walking. We don't even use them for transporting the rice. That's all done by barges."

"Well, I'll just have to find some other way to get my exercise, I suppose."

As they walked along the main river dike, they passed dense thickets of wild vegetation, inspiring Fanny to remark, "You certainly have beautiful shrubbery here in the South. It's now midwinter, and yet I see every shade of green, every variety of fern—all in full leaf. The dark-colored oak, the magnolias, bays, and myrtles are really beautiful. The magnolia, by the way, is my favorite. The birds are beautiful, too. I've seen partridges, ducks, and a variety of long-necked waterfowl.

You've got a variety of hawks, as well. I really find them beautiful in flight—that is, except for that kind over there. What is it?"

"That's a turkey buzzard, ma'am."

"Well, it's one of the most grotesque birds I've ever seen."

"It sure is," replied Oden. "It's a scavenger that'll eat just about anything. And it don't pay to shoot 'em; they don't taste good when they're cooked."

As they were completing their tour, Oden spotted a young male slave standing in the courtyard in front of the overseer's house.

"Good," he said, "there's someone I want you to meet." As they reached the young man, he said, "Ma'am, this here is Jack. He's going to be your personal servant while you're here. If there's anything you need him to do, just tell him, an' he'll do it."

"Well, I'm happy to meet you, Jack," she said, shaking his hand.

"I'se likewise, Missis."

"Thank you, Mr. Oden, for showing me around. I've worked up quite an appetite, and I'm looking forward to a good breakfast. I'll be seeing you later.

"Jack, I'll meet you right in front of the house here when I've finished eating, okay?"

"Yes, Missis."

*   *   *   *

"Now Jack, are you ready to go?"

"Go where, Missis?"

"I want to take a closer look at the cabins in Settlement No. 1. Follow me!"

The two left the main courtyard and walked past the cookhouse, into the settlement. Fanny could see upwards of twenty single-story frame cabins lining the main street, and at the far end, the two-story infirmary building.

Passing the first two cabins on the left, she entered the third through an open doorway. Her eyes immediately focused on three half-naked female children, ages seven to ten years old, who were squatting down around smoldering embers in the fireplace. Each child held a small infant in her arms. Fanny gasped at the sight and said, "Where's your mother?"

"She in de fields," replied the oldest child in a frightened, half-muffled tone.

The cabin's main room measured twelve feet by fifteen feet. There were two closets divided off by rough wooden partitions that were used as sleeping compartments. Each had a rudimentary bed with gray moss used as a mattress. Dirty, worn blankets were strewn everywhere. Firewood and shavings lay about the floor, as were chicken droppings and feathers. Through the open back door she could see an unsightly sanitation ditch running behind the cabin.

"These are the most miserable living conditions I've ever seen," she exclaimed. "How do you stand living like this?" Pointing at one of the older children, she commanded, "Put some wood on the fire, and warm this place up. You! Get a broom and start sweeping, and you, get these filthy chickens out of here and close the door behind them."

The children seemed bewildered; they did nothing. In frustration, Fanny threw wood on the fire herself, and, grabbing a broom, started sweeping the floor.

Looking up at Jack, who was standing motionless outside of the doorway, staring at her, she said, "Don't just stand there—find another broom, and help me." Jack did as he was told. The children, seeing all the activity, started laughing, but, in the end, tried imitating them.

After getting the cabin in fairly good order, Fanny and Jack proceeded to do the same for the next six cabins in the row. Fanny was exhausted and told Jack, "I think that's enough for one day. We'll have to do the rest some other time. Tomorrow, though, I want to take a look at the infirmary."

That night, she made the following entry in her journal:

The conditions I found today were abominable, filthy, and wretched in the extreme. They exhibited the most despicable conditions of ignorance and the inability of the inhabitants to secure even the pitiful comfort as might yet be achieved by them. Instead of the order, neatness, and ingenuity that might convert these miserable hovels into tolerable residences, there was the careless, reckless, filthy indolence, which even the brutes do not exhibit in their lairs and nests.

I shall in my small way attempt to alleviate the situation by going in and out among them. I shall teach, and they shall learn a thousand things of deepest import. They will also learn that there are beings in this world, with skins of a different color from their own, who have sympathy for their misfortunes.

On the following day, she visited the infirmary, a large two-story building made of whitewashed wood. It consisted of four large rooms, two on each floor.

As she entered the first of the ground-floor rooms, she found it to be dark, with only a small fire burning in a fireplace set in the middle of the room. There were six windows, three containing glass panes too dirty to see out of. The remaining three were without glass and had been shuttered closed to keep the cold air from coming in. The room was devoted exclusively to the care of pregnant women.

There were so many women lying about the room that it was difficult for her to move around. Those women who were strong enough were sitting up, crowded around the fire, mostly on bare ground. Other women too ill to move lay prostrate on the floor, buried in tattered, dirty blankets. There were no beds, mattresses, or pillows. Some women were still expecting, others had recently given birth, and still others were recovering from miscarriages.

Fanny was shocked by what she saw and said out loud, "Why, oh God, have you forsaken your people?" Finding the midwife in charge of the room, a woman in her sixties named Old Rose, she commanded, "Open the shutters on these windows that have glass panes, so we can get some light in this place!" She then grabbed a log and put it on the fire.

"Let alone, Missis, let be," exclaimed Old Rose. "What for you lift wood? You got niggers 'nough to do dat!"

Fanny resisted Old Rose's attempt to stop her, and threw several logs onto the fire. "Now, Rose, help me get rid of all the rubbish in here. And fold these unused blankets, too. When we're done with that, we'll tend to some of these women who are too ill to sit up and make them more comfortable." When this was finished, there seemed to be some semblance of order.

Looking more closely at the patients, Fanny was appalled by the dirty condition in which one mother was keeping her sick infant. The mother, named Harriett, had given birth to the child some two months prior. They had been readmitted to the infirmary when both she and the child had become ill. Fanny exclaimed, "You should be ashamed to treat your child in this manner. Look at her—she's as dirty as a pig. No wonder she's sick!"

"Oh Missis, I'se sorry," replied Harriett. "None of us mothers got no strength to keep our chillun clean. We's all work from daybreak till evening time, an' when we gets home, we's just too tired to do much wid de chillun. We just throws ourselves down an' goes to sleep."

Seeing the woman's poor physical condition, Fanny gave credence to what she was saying, and she asked Old Rose to give the child a bath. She then made a brief tour of the remaining three rooms, finding that the other first floor room was devoted to women with various disorders and that the two rooms upstairs were devoted to men. None of the windows upstairs had panes in them and were kept shuttered.

Upon returning home, she accosted Mr. Butler and Mr. Oden, giving vent to her indignation, "I have never seen worse conditions in any infirmary in my life!" In defense of the situation, Mr. Oden replied, "I agree they are not the best, but when I became overseer a little more than a year ago, I proposed to Mr. King that upgrades be made. But he gave me no encouragement to proceed. I therefore thought the owners were indifferent to the situation and decided to leave the infirmary in the condition I found it." Neither Mr. Oden nor Mr. Butler gave Fanny any encouragement to improve conditions at this time, either. She could only wonder, "My God, have these people lived like this during the entire nineteen years Mr. King was manager of this place?"

As far as Harriett's statement about women being too tired from work to care for their babies, Mr. Oden repeatedly assured her it wasn't true. And he appeared annoyed by the insinuation.

The next morning, Fanny paid another visit to the infirmary and found there had been some attempt at sweeping and cleaning. But, alarmingly, she found Harriett cowering in the corner, crying.

"My goodness woman, what ails you? Why are you crying?"

No words came from Harriett, but with a loud groan she pointed over her shoulder to her back. Then Old Rose interjected, "She's been whipped!"

"By whom? Why?" asked Fanny.

"By de overseer, Massa Oden," replied Rose. "He done it 'cause of de things she told you yesterday."

"What? Harriett, is that true?"

"Yes, Missis," replied Harriett, in a subdued voice. "He just left here an' he told me if I ever say nothin' mo' to you, he'll come back an' whip me again."

As Fanny looked around at the other women in the room, there seemed to be a great deal of nodding in support of what had been said. Fanny exclaimed, "This is horrible. The man is a beast." Indignantly, she left the infirmary.

That evening at dinner, with Mr. Butler present, she asked Oden, "Did you flog Harriett today?"

"Yes, ma'am," was the reply.

"I am told the reason for the flogging was because she had spoken with me about problems women were having caring for their children."

"Oh no, ma'am. That's not the reason at all. I flogged her for being impertinent. I went there this morning to check on her condition. After I looked her over, I told her she was well enough to go back to work, and I ordered her to get up. At first, she refused, but, after some prodding, she said in a very impertinent manner, "Very well, I'll go, but I'll be back again." It was for this reply that I gave her a good lashing. It was her business to have gone to the fields without answering me. Once she was there, we would have seen whether she could work or not. It's just another example of these people trying to get out of work by feigning illness."

Mr. Butler partially substantiated Oden's statement by saying, "It's impossible to believe anything these people say."

Fanny was stunned by the discrepancy between Harriett's and Oden's description of the same event. She didn't believe Oden's version, but she said nothing.

The next day, again seeing the uncleanliness of the infants, she contrived a bribery scheme to address the situation. Gathering together as many "baby nurses" as she could find, she announced a new system of wages. For every infant whose face was clean the next day, she would give the "nurse" a penny. And for any "nurse" whose face and hands were clean, another penny as well.

The following morning, she was surrounded by a swarm of children carrying their little charges on their backs—all with bright, shining faces. The bribe paid off handsomely, and, for the first time, Fanny realized that black babies were pretty. She thought they had beautiful eyes and eyelashes, pearly white teeth, and skin infinitely finer and softer than the skin of white babies. At one point, she picked up a small infant and gave him a kiss—much to the delight of all present.

Late that afternoon, she noticed a number of women field hands who had just completed their labor for the day. They were down by the river filling large buckets with water for household use. She told them, "I want you to go home and use this water to clean your children, and yourselves, too."

"But, Missis, we cain't do dat. We ain't got no soap," replied one woman. "If Missis only give us soap, we be so clean fo'ever."

The woman's response struck a chord with Fanny and she chastised herself for not realizing that such a basic need wasn't being met. Thereafter she made sure that soap was given to the slaves.

There was still one more thing she could do for the neglected infants, and that was to provide them with appropriate clothing. After inquiring where the clothes for plantation workers were made, she made a beeline to the sewing center located in the storehouse.

Abruptly slinging open the door, she entered a large room where five women were busy operating sewing machines. When the women saw Fanny, they stood up and, in unison, said "Good day, Missis."

"Who is in charge here?" enquired Fanny.

"I is," said the middle-aged woman who had been sitting at the machine near the front of the room. "I'se Raylin."

"Well, Raylin, I've come to see if you can make some infant's clothing for me. I need them for when new babies are born at the infirmary. Have you ever made anything like this before?"

"No, Missis. Ain't never been no need fo' dat. S'pose we could, though."

"Get me some flannel and some chalk and I'll draw the patterns."

Fanny drew outlines for an infants' wrap—complete with arms, small booties, and a diamond-shaped piece for use as a nappy. "There, do you think you can make these for me?"

"Yes, Missis. We just got done wid makin' de new clothes fo' de hands—dey all got distributed at Christmas time. We got lots of scraps 'round here we can use."

"Good, I'll need twenty-five pairs of each, then. And I need them as soon as possible."

"Yes, Missis. We'll get right to it."

That evening, while Fanny was sitting alone in the main room of the house writing in her journal, the door opened quietly. One after another, men and women slaves came silently in—some fourteen or fifteen in all. They squatted down in a semicircle around her, not making a sound. Their eyes were fixed on her as she wrote, but she took no notice. This went on for nearly half an hour. When she came to a stopping point and closed her papers, she looked up for the first time and said, "What do you want?"

All of the slaves stood up at once, and, almost in unison, said "We's come say 'how do,' Missis." And as silently as they had entered, they trooped out.

Fanny didn't exactly know what to make of this but supposed she had become somewhat of a curiosity to the slaves. They had come to get a closer look—to see what made her tick.

From that time on, slaves no longer maintained a passive demeanor when they met her during walks around the plantation. They accosted her with petitions of all sorts—from simple requests for sugar or a piece of flannel to requests for having Massa Butler reduce their workload. She simply couldn't avoid the masses of people who approached her.

To gain consideration for their individual causes, women slaves always tried to place themselves in the most favorable light. Invariably, they did this by making known to her the number of children they had produced. "Look, Missis! Little niggers for you an' Massa" or "You see many, many of my offsprings." On one occasion, she was visited by nine women, who had come to protest the shortness of time given to new mothers recovering from birthing. Fifty-five children had been born to these nine women—of which twenty-seven had died. They'd experienced twelve miscarriages, as well. They argued that they had proven themselves valuable to Massa, so their pleas should receive proper consideration.

Following up on her order for infants' clothing, Fanny made it a point to stop by the storehouse to talk to the head seamstress, Raylin. "Good afternoon," she said, as she entered. "I've come to see how you're getting along with my infant's clothing."

"Dey's all done," replied Raylin. "Dey's over here."

Fanny was taken by surprise. It had been less than two days since she had placed the order. After inspecting the items, she said, "These clothes look just fine. You've done a good job! How did you get them done so quickly?"

"Thank you, Missis."

Fanny, noticing a degree of pride in Raylin's demeanor, began taking greater interest in her. "How long have you been sewing here on the plantation?"

"Mo' den twenty years now."

"Well, you've learned your trade well. Do you have a family?"

"Oh yes, Missis. I'se got two sons. My oldest one, Christopher, he's an apprentice to engineer Ned at de rice mill, an' my youngun, Bran, is a carpenter. Dey's both got good jobs. Had two girls too, but dey died. Don't want no mo', though, they's too much trouble. My husband's de head cooper on de plantation, too."

Fanny was taken aback by the importance Raylin placed on the success of her family members. It was a trait she hadn't seen in other slaves. Before she could make a response, Raylin continued, "I'se sorry I didn't recognize you b'fore. I mistook you for yo' white lady servant. I thought she was you, since she was de one carrying yo' white child 'round. I'se glad I got it straight now. We's all glad Massa got married an' has chillun'. It's nice to have you visit dis island."

"Well, thank you, Raylin."

"You gonna give des clothes to new mothers? Dat's nice. I hears you been helpin' some poor niggers get food an' clothin' too—dat's nice, too."

"I just can't help feeling sorry for the poor souls—especially the women who are bearing so many children and haven't the time to properly care for them."

"Conditions ain't all dat good 'round here, an' we need all de help we can git. De reason women has so many chillun, is so's dey can get out of doin' work. When dey becomes "lusty," dar work gets cut back, an' dey gets three weeks off after de child is born. In my way of thinkin', dat ain't a good 'nough reason fo' havin' chillun. De babies dat lives long 'nough to grow up ain't got much to live fo', anyway. Most of dem ain't goin' be nothin' but common field hands, 'cause dar ain't dat many good jobs 'round."

"I agree. Under the conditions here, I'm surprised more people just don't run away from this place."

"Run away?" exclaimed Raylin. "What's de use? Dar ain't nowheres to go from here. Dar's swamps for miles and miles all 'round . When peoples try to get through dem dey either dies or gives up an' comes back. An' when dey gets back, what's waitin' fo them is a good whippin'. Some of dem get sent to Five Pound for mo' punishment too."

"I don't know the area around here very well, but from what I've seen, I'm sure what you say is true." Then, realizing she had made a connection with an intelligent woman who was willing to express her opinions, Fanny boldly continued, "Please explain another thing to me. I've often met people who seem to be happy with what they're doing, and a short time later I've seen the same people downcast and looking sad. Why is there such a big change in their demeanor?"

"Missis, all us niggers got two faces we puts on. One is fo' de white folk who 'spects us to be happy all de time. We smile a lot, sing happy songs sometimes, bows down or curtseys, and takes off our hats, 'cause that's how white folk wants us to act like. Our other face is for how we really feels. If you see people 'round here dat looks sad, dat's 'cause dey is sad."

"I feel the reason why so many are that way is because they lack self-respect. They don't seem to feel good about themselves. And I think it's mainly because of the color of their skin—they feel inferior to white people."

"I s'pose dar's all kinds of niggers 'round here. Plenty don't care much about what dey do—an' dey ain't very happy, neither. Dars plenty dat does care, though, and some is plenty smart—smarter den white folk even. But I'm mo' of de mind dat most don't think dey is inferior to whites just 'cause of de color of dar skin. I thinks dey feels inferior 'cause de white folk is mo' powerful den dey is. White folk can make us niggers do whatever dey wants."

"You may be right. The whole system is based on fear, isn't it? If you don't do what the master says, you're afraid you'll get punished. But look at you. You don't strike me as a woman who is afraid of anything."

"Well, I does speak my mind, Missis. Done dat all my life. Got me in a heap of trouble sometimes, an' I'se learned de hard way when to keep my mouth shut. But when I'se right 'bout something, peoples listen. Even Massa King listened once in a while—never whipped me, neither."

"I've heard a lot about Massa King. He wasn't a very good person, was he?"

"No, Missis, I'se surely glad he's gone from dis place. I hope he burns in hell."

Fanny was floored by the openness of Raylin's comments, and she had one more question she was dying to ask. "I surely appreciate your openness in talking with me. Be assured that not a single word you've said will ever get back to Mr. Butler or Mr. Oden. It will be my secret—but I have one more question for you. If you were ever given a chance to become a free person, would you take it?"

Raylin took a moment before responding, and finally she said, "I 'spect if you asked dat question to every nigger on dis plantation, you'd get de same answer. Dar ain't one of us dat wouldn't jump at de chance. But dar ain't no use for any of us even thinkin' 'bout it. We's slaves. We been slaves all our lives. An' we's gonna be slaves till de day we dies."

"Oh, I hope that's not true." Fanny then stood up and said, "Come on now, help me carry these clothes up to the infirmary. I need to instruct Old Rose on what to do with them. And, by the way, I'll need twenty-five more pairs soon."

$$\ast \quad \ast \quad \ast \quad \ast$$

On her walk one morning, as Fanny was passing a group of slaves working in a rice field, she heard someone yell out in a loud voice, "You, nigger. I say, you black nigger! You no hear me call you? What fo' you don't run quick?" She looked in the direction of the voice and noticed a driver with a whip in his hand accosting another slave. She immediately walked over and took the whip out of the driver's hand and held it. The expression on her face told what she was thinking, and the driver exclaimed, "Oh, Missis, me use it for measure. Me seldom strike nigger wid it."

Her mind focused on the fact that here was a black slave, who happened to be a driver. He was about to inflict physical punishment upon one of his own kind, merely because he had been empowered to do it. It was black on black—virtually identical to white on black. Human nature, she thought, has no color boundaries, and whenever a person is given physical empowerment over another, his evil nature comes to the fore.

Under plantation rules, drivers could whip a slave twelve times for any offense, the headman thirty-six times, and the overseer fifty. But from what she'd heard, these limits weren't being enforced. She had experienced firsthand the whipping given Harriett, and had heard of other whippings given to Teresa, Sarah, and a cook named John during the time she'd been on the plantation. She felt it was a disgusting practice, but one she was powerless to do anything about.

After looking the slave driver once again in the eyes, she handed the whip back to him without saying a word—and walked away.

*　　*　　*　　*

A well-respected slave named Shadrack was suffering from dysentery. Despite attention given by a doctor called from Darien, he sank rapidly and died within six days' time. It was clear his death greatly affected the slave community. And Fanny, wanting to show her sympathy, convinced Mr. Butler to accompany her to Shadrack's funeral service.

On the day of the funeral, Shadrack's body was wrapped in cotton cloth, placed in a pinewood coffin, and laid on trestles in front of the cabin of the man who was to conduct the service—Cooper London.

A large assemblage of slaves gathered around just as darkness set in. Many carried pine-knot torches to give light to the occasion. Fanny and Mr. Butler stood near the coffin, with the eyes of every slave fixed directly upon them. The slaves had never witnessed white folk attending a slave's funeral before. On a signal from a male slave who acted as song leader, the group sang a hymn—one that Fanny had not heard before. When it was over, London began a prayer, and all the slaves knelt down in the sand. Fanny knelt down as well—only Mr. Butler remained standing. The prayer, she thought, was a conventional Methodist prayer with a very unconventional ending tacked on, which invoked a blessing upon their master, Mr. Butler, and his wife and children. Several women cried. When the prayer ended, everyone rose, and London read portions of the funeral service from the Prayer Book, proclaiming to the living and the dead the everlasting covenant of freedom, "I am de resurrection and de life."

The coffin was taken up, and a solemn procession formed, heading toward the slave burial ground. Four men with lighted torches led the way, followed in order by Shadrack's family, six men carrying the coffin, Fanny and Mr. Butler, and the remaining slaves. All walked in a long double-file line—up through the slave settlement and along the river dike for a half mile. Midway, the slaves broke out into a rendition of "Swing Low, Sweet Chariot" with several verses of local origin.

This was followed by a beautiful spiritual:

> I know moonrise, I know star-rise,
> Lay dis body down.
> I walk in de moonlight; I walk in de starlight
> To lay dis body down.
> I'll walk in de graveyard; I'll walk through de graveyard,
> To lay dis body down.
> I'll lay in de grave and stretch out my arms;
> Lay dis body down.
> I go to de judgment in de evenin' of de day,
> When I lay dis body down';
> And my soul and your soul will meet in de day
> When I lay dis body down.

The burial ground was an open space, overgrown with high grass. A grave had been dug in one corner, close to the river. When everyone had gathered round, London read from the Bible, reciting the story of Lazarus—exalting his resurrection and giving hope to all those present.

And again, a short addendum was tacked on, exhorting the slaves not to steal, lie, or neglect to work hard for Massa.

When the coffin was lowered, the grave was found to be partially filled with water, being below the level of the river that surrounded the plantation. People groaned, and many cried. It was a touching scene. London threw the first handful of dirt into the grave and uttered the words, "From dust to dust." When the grave was completely covered, Shadrack's family placed trinkets and ornaments relevant to his life on top of the grave. There was no headstone.

The procession back to the settlement was just as solemn as the one coming out. Midway, the slaves broke into a song entitled "I Hear the Angels Singing." When Fanny and Mr. Butler parted from the group, there were shouts of "Farewell, good night, Massa and Missis." "God bless you, Missis, don't cry!" "Lawd, Missis, don't you cry so!"

Fanny couldn't sleep that night, sitting up alone in the main room, wrapped in a blanket. The religious significance of the evening's events played over and over in her mind. She had been spiritually moved by the experience. Although parts of the service had been crude and unpolished, nothing had taken away from the solemn influence of the scene. It was apparent to her that black slaves had the same beliefs and the same dependence on God as white people. And she had been especially impressed by the group's leader, Cooper London, who she thought was a person of great intelligence.

That night, her journal entry read,

That man, London—who, in spite of all the bitter barriers in his way, has learned to read, has read his Bible, teaches it to his unfortunate fellows, and is used by his owner and his owner's agents for all these causes—is an effectual influence for good over the slaves—of whom he is himself the despised and injured companion: like them, subject to the driver's lash; like them, the helpless creature of his master's despotic will and without a right or a hope in this dreary world. But the light he has attained must show him the most terrible aspects of his fate hidden by blessed ignorance from his companions; it reveals to him also other rights and other hopes—another world, another life—toward which he leads, according to the grace vouchsafed to him, his poor fellow slaves. How can we keep this man in such a condition? How is such a cruel sin of injustice to be answered?

The next morning, immediately following breakfast, Fanny made a beeline to the cooper's shed in an effort to find London. He was alone when she arrived, and she bid him sit down so they could talk. London acted graciously, but he was suspicious over the attention he was getting.

"London, I want to tell you how much I enjoyed the service you held last night. I was very touched by it."

"Thank you, Missis," he replied.

"One thing that surprised me was how well you read from scriptures. I haven't found anyone else on this plantation who can read nearly as well as you. How did you ever learn?"

London was taken aback by the question, not understanding the reasoning behind it, and he was fearful of getting either himself or others in trouble. Hesitantly, he replied, "Well, Missis, me learn; well, Missis, me tries," and, finally, "Well, Missis, me s'pose Heaven helped me."

Disappointed by his response, Fanny said, "Well, I'm sure Heaven has been helpful to you in many other ways during your lifetime as well. You certainly know how to give a good sermon, and I hear you hold services regularly here on the plantation."

London's eyes lit up, and he replied, "Yes, Missis, every Sunday. Some of de folk go to Darien once a month to attend services over at de regular church, an' I holds a service in de cookhouse fo' dem that's left. Usually thirty or forty come, sometimes mo'."

"How did you ever get started preaching?"

"Well, my mammy all de time read de Bible to me when I was growin' up, so's I got to know it real good as a child. An', back in dem days, we got to go to church over in Darien as much as we liked, so's I went 'bout every Sunday. Got to know de two nigger missionaries dat lived over dar real good, an' dey tol' me I should take up preachin'. An' I got to likin' it. Sometimes one of de missionaries, Reverend Sharper, preached here on de island, an' he helped me a lot."

"Do you still get help from him?"

"Oh no, no Missis. Ol' Massa King stopped Reverend Sharper from setting foot on de plantation, an' run him out of town long time ago. Ain't seen 'em since. But fo' a time, though, he let a white preacher come and preach to us 'bout once a month. He taught me de catechism."

"Pray tell, what is the 'catechism'?" inquired Fanny.

"That's de way religion's s'posed to be taught to niggers. We can read folk de Bible, but we's s'posed to follow de catechism when we's preachin' to dem. De catechism's been written by de Reverend Charles Colcock Jones. He's a great preacher from up in North Georgia."

"Can you give me an example of what this catechism's like?"

"Yes, Missis. Some of it is just questions and answers, like,

"What command has God given to servants concerning obedience to their masters?
'Servants obey in all things your masters according to the flesh, not in eyeserve as men pleasers, but in singleness of heart, fearing God.'

"How are they to do their service of their master?"
'Wid goodwill, doing service to the Lawd and not unto men"
An',

How are they to try to please their masters?
'Please them well in all things, not answering again.'"

"Do you follow the catechism when you preach?"

"Sometimes I does, an' sometimes I doesn't—dependin' on de situation."

"I see. I suppose you also perform wedding ceremonies, too."

"Oh yes, Missis. Do dat all de time."

"Once couples get married, do their marriages tend to last?"

"Most times I'd say. In de ceremony dars a part 'bout lasting till death do you part, an' dat usually holds. Sometimes it don't. Back when we had so many niggers being sold off de plantation, it broke up a lot of marriages. I thought 'bout changing de words to "death do you part or sold apart," but I never did. Massa King done broke up some marriages, too. He'd decide sometimes it was better to have someone married to a person different from de one dey was. He'd come in an' move dem to another cabin and say you is now married to dis other person."

"Baptisms?"

"No, Missis, don't do baptisms. Not less Massa's given permission. I'd get whipped if I did; so would de person I baptized."

"Well, you seem to be doing very well under the circumstances."

"Thank you, Missis. I appreciates what you's sayin'. Could always do better, though, if I had mo' help."

"How so?"

"Well, Missis, we sure could use a heap more prayer books and Bibles 'round here. We ain't got but two each."

"If that's what you need, I can certainly get you some when I get back to Philadelphia. How many do you need?"

"I would certainly be obliged if you did, Missis. Would it be too much to ask fo' twenty copies of each?"

✳   ✳   ✳   ✳

By mid-February, Fanny had been on Butler Island six weeks. This was the midpoint of their scheduled stay in Georgia, and it was time to move on to Hampton Point, the other Butler plantation on St. Simons Island.

After farewells were given to a number of slaves at the landing, the Butler party set out in the *Lily*, one of the plantation boats, with a crew of eight. The boat looked to Fanny like a "combination of a soldier's baggage wagon and an immigrant transport." Forward in the bow were miscellaneous livestock, kitchen utensils, and household furniture. Fanny, her two children, and nurse were seated amidships among beds and bedding. And, in the stern, Mr. Butler did the steering.

When the party had completed the fourteen-mile journey, they found themselves on dry land covered with towering live oak trees. Gray moss drooped from their sprawling branches. Peach trees were in full bloom, and tufts of silver narcissus and jonquils, violets, and myrtle bushes seemed to cover the ground everywhere. It was a beautiful sight.

They were met by the overseer, James Gowen, and his wife, who showed them to their quarters in the Big House. These quarters consisted of a few rooms in the only remaining section of the house that wasn't in a state of decay. It appeared the house had seen better days.

Hampton Point was on high ground—a sharp contrast to what Fanny had experienced at Butler Island. She was delighted with her new surroundings. The variety of flora and fauna appealed to her sense of beauty. And the fact that she was now on solid ground, with room to roam, meant she could once again indulge in her favorite hobby of horseback riding.

To her, the Hampton slaves looked healthier than those at Butler Island, although there was a much higher proportion of older slaves, many of whom were too frail to work. She attributed this to the need to have younger and stronger slaves assigned to the harder work required in the rice fields.

But, to her dismay, she found the housing for slaves to be in even worse condition than at Butler Island—particularly at St. Annie's, the most remote settlement on the plantation. The same conditions applied to the infirmary. It was a two-room structure with a dirt floor.

On her first visit to the infirmary, she found "lusty" women lying on the floor, covered by dirty rags. A pine wood fire was burning in the fireplace, but a clogged chimney was forcing the smoke back into the room, where it hung like a dark cloud. Fanny's eyes smarted from the smoke, and she had to move on. There was no fire at all in the second room—which was also cluttered with women and men lying about on the floor. The room was dark, with the paneless windows shuttered.

She immediately began opening the windows to let in light. In the process, she discovered an old, feeble-looking man lying in a corner of the room. "What's wrong with this man?" she asked the nurse, Mollie.

"Dat's Friday; he's dyin'," was the reply.

Covered only by a tattered shirt and trousers, with no blanket, Friday looked exhausted. From his glazed eyes and rattling breath, Fanny could tell he was at the point of expiring. His bed consisted of a handful of straw that didn't fully cover the earth he lay on. Two wooden sticks were used for a pillow, which raised his head a few inches above the ground. Flies were gathered around his mouth. She stood there staring at him and thinking, "Here lies a miserable creature—a worn-out slave whose life was spent on this plantation, and now, at the supreme hour of his mortality, he has not one physical comfort, one Christian solace, nor one human sympathy." She bent over him, and through tear-laden eyes watched as his eyelids quivered and his jaw dropped. "Thank God, he is free," she said out loud.

In going about the plantation, Fanny observed a large number of mulattos among the slave population, many more than she had seen at Butler Island. Asking Mr. Butler why this was so, he said he thought it was because Hampton, being on St. Simons Island, was in close proximity to several other plantations belonging to different owners. The number of whites who would visit from these places accorded greater opportunity for intercourse between blacks and whites. He seemed undisturbed about the matter and deemed it to be the mere outcome of normal human behavior—a matter of course.

While they were discussing the subject, they were met by a black slave woman carrying a small mulatto child. Fanny remarked, "I truly think this child has an extraordinary resemblance to Driver Jock, on this plantation."

"It is likely his child," was the reply.

"And," said Fanny, "did you ever notice that Driver Jock is the exact image of Mr. King?"

"Very likely his brother."

She felt uncomfortable in discussing the matter, and she dropped the subject.

A few days later, during one of her horseback rides, she was stopped by a slave woman named Jennie, who asked for food and clothing for the two mulatto children with her. The children, Ben and Daphne, were apparently twins. Again, Fanny felt they had a strong resemblance to Mr. King. Because of this, she asked Jennie who their mother was.

"Minda," was the reply.

"And who is the father?"

"Massa King."

"What? Old Massa King?"

"No, young Massa King."

"Who told you this?"

"Minda, an' she ought to know."

"Well, Mr. King denies it."

"Dat's because he never looked upon them, an' ain't done nothin' fo' dem."

"He's acknowledged Renty as his son—why would he deny these children?" asked Fanny.

"'Cause old Massa Butler was here when Renty was born, an' he made Betty tell all 'bout it, an' Massa King had to own up. But nobody knows nothin' 'bout this, so's he can deny it."

Upon hearing this, Fanny continued on her horseback ride. In all, she figured there were at least three mulatto children who could definitely be traced to Roswell King Sr. and five others to his son, Roswell King Jr. And there definitely had to be more, she thought.

Unlike on Butler Island, where it took several days before slaves approached her with petitions for food, clothing, and the like, the slaves at Hampton Point began as soon as she arrived. Word about her willingness to address grievances had preceded her here.

Whenever she walked about the plantation, and in the evenings when the work was done, slaves gathered around her, begging for rice, sugar, and flannel, and asking favors. Most frequently, women complained about having to go back into the field after only three weeks of confinement follow birthing. They wanted the old rule of four weeks reinstated. One slave, Molly, put it forcefully, "Missis, me had um pickaninny—three weeks in de 'ospital, an' den right out upon de ho' again. Can we be strong dat way, Missis? No!" She had had eight children and two miscarriages—all were dead but one. "Oh, Missis, you speak to Massa for us! Oh, Missis, you beg Massa, he do as you say."

Her journal entry for a single day recorded encounters with these slave women:

Fanny has had six children—all dead but one. She came to beg to have her work in the field lightened.

Nanny has had three children; two of them are dead. She came to implore that the rule of sending them into the field three weeks after their confinement might be altered.

Leah, Caesar's wife, has had six children; three are dead.

Sophy, Lewis's wife, came to beg for some old linen. She's suffering fearfully; has had ten children; five of them are dead. The principal favor she asked was a piece of meat, which I gave her.

Sally, Sciprio's wife, has had two miscarriages and three children born, one of whom is dead. She came complaining of incessant pain and weakness in her back. This woman was a mulatto daughter of a slave called Sophy, by a white man of the name of Walker, who visited the plantation. She also begged to be assigned to work other than field labor. She felt that being in the field was too hard on her, "on account of her color." Being a mulatto, she considered field labor to be a degradation.

Charlotte, Renty's wife, has had two miscarriages, and is with child again. She is almost crippled with rheumatism, and showed me a pair of poor swollen knees that made my heart ache. I have promised her a pair of flannel trousers, which I must forthwith set about making.

Sarah, Stephen's wife: this woman's case and history were alike deplorable. She had had four miscarriages, had brought seven children into the world, five of whom were dead, and was again with child. She complained of dreadful pains in her back, and an internal tumor that swells with the exertions of working in the fields; probably, I think, she is ruptured.

Fanny made it a point to bring most of the petitions to Mr. Butler's attention. At one point, though, the situation must have become overwhelming, and he blew up in a rage, shouting, "Why do you believe such trash? Don't you know that niggers are all damned liars?" He went on to make it clear that she was never to bring any slave's petition to him again. He was through with such foolishness.

Fanny was floored by his reaction. She acknowledged that he might be weary of hearing about unfavorable conditions, but the fact that he wouldn't acknowledge their existence repulsed her. Mr. Butler, she thought, did not think black slaves shared his humanity.

Another of her visitors, Die, said she had had sixteen children, fourteen of whom were dead, and four miscarriages. One of her miscarriages had been caused by falling down with a heavy burden on her head. Another was from being whipped while having her arms tied up.

Fanny asked her, "What do you mean, having your arms tied up?"

"My hands got tied up at de wrists and drawn up to de post so tight dat my feet barely touched de ground. An' den dey take de clothes off my back an' beats me wid a cowhide."

"Did they do this when you were with child?"

"Yes, Missis."

The woman said this in a calm, deliberate manner, as if it were a commonplace occurrence. Fanny gave her the meat and flannel she had come to ask for, and remained choking with indignation long after she left. In her journal she wrote:

> I, an Englishwoman, the wife of the man who owns these wretches, and I cannot say: "This thing shall not be done again; that cruel shame and villainy shall never be known here again."

The question of what slaves thought about having their freedom was always in the back of Fanny's mind. It wasn't a question that she felt free to ask, however, because of its sensitivity. Mr. Oden, the overseer at Butler Island, had warned her that her presence among the slaves was an "element of danger to the institution." But, on one occasion, the subject came up unexpectedly.

Fanny was sitting in the garden with her three-year-old daughter, Sarah; her Irish maid, Margery; and her slave chambermaid, Mary. Out of the blue, three-year-old Sarah said, "Mary, some people are free, and some are not. I am a free person. I say, I am a free person; Mary—do you know that?"

"Yes, Missis."

"Some people are free and some are not—do you know that, Mary?"

"Yes, Missis, here," was the reply. "I know it is so here, in dis world."

Margery, who had heretofore been silent, interjected, "Oh, then you think it will not always be so?"

"We hope not, Missis."

What had suggested the subject to Sarah, or where she had gathered her information, Fanny didn't know. She knew, however, that children were made of eyes and ears, and nothing, however minute, escaped their observation.

Another instance occurred during a conversation with Jack, the slave who had been assigned as her servant. Jack was the son of a former headman at Butler Island; he was very intelligent and articulate. In the midst of his asking a great many questions about her home in Philadelphia, Fanny responded to her urge, and abruptly interjected, "Jack, would you like to be free?"

A beam of light shot over his whole countenance like a bolt of lightning. He then hesitated, began stammering, and even seemed to be confused. At length, he replied, "Free, Missis! What fo' me wish to be free? Oh no, Missis, me no wish to be free." He then went on to say, "No Missis, me no want to be free; me work till I die fo' Missis and Massa."

Immediately, Fanny regretted having asked the question. Jack's initial countenance belied his later response. It was clear he was afraid to reveal his true feelings or show the slightest discontentment with his present situation. It was a sad spectacle to witness.

During their stay at Hampton, Mr. Butler made frequent trips back to Butler Island to take care of business matters. On one occasion, he fell ill, and, for a period of four days, Fanny made daily trips to the island to nurse him. This brought her in close contact with the boatmen who rowed her back and to, and with their unique custom of singing boating songs. An entry in her journal described the experience:

My daily voyages up and down the river have introduced me to a great variety of new musical performances of our boatmen, who invariably, when the rowing is not too hard, moving up or down with the tide, accompany the stroke of their oars with the sound of their voices. The way in which the chorus strikes in with the burden, between each phrase of the melody chanted by a single voice, is very curious and effective, especially with the rhythm of the rowlocks for accompaniment. Their voices seem oftener tenor that any other quality.

Most tunes seem to have some resemblance to tunes they picked up from white men. One for example was a very distant descendant of "Coming Thro' the Rye." The words, however, were astonishingly primitive, especially the first line, which, when it burst from their eight throats in high unison, sent me into fits of laughter.

> Jenny shake her toe at me,
> Jenny gone away.
> Jenny shake her toe at me,
> Jenny gone away.
> Hurrah! Miss Susy, oh!
> Jenny gone away;
> Hurrah! Miss Susy, oh!
> Jenny gone away.

What the obnoxious Jenny meant by shaking her toe, whether defensive or mere departure, I never could ascertain, but her going away was an unmistakable subject of satisfaction; and the pause made on the last "Oh!" before the final announcement of her departure, had really a good deal of dramatic and musical effect.

Most of the songs, though, don't seem to make any sense. For example, a very pretty and pathetic tune began with words that seemed to promise something sentimental

Fare you well and good-bye; Oh! Oh!
I'm goin' away to leave you; Oh! Oh!

—but immediately went off into nonsense verses about gentlemen in the parlor drinking wine and cordial, and ladies in the drawing room drinking tea and coffee, etc.

One of their songs displeased me not a little, for it embodied the opinion that "twenty-six black girls not make mulatto yellow girl," and, as I told them I didn't like it, they have omitted it since. This desperate tendency to despise and undervalue their own race and color, which is one of the very worst results of their abject condition, is intolerable to me.

On one occasion, on the return trip to Hampton, we were met with a storm and rough seas, and part of the time the tide was against us. The labor was tremendous, and I had to forego the usual accompaniment of their voices. However, the men were in good spirits, and one of them said something which elicited an exclamation of general assent from the others. When I asked what it was, the steerer said they were pleased because there was not another planter's lady in all Georgia who would have gone through the storm all alone with them in a boat, i.e., without the protecting presence of a white man.

"Why?" said I. "My good fellows, if the boat capsized, or anything happened, I am sure I should have nine chances for my life instead of one." At this, there was one shout of "So you would, Missis; true fo' dat, Missis," and in great mutual good humor we reached the landing at Hampton Point.

*   *   *   *

On the first Sunday in April, Fanny attended services at Christ Church, located midway down St. Simons Island. It was the first and only time she attended church in Georgia. She, along with Israel, a young slave, rode horseback down the plantation road, eventually coming to the intersection with Military Road. At that point, they proceeded a short distance in a westerly direction to the church. It was a small, rustic structure tucked away in the midst of magnificent live oak trees, with a small, picturesque graveyard nearby.

When she arrived, she was met by the Reverend Bartow. He was standing in his cleric robes on the path leading to the front entrance. He greeted her,

"Good morning, Mrs. Butler."

"Good morning," Fanny replied. "It is certainly a fine day the Lord has given us."

"Yes it is, and welcome to Christ Church."

"Thank you; it is a beautiful structure, and it couldn't be in more beautiful surroundings. It looks as if it's been here a long time."

"Yes, it has—nearly eighty years. There's quite an interesting bit of history that goes with it, too—all the way back to the colonial days when it was built by General Oglethorpe's men. It was intended to serve the religious needs of the troops that were stationed at Fort Fredrica, and it eventually expanded to serve the whole town that grew up near the fort. The old fort and town are just up the road apiece, around the bend, there. General Oglethorpe's old home is up near there, too. There's not much left of anything though—all fallen to ruin over the years.

"Do you see that large oak tree over there? We call it the Wesley Oak. Back in Oglethorpe's day, John Wesley and his brother, Charles, came here as Episcopal priests to conduct services and convert the local Indians. They used to hold services under that tree, before the church was built. They weren't all that successful in converting Indians, though. John went back to Savannah after being here only a month or two, and Charles left after a year."

"Well, that's very interesting. I wonder if, during the time he stayed here, John Wesley formed any of the principles on which he founded the Methodist religion."

"Perhaps he did…. Well, I see some others are beginning to arrive; shall we go inside?"

Upon entering the church, Fanny noticed the Litany of the Episcopal Church of England, lying on the altar in a worn, tattered state. There was no clerk, no choir, and no organ—a single clergyman handled the entire service. Fifteen white people were in attendance, with a few Negroes standing in the back of the church. Reverend Bartow's sermon on "love thy neighbor" was meaningful, but long, and seemed applicable only for the white members present. Communion was given to all, including the Negroes.

Fanny was in good spirits as she left the church and decided to take a tour of the quaint cemetery nearby. As she began walking along the brick walkway that meandered through the cemetery, she heard a voice call out from behind her.

"Mrs. Butler, I'm glad I caught you before you left. My name is James Hamilton Couper—I'm the son of John Couper, of Cannon's Point, whom I believe you've met."

"Yes, I can see the resemblance."

"I've been dying to meet you ever since I learned you were visiting our part of the world. I actually live at Hopeton, the plantation just up the river from Butler Island, but I've been away in England the past few months and just returned a few days ago. I didn't have the opportunity to call on you while you were staying over there. How have you been finding things since you've been here?"

"Very well, thank you. Most of the people I've met, including your father, have been very gracious."

"That's wonderful. And what do you think of our little church?"

"It's very quaint. I was just about to take a tour of its cemetery—it looks beautiful."

"Well, permit me to join you. I've lived on this island most of my life and have personally known just about everyone who's buried here."

As they proceeded down the walkway, Couper gave a little family background for the individuals whose tombstones they passed. Then, as they approached a new grave, Fanny remarked, "Oh, someone must have died recently."

"Yes—it's sort of an embarrassment for all of us, but I'll tell you about it. Mr. Wylly, the man lying here, and a neighbor of his, a Dr. Hazzard, had for years been arguing over the boundary line that divided their two properties. Their argument reached a boiling point about a year ago, and the two challenged each other to a duel to settle the matter. The terms of the challenge were printed in our local newspaper. They were to use pistols, standing at twenty paces from each other, and each was to wear a piece of white paper attached to his clothing, directly over his heart, as a point of aim. Whoever would kill the other would have the privilege of cutting off his head and sticking it up on a pole on the piece of land they had been arguing over.

"The duel never took place, but, at a chance meeting of the two over in Brunswick recently, I'm told Mr. Wylly either struck Dr. Hazzard with a cane or spit in his face—whereupon Dr. Hazzard pulled out a pistol and shot Mr. Wylly directly through the heart. And here he lies. Dr. Hazzard has been charged with manslaughter, but the prevailing opinion around these parts is that no jury will ever convict him."

"That certainly is an awful experience. When will men ever stop being brutes?"

"I suppose never, I'm sorry to say."

Reading from the erected tombstone, Fanny remarked, "It says here that Mr. Wylly 'fell a victim to his generous courage.' I would venture to say that some liberties were taken in coming up with that."

Fanny and Couper then parted company, promising to make it a point to get together when Fanny returned to Georgia the following year.

On the ride back to Hampton Point, Fanny remarked to Israel, "I saw that you didn't go into the church with the other Negroes during the service. Why was that?"

"I never go to church, Missis. Massa King never permitted it."

"Why?"

"He didn't want none of us niggers from Hampton meeting up wid folk from de other plantations."

"Well, from what I hear, he was a strict disciplinarian, but that doesn't make it right. Have you ever attended services on the plantation or read the Bible?"

"I cain't read, Missis."

"What? I know your father, Old Jacob, can read. Don't tell me he never taught his sons to read, too."

Pulling up his horse, Israel exclaimed, "Missis, what for me learn to read? Me have no prospect!"

Fanny was taken aback by this remark, but she rode on without saying a word. Finally she said, "You may think you are without prospect, but being able to read would make you more intelligent. You'd become better able to serve your people—and yourself, too."

Israel listened intently, and, after some thought, responded, "All you say very true, Missis, and me sorry now me let de time pass. But you know dat whatever de head white man seems to favor, de niggers find out very soon an' do it. Now, Massa King, he never favor us readin'. He'd always say, 'Teach 'em to read—pooh!—teach 'em to work!' Accordin' to dat, we never paid much 'ttention to readin'. But now it'll be different, wid him gone. It was different in de old days, too. De old folk, like my Mammy and Pappy, can read more den we can, and I 'spect de people will give mo' thought to it now."

"Good, I hope so. I've promised to send a supply of new Bibles here from Philadelphia. I dearly hope you'll make use of them by getting your father or someone else to teach you to read. It would please me very much."

"Oh yes, Missis. I surely do dat."

✱   ✱   ✱   ✱

In mid-April, Fanny realized her days in Georgia were coming to an end. She had time for one last tour of the slave quarters and infirmary. In doing this, she was gratified to find that considerable improvements had been made. The most significant were at St. Annie's, where cabins had been swept, children were tolerably clean, and chickens were kept out of the cabins.

One last thing remained before the Butlers could return north—attend the "Grand Ball" on Butler Island, which was being given in their honor by the slaves of the two plantations. It was scheduled for Sunday afternoon, the day before their scheduled departure.

On Sunday, boats loaded with slaves arrived all morning long from Hampton. One could tell right from the start that the "Grand Ball" would be grand indeed. Men were dressed in suits and formal hats, which they'd acquired secondhand from white people. Women were in their best finery: bright handkerchiefs bound around their heads, chintzes with sprawling patterns, beads, bangles, flaring sashes, and small, fanciful aprons. The mass of humanity portrayed an ever-changing kaleidoscope of colors.

The smell of fattened hogs being cooked hung over the gathering, and there was a great deal of excitement among the crowd. A loud cheer greeted the Butlers when they appeared. They were given seats of honor in the courtyard in front of the overseer's house. Fanny was both delighted and overwhelmed by the goings-on.

The meal, consisting of roasted pig, oysters, shrimp, black-eyed peas, rice, and turnip greens, was served first. Then came the music and dancing. A team of seven fiddle players warmed up the crowd. It was then complemented by an enthusiastic banjo player and two drummers. A mass of bodies went through all sorts of gyrations in what appeared to Fanny to be wild African dances. It was a sight to behold!

It wasn't until late afternoon that the Butlers finally excused themselves and retired to the overseer's house. At that point, some of the slaves went back to their cabins, while others continued the festivities at the far end of the settlement.

*   *   *   *

In the late evening on the same day, Fanny sat alone on the front porch of the overseer's house. She had just finished making the last entry in her journal and was carelessly thumbing through its pages. "What has all this meant?" she asked herself. "I've seen a great deal in the past three and a half months—but not all, I'm sure. Do these pages reflect accurately the conditions that exist here on these two plantations—and, for that matter, conditions in the entire South? I truly believe they do.

"If I came here with a prejudice against slavery, I am leaving with an even stronger one. Slavery is an evil institution. It is degrading for the Negroes who cower and suffer under inhumane conditions. It is furthermore equally degrading for the white owners, whose inhumanity toward members of the human race robs them of their moral dignity.

"I certainly wouldn't call Mr. Butler's plantations "paternalistic," especially under the reign of the Kings. There may be some plantations in the South that are, but, regardless, all suffer from the same hypocrisy. No amount of rhetoric that claims slaves live happy lives and are well treated can mask the truth about slavery itself. Slavery takes away the freedom of a human being. And that, by definition, is immoral. I suppose one's freedom isn't fully understood or appreciated until one loses it. But, in reality, it is the most precious gift given to man by God.

"While I've been here, I have in a small way tried to alleviate some of the suffering and hardships these people face. And I feel I have made progress. But, as Mr. Butler says, it probably won't last. As soon as I'm gone, things will go back to where they were before I came. Even so, I have made an effort, and, in God's eyes, that's a start. More must follow, and I vow to do my best to continue the effort during my visit next year—and every year thereafter, if necessary."

*   *   *   *

True to her word, Fanny asked to return to Georgia the following year. Her request was denied—this time by both Pierce Butler and his brother, John, as co-owners of the plantations. She would never set foot on Butler Island or Hampton Point again.

Ten years after their visit to the plantations, Fanny and Pierce Butler became divorced. Their marriage had been a stormy affair, involving several long separations, acrimony on both sides, and public notoriety. The slavery issue and Pierce's infidelity fueled the breakup.

Under prevailing laws, the father, Pierce Butler, was granted principal guardianship of the two children, Sarah and Fran. The terms of the divorce settlement granted Fanny the right to be with the children two months each summer, and she was to receive fifteen hundred dollars in annual payments. As a condition for granting her the right to see the children, Fanny agreed not to publish the journal she had kept while living on the Georgia plantations. If she failed to adhere to this condition, she would forfeit this right.

The divorce, coupled with the surrounding notoriety, tarnished Pierce Butler's social standing. In his defense, he published a long dissertation that set forth his side of the proceedings, and he circulated it among his friends. It included this statement:

One painful subject of difference between us was that of Negro slavery. Although we resided in Pennsylvania, where slavery does not exist, the greater part of my property lies in the State of Georgia, and consists of plantations and Negroes. Mrs. Butler—after our marriage, not before—declared herself to be in principle an abolitionist, and her opinions were frequently expressed in a violent and offensive manner; this was grievous enough to bear; however, I seldom opposed or combated them, but when it came to the point of publishing her sentiments, I offered the most unqualified opposition to it.

As a means of supporting herself, Fanny reestablished her acting career—as a reader of Shakespearean plays. She once again became a smash hit in both America and England.

CHAPTER 12—"DEEDS OF CRUELTY AND WRONG"

Financially speaking, the 1850s were not kind to Pierce Butler. His income failed to cover the cost of his extravagant lifestyle, and he found himself in debt over his head.

For more than thirty years, since the death of his grandfather, Major Pierce Butler, the operations of the Georgia plantations had provided ample income for him, his brother, John Butler, and his two aunts, Elizabeth and Frances—making them all very wealthy individuals. He and John had shares of 25 percent of the profits each. And when his aunts died, their 50 percent share was divided equally between the two brothers, doubling his income. But even this windfall didn't alleviate his worsening financial position.

Pierce Butler lived in grand style. He owned one of the finest town homes in Philadelphia as well as one of the largest country estates outside the city. With a consuming desire to maintain a respected position in high society, he threw lavish parties to entertain a large international circle of friends. His gambling escapades were notorious—once losing the enormous sum of fifty thousand dollars in a single wager. And he seemed addicted to the stock market, frequently investing in high-risk speculative ventures.

He lived his life with little regard to its financial consequences, feeling his Georgia income would always cover any obligations he might incur. It therefore came as a shock when he discovered he lacked sufficient funds to cover the debts he had accumulated. Creditors demanded payments he could not meet.

In an effort to avoid threatened legal actions for nonpayment—which would have adversely affected his social standing—he placed his assets in the hands of three trustees. From that moment onward, the trustees—George Cadwalader, Thomas James, and Henry Fisher—assumed responsibility for managing his affairs. Assets, such as the grand mansion on the corner of Chestnut and Eighth Streets in Philadelphia, and various properties in Tennessee and Pennsylvania, were sold to meet the most urgent creditor demands. Other assets were pledged as security for debts. And he agreed to a plan with creditors to pay off his remaining debts over time with proceeds he would receive from his Georgia plantations. Although painful for him to do, Butler also agreed to greatly reduce his living expenses until the debts were cleared.

It all seemed to be working well—right up until the stock market crash of 1857–58. The crash wiped out assets he had pledged as security for some of his debts. And, at that point, the trustees had no other choice than to direct the sale of a portion of his Georgia assets—namely, some of his slaves. This decision had a far-reaching impact on Butler's financial position, since it diminished the long-term viability of his primary source of income. Coincidently, it had a far-reaching impact on the lives of every slave living on his Butler Island and Hampton Point plantations, as well.

The trustees arranged for knowledgeable parties to make an evaluation, so that a dollar value could be assigned to each of the nine hundred slaves owned by the Butlers. This would serve as a basis for assigning ownership of specific slaves to either Pierce Butler or to the estate of his brother, John Butler. Slaves had heretofore been commingled. Thomas Foreman, James Hamilton Couper, and Thomas Pinckney Huger were chosen to perform the evaluation. The process involved physically inspecting each slave and, in the end, it resulted in a listing showing the name, family connections, age, skills, and monetary value of each slave living on the two plantations.

Armed with the results of this evaluation, on the morning of January 26, 1859, three men—George Cadwalader, Thomas James, and Captain Joseph Bryan—made an unannounced visit to Hampton Point, arriving by chartered steam packet from Savannah. They carried with them a letter of introduction from Pierce Butler. The plantation manager, Alexander Blue, was surprised by their arrival—and even more surprised when he learned the purpose of their visit.

Cadwalader, serving as representative of Pierce Butler's creditors, initiated the conversation, "Mr. Blue, because of certain financial difficulties Mr. Butler is experiencing, which are outside his control, he is being forced to sell slaves he owns here on the two plantations in Georgia. Our purpose in being here is to identify which particular slaves are to be considered the property of Mr. Butler, so they can be sold at auction in Savannah. The auction will be conducted by Captain Bryan, here. Mr. James is here representing the interests of the other owner of the plantations, the estate of John Butler. Between us, then, with your assistance, we are to determine how the slaves are to be divided between the two parties."

"Well, sir, this certainly comes as a big surprise. How many slaves are you planning to sell? "

"Mr. Butler's entire share," replied Cadwalader, "—all 450."

"My God! That would cripple the entire workforce on these plantations. How can we keep operating?"

"The best you can, I suppose," replied Cadwalader. He then produced the listing of slaves that had been prepared, and began reading the names: "Headman Frank, age 61. He's classified as being 'bedridden and superannuated' and has no assigned value. His wife, Betty, is a poultry-minder with a value of $200. Now, I must insist right from the start that families like this, having a person with no value, must not be included in the group to be auctioned. They would bring down the value of the entire sale. This first family must, therefore, be assigned to the John Butler Estate. We don't want any mulattos either—their appearance at the auction would tarnish the Butler family name. Only prime field hands and skilled workers are to be included. If necessary, Mr. Butler will compensate the estate of John Butler for taking more than a fair share of able-bodied workers. I hope this is agreeable with everyone."

It was agreed, and with assistance from Mr. Blue, a division of all the slaves was made and agreed upon by the parties.

"Now comes the hard part," said Cadwalader. "How do we go about getting all these Negroes up to Savannah to be sold? For that we will rely on your expertise, Captain Bryan."

"Well, sir," replied Bryan, "this situation certainly presents some unique challenges. I believe it will be the largest sale of slaves ever held in America, and it'll require good organization to pull it off properly. My establishment, however, is fully experienced in handling large sales, and you can be assured this one will be handled professionally."

"Good," replied Cadwalader. "Now let's talk specifics."

"Okay. First of all, it'll take at least two full days to sell this many niggers. We've chosen March 2 and 3 as the dates. That'll give us a little more than five weeks to get everything in order. We'll use most of the time to do advertising in newspapers all over the South, so we can attract as many qualified buyers as possible.

"As far as getting all 436 niggers we've identified here today up to Savannah, we'll transport them in groups of thirty or so from both Butler Island and Hampton Point. We'll use the railroad out of Darien for the ones from Butler Island and a small steamboat for the ones from Hampton. We'll move one group from each of the plantations every two days, till we get 'em all transported. That'll give us ample time to get 'em settled properly once they get to Savannah. It'll take a little more than two weeks to get it all done.

"Now, with a group this large, we can't make it known to them all at once that 436 niggers are going to be sold. If we did, we'd get 'em real upset and cause a big disturbance. So, we got to announce it piecemeal—one group at a time. And, furthermore, we've got to make sure that all the potential troublemakers and leaders in the slave settlements are included in the first groups transported out of here. That'll minimize the possibility of the remaining niggers causing any trouble. Mr. Blue, we'll need help from you in identifying who these are."

"I can do that," replied Blue.

"I see we got two slave drivers from Butler Island and one from Hampton Point included in the group to be auctioned. We'll plan to include them in the last group transported without telling 'em in advance they're going to be sold. That way we'll maintain their cooperation right up to the end, and they can help us maintain order.

"We'll need to get the niggers ready for sale while they're still here on the plantations, so we've got to make arrangements for bathing and separate sleeping facilities, as well as good clothing for them to wear at the sale.

"I'll have plenty of men for handling the transporting and getting them ready. You'll have to take responsibility for maintaining order among all the niggers who'll remain here. It's got to be a combined effort on both our parts."

"Captain Bryan," interrupted Blue, "if you don't mind me saying so, all this seems a bit risky. If it doesn't go off perfectly, we could have a riot on our hands."

"I share your concern, Mr. Blue. That's why it's got to be done piecemeal rather than all at once. And it's important we maintain strict control over the niggers being transported, those waiting to be transported, and those who will remain behind. If we do this, I'm confident everything will be all right."

"I certainly hope you're right, Captain Bryan," said Cadwalader. "The last thing we need to have is some sort of uprising. Just the mention of one would scare away a huge number of potential buyers and reduce the prices we'll get for the Negroes.

"Well, Mr. James," continued Cadwalader, "I think that concludes all the business you and I came here to do. We can leave the details of how to handle the Negroes to Captain Bryan and Mr. Blue here and be on our way back to Savannah, don't you agree?"

"Yes, I think we've done a good job."

✳   ✳   ✳   ✳

Although some of the housekeeping staff at the overseer's house had noticed the three strangers on January 26, they were unaware of the conversations that had taken place. It appeared to be some sort of business meeting. And since it had lasted less than a day, it was of little consequence. They didn't mention anything about the event to other slaves in the community.

The significance of the meeting, however, became clear to everyone two weeks later. On a cold, overcast day in February, shortly after the slaves had begun their tasks, Captain Bryan and eight strong-looking Negro men disembarked from a small steam packet at the Butler Island landing. They were wearing black pants, shirts, and coats. After unloading their gear, they proceeded directly to the overseer's house for a meeting with Mr. Blue. A short while later, they went to the threshing building, where they were seen arranging various items inside, closing windows, and making sure doors could be shut and locked. Then at two o'clock in the afternoon, well before normal quitting time, the large plantation bell was rung, as a signal for all slaves to assemble in front of the overseer's house. All able-bodied hands immediately began making their way to the assembly area. To say the least, the signal to quit work early was highly unusual, and it caused a great stir among the slaves as they gathered. Everyone was eager to find out what was going on. Some were excited, most apprehensive.

Precisely at three o'clock, Mr. Blue, accompanied by all four of the Butler Island slave drivers, came out of the overseer's house and proceeded to the center of the assembly area, where a small platform had been erected. An abrupt stillness came over the crowd, as he mounted the platform. "We're all gathered here," began Blue in a loud voice, "so I can give you a message from your master, Mr. Pierce Butler. It seems that Mr. Butler, through no fault of his own, has experienced some hard times in his financial dealings. Although he desperately doesn't want to do it, he needs to sell some of you niggers at auction in Savannah. He knows this will present some hardships, and he wants to make it as easy as possible on those of you being sold. He will do everything he can to find good masters for you. In every case, entire families will be sold together as a unit. No family will be broken up."

A great murmur erupted among the slaves.

"Now, quiet down, while I read out the names of the families that'll be sold," continued Blue.

"Bernard, his wife Elizabeth, and his two children, John and Joe."

"No! No!" cried out Elizabeth. "You cain't sell us. Dis our home—we's lived here all our lives!" She burst into tears and began wailing. Several slaves nearby tried to comfort her.

"Andrew and his wife, June," continued Blue.

The slaves stood in silence, astonished by what was happening. In total, the names of eight families were called out—thirty-one men, women, and children. Blue then told them, "I want each of you whose name I just read to go to your cabin and collect your belongings. Bring them to the threshing building by five o'clock this evening. You'll be spending the night there." After motioning to his four drivers to spread out around the crowd, he then walked back to the overseer's house.

Some of the slaves gathered around those who were being sold, to offer condolences. Most, though, stood motionless in disbelief. Never before in their lifetimes had anything like this happened. It was a shock to the entire community.

When Blue got back to the overseer's house, he met with Captain Bryan, who had been observing the scene from a window in the parlor. "It looks like it went okay," said Bryan. "There's no sign of trouble."

"I think so, too, but I've got three loaded pistols here just in case. I think we should wait here tonight and make sure things don't get out of hand. We can go over to Hampton Point in the morning."

*   *   *   *

Every member of the slave community stood waiting at the entrance to the settlement when the eight families came out of their cabins at the appointed hour of five o'clock. When they were all together, Cooper London led them in prayer, telling the families that God was with them and they need not be afraid. He then read aloud the twenty-third Psalm:

De Lawd is my shepherd; I shall not want.
He maketh me lie down in green pastures; he leadeth me 'side de still waters.
He restoreth my soul; he leadeth me in de paths of righteousness fo' his name's sake.
Yea, though I walk through de valley of de shadow of death, I fear no evil; Fo' thou art wid me; thy rod and thy staff dey comfort me.
Thou preparest a table before me in the presence of mine enemies; thou anointest my head wid oil; my cup runneth over.
Surely goodness and mercy shall follow me all de days of my life; and I will dwell in de house of de Lawd fo'ever.

"God bless you all, my chillun," London added.

The slaves formed into two side-by-side lines, stretching out from the entrance of the settlement, past the cookhouse, and all the way to the carpenters' shed. As the families passed between the lines, one could hear people crying, as good-byes were said and hugs exchanged.

When the last family had passed through the lines, the whole group followed behind to the threshing building and watched them enter and disappear from sight. Several women wanted to "sit up" with the families, but the drivers forced them to return to the settlement, saying "Dar's nothin' mo' you can do here tonight."

The settlement was all abuzz. The reality of the situation had set in, and large numbers of slaves gathered around campfires to talk. Initially, everyone expressed deep resentment, calling the sale of innocent people cruel and inhumane. They wanted to stop it—"Do somethin'." "Burn down de rice mill!" "Bust open de main river dikes!" "Kill Massa Blue!" It appeared this feeling would get out of hand, until cooler heads began explaining the realities of the situation. They reminded everyone of what had happened to the slaves who had participated in the Nat Turner rebellion—all had been killed, along with many innocent people, as well. Feelings then settled down, with most of the discussion centering on prayers and expressions of sorrow for those being sold. Everyone, too, felt a sense of relief that the number of families had been limited to eight and that they themselves hadn't been included. At least they were safe.

*   *   *   *

A normal workday began at dawn the next day, as drivers marshaled the slaves into the fields. It was planned as a "ditching day," when dikes and drainage channels were to be repaired. At ten o'clock, Captain Bryan and Mr. Blue began their trip to Hampton Point to deliver a similar message to the slaves there.

Inside the threshing building, the slaves were being made ready for sale. A hardy meal of cornbread, hog jowls, turnip greens, and milk was served during the morning hours. Bryan's men then made sure that every slave was bathed in warm water, with soap. Hair was trimmed. Gray hairs were plucked from the heads and beards of older slaves, and sometimes hair was dyed. Everyone was given new clothes to wear.

At the end of the workday, some hands approached the threshing building, attempting to visit with the slaves being held inside. They were turned away by Bryan's guards and not allowed to make contact.

The next day, immediately following the morning meal, the slaves were organized in coffles. Men, with iron shackles on their wrists and legs, were connected together by a long chain, forming one group. Women were in another. Only small children were allowed to go without irons. The groups were marshaled onto separate rice barges and transported to Darien, where they were loaded into a railway boxcar for the trip to Savannah. A similar process was carried out the following day at Hampton Point, using a small steamboat for transportation. At both locations, the process went without a hitch.

To those remaining on the plantations, it seemed as if the slaves who were being sold had just disappeared off the face of the earth. Campfire meetings resembled prayer meetings, and old spirituals were sung.

> See these po' souls from Africa
> Transported to America;
> We's stolen, and sold in Georgia,
> Will you go along wid me?
> We's stolen, and sold in Georgia,
> Come sound da jubilee!

> See wives an' husbands sold apart'
> Their chillun's screams'll break my heart.
> Dar's a better day a comin'
> Will you go along wid me?
> Dar's a better day a comin'
> Go sound da jubilee!

*   *   *   *

Just as the Butler Island slaves were about to enter the cookhouse for the evening meal on the following day, the command to assemble was again signaled by the large plantation bell. Blue addressed the gathering, "I'm going to read off the names of the next group of niggers to be sold."

Immediately, a loud roar erupted—like a bomb exploding in the middle of the crowd. "What he talkin' 'bout?" "Dar ain't s'posed to be no mo' niggers sold!" "Dar gotta be some mistake!" "Lawd, can dis be true?"

"Now, quiet down! Quiet down! Quiet down all of you, and listen! Here's the names:

"Mike, his wife Susan, and his three children, Paul, September, and April..."

The slaves stood in a state of shock as they listened to the names being called out. One could hear muffled sounds of women crying in the crowd, but most stood in utter silence. When the last name had been called, Blue instructed them to go to their cabins to collect their belongings and report to the threshing building right after supper.

It took a long time for the gathering to break up. Everyone had believed the previous group of slaves would be the only ones sold. No one had ever dreamed there'd be more—and all were speechless.

After supper, the entire community again gathered at the entrance to the slave settlement, as those being sold came out of their cabins carrying their belongings. And, just as before, Cooper London prayed over them, lines were formed for them to pass through to say good-byes, and everyone accompanied them to their confinement in the threshing building.

Unlike the first time, though, there were no gatherings around campfires that night. Almost all the slaves returned to their cabins early, contemplating whether or not more slaves would be sold, and what their own fates might be. No one got any sleep that night—and no sleep during the next ten nights, either! Announcements of additional slaves to be sold were repeated every other day. It kept the whole community in a heightened state of anxiety. No work got done on the plantation. Workers moped around, merely going through the motions of carrying out their tasks. Everyone expected to be included in the next group to be sold, accepting it as their fate without complaint.

The third group called at Hampton Point included the family of Primus, a plantation carpenter. His wife, Daphney, had just borne their second child five days earlier. She was still in the plantation infirmary when she heard the news of her sale, and she pleaded with Mr. Blue to let her stay there for the remainder of her three-week confinement. Her pleading fell on deaf ears, and she and her family were included in the group shipped off to Savannah.

Margaret, the wife of Doctor George, received more favorable treatment. She had been confined on February 16 and gave birth on the very day the last group was to be transported to Savannah. She had been assigned to go in the last group, because of her circumstances, in hopes that both mother and new baby would be able to travel by that time. She, however, adamantly refused to be moved from her confinement so soon after the baby's birth. "Dey gotta kill me 'fore I'se movin' nowheres." As a result, she and her family—a total of six—were not included in the sale.

Raylin's son, Bran, who was the head driver at Hampton, and his family were included in the last group from Hampton Point. This came as a surprise to Bran, since he believed his services would be needed to pull together the remaining pieces of the plantation's operations once so many slaves had departed. This was not to be the case.

In total, 430 slaves, including thirty babies, were transported to Savannah. For those remaining on the plantations, it was as if "de whole world has come to an end."

✳   ✳   ✳   ✳

Captain Bryan originally planned to hold the auction at his slave pen on Jackson Square in Savannah. But the response from prospective buyers was overwhelming, and he feared he couldn't accommodate them all on the days of sale. He therefore made arrangements to use more commodious facilities at the Ten Broeck Race Course located three miles west of the city. For weeks prior to the sale, advertisements like this appeared in newspapers throughout the South:

For Sale

Long Cotton and Rice Negroes

A gang of 430

Accustomed to the culture of rice and provisions, among whom are a number of good mechanics, and house servants, will be sold on the

2nd and 3rd of March next in Savannah. The Negroes will be sold in
families.

Persons desiring to inspect these Negroes will find them at the Race
Course, where they can be seen from 10 A.M. to 2 P.M., from 3 days
prior until Day of Sale. Catalogs will be furnished.

Terms of Sale

One-third cash, remainder by bond bearing interest from day
of sale, payable in two equal annual installments and secured
by mortgages on the Negroes and approved Personal security
. **Joseph Bryan**

No mention was made of the fact that all the Negroes were being
taken from Butler plantations. There was no need to do this. Through
word of mouth and a great many newspaper articles, the fact had
become widely known. Butler slaves were thought to be a choice lot
and highly desirable property.

Days before the sale, eager buyers seeking information and making
sure their securities met with approval thronged Bryan's offices. In bars
and public rooms throughout the city, there was nothing but talk of
the great sale and speculation as to the probable prices the stock would
bring.

This was to be the largest sale of slaves in the history of the United
States, and Bryan's enthusiasm grew daily.

*   *   *   *

A large stable at the racecourse was used to house the slaves. It
was designed to accommodate the horses and carriages of gentlemen
patrons. There were no tables or chairs in the stable, only a thin
scattering of straw that barely covered the floorboards. The belongings
of slave families were piled in bundles scattered about the floor. Some
slaves sat or reclined near their bundles, some restlessly moved about,
and some gathered in small groups, talking among themselves. As a

show of authority, Bryan's men kept moving among the group, keeping a close eye on what was going on.

Buyers came from Georgia, North Carolina, South Carolina, Tennessee, Virginia, Alabama, and Louisiana—every hotel in the city was filled to capacity. Most of the buyers were from inland and back-river regions—generally, they were a rough breed. Many carried whips and wore revolvers strapped to their sides.

During inspections, little concern was shown for a slave's comfort or dignity. Buyers pulled their mouths open to see their teeth, pinched their limbs to see how muscular they were, walked them up and down to detect signs of lameness, ordered them to stoop and bend in awkward positions to detect concealed ruptures or wounds, and asked pointed questions about their skills and experience. Frequently, while breathing directly into a slave's face, they would make demeaning remarks to him. All this was submitted to without a murmur, and the slaves remained docile and under control at all times.

Women slaves never spoke to a white man unless spoken to first, and then only to make brief responses to questions. On some occasions, though, a male slave, when he spotted a buyer he thought would be a good master, would aggressively try to persuade him to buy his family. On one such occasion, Elisha made a pitch that made no appeal to the prospective buyer's sympathy. He concentrated solely on showing the business value of the proposed purchase:

"Look at me, Massa—am prime rice planter; you won't find a better man den me; no better on de whole plantation; not a bit old yet; do mo' work den ever; do carpenter work, too. Molly, too, my wife, she first-rate rice hand; 'most as good as me. Stand out here, Molly, an' let de gentleman see. Show Massa yo' arm—good arm, dat—she do heap work mo' wid dat arm yet. Let him see yo' teeth—see dat, Massa, teeth all regular, all good. Little Vardy here is only child yet, make prime girl by-an'-by. Better buy us, Massa, we's first rate bargain."

Sometimes emotional pitches like this resulted in a sale, with a happy ending. Sometimes they didn't.

Once Bran had settled his family in a corner of the stable, he began walking around, nodding to all, and talking with some he knew. Over the past several years as head driver, he had served as an authority figure to Hampton slaves. Now they looked up to him as their protector and advisor. "What dey gonna do wid us?" "We gonna be taken to de slave market in New Orleans?" "Every one of dem buyers looks mean—what'll happen to us?" "Dey ain't gonna take our chillin away from us, is dey?" Bran couldn't answer most of their questions. He merely tried calming everyone down and assuring them they'd get good masters and like their new homes.

When he came across Robert, a slave from Hampton, he noticed that he and his wife, Joanna, were sitting in a place removed from the rest of their family, and he asked him why. Robert told him that he and Joanna were to be sold as one family, and his two grown sons who were married would be sold separately as different families. This disturbed Bran, and he hurried back to where his own family was sitting.

"I'se just found out we could be in a heap of trouble," he said. "Dey is selling everybody in families, but if any of de chillun is married demselves, dey is considered to be in a separate family. Dat means John an' Mary an' Sarah could be sold apart from de rest of us." The news upset everyone. After all, they'd all been called up as one family unit—why couldn't they all be sold as one? They suddenly realized that if they did get separated, they needed to find a way to keep in contact with one another, no matter where they ended up.

*　　*　　*　　*

Captain Bryan was the largest slave trader in Savannah, having carried out hundreds of auctions in the past. He interacted easily with buyers and sellers from all levels of society, and he knew how to motivate buyers. A short, dapper man, who wore spectacles and a yachting cap, he was very precise in his movements and speech. He seemed always to have planned his actions thoroughly in advance and to be in control of every situation.

During auctions, Bryan supervised the overall operation, from getting slaves ready for presentation to making sure the bidding was carried out in an orderly fashion, with all financial transactions being handled properly. An employee of Bryan's, Mr. Albert Walsh, served as auctioneer.

In appearance, Mr. Walsh was the direct opposite of Bryan. Careless in his dress, he was a large man, fat, and good-natured—a rollicking "ol' boy," with a clever eye that never let a bidding nod escape him. Skilled in what he did for a living, he underplayed a sharp intellect in a manner that worked well with the lower class of individuals he dealt with as buyers. He was a source of unending jokes whenever bidding became slack.

On the morning of the auction, the slaves were moved to a large room underneath the grandstand, one hundred feet by twenty feet in size. They were aligned in accordance with their order of sale.

At this point, moments before the sale was to begin, an unexpected visitor came into the room, causing a stir among the slaves. It was Pierce Butler! He began moving among the group, nodding and talking to some, and on occasion extending his gloved hand to those he recognized. The slaves obsequiously pulled off their hats as he passed; men bowed, and women curtsied. They seemed delighted by his presence, perhaps in the belief that he would somehow make everything right for "his people."

The auction was held in an open area of the grandstand proper, where punters normally placed their bets on race days. It was open to the elements, but the grandstand's overhanging roof provided shelter from the rain. A large platform commanded the center portion of the area, and there was a doorway on the side that connected to the room underneath the grandstand where the slaves were being held.

It had rained heavily since early morning, and buyers experienced difficulty getting to the racecourse from their hotels. The lower-than-expected attendance cast a pall over the auction scene, and, as a result, the sale opening was postponed two hours beyond the advertised time. But as more and more buyers trickled in, the prospects for a successful sale became brighter for Pierce Butler.

The sale officially began when Mr. Walsh mounted the platform, and, in a loud voice, announced the terms of sale. The first family to be sold was then brought out from the adjoining room. Amidst the loud noise that arose from the crowd of buyers, the two Negro children in the family became frightened and began to cry, and the mother's knees buckled. The family of four was then made to stand on the platform in full view of the crowd.

George, age 27, prime cotton planter
Sue, age 26, prime rice planter
George, age 6, boy child
Harry, age 2, boy child

The auction rules called for bids to be made at a set unit price for every member of the family. In this case, bidding started at three hundred dollars per person and ended at six hundred dollars. The total amount paid for the family was therefore twenty-four hundred dollars. The sale then proceeded in accordance with the published catalog:

Kate's John, age 31, rice, prime man
Betsy, age 20, rice
Kate, age 6
Violet, age 3 months
SOLD for $510 each

Wooster, age 45, hand and fair mason
Mary, age 40, cotton hand
SOLD for $ 300 each

Commodore Bob, age 42, rice hand
Kate, age 37, cotton
Linda, age 19, cotton, prime young woman
Joe, age 13, rice, prime boy
SOLD for $600 each

As the sale proceeded, the expressions on the faces of most slaves showed their sorrow at being put through the ordeal—many of them were crying. Some, though, seemed to regard the sale with complete indifference. All stood motionless throughout the process, reacting only to instructions issued by Captain Bryan to turn from one side to another so the crowd could get a better view of their physical properties.

When a sale was made, the family stepped down off the platform without casting an eye toward the person who had bought them. They began making their way to the room under the grandstand to collect their belongings and await their new owner. In the process of doing this, their former owner, Pierce Butler, met them at the doorway exit. He was holding a sack of coins, and, as they passed through, he offered each a dollar in newly minted twenty-five-cent pieces. It was his parting gift, given to clear his conscience. Some slaves accepted the money, others rejected it.

Bob and Mary, married for almost a year, were listed in the catalog as "prime," but they had no children. One of the buyers questioned whether Mary was capable of bearing children. This caused a big discussion, which held up the sale process. In the end, though, each was sold for $1,135—a handsome price.

When the family of Mingo—consisting of his wife, two sons, and a daughter—was called up, the auctioneer, Mr. Walsh, announced there had been a change in plans. Dembo, the older son, aged twenty, had during the previous evening procured the services of a minister. The minister had performed a marriage ceremony uniting him and Frances, a female aged eighteen, who was part of another family scheduled to be sold later in the day. As a consequence of this marriage, the two newlyweds were placed on the block together as a new family unit. Amid a volley of course comments from the crowd concerning their forthcoming honeymoon, they were sold for $1,320 each.

A not-so-happy ending occurred when Jeffery, age twenty-three, prime cotton hand, was sold for $1,310. He and a female slave, Dorcas, were engaged but not yet married. Following his sale, he approached his new master, hat in hand, "I loves Dorcas; I loves her well and true. She says she loves me, an' I knows she does. De Lawd knows I loves her better den I loves anyone in de whole world—never can love 'nother woman half as well. Please buy Dorcas, Massa. We'd be good servants to you long as we live. We'd be married right soon, an' the chillun'll be healthy and strong, an' dey be good servants, too." After examining Dorcas, the buyer agreed to purchase her, to the delight of Jeffery. But, when Dorcas was brought onto the block, she was designated to be sold as part of a family of four—a burden the buyer hadn't contemplated and wouldn't assume. The deal with Jeffery was called off. And so was the union of Jeffery and Dorcas, who went their separate ways.

Bob, age 30, rice
Mary, age 25, rice, prime woman
SOLD for $1,135 each

Anson, age 49, rice, ruptured, one eye
Violet, age 55, rice hand
SOLD for $250 each

Allen Jeffery, age 46, rice hand and sawyer in steam mill
Sikey, age 43, rice hand
Watty, age 5, infirm legs
SOLD for $250 each

Rina, age 18, rice, prime young woman
Lena, age 1
SOLD for $650 each

Goin, age 39, rice hand
Cassander, age 35, cotton hand—has fits
Emiline, age 19, cotton, prime young woman
Judy, age 11, cotton, prime girl
SOLD for $400 each

Tom, age 22, cotton hand
SOLD for $1,260

When the family of Primus came on the block, his wife, Daphney, had a large shawl wrapped around her body. This caused outcries from some of the buyers, "What do you keep your nigger covered up for?" "What's the matter with that gal?" "Pull off her blanket!" Daphney had given birth to a new infant just days prior to her being forced to make the trip to Savannah. When her shawl was removed, the new infant was disclosed, suckling at her breast. Astonishingly, over a period of just fifteen days, this woman had endured giving birth to a child, being forced to leave her confinement, making the long journey to Savannah in the bowels of a steamboat, being exposed to rough physical inspection from prospective buyers, and being put on the block and sold. The family of four brought a price of $625 each.

Guy, age twenty, a prime young man, sold for $1,280. Andrew, the next in line, was of the same age and had similar physical attributes, except he had lost his right eye. He was sold for $1,040. The "value of a right eye" was then firmly established to be $240, the difference in the two sale prices.

Bran, Raylin's son, the head driver at Hampton, saw his family separated and sold in two units, as he had suspected. He, along with his wife, Doris, and his unmarried son, Luke, were sold for $900 each. His married son, John, and his family were sold separately for $850 each.

Dorcas, age 17, cotton, prime woman
Joe, 3 months
SOLD for $1,200 each

Lowden, age 54, cotton hand
Hager, age 50, cotton hand
Lowden, age 15, cotton, prime boy
Silas, age 13, cotton, prime boy
Lettia, age 11, cotton, prime girl
SOLD for $300 each

Tom, age 48, rice hand
Harriet, age 41, rice hand
Wanney, age 19, rice hand, prime young man
Deborah, age 6
Infant, age 3 months
SOLD for $700 each

Finally, the last slave had been sold, and the auction officially came to a close. Captain Bryan ordered baskets of champagne brought out and served to all present. It was a grand ending to what had been a long, arduous process. And, to everyone's delight, the sun broke through the dark clouds, and the heavy rain stopped abruptly.

In all, 429 men, women, and children had been sold. The sale grossed a total of $303,850.

No one knew for sure what the final disposition of each slave would be. Where would they end up? Would families be divided in subsequent sales? Would they have good owners or bad? ... And, what's more, no one seemed to care.

Symbolized by the heavy rains that had fallen throughout the auction—and which abruptly stopped at its conclusion—the slaves from that time on referred to the auction as a "weepin' time." They had experienced a deep weeping in their hearts. Their lives had been ripped apart, and they had been separated from those they had known and loved all their lives—never to be joined again.

Sidney George Fisher, a social butterfly in Philadelphia, who enjoyed recording gossip about prominent socialites in his diary, wrote this commentary on the sale:

> It is a dreadful affair, selling these hereditary Negroes. There are 900 of them belonging to the estate, a little community who have lived for generations on the plantation, among whom, therefore, all sorts of relationships of blood and friendship are established. Butler's half, 450, to be sold at public auction and scattered over the South. Families will not be separated, that is to say, husbands and wives, parents and young children. But brothers and sisters of mature age, parents and children of mature age, all other relations and ties of home and long association will be violently severed. It will be a hard thing for Butler to witness, and it is a monstrous thing to do. Yet it is done every day in the South. It is one among the many frightful consequences of slavery and contradicts our Civilization, our Christianity, our Republicanism. Can such a system endure; is it consistent with humanity, with moral progress? These are difficult questions, and still more difficult is it to say, what can be done? The Negroes of the South must be slaves, or the South will be Africanized. Slavery is better for them and for us than such a result.

Unknown to anyone attending the sale, a spy had been operating among the crowd of buyers. He was Mortimer Thomson, a star reporter for Horace Greeley's *New York Tribune*, who wrote exposé articles under the pen name "Doesticks." Disguised as a potential buyer, he had moved freely among the crowd, observing what was going on. The articles he wrote detailed the proceedings in a manner highly critical of Pierce Butler and the institution of slavery. Reprinted in Philadelphia, Boston, and London newspapers as well, they had a damaging affect on Butler's reputation. As an ending to his last article, describing the closing of the auction, he wrote:

> That night, not a steamer left that Southern port, not a train of cars sped away from that cruel city that did not bear each its own sad burden of those unhappy ones, whose only crime is that they are not strong and wise. Some of them maimed and wounded, some scarred and gashed, by accident, or by the hand of ruthless drivers—all sad and sorrowful as human hearts can be.

> But the stars shone out brightly, as if such things had never been; the blushing fruit trees poured their fragrance on the evening air, and the scene was as calmly sweet and quiet as if Man had never marred the glorious beauties of the Earth by **deeds of cruelty and wrong**.

Pierce Butler once again became a wealthy, cash-rich individual capable of maintaining the high position in society he desired. His decision to sell all his Georgia slaves, instead of merely enough of them to cover his immediate debts, proved fortuitous. The timing could not have been better. Just two years after the auction sale, civil war would break out between the North and South, which, in the end, would have rendered his total investment in slaves worthless.

CHAPTER 13—CIVIL WAR

On December 20, 1860, South Carolina seceded from the Union. There had been pro-secession sentiment in the South for some time, but this was the first step taken by any state to formerly break ties with the Union. It sent shock waves throughout the northern states—and the whole world.

For several months prior to this event, Pierce Butler and his daughter, Fran, had been planning a trip to Georgia, which was to take place in January 1861. Pierce had important business involving the estate of his late brother, John, and it was mandatory that he appear at a Supreme Court hearing in Savannah. Fran, sensing danger, became hesitant, but, in the end, ignored her concerns and accompanied her father in late January.

During the course of their journey, the secession movement in the South gained momentum. On February 4, seven Southern states met in Montgomery, Alabama, and adopted a constitution for the Confederate States of America. Four days later, South Carolina formally ratified the constitution and joined the Confederacy. Georgia quickly followed.

Pierce and Fran's trip to Georgia was uneventful, and, on their return home, they stopped over in Charleston to visit friends. Coincidently, during their stay, Pierce was given a personal tour of the Charleston harbor fortifications by General P. G. T. Beauregard, commander of the South Carolina Militia.

A few days later, on April 15, Fort Sumter, the Union fort guarding the entrance to Charleston harbor, was attacked by Confederate forces. This marked the beginning of the war between the North and South.

The war created a sharp division among members of the Butler family. Pierce and Fran strongly supported the South's cause. Sarah and her husband, Dr. Wister; John Butler's widow, Gabriella; and, of course, Pierce's former wife, Fanny Kemble, supported the North.

*   *   *   *

A call to arms rang out all over Georgia following the attack on Fort Sumter, and a great many young men from the coastal region responded. They included the five sons of James Hamilton Couper and two sons of the Page-King family. The sendoffs given these young men caused a great deal of excitement on St Simons Island and in the surrounding region. The men were going off to fight a war against the North—to kill Yankees and preserve the South. "It's a known fact that for every Southern boy killed in the war, ten Yankees will die." It wouldn't be long before the North got tired of the war and wanted out, was the popular opinion. "Our boys will be back home in less than a year."

All the activity caused a stir among the slaves at Hampton Point and Butler Island. "Why dey go and start a war fo'?" "Lots of folk gonna get killed." "Why dey sendin' men from here way up North?" "It don't sound good to me." "What dis war mean to us?" There were a lot more questions than answers. About all the slaves could understand was that the Southern states wanted to break away from the North, and the North didn't want them to. It didn't seem to make much sense, but, since it didn't affect them, they weren't overly concerned.

In preparation for defending Georgia against a possible Yankee attack, Governor Joseph E. Brown ordered fortifications built to guard the harbors of Savannah and Brunswick. Colonel Carey Styles was placed in charge of the defenses for Brunswick. He immediately began building fortifications at the south end of St. Simons Island, on land belonging to the Page-King plantation. From this strategic position, the Confederate army could command the entrance channel leading from the ocean to St. Simons Sound and Brunswick harbor.

Slaves were commandeered from nearby plantations—including twenty men and women from Hampton Point—to help build the fortifications. Within three months, five earthen batteries, overlaid with palmetto branches and iron rails, had been constructed. A company of soldiers, the Jackson Artillery from Macon, was assigned to man the facility. They brought with them fifteen large cannons capable of shooting across the entire width of the entrance channel. At this point, the South stood ready to defend the area against anything the North could throw at them.

*   *   *   *

Upon his return from Georgia, Pierce Butler didn't attempt to conceal his strong support for the South. His frequently stated opinions in favor of Southern secession and his criticism of the North eventually came to the attention of Simon Cameron, Secretary of War—as did news of his recent journey to the South immediately prior to the war. On August 15, 1861, Cameron issued a warrant instructing the U.S. Marshall in Philadelphia to place Butler under arrest and to search his personal files for information linking him to the Confederacy. He was jailed at Fort Hamilton, New York.

Pierce's friend, Sidney Fisher, felt that Pierce's recent behavior was sufficient cause to justify his arrest. He thought, too, that it would be a good thing for him, "as it will keep him quiet and out of harm's way."

Fanny Kimble, in writing to a friend, was more direct in her feelings.

> The charge against him is that he acted as an agent for the Southerners in a visit he paid this spring, having received large sums of money for the purchase and transmission of arms. Knowing Mr. Butler's Southern sympathies, I think the charge very likely to be true; whether it can be proved or not is quite another question, and I think it probable, that, if it is not proved, Mr. Butler will still be detained till the conclusion of the war, as he is not likely to accept any oath of allegiance tendered to him by the Government, being a determined democrat and inimical, both on public and private grounds, to Mr. Lincoln and his ministers.

The government failed to find any incriminating evidence against Butler. And, based on Henry Fisher's intervention with government officials and a direct appeal to President Lincoln by his daughter Sarah Wister, he was released from prison on September 21. As a condition for his release, he signed a statement that he would "do no act hostile to the United States" and would not visit South Carolina without a passport from the secretary of state.

Pierce and his daughters were elated over his release. This feeling, however, wasn't shared completely by members of Philadelphia's high society. Opinions were mixed, with some people feeling that his refusal to take the oath of allegiance made him "morally as much a traitor as any man in the Confederate army." His social standing suffered greatly during the remainder of the war.

*   *   *   *

One of the first military actions taken by Union forces was the establishment of a naval blockade along the Southern coastline. This was aimed at preventing Southern exports from being shipped to England, and, more importantly, to prevent the import of arms and other material that would be useful to the Confederate army. To support the blockade, they invaded South Carolina and established a base of operations at Port Royal Sound, south of Charleston. A squadron of warships was stationed there and given responsibility for blockading the entire coastline of South Carolina, Georgia, and Florida.

Within days, warships were patrolling off the coast of St. Simons Island. Local plantation owners, fearing an imminent invasion, hurriedly evacuated the island. Some attempted to take their slaves with them, but most merely left them to fend for themselves.

At Hampton Point, the overseer, Martin Hanks, who had been on the job less than six months, packed up his belongings and abruptly moved his family to the interior of Georgia. This was done in broad daylight, in full view of the slaves, but without any word being given as to what was happening. When Hanks failed to return after four days, his two slave drivers became nervous and left the plantation as well. All work came to a standstill.

Word began filtering in from other plantations that owners all over the island had evacuated. They had left to get away from the Yankees, who were about to invade the island. "Yankee ships is just off de coast!" To judge for themselves, a group of Hampton slaves rowed boats over to Little St. Simons Island and stood on the beach looking seaward. Sure enough, there were Yankee ships everywhere, and it looked like an invasion was imminent.

"De Yankees is comin' to set us free!" was the word brought back to the plantation. This was a joyous message for the nearly one hundred slaves still resident at Hampton. It caused a spontaneous eruption of whooping and hollering, dancing, and praying that went on for hours.

All of a sudden, though, the celebrating abruptly stopped, and a hush fell over the group. Everyone felt a sense of restraint. "What if de Yankees don't come? Dey could pass right by us." "What if de overseer comes back—maybe tomorrow?" "We don't want no trouble—no whippin's." It was as if everyone, all at once, felt guilty over the way they were behaving. "Maybe we oughta get back to work."

Then a young boy, Amos, was seen carrying a chicken he'd taken from the hen house—its neck had been wrung. When he was asked about it, he said he was taking it home to be cooked for supper. All heck broke loose! Slaves forgot any inhibitions they had and started breaking into every locked building on the plantation, taking anything and everything they fancied. Things got totally out of control—people were running everywhere, doing whatever they pleased. The looting and breakage lasted nearly three days—until nothing was left. Both the portion of the Big House that had remained standing and the overseer's house were burned to the ground.

Four days after the overseer, Martin Hanks, had left Hampton, the overseer at Butler Island left too—stealing away in the middle of the night. This caused a similar reaction from the nearly three hundred slaves resident there. Looting, though, was more restrained, and the overseer's house and main buildings were left standing.

*   *   *   *

In February 1862, General Robert E. Lee, who was then on staff to President Jefferson Davis, visited Georgia to inspect coastal fortifications. Viewing installations around Brunswick, he determined the area couldn't be successfully defended, due to the many waterways leading into the harbor. He felt the gun placements on St. Simons Island would be merely bypassed by Union forces. He, therefore, ordered the guns and soldiers stationed there to be redeployed to Savannah, where they could be better utilized. Within days, the Confederate forces evacuated the island. And, as they departed, they destroyed the St. Simons Island lighthouse to prevent its use by Union naval forces.

One month after the departure of the Confederates, Union forces landed at the south end of the island and established a base of operations in the exact location the Confederates had evacuated.

News of the Yankee invasion spread quickly. And, immediately, the Union forces became inundated by slaves leaving their plantations on the island, coming to seek protection.

A mass exodus occurred at Hampton Point, with most of the nearly one hundred slaves making the fourteen-mile trek to the south end of the island to join the Yankees. The plantation was deserted.

Existing slave quarters at Retreat plantation, near the Yankee base of operations, were used initially to house the arriving slaves, but these facilities proved totally inadequate. By May of 1862, there were over three hundred slaves in custody; by August, five hundred—and the number was growing rapidly. Feeding this large number of slaves became a serious problem for the Union forces.

To address the situation, the First South Carolina Regiment Volunteers, a black Union army regiment made up of former slaves, was brought in and assigned responsibility for managing the slave collection center. They immediately began a widespread foraging campaign on plantations in the general area—taking all the food they could find.

Around noon on a sunny day in September, two Union frigates pulled up to the main landing at Butler Island, and a company of Negro soldiers disembarked. "Where's de owner of dis place? Who's in charge here?" asked a staff sergeant.

There was murmuring among the group of slaves who had gathered to see what was going on. Finally, an elderly Negro woman stepped forward and said, "Dar ain't no owner here. He's done gone away. My name is Raylin. What you want here?"

"We's soldiers of the United States Army, and we's come to set all you niggers free. We got a refugee camp set up on de south end of dat island over dar, and if you want, we'll take you dar so's you can be free. We's also here to fetch any food supplies you got so's we can feed all de niggers at de camp."

"It's mighty nice of you to come an' set us free, but dar ain't no food supplies around here dat we can give you. We needs all we got so's we can live."

"Well, from de looks of things 'round here, dar's more you can give den you think," replied the staff sergeant. He then ordered his men to scout around and bring back whatever they could find and load it on the ships. "An' get some of des niggers here to help you wid de loadin'."

"Now, you ain't gonna steal food right out of de mouths of yo' own kind, is you?" exclaimed Raylin.

"Ain't got no choice, ma'am. I'se just followin' orders. Now, please get out of our way."

The troops proceeded to load a number of cows and pigs on board the ships, along with eighty tierces of rice they found stored in a warehouse. When they finished, the staff sergeant addressed the slaves who had gathered around—now numbering about 150. "We's takin all dis food back to our camp. If you wants yo' freedom, you can go wid us. We'll wait right here fo' one hour more. Any of you who wants to go, hurry and collect yo' belongin's and get on de ships right away."

More than half of the slaves still resident on the plantation accepted the staff sergeant's offer. Some were enticed by the prospect of joining the Union Army and being given a uniform and gun.

Raylin saw the gleam in Christopher's eyes when the soldiers talked about freedom. She said to him, "Dey's lyin' to us, son. I don't believe dem, an' I ain't goin' nowheres! When I was a child, during de last war we had 'round here, my two brothers went off wid de British soldiers, and I ain't heard nothin' back from dem since. Fo' all I knows dey is dead—maybe de soldiers killed 'em. Christopher, since yo' pappy died an' yo' brother got taken away, you's all I got left in dis world, so's I don't want you goin' nowheres, neither. You gotta stay here wid me. We'll make do right here."

Christopher, nodding his assent, said, "Yes, Mammy, I will."

After the soldiers had departed, Raylin ordered a number of slaves to take inventory of what was left of their food supplies. She then announced there would be a "camp meeting" that evening. "An' I hopes those nigger soldiers all rot in hell fo' what dey done here today!" she exclaimed to the whole gathering.

✶   ✶   ✶   ✶

Ever since the overseer had departed Butler Island, the slave community had been in a state of flux. No one had a clear idea what they should be doing or not doing. The group was leaderless. Most of the slaves had remained on the plantation initially, but over the past three months the number had dwindled down from nearly three hundred to less than two hundred. Now half of those had just left with the Union soldiers.

At the camp meeting, Raylin sat alone on the bench in front of the fire. The bench was normally reserved for the Council of Elders, but the council no longer existed. When the slaves had assembled, she rose and began to speak.

"I don't know 'bout ya'll, but I'se awful mad 'bout those nigger soldiers comin' in here and stealin' all our food. Dey is Yankees who's s'posed to be helpin' us—not causin' us to starve to death. Seems we cain't trust de Yankees no more den we can de Rebels.

"Best I can count, sixty-four of us niggers is still left on dis plantation—twenty-four full hands. An', as I sees it, if we don't start lookin' out fo' ourselves, we is all gonna starve to death widout no food. So's we better get organized.

"Now, we still got eight tierces of rice left, and we better hide dem somewheres the Yankees cain't find dem—case dey come back here. We ought to move all de livestock and chickens we got left up in de piney woods and get 'em out of sight, too. An' we got to tend to growin' some crops. De corn up in de north fields don't look all dat good, but what we got needs harvestin' in 'bout a week's time.

"According to Henry here, dar's maybe two or three rice fields dat's worth savin'. We need to drain dem soon an' do de harvestin'. We's gonna need all de rice we can get to carry us through till next year."

A great deal of grumbling arose among the slaves as Raylin talked about all the work that needed doing. "If we's free now, why we gotta work so hard fo?"

"I knows, I knows," said Raylin. "Dar sho' is a heap of work to git done. But I'se gonna tell you dis one mo' time. If we all don't come together as a group, we's all gonna starve to death. We only got 'nough food to last maybe a month or two. What we gonna do when dat's all gone? We grows some mo'! Now, I'se sixty-three years old an' maybe de oldest nigger left here. If I can hold a grubbin' hoe an' do de work, so can you. If any of you don't want to do no work, my advice is fo' you to get off dis plantation right now. We won't have no freeloadin' niggers 'round here."

Without asking for approval, she began issuing directives, "Christopher, you'll be in charge of running de rice mill. You gotta make sho' it's runnin' good by harvest time. You'll be in charge of de corn shuckin' too. Harold, you'll be de head trunk minder. Jupiter, you and yo' two boys is in charge of all de livestock—get 'em moved as soon as you can. Caesar, you form a gang of hands dat'll do de rice harvestin'. Nero, you's in charge of movin' de rice tierces we got left—hide 'em down in de quarters at Settlement No. 4."

By the time she finished, every slave had an assignment. There was no longer any grumbling among the group, and a sense of determination prevailed.

As they were walking back to their cabin, Raylin turned to Christopher and said, "You know, son, I'se spent my whole life doin' my best to keep from being a common field hand, an' now, in my old age, I'se goin' to be one. An' you know what? I thinks I'se gonna like it."

*   *   *   *

In June 1862, Fanny Kemble travelled to England on one of her periodic visits. She arrived at a time when England's position of neutrality in the American Civil War was being questioned and possibly changed. Public opinion was shifting more in favor of the South. The war had dragged on far longer than anyone had expected, but finally Southern forces were beginning to take the advantage by moving north across the Potomac River into Maryland and Pennsylvania. Britain's chancellor of the exchequer, W. E. Gladstone, publicly stated, "We may anticipate with certainty the success of the Southern states, so far as regards their separation from the North," implying that recognition was only a matter of time.

Southern forces received a setback at the hands of the Union Army, at Antietam, on September 17. Then on September 22, Lincoln issued his Preliminary Emancipation Proclamation, announcing his intention to free slaves in all states that were in rebellion against the Union. However, these events didn't curb Britain's appetite for ending its position of neutrality. A petition from the "People of the United Kingdom of Great Britain and Ireland to the People of the United States of America," signed by tens of thousands of British citizens, stated that the South was entitled to establish its own government. It called on the Union to make peace—"in the name of religion, humanity, civilization, and common justice." As far as the "Emancipation Proclamation" went, the general feeling in England was that it wasn't worth the paper it was printed on.

Fanny was appalled over the hysteria that had been created. She thought the true Northern position on slavery, and the very injustice of the slavery system itself, wasn't understood by the general public, nor adequately presented in the English press. Because of this, she decided to publish the journal she had kept of her experiences while living with slavery in Georgia. A condition in her divorce settlement with Pierce Butler had prevented her from publishing it earlier. But now that her daughters were of majority age, she was no longer under any constraint. Her journal, entitled *Journal of a Residence on a Georgia Plantation in 1838–1839*, was published in both England and America in May and July 1863 respectively.

It was said that the journal was "read and discussed, with anger and tears from one end of England to another." In America, the northern press gave it high acclaim, as noted in this review appearing in the *Atlantic Monthly*.

The tumult of the war will be forgotten, as you read, in the profound and appalled attention enforced by the remarkable revelation of the interior life of slavery.   The spirit, the character, and the purpose of the rebellion are here laid bare. Its inevitability is equally apparent.   The book is a permanent and most valuable chapter in our history; for it is the first ample, lucid, faithful, detailed account from the headquarters of a slave plantation in this country, of the workings of the system—its persistent, hopeless, helpless, crushing of humanity in the slave, and the more fearful moral and mental dry rot it generates in the master.

Britain ended up by not changing its position of neutrality in the Civil War, nor did it ever recognize the sovereignty of the Confederacy. It's unclear exactly how much influence Fanny's journal had on the British government's decision—perhaps not as much as the events of the war itself. But the prevailing opinion among most Southerners in America was that Fanny Kemble "single-handedly" prevented England's recognition of the Confederacy. "If England had recognized the Confederacy, the tide of the war would surely have turned in favor of the South."

*   *   *   *

One morning in June 1863, slaves at Butler Island saw heavy black smoke rising from the direction of the town of Darien, two miles away.   They couldn't tell exactly what was going on, but they thought it must have something to do with the war.   Fearing that whatever was taking place in Darien might spread over to them, they began taking defensive measures.   Hands were brought in from the fields, all tools and foodstuffs hidden, and women and small children shut up in their cabins.   They then waited—but, luckily, nothing happened.

As it turned out, a large contingent of Union Negro soldiers had attacked Darien and found that all the town's white males had previously evacuated—only women, children, and slaves remained.   They took over the town without resistance, and then proceeded to burn it down. Not a building, house or business was left standing.   It was an act of war taken against a defenseless town. Southerners became enraged over the action, as reflected by this report in Savannah's *Daily Morning News*:

> The accursed Yankee vandals came up yesterday with three gunboats and two transports and laid the city in ruins. They carried off every Negro that was in the place.

> The destruction of Darien was a cowardly, wanton outrage, for which the Yankee vandals have not even the excuse of plunder. The town had for a long time been nearly destroyed, and there was nothing left in the place to excite even Yankee cupidity. It afforded a safe opportunity to inflict injury upon unarmed and defenseless private citizens, and it is in such enterprises that Yankee Negro valor displays itself.

Three days later, a party of Butler Island slaves made the trip over to Darien to get a firsthand look at what had happened, and their report back alarmed the slave community. It was clear that a devastating war was going on all around them, and they had to do their best to isolate themselves from it. The Yankees were not to be trusted.

Three months after the raid on Darien, all Union forces in the coastal Georgia region were ordered to relocate north, to Port Royal Sound, in South Carolina. This was in preparation for a major forthcoming attack on the city of Savannah to be lead by General William Tecumseh Sherman. As ordered, the troops quickly abandoned their base on St. Simons Island, and the nearly one thousand former slaves who were being held there in custody were transported to holding facilities on St. Helena Island, in Port Royal Sound. These included the large number of former Butler slaves who had deserted the plantations in order to follow the Union troops.

*   *   *   *

Having secured a Union victory at Atlanta, General Sherman began a three-hundred-mile march through the heart of Georgia, with the objective of capturing the city of Savannah. His 62,000-man army faced a moderate force of 10,000 men under the command of Confederate General Joseph Wheeler, which provided little resistance to their movement.

Wanting to reduce his army's dependence on traditional supply lines that would stretch all the way back to Atlanta and beyond, Sherman's strategy was to have his troops "live off the land" by foraging from local farms as they moved through Georgia. At the same time, he planned to deal a severe economic and psychological blow to the South by destroying whatever civilian infrastructure they came across. His specific orders directed:

> The army will forage liberally on the country during the march. To this end, each brigade commander will organize a good and sufficient foraging party, under the command of one or more discreet officers, who will gather, near the road traveled, corn or forage of any kind, meat of any kind, vegetables, corn meal, or whatever is needed by the command, aiming at all times to keep in the wagons at least ten days' provisions for the command and three days' forage.
>
> To army corps commanders alone is entrusted the power to destroy mills, houses, cotton gins, etc.

Sherman's troops moved swiftly in two columns, carving a fifty-mile-wide path of destruction. Almost every structure they encountered was destroyed. Homes and farms were stripped of their belongings—food and otherwise.

Dolly Lunt, the owner of a plantation in Covington, Georgia, that lay directly in Sherman's path, wrote the following account of what happened at her plantation as the Union troops passed through:

> They are coming. I hastened back to my frightened servants and told them they had better hide, and then went out to my gate to claim protection. But like demons they rush in! My yards are full. To my smokehouse, my dairy, pantry, kitchen, and cellar, like famished wolves they come, breaking locks and whatever is in their way. The thousand pounds of meat in

my smokehouse is gone in a twinkling; my flour, my meat, my lard, butter, eggs, pickles of various kinds—both vinegar and brine—wine, jars, and jugs are all gone. My eighteen fat turkeys, my hens, chickens, and fowls, my young pigs, are shot down on my yard and hunted as if they were rebels themselves. Utterly powerless, I ran out and appealed to the guard.

"I cannot help you, Madam; it is orders."

Sherman himself and a greater part of his army passed my house that day. All day, as the sad moments rolled on, were they passing not only in front of my house, but from behind; they tore down my garden palings, made a road through my back yard and lot field, driving their stock and riding through, tearing down and desolating my home—wantonly doing it when there was no necessity for it.

It wasn't till after ten o'clock in the night when the last of the soldiers came by, ending the passing of Sherman's army by my place, leaving me poorer by thirty thousand dollars than I was yesterday morning. And a much stronger Rebel.

Sherman's "scorched earth" tactics proved successful, and within less than a month, his forces were in position to attack Savannah. In preparation for what might become a long siege, Union foragers spread out in quest for supplies. They ravaged Chatham and Bryan counties, which surrounded Savannah, part of Liberty County along the coast south of Savannah, and they were poised to move farther south into McIntosh County, whose county seat was the town of Darien.

*   *   *   *

As night was approaching on December 9, a disturbance was created at Butler Island. A former Butler slave suddenly appeared out of nowhere, shouting, "De Yankees is comin'! De Yankees is comin'!"

Hearing the commotion, Raylin rushed out of her cabin and exclaimed, "What you mean, de Yankees is comin?"

"Raylin! Don't you know me? I'se Pinder. I used to live here till Massa King took me up to Liberty County eighteen years ago." After receiving a sign of acknowledgment from Raylin, he continued, "De Yankees, dey's destroyed 'bout everythin' on Massa King's ol' plantation, and just 'bout everythin' else in de county. Dey's lookin' for food and burnin' down all de houses and barns dey can find. I 'scaped 'fore dey could catch me, an' I'se come all de way down here to warn you."

"Well, Pinder, it's mighty nice to see you again, and we 'preciates you givin' us de warnin'. How close is de Yankees from here now, do you think?"

"Dey's done all de damage dey can up in Liberty County, an' dey was headed south into McIntosh when I seen 'em last. S'pose dey'll get as far as Darien by tomorrow or de next day."

"Dat don't give us much time to hide all de food and things we got layin' 'round here," remarked Raylin. Turning to the slave standing next to her, she commanded, "George, ring de plantation bell so's we can get everybody together. We got lots of work to do tonight.... Christopher! I needs you to take a boat over to Darien an' keep an eye out fo' de Yankees. When you see's dem, hightail it back here and give us a warnin'. You understand?"

"Yes, Mammy."

✳   ✳   ✳   ✳

Christopher rowed a small fishing boat over to Darien, arriving at daybreak. Tying the boat up in a clump of bushes at a point some hundred yards upriver from the city dock, he stealthily made his way down along the river until he reached the end of the town's main street. The town was deserted. Only the burned-out rubble of buildings remained—casualties of the Yankee attack some five months earlier. There were no signs of Yankee foragers. He then picked a spot behind a pile of rubble where he could sit down and view the full length of the main street, while at the same time be out of sight.

He remained there throughout the morning, but by noon the sun was beating down on him, and he was getting uncomfortably warm. Looking for some shade, he spotted a half-burned building with a portion of its second story leaning down to the ground. "It'd make a good lean-to shelter," he thought, "wid some good shade." He stripped a bundle of Spanish moss from a nearby oak tree, used it to make a headrest under the lean-to, and then layed down to continue his vigil in comfort.

About an hour later, the loud noise of hoofbeats from a dozen horses broke the silence and awoke Christopher from his unintended slumber. A Yankee cavalry patrol had galloped through the town and come to a halt at the end of the street, directly in front of Christopher's makeshift lean-to. The commotion startled him, and he abruptly sat up. His movement caught the eye of one of the horsemen, who yelled, "Hey, you, what are you doing? Captain, there's somebody hiding next to this building over here." The soldier dismounted and pulled Christopher out into the open.

The captain in charge brought his horse up to within a few feet of Christopher and said, "Boy, who are you? What are you doing here?"

"I'se Christopher, Massa. I'se just layin' down here takin' a rest, not doin' nobody no harm."

"You're the only living person in this entire town. How come you're here?"

Christopher, collecting his wits about him, responded, "I ain't got nowheres else to go. My massa, Dr. Holbrook—he lived in dat house dat's burned down over dar—went away when dey burned de town down 'bout five months ago, an' I ain't seen him since. I'se just waitin' fo' him to come back."

"You been here alone all that time?"

"Yes, Massa"

"What you been doing for food?"

"Been doin fishin—mostly catfish an' oysters. I'se nearly starvin'. You ain't got no spare food, do you?"

"Hell, no, that's what we're looking for! And it don't look like we're going to find any in this town either. You know this area pretty well, boy?"

"Yes, Massa, 'bout as well as anybody. I'se lived here my whole entire life."

"Tell me then, what's the best way to get across this river here—we want to take a look at what's on the other side."

"You'll need some boats to do dat, an' dar ain't none left in dis town…. Ain't much use in crossin', though."

"Yeah, why not?"

"'Cause there ain't nothin' but swamps on de other side—den 'nother river and some mo' swamps after dat—an another river and another river. Dar's four rivers in all fo' 'bout twenty mile. Ain't no place to take a horse."

"How do we get around the swamps?"

"Well, now, I s'pose you gotta go back de way you come—'bout three or four mile, to de old Sunbury Road. You follow dat goin' west for 'bout twenty mile to de Brunswick Road and take dat south. 'Bout another twenty mile you can cut back to de coast—ain't much swamp after dat."

"Well, that won't do. Saddle up, men, and let's get out of here. It looks like we've hit a dead end."

The horsemen directed their horses back down the main street—at a slow walk. A block down the street they broke into a canter. Christopher stood watching them until they disappeared from sight. He then took in a deep breath of air and slowly exhaled. A broad smile beamed across his face. The boat ride back to Butler Island was going to be pleasant, indeed, he thought.

*   *   *   *

By December 17, Sherman had surrounded Savannah and demanded surrender by the greatly outnumbered Confederate forces defending the city. Instead of surrendering, Lieutenant General William Hardee and his troops secretly evacuated the city during the night and escaped northward in boats into South Carolina. The next morning, Mr. R. D. Arnold, mayor of Savannah, rode out to formally surrender. Sherman telegraphed President Lincoln: "I beg to present you, as a Christmas gift, the city of Savannah, with one hundred and fifty guns and plenty of ammunition, also about twenty-five thousand bales of cotton."

The dilemma Sherman then faced was what to do about all the human "contraband" he had accumulated during his march to the sea. As the army moved through Georgia, slaves on the plantations they passed had looked upon the Union forces as liberators who would lead them to freedom. They had left their plantations and followed the troops in droves. By the time Savannah surrendered, more than forty thousand slaves were in the army's custody, including the former Butler slaves being held on St. Helena Island. Sherman didn't want to be encumbered with so many dependents during his upcoming campaign into South Carolina—they'd be too much of a hindrance.

To address the issue, the secretary of war, Edwin Stanton, traveled to Savannah to meet with Sherman. The two held meetings with groups of Negro ministers from the Savannah community to gain local input. As a result, Sherman issued Field Order No. 15 to deal with the situation. The field order, approved by President Lincoln, ordered the setting aside of abandoned plantations along the coast of Georgia and South Carolina for the establishment of home sites for former slaves. Understandably, the Field Order created considerable excitement among the "contraband" Negroes.

$$\ast \qquad \ast \qquad \ast \qquad \ast$$

Two months later, in March, Raylin was told by a young Negro boy, Freddy, that a group of niggers were over in Darien looking for transportation to Butler Island. He didn't know who they were, only that they said they were former Butler slaves. Raylin directed the boatmen to take a rice barge and go over and fetch them.

When the group arrived, she knew immediately who they were— Peter the blacksmith, with his wife, Anne, and their three children; and Sirius and his wife, Joan. They had been slaves on Butler Island at the time the Negro Yankee soldiers had first appeared at the plantation and had elected to go with them to "freedom." They had subsequently been transported to a holding camp near Port Royal.

"It's good to see ya'll again. But what brings you back to dis place?"

"We's come back to claim our land," said Peter.

"What you mean?"

"We's entitled to forty acres. General Sherman's ordered it. All us niggers gits forty acres.... Don't you know nothin' 'bout dis?"

"No, I don't. But General Sherman, he's a Yankee, ain't he? I don't pay no mind to what no Yankee ses. Dey ain't nothin' but liars."

"Oh no! Dis de truth. It's fo' real," interrupted Peter's wife, Anne. "It's all been 'proved by President Lincoln. He's a great man—de one dat's 'mancipated all us niggers an' set us free."

"President Lincoln, hmm? What 'bout dis 'mancipated? Ain't heard nothin' 'bout dat, neither!"

"Peter, show Raylin de newspaper 'bout 'mancipation, an' dat paper 'bout General Sherman's order too," said Anne.

Peter pulled from his pocket a well-worn copy of an article that had appeared in a Savannah newspaper, along with a printed copy of Sherman's Field Order No. 15, and handed them to Raylin.

Raylin in turn, handed them to Christopher, "Here, you read dis an' tell me if what dey's sayin's true."

After he had read the papers, a broad smile erupted across Christopher's face, and he exclaimed, "Sho' 'nough—it's all true. President Lincoln's set us all free! It look to me, dat all de islands along de coast here in Georgia is gonna be given to us niggers, too. We all git forty acres apiece. An dar ain't gonna be no white folk livin' round here, neither. Dis is what we been waitin' fo', Mammy!"

"You sho' dat's right?" asked Raylin.

"Yes, Mammy, I'se sho'!"

"Well, hallelujah! Dis sho' is good news. Ring de plantation bell, so's we can tell all de folk!"

When all the slaves had gathered, Raylin, trying hard to contain her excitement, addressed the gathering: "We's got some good news to tell you. We's all been 'mancipated by de great man, President Lincoln. Dat means we's all free—ain't gonna be slaves no mo'!"

A great roar erupted—people began jumping, whistling, yelling, and dancing all around.

"Quiet down now! Dat ain't all—de government's gonna give all us niggers de land right here on dis island, too. It ain't gonna belong to de white folk no mo'. It's gonna be ours!"

Again, a big roar went up, and the crowd went out of control.

"Now! Now wait a minute! Calm down." When order was restored, she continued, "Christopher here is gonna read you de official government papers 'bout all dis."

Christopher began reading from the newspaper article: "President Lincoln's 'mancipation proclamation states dat all slaves in the State of

Georgia shall be fo'ever free. De 'Xecutive Government of de United States, includin' de military and naval authority thereof, will recognize and maintain de freedom of such persons."

He then read from General Sherman's Field Order No. 15:

De islands from Charleston south, de abandoned rice fields along de rivers for thirty miles back from de sea, and de country bordering de St. John's River, Florida, are reserved and set apart fo' de settlement of de Negroes now made free by de acts of war and de proclamation of de President of de United States.

At Beaufort, Hilton Head, Savannah, Fernandina, St. Augustine, and Jacksonville, de blacks may remain in dar chosen or accustomed vocations; but on de islands, and in de settlements hereafter to be established, no white person whatever, unless military officers and soldiers detailed for duty, will be permitted to reside; and de sole and exclusive management of affairs will be left to de freed people demselves, subject only to de United States military authority and de acts of Congress.

Whenever three respectable Negroes, heads of families, shall desire to settle on land, and shall have selected fo' dar purpose an island or a locality clearly defined within de limit above designated, de Inspector of Settlements and Plantations will give dem a license to settle upon de land, which will be divided equally among dem, so dat each family shall have a plot of not more dan forty acres of tillable land."

When Christopher finished, a sense of great joy came over the former slaves. There were many questions, too, and discussions carried on well into the night.

✱   ✱   ✱   ✱

No one was more excited about the news than Raylin. She went around all the following day exclaiming to everyone, "Hallelujah!"

"Praise de Lawd, brother!" "Thank you, Jesus!"   To her, this was "deliverance day" for all the slaves who had spent their lives laboring for rich white folk. The Lord had finally answered their prayers—and they were now free.

Then, at one point, all the excitement seemed to catch up to her. While doing an impromptu dance, she collapsed. She was feeling ill, and Christopher, with the assistance of two women, helped her to her cabin—where she immediately fell asleep. She slept most of the following day, too, not showing any sign of improvement.

During a period of consciousness, she called Christopher to her bedside and spoke to him: "I cain't tell you how happy I is over how things has turned out. To be a free woman means a powerful lot to me. I'se truly glad it happened in my lifetime. I only wish yo' Pappy was still alive to see it, too. Dar wasn't nobody on dis whole plantation dat prayed fo' freedom more den he did. He was a good man and deserved to be free.

"We's sho' lucky to have a great man like President Lincoln lookin' out fo' us, ain't we? He won't go back on his promises. We gotta thank de Lawd fo' him."

Taking Christopher's hand, she continued, "You knows, Christopher, I'se getting mighty old now—goin' on sixty-five. Been feelin' poorly for some time now, an' maybe I ain't gonna last all dat much longer. Don't know if I'se got de strength to do all de work dat's needed doing to settle de land General Sherman's givin' us, neither. I wish I did. But I knows you do, an' you's gonna make a mighty fine farmer, an' raise a good family too. It's important dat you gets yo' share of de land, 'cause it'll be difficult to make a life fo' yo'self widout ownin' yo' own land. You deserve to own it, an' you cain't let nobody take it away from you—ever! You understand dat, don't you? Now, promise me you won't let nobody take it away from you."

"I promise, Mammy, but I don't like hearing you talk like dis."

"Nonsense, now go away, and let me get some rest."

That night Raylin passed away in her sleep.

CHAPTER 14—A BUMP IN THE ROAD

"What you mean, dis land don't belong to us?"

"I mean just that. I'm very sorry, but circumstances have changed, and we're no longer in a position to give you the land."

"Well, dat ain't so. Look here, I got dis official order dat come from General Sherman dat ses we own it. It's mighty official, an' 'proved by President Lincoln hisself. 'Sides, when you was here last, you told us fo' certain we owned it, an' you was gonna give us de deed to prove it."

"President Lincoln is dead, and all that's changed now."

The two men having this heated discussion were standing face to face at the main landing on Butler Island. One of the men was Christopher. The other was a representative of the Freedmen's Bureau, Mr. Alexander J. Wilcox, who was head of operations for the area that incorporated the central coast of Georgia. The Freedmen's Bureau, more formally titled the Bureau of Refugees, Freedmen, and Abandoned Lands, had been established by Congress to manage and assist the emancipated slaves' transition to freedom. Its role was to provide food and medical supplies, education, hospitals, employment, land acquisition, and financial assistance. It was a young organization, understaffed and underfunded, but eager to help former slaves become assimilated into white society. As guidance in carrying out their mission, agents used both the newly ratified 13th Amendment to the Constitution, which formally abolished slavery in the United States, and General Sherman's Field Order #15, which granted ownership of property along the coast of South Carolina and Georgia to former slaves.

Two months earlier, Wilcox had paid a visit to Butler Island to introduce himself to the former slaves and to explain the purpose of the Freedmen's Bureau. During his visit, he had passed out copies of Sherman's order and the 13th Amendment. The slaves' response was very positive, and he felt the bureau would be able to make significant headway on the plantation. As he was leaving, he had told them he'd be returning to formally convey deeds of ownership to those families who qualified for the land grant.

However, in the interim, the situation had changed dramatically. Following the assassination of President Lincoln, his successor, Andrew Johnson, objected to any provision that would take property away from its original owners. He issued a proclamation of amnesty and pardon to all Southerners, with only a few exceptions—who would take an oath to support the Union and abide by its laws. For those who took the oath, ownership of their former lands would be restored. Therefore, the land that had been set aside and promised to former slaves along the Georgia coast could now not be given to them. It would be returned to its former owners.

This change in the government's position placed Wilcox in a difficult and embarrassing position. He now had to renege on promises he'd made to the former slaves on Butler Island, and elsewhere, and either get them to accept the situation as it now stood or remove them from the property.

"President Lincoln's dead? Dat cain't be!" exclaimed Christopher.

"I'm afraid it's true; he was shot by a man named Booth. We've got a new President, Andrew Johnson, and he's changed things all around. The federal government has now decided not to give any land to freedmen. It's giving it back to the former owners. This island will be given back to Mr. Butler," said Wilcox.

"Well, dat ain't right. We's de ones dat did all de work to build dis plantation. We's de ones dat grew all de crops. We's de ones dat lived here all our lives. An we's de ones dat are de true owners—not Mr. Butler!" replied Christopher.

"I understand your feelings, but there's nothing I can do about it. It's the law, and I've got to follow it."

"Dar's plenty we can do about it, Mr. Wilcox! Dar's no way you or nobody else is gonna take dis land away from us. We's prepared to fight fo' it!"

A load roar went up from the crowd of Negroes that had by then gathered around the two men. Many were brandishing pitchforks and axes, and one had a gun. They began yelling and jumping—crowding in on Wilcox.

"You'd better get off dis island pretty quick, Mr. Wilcox, fo' you get hurt—an' don't come back," warned Christopher.

Wilcox backed up and got into his boat. "I'm sorry, but this won't be the last you'll hear from me. I'll be back," he said as he pushed off into the river.

*　　*　　*　　*

Four days later, the noontime quiet was shattered by three long blasts from a steam whistle near the main landing. The noise was heard for miles around. Negroes on the plantation stopped what they were doing and hurried in the direction of the landing to see what was happening.

Two small steam-driven naval frigates had maneuvered up the river and approached the landing. The lead boat pulled parallel to the landing, some seventy feet offshore. Its engine was kept running to keep it stationary against the river current. A cannon, manned by a crew of artillerymen, was mounted on the ship's foredeck.

When fifty or so Negroes had gathered near the landing, the cannon was fired in an upriver direction. The shot crashed into a clump of cypress trees one hundred yards away—cutting a large tree in half. A loud gasp came from the crowd of Negroes, and many became frightened.

In a flurry of activity, the artillery crew reloaded the cannon and turned it to face directly at the Negroes. The trailing boat then moved up alongside the landing and tied up. A gangplank was lowered, and three soldiers—a drummer and two flag carriers—rushed out and stood alongside the boat. At the drummer's signal, soldiers—forty in all—came out on the double, carrying rifles with fixed bayonets. They formed into three rows, standing at attention. A saddled horse was then off-loaded, followed by a military officer, and Mr. Wilcox—the Freedmen's Bureau agent.

The officer mounted the horse, rode to the front of the assembled troops, and yelled the command, "Right shoulder arms!" Up went the rifles, bayonets gleaming in the bright sunlight. "Left face!" commanded the officer. "Forward march!" The procession moved out from the landing toward the clearing at the center of the plantation. The two soldiers carrying flags and the drummer led the way. They were followed by the officer on horseback, with Mr. Wilcox walking alongside, and the troops in marching order. The loud drumbeat, coupled with the sound of marching feet, riveted the Negroes' attention.

Christopher, who had been observing the activity from among the crowd, was overwhelmed. He had never seen such a display of military force before and was frightened, as were the rest of the Negroes.

The procession came to a halt in the middle of the clearing. The officer, still on horseback, addressed the Negroes: "Is there a Mr. Christopher here?" After a brief silence, a young man replied, "I'se Christopher," as he stepped out from the crowd. "What can I do fo' you?"

"I'm Lieutenant James Anderson of the United States Army. I'm here to carry out orders to secure this island for its rightful owners, the Butler family, and to establish who among you will have the right to remain here on the property. We have come peacefully, but, as you can see, we are armed and are prepared to forcibly carry out our orders, if necessary. You, sir, I'm told, are the spokesman for these people."

"Well, Massa, we gotta whole committee dat speaks fo' all. Not just me."

"How many on this committee?"

"Dar's five of us, Massa."

"Assemble them together, then, and find a place where we can talk."

"Yes, Massa—s'pose de cookhouse be de best place."

Inside the cookhouse, Lieutenant Anderson sat directly across the table from Christopher; Mr. Wilcox sat at one end. The four other members of the committee stood behind Christopher, and four armed soldiers stood behind Lieutenant Anderson.

"How many Negroes are there living on this island?" asked the lieutenant.

"Well, 'bout three months ago, we counted 90, but new ones been comin' in almost every day. Dar's maybe 150 or 160 now."

"Are all of them former Butler slaves?"

"Yes, Massa, 'cept maybe some who has new wives and chillun dey got when dey was livin' off de island."

"Well, I'm sure you understand why we're here. Our orders come from the President of the United States, and we must carry them out."

"I realizes dat, but, Massa, dar must be some mistake. We been told we owns dis island—not Massa Butler. Dis is our home—we's lived here all our lives."

"Believe me, there is no mistake. Mr. Butler is the rightful owner of the property, and we're charged with making sure he gets it back. I'm sorry for any misunderstandings that occurred in the past, but this is the way it is today. You can either agree to stay here peacefully, working for Mr. Butler as free men, or get off the property. If necessary, we are prepared to use force to make you comply. We have sufficient men here today to do this, and there are a lot more to back us up in Darien and Savannah. A great many of your people will be killed or wounded if you try to resist."

"Oh, Massa, oh Massa, we don't mean to fight wid you. We wanna do what's right. But we don't want to give up our land if we don't have to, dat's all."

"Well, you have to! You better understand that right now."

Pausing a moment, Christopher replied, "I think we better talk dis over wid all de folk here, fo' we agrees to anything. Dat all right wid you?"

"Yes, but make it quick, please."

When the committee returned, Christopher began, "All de people has taken a vote, an we's decided to accept yo' offer. Most people is willin' to stay here an' work fo' Mr. Butler—but only as free people, not as slaves. Dey don't want no mo' whippin's, an' dey want to be able to quit dis place an' leave, if dey don't like it."

"That's fine. They can be assured that they will be treated as free people and paid good wages."

"Dar's one mo' thing, Massa."

"What is it?"

"Well, Massa, we's got some food stored here and we's fixin' to plant some more crops dis spring, but wid all de new folk dat's been comin back here lately, we ain't got 'nough food to last us much. We'd greatly appreciate you givin' us some mo'."

Looking at Wilcox, the Lieutenant responded, "I think we can help you with some rations to carry you over. Mr. Wilcox will arrange for delivery in the next week or two—possibly some medical supplies, as well. Then we have agreement?"

"Yes, Massa."

"Good. Before we leave here today, Mr. Wilcox will need to get the name of every Negro who is going to remain here. And if more come in, you must notify him as well."

Once they'd returned to their ship, the Lieutenant told Wilcox to do his best to get Mr. Butler or his representatives down to Georgia as soon as possible. "Someone needs to take charge of these people before they get rebellious again."

Chapter 15—Trying to Pick up the Pieces

Pierce Butler was encouraged by the news he received from Alexander Wilcox. It had been nearly a year since the war had ended and more than four since he had abandoned the plantations. He thought the former slaves had all left after they were emancipated, and he was surprised to learn that many were still there. If Wilcox was right, maybe something could be done to bring the plantations back to life. It was certainly worth a try. Besides, the additional income would come in handy.

Wilcox's letter stated that there were 164 former slaves in residence at Butler Island and twenty at Hampton Point. "They are all desirous of working for Massa Butler, and no one else." However, time was of the essence. The Negroes were impoverished and would have to be moved elsewhere, if he didn't come to Georgia at once. Wilcox also pointed out that it was getting late in the planting season, and a crop would have to be planted soon if it were to have any chance of success this year.

Pierce Butler and his daughter Fran left Philadelphia on March 22, 1866, enroute to Georgia. Some of his friends in Philadelphia, though, held little hope for his success. Sidney Fisher wrote:

> Pierce Butler has been offered a reasonable sum for the rent of his land in Georgia. He has been so unwise as to refuse the offer and is going, or says he is going, down to manage the estate himself, in which case he will soon make ducks and drakes of it. He has an unfortunate propensity for attempting to manage business, comprised with a total incapacity for such work.

When the Butlers arrived in Darien, they were joined by Alexander Wilcox for their final leg to Butler Island. Wilcox had insisted he be involved with the impending negotiations for a new labor contract with the Negro workers.

They found the property in a desolate condition, with weeds and high grass growing everywhere. The overseer's house was intact but stripped bare of all furnishings. The rice mill was in working order, but guild shops, barns, and rice fields were in need of significant repairs.

The labor contract with the Negro workers was negotiated between Pierce Butler and Christopher. It acknowledged that the crops from the three rice fields that had been previously planted by the Negroes would belong exclusively to them. A limited number of additional rice fields, ten in all, would be cultivated as soon as possible, since the planting season was nearly at an end. Unless there was an absolute necessity for ditching or banking due to emergencies or malfunctions, it would be postponed until the next winter. The Butlers were to provide the necessary rice seed and tools; labor was to be provided by the Negroes. Proceeds from the crops would be shared equally between the partners—a major divergence from slavery days.

Another major divergence was that the Negroes would now be responsible for providing their own clothing, food, and medicine.

Mr. Wilcox, acting as agent for the Freedmen's Bureau, approved the contract—as did the Negro community. And the parties began what was to them a mutually beneficial relationship.

*　　　*　　　*　　　*

With some hard work, Fran slowly brought the overseer's house back into a livable state—which included hanging her prize picture of General Robert E. Lee over the mantelpiece. Two months after their arrival, though, plaster was still missing from interior walls, and most windows were without panes of glass. Cooking was done over an outside fire pit.

Early on, the Butlers received some good news. Jupiter, one of their former slaves, who had been in charge of minding the livestock before the war, had moved the animals up into the piney woods to get them out of reach of Rebel and Yankee foragers. He had ninety sheep and thirty cows still in his care. The problem was, they were on a tract of land some twelve miles upriver, and there was no way to transport them back down. They would have to remain there until boats were available the following year.

Fran also had a heartwarming experience when two old Negroes, Uncle John and Miss Peggy, came over from Hampton Point. They brought with them five dollars in silver coins, which they said a Yankee officer had given them for chickens he'd taken from the plantation during the early days of the war. The two Negroes were bringing the money to the Butlers. And, to the amazement of both Fran and Pierce, there was a continual influx of former slaves trickling in from places they'd migrated to before or during the war. When they arrived, the exchange with Fran would typically be:

"Thank de lord, Missis; we's back and sees you and Massa again."

"You know, don't you—you are free and can be your own masters now," Fran would reply.

"No, Missis, we belongs to you; we be yours as long as we live."

It soon became apparent, however, that dealing with the Negroes was't all a bed of roses. To many, freedom from slavery meant freedom from having to do work, and they contrived means to do as little as possible.

When Fran remonstrated her laundry maid, Phillis, for taking all day to wash a few towels, Phillis responded by telling her, "De fleas was so bad I couldn't get much of nothin' done. Dat's true, Missis; de fleas ain't got no principles; dey bites me so all de time. I just gotta keep stoppin' to scratch." Fran found that if she didn't closely supervise the work, it would probably not get done. After directing a man, Cato, to churn butter, she returned an hour later to see how he was doing. She found him sitting on the floor with the churn between his legs, turning the handle about once every minute. "Cato, that will never do," she exclaimed. "You must turn the handle as fast as you can to make butter." Looking up gravely at her, he said, "Missis, in dis country de butter must be coaxed; ain't no use to hurry." Often, when she needed something done, she would first tell the Negroes to do it, then show them how to do it, and then, finally, do it herself.

Pierce had similar problems. On many days, he would come in from the fields and report that half the hands had stopped work early at one o'clock and the rest by three o'clock. This was taking place right in the middle of critical planting and sprout flow operations. To Fran, Negroes had little appreciation for what it took to raise a cash crop—they wanted only to work long enough to grow a crop they could live on. Instead of cultivating the ten rice fields that had been agreed to at the time the labor contract was signed, they cultivated only six

By the time fall arrived, it was evident that the crop would be poor. This meant there would be only a small payout to the Negroes for their labor, and the Butlers wouldn't cover their expenses.

Under new regulations issued by the Freedmen's Bureau, a change was made to pay Negroes by the day, instead of on a crop-sharing basis. This didn't sit well with Butler Negroes, and the change was scrapped in favor of payment by the task. The workforce—now numbering 220—had to be divided into multiple groups, each under the direction of an appointed captain, the newly accepted term for slave driver. The former daily reporting on work performed was also reinstated. Every day after work, captains would report, as each worker's name was called out: "He done his work." "He done half his task." or "He didn't show up."

Early one morning, Pierce came into the plantation house all excited—"Bran is back! Bran has come back!" Bran, the son of Raylin and Cooper London, was one of the slaves Pierce had sold at auction in 1859. Prior to his being sold, he had been the best driver on the plantations and was in charge of cotton production at Hampton Point. He had been sold to a plantation owner in North Carolina, and, after being emancipated, he had made his way back to Georgia.

When she met him, Fran said "Welcome home, Bran. I've heard a lot of good things about you."

"Thank you, Missis; it sho' is good to be home again."

"Bran has agreed to be the captain over at Hampton," interjected Pierce. "This will free me up to concentrate on things here on the rice island. We couldn't have found a better man—he'll really straighten things out over there."

"That's good news. We can certainly use all the help we can get," said Fran. "I only wish you'd been here to help with last year's crop."

"Well, I wish I could, too, Missis, but my massa in Carolina said he needed me to help finish de crop we'd planted and didn't want me leavin'. So's I stayed on dar an' helped him. But I'se here now, an I brought most of my family wid me—my wife, an' one of my sons, an' his family. My other son an' his family's bound to be here soon, too. Dey's all good workers."

"I'm sure we'll have a good crop," replied Fran. "And, by the way, if you're Raylin's boy, you must be related to Christopher, our rice mill engineer."

"Oh yes, Missis. He's my brother. I'se dyin' to see him."

"Well, you'll probably find him over at the mill."

"Thank you, Missis, an' good-bye."

✳   ✳   ✳   ✳

It had been seven years since the two brothers had last seen each other. There was a lot of hugging and crying for joy when they met.

"You don't look a bit older, little brother!" exclaimed Christopher.

"You don't look bad yo'self, big brother!"

"My goodness, a lot sho' has happened since we's seen each other—de war an' all. What was it like up dar in Carolina?"

"Not all dat bad. I had a good massa. Almost decided to stay dar wid him, but I knowed dis was my home, an' I needed to come back. My son John's been in Tennessee, an' he's comin' back too—probably be here in a couple of weeks."

"It sho' was good you could keep in touch wid him after you was separated at de auction in Savannah," said Christopher.

"It sho' was. When we was sold apart, we didn't know where we was goin' an' we promised each other dat once we found out, we'd have our new masters write a letter to Pappy an' tell him where we was at. Pappy was our link."

"I knows," replied Christopher. "At de time he got de letter from John, his eyes was so bad he couldn't read it. I had to read it to him, an' he told me what to write back to you."

"You know, I sho' do miss him—an' Mammy, too. Wish dey could be here wid us now."

"Me, too. Pappy's been dead four years now, Mammy two. Dey's buried together up at de ol' graveyard."

"Mind if we go up and visit wid dem?" asked Bran.

"No, let's go."

The two brothers made their way up past the main landing, the corn barn, and the horse rice mill to the river. They then followed the path along the dike for a half mile to the old slave graveyard. When they got there, Christopher pointed to two side-by-side graves, each outlined with whitewashed rocks and clamshells. A wheel used to power a sewing machine and various trinkets were evenly spread over one grave. A one-foot thick section of a cypress tree trunk was on the other. The tree section had a cross carved on its top, with a cooper's chisel stuck firmly into it. The grass around the graves had recently been cut, and they seemed to be the only graves in the entire graveyard that were maintained.

"Dey sho' was good to us, little brother," said Christopher.

"Dey sho' was. Too bad dey didn't live long 'nough to see de freedom we has now. I knows dey really wanted it bad."

"Yes, dey did. Mammy wanted even mo' dan dat. She thought freedom wasn't 'nough. To be really free, she thought we needed to own de land we lived on. At de time when she was dyin', we thought we was gonna own all de land on dis island and she was happy 'bout dat. An', wid her dyin' breath, she made me promise never to let nobody take it away from us. An' now I feels awful bad, 'cause I'se let her down. Didn't have no choice, though. President Lincoln died, an' de government changed its mind 'bout givin' us de land. An' dey sent a bunch of soldiers here to take it back. Didn't make no sense to fight 'em. Dey was jus' too powerful.

"Dat's de whole trouble wid 'mancipation. Us niggers still ain't got much power. De white folk done kept all de power an' can make us to do whatever dey wants. It ain't all dat much better den de slavery we was under."

"I s'pose I ain't too much concerned 'bout having power," replied Bran. "I'se just glad to be free. 'Sides, how you gonna take power away from white folk, anyway?"

"Well, dar may be a way, little brother. Dar's been folk at de Freedmen's Bureau from up north dat's been talking 'bout votin' in some election next year. Dey been holdin' meetings for all us niggers over in Darien. Dey ses dar's more of us den dar is white folk in Georgia, an', if we all git together, we can elect our own people to de government. If we do dat, we'd be usin' de white folks' own system to take power away from dem widout no fightin'. We'd all be equal."

"Dat sounds good, but I ain't all dat excited about it right now. I'se more interested in gettin' somethin' to eat."

"Okay, come on den. But we gotta talk 'bout dis some mo'."

✴   ✴   ✴   ✴

In July 1867, Fran left Georgia to spend the summer in the north. She wanted to make several purchases for the plantation homes, visit with her sister and mother, and, most of all, take a break from the chaotic existence she'd led over the past fifteen months. Her father, Pierce, remained to supervise the cultivation of the second year's rice crop. It was essential that it be a good one financially.

Pierce devoted himself fully to the task, remaining on Butler Island long after the start of the summer miasmas season. As a result, in mid-August, he fell victim to the sickness. He was taken to Darien and placed under the care of a physician. By that time, though, it was too late to do anything for him, and, within days, he died. He was buried at a gravesite in Darien.

Commenting on his death, his friend Sidney Fisher wrote:

Pierce Butler died at his plantation in Georgia of the country fever. He was a man of strongly marked character, with some good qualities and many faults. He led an unsatisfactory life and threw away great advantages. He was handsome, clever, most gentleman-like in his manner, but uneducated, obstinate, prejudiced, and passionate. His daughters are in great grief.

Chapter 16—Come Hell or High Water

Fran's grief over the loss of her father didn't last long. In the fall of that year, she returned to Georgia more determined than ever to finish the work she and her father had started. She would make a success of the plantations, "come hell or high water."

In doing this, her role changed dramatically. She now became the mistress of the plantations—in full charge of producing crops and managing the Negro labor force. And the challenges she faced became more demanding.

Immediately, she became embroiled in the settlement of accounts with the Negroes for their work over the past two years. Her father had given each Negro a personal pass-book, in which he had entered the amounts for food, clothing, and cash given to them from time to time on account. The total of these amounts represented the Negro's debt to the Butlers. Another ledger, the master's plantation ledger, contained a record of the days each Negro had worked. This represented his earnings. The balancing of these two accounts—debts versus earnings—took Fran several days to complete, working until two or three o'clock in the morning. She was intent on making the results absolutely fair and accurate for each Negro.

In retrospect, she could have saved herself the trouble. Few Negroes understood what she was talking about, and all were convinced they'd been cheated. A typical encounter went like this:

"Well, Quash, you got on January 16 ten yards of homespun from your master and on March 4 a new suit and shoes."

"Yes, Missis; Massa give me dat."

"Then, on March 13, you got ten dollars and on September 30, you got three bushels of corn and two chickens."

"Yes, Missis; dat so."

There was almost no disagreement over the amounts owed as debts, but it was an entirely different story when it came to discussing wages earned. Every one of the Negroes insisted he had not missed a single day during the whole two-year period and had done full work every day. It caused endless discussions. After a while, Fran stopped discussing the matter entirely, and merely paid the Negroes the amounts due them. Most were dissatisfied and said, "Well, well—work for Massa two whole years and only git dis much."

"But I am paying you from your master's own books and accounts."

"No, no, Missis; Massa not treat us so."

Notwithstanding their dissatisfaction, more than six thousand dollars was paid out to the Negroes. Many got as much as two or three hundred dollars. This was far more money than any of them had ever earned in their lifetimes. And, as a result, nearly thirty families decided to leave the plantation with their newfound wealth. They used the money to buy land of their own in the town of Darien or in the upland piney woods—"to live the rest of our lives as gentlemen." The big exodus gave Fran concern over whether or not she'd have sufficient hands to work the following year's crop.

*   *   *   *

Her dealings with the Negroes didn't become any easier following settlement of the pay issue. The Freedmen's Bureau issued new regulations requiring plantation owners to enter into labor contracts individually with each Negro they employed. These contracts, the form of which was approved in advance by the Bureau, were binding on both parties. At first, the Negroes flatly refused to sign any contract whatsoever, saying that it would make them slaves again. To Fran, this simply meant they were willing to live on the plantation but not to work. She firmly took the stance: "You must either sign the contract or leave."

On the first day of signing, the large plantation bell was rung at ten o'clock as a signal for workers to come in and sign their contracts. For a period of six hours, Fran sat in her office listening to long explanations, objections, and demonstrations made by each Negro. Even those who came in fully prepared to sign had to have their say. On one such occasion, when she had interrupted a long speech, the man said, "Stop, Missis—don't cut my discourse!" Almost all wanted some change made to the contract: one was willing to work in the mill but not in the fields; many wanted Saturdays off.

Fran was immovable. "No, you must sign the contract as it stands." "No, I cannot have you work here without signing." "No, you must work six days a week." Her demeanor remained calm throughout this process—right up until the point when an insolent male said, "You sign my paper first; den I'll sign yours." "No!" she replied in a rage, "I won't sign yours—nor you mine. Get out of this room, and get off the plantation—immediately!" Afterward, she felt sorry over the way she had treated the man. But, within five minutes, she looked up and saw him standing in the doorway, with a broad grin on his face. "I'se come back to sign, Missis." By the end of the day, sixty-two contracts had been signed.

On the next day, the process was repeated, which left only a few stragglers on the third day. The very last man arrived carrying a large multicolored umbrella. He stated flatly that he wouldn't sign any contract unless he was given Saturday off as a holiday. With a flourish of his umbrella, he said, "Five days I'll work, but I works fo' no man on Saturday."

"Then, William, I am sorry, but you cannot work for me. Any man who works for me must work on Saturday," replied Fran.

"Good morning, den, Missis," he said, and, with another flourish of his umbrella, he departed.

Within an hour, he reappeared with his umbrella shut and informed Fran that "after much consideration wid myself," he had returned to sign. At the end of the entire process, only two Negroes hadn't signed their contracts. With this behind her, Fran was in a position to turn her attention to other matters.

The plantation store was one of the first things she was drawn to. During the previous year, the Butlers had stocked the store with items they felt would be useful to the Negroes. Goods were sold to them at cost. The plantation bore the cost of transportation from Philadelphia and absorbed the cost of spoilage. In so doing, the store had incurred a loss of more than three thousand dollars. Fran's decision was to close it down. And, interestingly enough, this didn't bother any of the Negroes. They seemed to prefer going to Darien to make their purchases—even for lesser quality goods at higher prices. It was a sign of their independence.

*   *   *   *

Near the end of her fourth year in residence on the plantation, and her second as mistress, Fran noticed a marked change in the Negroes' demeanor. All of a sudden, they began referring to her father by his last name only, without any title before it; dropping the term "Mistress" and calling her "Miss Fran"; walking around with guns on their shoulders; working only as much as they pleased; and speaking to her with their hats on, or not touching them as they passed.

As a counter to this, she deliberately became more demanding and a stricter disciplinarian. In her own words, she became "the supreme dictator of the place." In regard to their hats, she would command sharply, "Take your hat off this instant!" When a Negro was insolent to her, she would immediately dismiss him, saying, "You are free to leave the place, but not to stay here and behave as you please—for I am free, too, and moreover, I own the place. I have the right to give orders and have them obeyed." This new approach brought with it a high degree of anxiety, and she began sleeping at night with a loaded pistol at her bedside.

There was one problem, it seemed, she couldn't solve—the Negroes' refusal to do the "dirty work" involved with ditching and banking rice fields. This was the most physically demanding task on the plantation. Once the Negroes had been emancipated and could no longer be forced to perform such work, they refused to do it. In desperation, Fran searched for an alternative and found a silver lining.

There had been a large influx of Irish immigrants into the Philadelphia area during the previous year, and many were having difficulty finding employment. She hired a gang and transported the lot of them to Georgia. The Irish workers were thankful for the opportunity to get work and actually did a better job at ditching than the Negroes had done. It worked out well for all parties, and trips to Georgia became an annual event for the Irishmen.

On the brighter side, the rice crop at Butler Island was looking good, as was the cotton crop at Hampton. This gave Fran a sense of accomplishment and a feeling that she was finally making a success of the operation.

*   *   *   *

None of the disciplinary problems Fran encountered at Butler Island were present at Hampton Point. The plantation, with fifty Negroes, was under the supervision of Bran and ran smoothly. About 125 acres of cotton were under cultivation.

Over the previous two years, though, the cotton crops had been attacked by caterpillars just as the bolls were coming into full bloom. Both crops had been destroyed, causing severe financial losses. This year—the third since Bran had been in charge—Fran hoped things would turn out differently. And, with harvest time approaching, the crop looked good. Everyone had high hopes that it would be successful.

Unfortunately, the bad news came in a note one morning from Hampton. After reading it, Fran immediately ordered a boat to be prepared for the trip over. "I don't care whether the tide is coming in or going out. I must get to Hampton at once!"

When she arrived, she commandeered a mule wagon and had the driver take her to the cotton fields just south of the Jones Creek settlement. When she got there, she saw Bran sitting alone on a large tree stump at the edge of one of the fields, seemingly staring off into space. He didn't move or say anything as she approached. And, as she sat down next to him and put her arm on his shoulder, she could see tears flowing down his face.

"Oh Missis, I'se so sorry," he said in a broken voice.

"I know ... I am, too. But it's not your fault. None of us can control these pesky caterpillars."

"It ain't fair. Work so hard to bring in a good crop, an' now dis! Look out dar Missis—see de bare twigs on dem plants at de far end of de field, an' 'long de edge, here. All dat's happened in just one night. Won't be but a day or two more dat de whole field is gone. Once dey gets started, dar's no stoppin' 'em."

"It sickens me to see it happening, but we can't do anything about it, Bran. So we've got to put it behind us. Come, let's go up to the house and get us a good cup of tea." Fran held onto Bran's arm as they walked slowly up to the house together.

After tea, when Bran was calmer, she said, "Bran, I want you to know that I think you're one of the best and most reliable workers I have on my plantations—and I appreciate all the hard work you've done for me."

"Thank you, Missis."

"Unfortunately, this is the third crop in a row that's been destroyed by caterpillars, isn't it?" Receiving an affirmative nod from Bran, she continued, "It's cost me a lot of money to do all the planting, and I haven't gotten anything back in return. Financially, it's been a burden, and I can't afford to keep it up any longer. I've just got to shut the whole plantation down, or I'll go out of business."

"Oh no, Missis."

"I'm sorry, but I have to. But don't worry. I'll take care of you and your family. I'll find good jobs for all of you over at Butler Island."

"Dat sho' is nice of you Missis, but I don't want to leave dis place— it's home to me an' my family."

"I know it is, but things just have to change. You may find that you like working at Butler Island even more than you do here."

"Maybe so, I'se just got to think 'bout it some—talk it over wid my family."

"You do that, and then come and see me."

Three days later, Bran was standing on the front steps to her office at Butler Island when she opened the door to begin the day's business.

"Oh my goodness, I didn't expect to see you here," she said.

"Yes, Missis. Good morning to you."

"Good morning to you, too. Please come in."

Taking his hat off as he entered, Bran said, "I got up early dis mornin' and caught de six o'clock tide comin' in, 'cause I needed to talk wid you. I'se got somethin' important to say."

"Well, what is it, for goodness sake?"

"I'se awful sorry Missis, but after careful consideration on de part of my entire family, we's decided not to come over an' work here on de rice plantation. We's decided to move away—go to Savannah."

"My goodness—what made you decide that? You know I would give you good jobs here."

"Yes, Missis. I s'pose we's just wantin' to do somethin' different—to improve our livin' now dat we's got our freedom. We hears dar's good jobs in Savannah, an' dar's schoolin' for de chillun. De Bureau man has promised to get us transported up dar an' help us get jobs. We's all plannin' to leave in two weeks' time."

"Well, you better be careful about what the Freedmen's Bureau agents tell you. It's been my experience they don't always tell the truth. And the last time I was in Savannah, I saw a great many Negro men sitting around all over the place as if they couldn't find work."

"We's all strong and good workers, so we's willin' to take our chances. 'Sides, we don't cotton to workin' in de damp mud dat's in de rice fields—it ain't healthy."

"I don't know what to say. But I sure wish you the best of luck. I'm sorry to be losing you."

*   *   *   *

During late 1870 and early 1871, in Fran's third year as mistress, an abnormally high number of marriages took place on the plantation. There seemed to be a large number of Negroes reaching the "marrying age." Several older couples, who had been married during slavery days, also retook their marriage vows. Under slavery, Negro marriages were not recognized by the State of Georgia, and, following emancipation, the couples wanted to legalize their relationships by getting married a second time.

Marriage ceremonies were important events on the plantation: morally, for the bride and groom; and socially, for attendees. Brides dressed in white, bridesmaids in either white or light-colored dresses, and the groom and groomsmen in black frock coats with white waistbands and white gloves. Most of the attendees dressed in their finest as well, and the event was a social highlight of the year.

The parson, John Bull, was an old Negro man highly respected in the community. He performed all the ceremonies held on the plantation—with both solemnity and unexpected humor. He would typically receive the couple at the reading desk in the small chapel, and, after a great deal of arranging and rearranging of the candles, his book, and his large-rimmed spectacles, he would proceed to read the marriage service of the Episcopal Church. Part of the reading he knew by heart, part he guessed at, and part he read with great authority— mistakes and all. Often he would read aloud the portion to be spoken by the minister, and in addition, the written directions for actions to be taken by participants. "Here de man shall take de women by de right hand." He would then pause, and, looking over his spectacles, say, "Take her, child, by de right hand and hold." On one occasion, after he had read " ... this ring to be given and received as a token and pledge," he said with emphasis, "Yes, children, it is a plague, but you must have patience."

If, during the ceremony, attendees tittered in response to a mistake either he or the couple made, he'd immediately slam his book shut, and, in a severe tone, would say, "What you laugh for? Dis not triflin'; dis business!" This would cause everyone to quickly quiet down. And as an ending to the ceremony, he would say to the bridegroom with great solemnity and a wave of his hand, "Salute de bride." The happy bridegroom would then give his bride a kiss that could be heard all over the chapel.

As acting parson on the plantation, Bull performed a valuable service for the Negro community. He had done this for several years. But when the State of Georgia passed a law that required marriage ceremonies to be performed only by ministers or magistrates who were licensed by the state, he was forced to stop his ministry. Fran, not wanting to loose her local parson, sent him to Savannah to become licensed. But unfortunately, the authorities found him unqualified, and he had to retire permanently to private life.

*   *   *   *

Speaking of marriages, there was one in Fran Butler's future as well. During a trip north one summer, she had met a young Episcopal minister from England, who was in America visiting friends. He was the Reverend James Wentworth Liegh. The two got along well that summer. So well that James, or Jimmy, as he was better known to his friends, was invited to visit Fran at her Georgia plantation the following winter. This visit went well, too, and Fran followed it by traveling to England in May. The two were married in June.

The newlyweds began their married life in England at the parish of Stoneleigh. It was their intent to remain there long-term and leave the operation of the Georgia plantation in the hands of an overseer.

In the beginning, this arrangement worked well. The new overseer managed to reduce expenses, and the first year's crop proved satisfactory. After that, though, conditions deteriorated rapidly. Negroes began leaving the plantation at a higher rate, and less acreage was planted. Worst of all, a fire destroyed the rice mill and the entire supply of rice seed for the coming year's crop, amounting to fifteen thousand dollars in damage.

According to the overseer, the fire had been deliberately set by a disgruntled Negro worker who had been reprimanded for poor work. Having had a dollar deducted from his wages, the man had thrown a fit and refused his wages altogether. On the morning of the fire, he'd been spotted near the mill, but it couldn't be proved conclusively that he was the culprit. The sight of the fire excited the Negroes into a frenzy, and they made no attempt to put it out.

Because of these circumstances, Fran gave serious consideration to abandoning the plantation, but, at the urging of her husband, decided against it. The couple returned to Georgia in the fall of 1873 to resurrect the operation.

The good news following Fran and Jimmy's return was how quickly Jimmy took to managing the plantation. Without any prior experience in rice cultivation, he immersed himself in learning the details of the operation and in learning how to deal with the Negro workforce. Making a number of changes in work practices, he improved the efficiency of the operation. And, more importantly, when he changed the wage payment scheme to weekly, the Negroes' recollection of how many days they had actually worked improved greatly. Disputes over how much was owed disappeared.

The rice yield doubled the first year under his management, much to the astonishment of other planters in the area. The Negroes liked him, too—one was heard remarking, "Miss Fran sho' made a good bargain dis time."

* * * *

Jimmy also began a concerted religious program for the Negroes. He conducted regular Sunday services and twice-weekly evening educational programs in a small chapel he built on the plantation. In addition, he became a regular pastor at the white Episcopal Church in Darien, which also served Negroes in the area.

At a point when the Negro attendance at the Darien church became too large to accommodate, he received permission to construct an independent church for them. He obtained plans from a friend in England, and volunteers helped build the structure, which was completed in March 1876. It was named St. Cyprian's, after a third-century black saint who became bishop of Carthage. The church was officially opened and consecrated by Bishop John Beckwith of Savannah. Negro attendance was strong from the very beginning.

* * * *

Jimmy was able to achieve these early successes despite laboring under difficult circumstances. He described some of these circumstances in a letter to a friend in England:

Since the war, owing to want of capital and labor, much of the country in the Southern States has returned to its natural state. Whereas, formerly, in six states 180 million bushels of rice were produced, only 72 million were produced in 1870. Even less is produced today. The original planters were completely ruined by the war.

In Carolina and Georgia, planters were driven from their plantations along the coast, labor was placed in a chaotic state, and plantation infrastructure, such as dams, floodgates, canals, mills, and houses, was destroyed or allowed to decay. Rice fields became entangled in weeds and shrubbery, making it impossible to plant crops and much more labor intensive to reclaim.

In our own neighborhood, there is scarcely a planter whose plantation is not mortgaged and whose crop is not the property of his factor, who has advanced him money to plant with. They plant on sufferance and live from hand to mouth the best they can.

With regard to our own laborers on the plantation, we had at the beginning of the year seven Irishmen for ditching and banking, at two dollars per day; an English carpenter and blacksmith, at two and a half each; six English laborers, at one and a half each; two colored carpenters, at one and a half; and about eighty negroes, full hands, three quarter hands, half hands, and quarter hands, rating at twenty four, and eighteen, twelve, nine, and six dollars per month; added to which we have a trunk minder to look after the trunks or locks which shut out the water from the ditches, a cow and sheep minder, an hostler, a flat man, and a boatman. This seems to be a large staff for the cultivation of 500 acres; but we do not find it enough, as most of the Negro hands are women and children and the men do as little as they can.

*   *   *   *

The most troubling problem Jimmy faced in managing the plantation was the dwindling labor force. In 1874–1875, plantation operations were a far cry from what they had been in the antebellum period. The U.S. census had shown a total of 505 Negroes living on the plantation in the year 1860. The number had dropped to 216 in the 1870 census, and now there were only 90! Over the years, there had been a steady migration of Negroes off the plantation, and there were no signs of the trend abating. They were coming dangerously close to the point when they wouldn't have enough hands to operate the plantation.

Jimmy also encountered problems of an unusual nature. A large consignment of rice he had shipped to their Savannah agent was lost when the agent's business was forced into bankruptcy. And when a stronger-than-usual spring freshet came down the Altamaha River unexpectedly, it breached the outer dikes of the plantation. Massive flooding occurred, and most of the year's rice crop was lost.

At that point, it seemed as if nothing was going right, and the plantation was becoming a huge financial drain for Fran.

To make matters even worse, the city of Savannah, which served as their main link to the outside world, was experiencing difficulties, as well. The city's population of thirty thousand people included fourteen thousand Negroes. Twelve thousand of these Negroes were unemployed! The city defaulted on its public debt and its commerce became almost nonexistent. And, worse yet, a yellow fever epidemic struck the city, killing three thousand inhabitants.

In the fall of 1876, faced with these difficulties, Fran and Jimmy made the fateful decision to shut the plantation down and leave Georgia permanently.

For ten years, Fran had made a valiant effort to save the plantation and restore it to a modicum of its former self. But, like the rest of the plantation owners along the Georgia coast, she'd failed. Her efforts and successes were better than most who'd tried. But, in the end, the cotton and rice dynasty created by her great-grandfather, Major Pierce Butler, was no more.

Epilogue—Two Years Later

In early May of 1878, a Negro woman was sitting on a small wooden chair outside a former slave cabin at Hampton Point; she was shelling peas. In the distance, she heard the muffled sound of a steamboat. And, as she looked up, she could see smoke rising over the far reaches of the marsh some two miles away. The boat had just entered Buttermilk Sound and was heading south. She could barely make out the top of its smokestack. "Must be a small boat," she thought. "Maybe de mail boat goin' to Brunswick." Other than glancing up again just as the boat disappeared from view beyond the end of the island, she paid no further attention to it. She had seen many boats go by in the past and knew that in a few minutes the noise would go away.

The noise abated somewhat, but then it seemed to get louder. It startled the woman when she realized this. "Oh my Lawd! Did dat boat make de turn an' come up de river here? What it do dat fo'? Maybe it's my 'magination."

Suddenly, the boat appeared around the bend in the river, a half mile away. "It's headin' dis way," she thought, as she stood up abruptly, dumping the unshelled pea pods from her apron into her wooden bowl. "Cain't let dem see me." She hurried into the cabin and shut the door.

"There's someone there! I think I saw someone go into that cabin," said the well-dressed woman passenger in the boat as she looked through a spyglass. "The place is a shambles—looks deserted. I may be mistaken."

The boat, a small steam packet chartered out of Savannah, was manned by a captain and two Negro crew members wearing black uniforms. The woman was the only passenger. When they reached the landing, the captain helped the woman out, and she began making her way toward the cabin.

"Hello, is anyone here? Hello! Hello!" she shouted.

No answer came from the cabin, but she heard a rustling noise off to her right and saw a man coming through the palmetto undergrowth. He was a barefoot, elderly Negro with a gray-speckled beard. He wore overalls, a tattered shirt, and a loose-fitting hat. He was carrying a bucket and a fishing pole. The woman's eyes focused intently on the man as he approached, and a quizzical expression came over her face, "Bran? Bran, is that you?"

"It's me, fo' sho'," was the reply. "Oh my Lawd, is dat you, Miss Fran?"

"Yes, it is. My goodness, it's good to see you," she said, giving him a big hug. "You sure are a sight for sore eyes. It's been years since I've seen you. What on earth ever brought you back to this place?"

"I'se just come back home, Missis."

"But this place is deserted. How can you manage living here? Are you by yourself?"

"No, Missis. Mary, my son's wife, an' her daughter, Sarah, is here wid me. We gets along just fine."

"Well, it must be six or seven years since we've seen each other. I'm sure a lot has happened to you in all this time, and I'm dying to hear about it. Why don't I get the boat captain to make us a cup of tea, and let's you and me sit down under this oak tree here where we can talk some."

When they were settled, Bran asked, "Missis, has you come back to start up de plantation again?"

"Oh no, Bran. I live in England now. Reverend Jimmy and I are very happy there, and we plan to make it our permanent home. We gave up working the plantation almost two years ago now. We just couldn't make a go of it, and we had to abandon it. It's a sorry fact, but I've been up in Savannah over the past two days with my sister, Sarah, making arrangements to sell the property. I just came down here for a brief visit, so I could take one last look at the place before I go back to England."

"Well, dis place sho' misses you. De plantation was sho' nice when you was runnin' it. S'pose I was jus' hopin' you was comin' back."

"Thank you, Bran. But I want to hear about you. How have you been?"

"Well, wid de Lawd as my witness, I gotta say dat since 'mancipation, things ain't been all dat good. It's been a "weepin' time," Missis."

"Oh, I'm sorry. Tell me about it."

"Well, s'pose I oughta start at de beginnin', back at de time when I left de plantation. You probably 'member dat's when de caterpillars eat all de cotton—third year in a row. Dat's when my whole family, we's packed up all our belongin's an' hitched a ride on a mule wagon dat de Bureau man arranged fo' us. We got to Savannah in three days time an' was put off at de Bureau job center right in de middle of de city. De driver tol' us to get in line dar so's we could get jobs. Dat's when everythin' started goin' wrong. We didn't know nobody, an' de line gettin' into de center was so long it'd take fo'ever. So's we left my son Luke dar, an' de rest of us went off, tryin' to find my brother Christopher, to get some help findin' a place to stay. We didn't find him till de next day. He was livin' out in Baldwin camp, one of de shantytowns fo' niggers out west of de city 'bout two mile. He took us in to live wid him.

"It was de day after dat when we finally got in to talk to de man at de job center. When we told him we was lookin' fo' jobs an' we'd take anythin' dat paid money, he just laughed at us. He said dar was three thousand niggers just like us lookin' fo' dem same jobs, an' dey was all on de list ahead of us. He just wrote down our names an' said he'd tell us when a job come up.

Baldwin camp, de place Christopher lived at, was one of 'bout six or seven camps all 'round de city. Dar must have been a thousand, maybe two thousand niggers all crowded together livin' dar in small wood shacks. Weren't nowheres as good as what we had here on dis plantation. De city wouldn't allow no fires inside de shacks, on account of dem burnin' down, so's all de cookin' had to be done outside. At mealtime, de smoke all 'round was so thick you could hardly see de shack next to us. Dar was one good thing, though. Dar was a well wid a hand pump 'bout a quarter mile away where we could get water. Couldn't trust nobody in de camp, though. Peoples was always stealin' anythin' they could find.

Christopher, he had a good job workin' fo' de Union League, an' he knew his way 'round de city real good. He found jobs fo' all of us—payin' a dollar a day. Luke, he worked fo' de city in road buildin', an' John an' me worked in de big flour mill jus' outside de city.

"De quarters at Christopher's shack was too small fo' us to keep livin' dar, so's I bought de shack right next to his—paid ten dollar fo' it. Livin' was a whole lot better den. 'Nother good thing was de school dey had at de camp fo' nigger chillun. Both of John's chillun went dar an' had good teachers. De school was set up by de Bureau, an' all de teachers was missionaries from up north. Trouble was, de school closed down 'bout a year after we got dar. De white folk was complainin' 'bout havin' schools fo' niggers out in de camps an' wanted de money spent fo' schools in de city. De Bureau said it didn't have 'nough money to keep all de schools runnin', an' if de state didn't help out some dey'd have to close dem down. The state didn't help, so they closed dem, an' all de teachers left."

"It sounds to me that the white people kept all the political influence for themselves," said Fran. "Why, when you had the right to vote, didn't all the Negroes band together and vote for the things you needed?"

"Oh, we tried, Missis. It's true we had de right to vote, an' dar was mo' niggers in Savannah den dar was white folk—probably de same all over Georgia. But dat didn't do no good. First de government started makin' us pay a poll tax—two dollar an' fifty cent each time we voted. An' if we didn't vote in one election, it was double in de next. Not many niggers could pay dat kind of money, so's dey didn't bother to vote. I'se not sho' if de poll tax applied to white folk, 'cause dey all voted.

"White folk wanted everybody to vote de Democrat ticket, an' dey got awful mean when us niggers didn't do it. Most of us wanted to vote de Lincoln ticket, an', when we got to the pollin' place, it got mighty rough when we went to put our votes in de box. You had to pass by a whole lot of white men dat was standin' in de way, an' dey shoved an' pushed you when you got close to de box. One time I got knocked down real hard. An' 'nother time, a man pulled out a gun an' pointed it right at my head. He said he'd shoot me if I put my vote in de box. I'se sho'ly scared, an' got out of dar in a big hurry. Never tried votin' again."

"What they did was illegal, Bran. Why didn't the Freedmen's Bureau stop them?"

"I don't know, Missis. S'pose dey didn't have 'nough people to look after all de pollin' places. Dar was a lot of soldiers in de city, too, an' dey didn't help none, neither. Both de soldiers an' de Bureau was mo' help when Christopher was 'round. He could get dem to do things fo' us. But, after he died, we hardly seen dem no mo'.

"Christopher—did he die?" asked Fran.

"Oh yes, Missis. De Ku Klux killed him."

"Oh no! He was one of my favorite persons. Very smart, too. Tell me what happened, please."

"He sho'ly was smart, an' he did mo' to help all us niggers den any other man I knows. We's all worse off since he got killed. But I s'pose I better start at de beginnin'.

"Christopher, he left de plantation here 'bout a year or two after 'mancipation. He was itchin' to get into politics over in Darien. Dar was an important leader dar by de name of Tunis G. Campbell, who he liked. De two of dem started registerin' niggers in McIntosh County an' gettin' dem to vote in de elections. Dey done real good. Most of de niggers in de area voted fo' President Grant on de Lincoln ticket, an' a whole bunch of niggers got elected in de county election, too.

"Tunis G. Campbell, he got elected to de state senate. Dar was five or six other niggers dat got elected to de senate from other places in de state, too. Trouble was, de federal government law dat gives us niggers de right to vote didn't say nothin' 'bout givin' us de right to hold office. So de state government passed 'nother law dat said we couldn't hold office. Dat meant dat Tunis G. Campbell an' all de other niggers wasn't legal, an' dey got thrown out of de state senate. 'Bout a year later, though, de "Big Judge" up in Atlanta ses dey *was* legal an' dey all could go back to de senate. But Tunis G. Campbell didn't go back. Instead, he became de magistrate fo' all of McIntosh County, an' he did a good job upholdin' de law to protect us niggers."

"I remember him well," remarked Fran. "He was a big troublemaker around here. Always arresting white people for minor infractions. I seem to recall he got his comeuppance when he illegally arrested someone and got put in jail himself. Isn't that right?"

"Yes, Missis. But de charges wasn't true. Tunis G. Campbell was a great leader. Ain't seen de likes of him since."

"Well, I guess we can disagree on that point," said Fran. "But continue telling me about Christopher."

"When Tunis G. Campbell got elected to de senate, Christopher, he went up to Savannah an' started workin' as an organizer fo' de Union League. Dis was a mighty good job—paid fifteen dollar a week.

"Christopher done a good job, too. Almost all de niggers in Savannah was registered to vote. Most voted fo' de new state constitution an' fo' President Grant on de Lincoln ticket. He run a lot of big rallies all 'round de city to get folk to vote—mo' den three hundred niggers usually showed up at dem. An' he probably knew just 'bout every nigger in de city.

"After one of dem big rallies, he decided to go up to an even bigger rally in Macon, where folk was comin' from all over de state. Christopher got 'bout a hundred niggers from Savannah to go up dar in mule wagons. My son Luke went wid him.

"'Bout a day's ride out of Macon, dey stopped over fo' de night near a little town called Doby. At evenin' time, Christopher and Reverend Samuels was holdin' a prayer meetin' for all de folk, when 'bout thirty horsemen rode into de camp, shootin' dar guns in de air. Dey was all wearin' white robes an' big white hats dat covered dar faces. Everybody knowed dey was de Ku Klux, an' dey was all scared.

"De horsemen saw Christopher and Reverend Samuels leadin' de meetin', an' dey grabbed dem an' started beatin' dem wid sticks.... An' den dey took 'em to a big tree, an' put nooses 'round dar necks, an' strung 'em up. All de other horsemen formed a big ring 'round de tree, wid dar horses facin' de crowd, an' dar guns was pointed at de niggers. Nobody dared do nothin'. When dey was done, dey told everybody to go back to where dey come from, or dey'd be back de next day an' hang 'em all. Den dey rode off, shootin' dar guns in de air.

"Luke ses de hangin' was de awfulest sight he's seen in his entire life. He barely could stand cuttin' Christopher down from de tree an' bringin' him back home to be buried."

"That was awful!" exclaimed Fran. "Didn't the sheriff in that town know what was going on? Couldn't he have stopped it?"

"Luke ses de sheriff claimed he didn't know nothin' 'bout it, an', since it was just a couple of niggers dat got killed, he wasn't goin' to do no investigatin' 'bout it, neither."

"My God, that's hard to believe."

"My son John, he died too, 'bout three years later. We's both workin' in de flour mill when de roof caught fire. I'se in de back near de loadin' dock an' got out 'fore de roof fell in. But John was in de front, an' he didn't make it. His wife Mary an' his daughter, Sarah, has been livin' wid me ever since. De mill never opened back up again, an' I was out of work fo' almost three year—takin' day jobs when I could find dem."

"My wife, Doris, died too—two years ago, now. Dar was a lot of sickness goin' 'round from de yella' fever, an' folk was dyin' all over de place, maybe thousands of dem. Finally, Doris got it too, an' dar was nothin' we could do to help her. It was de saddest day of my life."

"Bran, I'm sorry."

"Didn't know what to do wid myself after dat. Almost come back here den, but I decided to stay. Dat was a bad decision on my part, 'cause de situation got a whole lot worse in Savannah. De new president, I think his name is Hayes, said dat de federal government was all done helpin' niggers, an' he closed down de Bureau an' took away all de soldiers dat was protectin' us.

"Seems after dat, de state government passed laws dat completely changed 'round all de changes de Bureau done put in place. De laws makes niggers sign a one-year contract fo' jobs dat we cain't get out of fo' no reason. De sheriff's got de power to put niggers in jail fo' bein' idle an' out of work, an' he can sell any of de niggers he arrests to someone to do work fo' nothin'. Niggers cain't sit on no jury dat's tryin' white folk, or testify against white folk, neither. We cain't hold rallies ... Cain't insult a white man, neither—gotta git outta dar way when dey's passin'—it's just like being back in de slavery days 'fore 'mancipation. We's free, but it don't mean nothin'."

"My Lord, you've been through some hard times, Bran."

"Yes, Missis. I'se sho' feelin' mighty low 'bout it, too. S'pose de decision to leave dis plantation in de first place was a bad one. Wish we hadn't done it."

"I do, too. Things would have turned out better for you if you'd stayed."

"Dat's de same conclusion we's come to. Dat's why me an' Mary an' Sarah has come back here. We hoped you'd still be workin' de plantation, an' we could get jobs. But de place was all deserted when we got here."

"I'm afraid it's been deserted for some time now. We tried hard to make a go of it, but we kept having setbacks, and our labor force dwindled down to where we didn't have enough hands to keep it going," said Fran. "It's sad to see how the place is so overgrown and run-down now—no sign of crops anywhere. It's almost as if Mother Nature has reclaimed the land and taken it back from the people she entrusted it to."

"Probably looks de same as it did 'fore any man ever set foot here," remarked Bran.

"You know, as far back as I can remember, these islands have been called the Golden Isles. It's a name that probably got started 'way back in the early days. And maybe, in the heyday of the rich cotton and rice plantations, the days of my great-grandfather Major Butler, they really were golden isles. But not anymore. They're worthless as they stand today. It's a bloody shame, too."

"Cain't say dem days was all dat good fo' niggers, 'cause of de slavery. But dey sho' was better den what we got now. Least den we had food, an' clothin', an' a place to sleep. An' de settlement was like home, 'cause we was wid friends. Ain't got none of dat now.

"Seems dat white folk is doin' all dey can to keep us niggers down. We ain't got no schools or no jobs to better ourselves; we don't own no land, an' de new laws is makin' us mo' like slaves den when we's under slavery. Just seems dat dar's nowheres fo' us to go. Don't know what'll become of us, neither. We's just niggers, an' I s'pose dat's all we'll ever be ..."